Cassandra Steel's passion for science opens doors to an incredible opportunity—a study abroad program in Colombia's Amazon Rainforest. Still reeling from a devastating breakup, Cassie throws herself into research, convinced that love is not in the cards. However, fate has other plans.

Enter Zhang Xuan, a captivating fellow scientist who unexpectedly captures Cassie's heart. As they begin to explore their feelings for each other, they are forced to confront the harsh reality that their time together may be limited.

With their time abroad coming to an end, Cassie undertakes a final humanitarian project, delivering school supplies to local children. But tragedy strikes when a devastating mudslide hits. Against all odds, Cassie and Xuan cling to the hope that their connection is more than mere chance—a result of a powerful twist of fate.

Join Cassie and Zhang on a journey of true love, blazing as fiercely as the stars, as they navigate the complexities of destiny and defy the odds that stand in their way.

Fated to Love You

ISBN: 978-1-4874-3763-3
Cover art by Martine Jardin

Published by eXtasy Books Inc

Look for us online at:
www.eXtasybooks.com

Fated to Love You
Chasing the Comet 1

By

Kayla Cunningham

Dedication

For my parents, Craig and Robbie Cunningham – No one has ever been given more loving and unconditional support than I have been given by you. Thank you for showing me the world, and for empowering me to follow my dreams.

For my husband, Brayan Trujillo Suarez, who, like the comet, is the brightest star in my sky. Considering the way our lives mysteriously wove together, I have a hard time believing it wasn't fate that led you to this country, and to the same school as me. Thanks for proving to me that true love exists.

For the Newton and Valerio family – with deep respect and a lifetime of love. I am thankful for each one of you. You have been a blessing to me, and to the Cunningham family. You'll always have a special place in my heart.

"With relatable characters, a compelling plot, and thought-provoking themes, *Fated to Love You* is a book that will stay with readers long after they have turned the last page." —Manhattan Book Review

"*Fated to Love You* starts off with one of the closest things to a literal bang I can think of."-Seattle Book Review

"The author's creativity in exploring strong themes in this engrossing tale made it possible to award the book a perfect rating. I recommend this book to lovers of romance fiction and also to persons whose relationships may be going through certain upheavals."-*OnlineBookClub.org* Review

"More than just a romance, *Fated to Love You* brings to life the struggles of two very realistic characters."
-Portland Book Review

"Fans of Nicholas Sparks and John Green's *The Fault in Our Stars,* pick up this book!"-Author Miranda Lee

"Cassie and Xuan's relationship is one worth mimicking, as it shows the devotion and love they hold for each other, while not letting anything or anyone get in the way."
-San Francisco Bay Area

"This book discloses the fundamental mystery of where the very core of love germinates from and the elements that keep it prevailing, despite the odds."
- OnlineBookClub.org Review

Read for a Better World:
Every Book You Buy Gives Back!

Indulge in a heartwarming tale of love while making a positive impact on the world. With every purchase of *Fated to Love You*, a percentage goes directly to supporting charitable organizations that make a difference in our world communities. Not only will you be enjoying a great read, but you'll also be making a positive impact on the world.

The story begins in Colombia, where the protagonist, Cassandra Steel, goes on a science study abroad. She visits the rainforest and raises school supply donations to take to kids.

With every copy sold of this first novel, a percentage of the proceeds will be donated to two organizations that are close to the story and the protagonist's heart: the *Amazon Conservation* and *Save the Children*. These charities are tirelessly working towards conserving the Amazon rainforest and improving the lives of underprivileged children in Latin America. Find out more about these amazing organizations, here:

https://www.amazonconservation.org/

https://www.savethechildren.org/us/where-we-work/latin-america

Join me on a mission to create a better world, one book at a time. Purchase Fated to Love You today and experience the joy of giving back to society. Let's make a difference together!

A Note to My Readers on Language

I hope you will find yourself completely absorbed in the world of *Fated to Love You* and find this novel to be a captivating and enjoyable read. Before we begin this incredible journey together, I wanted to clarify a few key language points in this novel because you will come across a mixture of phrases and conversations. As an author, I choose to follow the grammar rules of other languages, as an important sign of respect, and it is my way of acknowledging cultural differences. The main characters in *Fated to Love You*, travel to the country of Colombia for a study abroad program. It is important to know that Spanish titles like señor—sir or Mr., señora—ma'am or Mrs., and doctor—doctor are not capitalized in Spanish, except when used as abbreviations or at the start of a sentence. Because of this, you will see lower case personal titles like, señorita Steel, señora Gálvez, and señor Nieto, instead of Señorita Steel, Señora Gálvez, and Señor Nieto, which we would typically capitalize in English.

The narrative is presented from Cassie's perspective, as she writes this story and reflects on the events long after they took place. It is of great importance to me to pay homage to the cultures that played a significant role in her experience. As a result, you will often find translations of foreign words that she didn't comprehend at the time, or even words that I believe you, the reader, may not be familiar with. This approach ensures that the genuine expressions of the characters are preserved and not lost in translation.

Overall, the beauty of language lies in its ability to express the full range of human experience and to connect with one another in meaningful ways. I hope *Fated to Love You* becomes a treasured read for you, full of memorable moments and cherished characters.

Prologue

Do you believe in fate? Fate . . . as in the universe has everything planned for you . . . that there is some predetermined path laid out for you from birth. If I'd ever been asked to predict my future, weave my own story—the story of Cassandra Steel—the outcome would have likely been much simpler than the narrative that is about to unfold. My answer as a young child would likely have been the common vision of an unextraordinary white picket fence in a suburban neighborhood, with Mr. Right and one, maybe two kids. You know, *that* kind of dream—the same one almost all girls in America are taught to want early on as they play with their beautiful Barbies and mansion-sized dollhouses, meant to replicate a make-believe, princess-like future. But that wasn't meant to be my fate, nor could I escape the path laid out for me by the *powers that be*.

Sometimes when I look back and analyze my past, I think the catalyst behind this story was my passion for science. I remember looking at seaweed and pond water microorganisms under a microscope during my Physical Science class my freshman year in high school and I felt exhilarated. My curiosity was awoken and I found myself instantly in love with the subject. Then, during my sophomore year in Biology, I single-handedly dissected a cow's eye and heart while my lab partner—and half the class—were busy passing out or vomiting in the bathroom, and that was it. The road ahead was clear. Set. I knew exactly what I wanted to do with my life. Science wasn't just accumulating observations and data of the physical world . . . it was the doorway to help battle things like disease, global warming, hunger and poverty when applied properly. Science was discovery and possibility, and more than anything, I wanted to be a part of it.

I spent the next few years planning accordingly. A 4.0 GPA,

Varsity athletics, and extracurricular activities, allowed me to attend the University of California in Santa Cruz on an academic scholarship. I was book-smart and totally self-confident in anything related to my studies. A total nerd. A know-it-all. I have never feared taking a risk when it came to science. But socially I was the opposite of assertive, despite the clubs I belonged to or the athletic teams I played on. Outside of the classroom, I tended to be insecure and conservative. Shy, even. Usually an outcast. In fact, I've been told I'm socially timid. An introvert. An INFJ on the Myers–Briggs Type Indicator test. I'd even been bullied up until I made the Varsity basketball team. And then my reputation changed entirely when I finally entered the high school dating scene. Well, not exactly dating in the plural sense. Just one guy really—Raylan Thompson who, for whatever reason, had taken an interest in me despite his superstar status in high school.

A few years later, Raylan and I went our separate ways. He joined the military and I started the science program at the university. It was after our breakup that the thread of my life, woven from Fate's loom, finally started to take shape. And it was because of science that I met *him*. *The one.*

The spinner of my story set me on a collision course that began the night I walked into the Red Iguana, and it was sealed after escaping death's clutches the day of the comet, but none of those fateful events would have happened if I hadn't fallen in love with science. Just like in the movie, *The Curious Case of Benjamin Button,* I believe a series of events resulted in leading me to find my soulmate.

In a way, I blame my teachers. Yes, definitely my teachers. If my freshmen and sophomore teachers had just read out of a stupid book and been less interesting, I wouldn't have been introduced to microscopes, labs, and dissection. The first time I looked into a microscope at seaweed and pond water microorganisms, there was something inside me that shifted—like the way people describe falling in love. And if I hadn't been given the opportunity to cut into a cow's eyeball at the age of fifteen, maybe I would have never majored in science, or gone on the semester study abroad trip to Colombia with the UC Santa Cruz biology department. So yes, I blamed seaweed and pond water microorganisms, a cow's eyeball, and my teachers, the real culprits, for starting me down this path. Just like accident investigators put together a timeline, I call this *the causation analysis of my love life.*

To the skeptics, perhaps the events that are to follow were just a coincidence and nothing more than a series of random accidents that led me to where I am today. But to the lovers and poets and dreamers, perhaps you might agree that the story about to unfold is something more. You might even agree that there are times when coincidences are so powerful that they don't really seem like coincidences anymore. Times when you come across events that seem too strange, or too strong, to be anything other than Fate—a grand design that incorporates everything from the career paths we take, the friends we meet along the way, and the partners we choose to spend our lives with. Times like these make you question that maybe nothing in this world happens by accident. Maybe everything really does happen for a reason, as some prewritten destiny slowly takes shape and shoves you down a path—or in my case, a mountain side.

My story begins in the foreign country of Colombia, where I found myself newly single and embarking on a semester study abroad program for science . . .

Part One: The Spinning Wheel

Chapter One: The Reaper of Souls

Medellín-Bogotá Highway, Colombia
October 15, 2016

All around, silvery rain fell, mixed with mud and earth and the screams of helpless people trapped on the muddy highway headed away from the city of Medellín, Colombia.

Trapped inside my smashed vehicle, I tried to breathe normally. Each inhalation was painful, but the sharp exhalation was even more excruciating. Raising my shirt slightly to better examine the bruises on my ribs, I knew my skin would look a deep Barney purple tomorrow by the time I woke up—that was, if I somehow survived today's catastrophe. Even grazing the bruise made me wince, but fractured ribs and trouble breathing were the least of my concerns right now.

As the angry earth started to rumble again, I clawed my bloody fingers through my hair and watched helplessly as several vehicles and their passengers were swept away by the muddy current and then tossed off the side of the cliff, like small toy boats on the waves of the sea. Then my car started to move.

I braced myself against the seat as much as possible. Absolutely terrified at what would come next. Fully aware that I was about to be thrown over the edge . . . and there would be no escape.

At second impact, the world seemed to shatter as more debris collided with my car. The front bumper scraped against *something*. I leaned forward in my seat to see only some kind of old, half-demolished guardrail near the edge. Fifteen feet in front of me were several orange traffic cones but no rail, only scaffolding. If I had to guess, it looked as though a section of the guardrail had been taken down so construction workers could replace it with something new and better.

The metal below the car creaked as it bent, but the friction had created a sort of resistance that kept me from falling straight off the cliff. The car moved ever so slightly forward—it felt like several feet but must have been only a few inches. I had a *National Geographic* front row view of the lower valley as the car stopped.

No . . . no . . . no. This can't be happening. Dread coiled in my gut like a snake full of denial and regret. *If I die now, what was the point of it all? I haven't done anything with my life yet. I've wasted the last five years buried in books. I haven't traveled anywhere outside of the United States. And I've only ever kissed two guys—real kisses. I've never even been in love.*

I had the fervent desire to turn back time, and reverse fate. To be better than I was. To live. In high school I never once skipped class or received detention. I worked hard and gladly skipped the bar nights and raves to focus on my work, because I thought one day my research would matter. I wanted to help people.

Now with my existence suspended on the edge, I realized my life up to this point had been pointless. I hadn't achieved anything in science yet. And all those self-sacrifices were inconsequential when weighed against the grander scale of my inexperience.

Please. I can't die . . . not yet. I'm only nineteen. I want my life to have meaning. I gave up everything because I wanted to make a difference. But I'll change. I'll do whatever you want, please just let me survive this . . .

The minutes ticked by slow as hours, and a cold wind rattled the car windows. I could hear the snap of steel from the guardrail giving way. The metal groaned like a door on rusty hinges. As the steering wheel jerked to the right side, the front two tires of the car slid off the embankment.

I tried to remain as still as possible as the car hung there like the Scales of Justice beam, teetering on the edge of the cliff. The car did not immediately tip—instead the vehicle dangled there like a pendulum. I could imagine the Fates of old, watching and weighing the balance of my life against some imaginary scale. Knowing that my life and death were no longer in my hands was scary. There was nothing I could do but repent and pray.

I let out a deep, whimpering sigh. *I wish I'd been braver and realized how little time I had. I would have done more. I would have –*

Pop, pop, pop – my weight combined with the pressure of the car and the gushing sludge was too much. In the equation $F=\mu N$, mass had won against friction, sending my vehicle careening toward the edge and then over. Like a missile, I plummeted. Mountain and trees and thousands of dollars in ruined backpacks and school supplies flew past. I remember screaming as my conscience roared with should-haves and could-haves.

A loud crunch sounded like a bomb going off as I was thrown back hard into the seat and then forward into the steering wheel as the car's frame hit something sharp and hard. This happened again and again as the underbelly of the vehicle scraped against every rock and bush, resulting in the horrific grinding and smashing of twisting, shrieking metal.

Falling seemed to go on forever. Incredibly, the car felt as though it was picking up speed – I knew I would not be spared.

Just before the car reached the bottom, I tried to remember the faces of my family. I'd heard people say that in their final moments they watched their life flash before them, but that did not come naturally. Being an only child, my family was small. I forced myself to see my mother Stella's face. I could picture my father, Richard Steel . . . or at least the last image of him I remembered. He'd been overseas for most of my life, defending freedom.

After the imposed visions of my parents, I spent my last moments thinking about science – an equation, to be precise: $F = mv^2/2d$. I know it's not possible to cheat death, but I hoped for a last-minute ingenious MacGyver moment where I could somehow improvise or find my way out of this mess. But it didn't matter how many scientific equations – or terms like force of impact, kinetic energy, and all three of Newton's laws of motions – swam through my useless brain at that moment. The chance of me surviving was highly unlikely—less than 5%. And none of the years I spent studying or memorizing scientific facts or mathematical equations would save me now.

Acting on pure instinct, I threw my arm up in front of my face. *Bam*! The airbag finally deployed right before the car reached the bottom. The car finally stopped plunging downward and came to a standstill . . . but I was still not safe. I hurt everywhere as I continued to gasp for air. Pressure all around me, tightening, squeezing . . . as if hundreds of pounds sat across my lap, keeping me from moving my legs. Half my body felt paralyzed, but I knew the pain radiating from my leg was a good sign. I curled my toes into the brakes, clenching rubber and metal just to make sure I could feel. I was instantly relieved by the sensation.

I looked out the window, unable to believe how far I'd fallen.

In my head I could hear my military-minded father, telling me "Toughen up, soldier, and focus. If you're in pain, embrace it. It means you're still alive. Use that big brain of yours and think." My jaw locked as I gritted my teeth to hold myself together. I certainly wasn't a soldier, but the absentee figure yelling at me was right. Somehow, against all odds, I had survived. *I have to find a way out of this,* I repeated again. *I'm an only child – it would destroy my parents if I was killed in an accident. I can't do this to them . . . I can't give up.* When you love someone, you fight for them in every way you can . . . I started thinking numbers.

Newton's 1st Law maybe? My leg was pinned and wouldn't budge unless I could force it loose. I needed an object or net external force to help set me free, but there was nothing within reach.

Grinding my teeth, I ripped at the fabric of my jeans and then my leg, pulling muscle by muscle as I tried to get free. My hands started to shake. I cursed as a sharp clawlike pain tore through my ankle. Movement made me want to vomit—or worse, cry like a baby. I was having a hard enough time keeping it together as it was. I crammed my palms into my eyes and breathed away the gut-churning nausea. Minutes passed. The initial pain subsided and I tried to shake off the lingering dizziness.

Determined to survive, I tried again to the point that my entire body quaked and my shallow breath huffed violently. This time the pain radiated all the way up to my hip bone and then spread like wildfire throughout my body.

Blood soaked my arm from a large cut, and the tips of my long blonde hair were now dyed rockstar red. Bright blinding lights tunnel my vision—*was this it? Was this the light at the end of the road that everyone talks about? Am I dead?* In the next second, something smashed into the driver's side of the car—another vehicle. My ears roared from the deafening sound vibrations and my leg twisted.

Cold and confused, I moaned in pain as my ears continued to ring and my eyes began to darken. There was so much blood. Shadows lurked nearby—as if Death herself were stalking me. A Reaper—a farmer of souls, loitered in the back seat, waiting to take me. I could feel her presence as she waited to harvest.

My name is Cassandra Temperance Steel, I said to the beautiful imaginary Death Angel, as if my name wasn't already on her Santa Claus-like list of souls to collect that evening. *Spare me.*

Then my world went dark.

The last thing I remembered before oblivion claimed me was that I was not alone in the car. There was somebody inside the vehicle with me in the passenger side seat . . . and that person was going to die because of me.

Chapter Two: The Force of Attraction

Fourteen hours before the accident
October 14, 2016; El Poblado, Colombia

What can I say about my first real relationship, the one I had with Raylan Thompson? That he was charming, and easy on the eyes . . . a brave military man like my father. However, if I was being honest with myself, he wasn't my Pierre Curie or Frederic Joliot. I never felt the way the songs say you're supposed to feel if you love someone. Sure, I really liked him, but I always knew I could live without him. Our relationship was unstable, like radioactive decay, or boron-7—a substance that didn't last, as though it had never been there at all.

Private Raylan and I ended things the day before I took a jet plane to South America for a college study-abroad program. So I did what any reasonable person would do. I dug into my studies and focused myself on anything but the handsome soldier. I refused to spend my semester beaten, defeated. I was brokenhearted—I wasn't broken. I worked hard over the course of my trip, but I also made new friends like my roommate, Amanda, and explored several new cities. Despite my failed relationship, I had plenty of amazing, novel-worthy stories to tell everyone when I returned home. And, just like that, four months passed. Slowly but surely my heart mended and I found beauty in the country of Colombia. But tomorrow night my classmates and I would be returning to the States. That meant I had exactly five hours left to finish recording the necessary experiment data before the building's security officer kicked me out for the night.

Inside the science lab, I finished recording the final numbers on my samples, but the data refused to make sense. Adjusting my glasses, even though they didn't need it, I thumbed a pen against the counter. Linear mixed-effect modeling and structural equation modeling ran through my head. My professor, señora Gálvez, had warned me that testing a network of complex ethnobiological hypotheses would be difficult, particularly for data sets with non-independent observations due to species phylogenetic relatedness or socio-relational links between participants. I always did like a challenge and tended to obsess over problems I didn't understand.

I was operating on zero coffee, but my body was used to running on autopilot. I took my shoes off as I ran the numbers again. The task señora Gálvez had assigned me was intriguing. I looked at the data I'd formulated until my eyes blurred and began to rerun the function and equations. *What am I missing?*

There was only one solution. I needed to run the tests again for accuracy, even if that meant being here all night. Honestly, I didn't mind. Weekends and evenings were the times I actually preferred working at the lab. The space was comfortable. Everything was quiet. Clean. I could focus just on my work without interruptions, particularly from my verbose roommate who also happened to be my lab partner. As I eagerly threw myself into my work, unlocking the cabinet of supplies and setting up for a second test experiment, the solitary echo of my bare feet against the stone floor resonated through the room.

"Oh hi, Ms. Steel. I figured that was you."

Looking over my shoulder, I was jarred by the sight of Zhang Xuan. His name was pronounced similar to Jong I-yen, even though it sounded like John Shen in English. He was one of the Chinese international students in the science program at the university.

"Hi Xuan. You're here late."

"I could say the same about you." He'd stepped into the door frame and was now leaning against the jamb. Underneath his lab coat, he wore a white shirt tight across his chest. His intense, dark eyes under his black hair emphasized his jaw. He looked smart and sophisticated, and as hot as a K-drama star. Suddenly a switch flipped inside me, and the change was dramatic. My stomach knotted and my heart tripped, stumbled, then raced, just at the sight of him standing there nonchalant. Truthfully, there was something I'd always found sexy about him.

Images of Xuan came to me as I remembered that we'd attended the same high school but I was always too shy and nervous to talk to him much outside our senior science class. General conversation was never my forte, especially when it came to boys. My two best friends, Roxy and Sky, never seemed to mind, because they were both really good at talking. In fact, it seemed as though they always had something to say about everything.

Roxy and Xuan were in several classes together in high school. She always said he was like an independent cat—aloof, indifferent, and reserved.

Even though Xuan and I weren't close, I'd been relieved to see him, a familiar face, on the plane headed to Colombia. He'd grown more handsome, and his face had become more defined since high school, but his personality hadn't changed much since our senior AP Physics class. Xuan had always been kind but super quiet and super studious. We had walked together to class a few times, in silence. I think he was shy too, and so we never made much progress as friends.

"Does it smell like diluted Gatorade in here to you as well?" Xuan asked.

"Yeah, I think it's from Rachel's experiment earlier."

Xuan moved to the cabinet and grabbed a microscope and test kit. I thought he'd sit somewhere else. Instead he circled around the table, came to stand behind me, and then slid his equipment next to mine.

Sitting down next to me, he folded his hands on the table. There were fifteen *other* long tables inside the lab. All vacant. Yet he'd decided to set up next to me, close enough that our thighs accidentally touched.

I took a desperate breath and then crossed one leg over the other. "So what are you doing here?"

He sent me an amused look as he stared down at my periwinkle-colored toes, which were slightly visible from under the table. "I needed to check the results on something."

My face heated as I realized he'd caught me working after hours barefoot. I couldn't look him in the face and instead focused on his petri dishes. "What've you been working on?"

He leaned closer, as if he was going to whisper some top secret information . . . his proximity drew me in like a magnet. "I started out studying the use of the Paullinia cupana as a heart tonic, but I decided to test different plant species used by the indigenous peoples for medicinal purposes."

"Sounds interesting."

"It has been. So why are you here so late?" he asked. "You're down to the wire with the submission deadline. It's not like you to cut it so close."

"Actually, I finished my project a few days ago. Señora Gálvez asked me if I'd be interested in collaborating on a side project related to my research. She thought I might enjoy the task since I'd already finished my assignment and the subjects were closely related. I finished the first step in the process, but the results were inconclusive. I decided to rerun the data to check for accuracy before sending her my conclusion."

"Of course you'd do extra work."

"What does that mean?" I'd been called a teacher's pet before, but coming from him the term stung a little. The difference between Xuan and I was that he was a natural. I'd believed that hard work beat talent, when talent wasn't working very hard, but Xuan was just as much of a perfectionist as I was.

"It means you're a hard worker." I heard no judgment or criticism in his tone. "I wasn't at all surprised to find you here when I saw this was the only light still on. You're definitely going to be the top of our class this semester."

I tried not to let his words go to my head. "I have to work extra hard to keep up with you," I said playfully. "You always outrank me. And you make it seem so . . . so painless." I sounded idiotic to myself, but he seemed flattered.

"Luck, I guess."

Hmph. *Overachiever.* He was unrelentingly good at everything. I doubted his scores were luck, but I didn't press the matter. Back in the States, Xuan had always been rather intimidating, and I'd been silently competing against him to be at the top of our class in grades and exam scores. My dream was to eventually get my doctorate. But that would come later, much later. First I had to finish my bachelor's and get accepted into my master's program, an expensive goal that wasn't really feasible without a scholarship. Unfortunately, scholarships are much harder to come by for a master's, meaning I would have to take out student loans too. Despite the money barrier, I knew exactly what I wanted in life and I had everything all planned out. I was aiming for that perfect grand slam of a future. Like grasping and getting the brass ring on a merry-go-round—education, career, travel, discovery. Maybe one day I'd even fall in love and start a family—if there was time.

"Maybe you're focusing too much on the problem or letting your bias get in the way of the data," Xuan suggested. "If you focus on the problem too much, you can't see the solution."

I kept my eyes cast down on the table, staring absentmindedly at numbers. "Good to know."

"So what are your plans after UC Santa Cruz?"

"Definitely Berkeley. And you?"

"Berkeley or Stanford."

Reaching blindly for an inoculating loop, our fingers briefly touched. My heart unexpectedly raced as though it was playing a tennis match against Venus Williams. I quickly retracted my hand. "Sorry."

"No worries." Xuan stared at his own hand with an amused expression. "By the way, how did you get in here so late? I expected to see señor Nieto or one of the other professors here, but the building's empty."

"Señor Nieto gave me the keys to lock up the lab."

"Since when?"

"The first week of class. He stayed until closing with me the first few days. But once he realized it was going to be a regular routine, he decided it was best to go home to his pregnant wife before she threatened to stop making him dinner. He had me sign some paperwork and then gave me a copy of the lab key. I just have to leave before the building security officer checks all the locks at midnight."

"If I'd known I could have stayed late, I would have joined you."

Xuan was focused and intense as he quietly finished taking notes and examining his labs under the microscope. The silence dragged on. Keeping my head down, I couldn't stop myself from occasionally peeking sideways at him through the upper rim of my glasses and hair.

Xuan suddenly stood up. "Well, I'm out of here. Do you want me to wait for you?"

"No, that's okay. I still have a few tests to run. Go enjoy your night."

He bit his lip pensively. "I hope to see you at the salsa club later. Your roommate said everyone from the science department is going to celebrate. I—we'd miss you if you weren't there."

My roommate Amanda and a few friends from our study-abroad course had all tried to convince me to join them in a final Friday night of cocktails and sin to celebrate our last evening in the capital of the Antioquia province.

"I don't know if I'll be done in time." I winced at how boring I sounded. I could picture Amanda shaking her head at me.

Xuan's mouth tilted up at the corner. "I understand. But if you do end up going, will you save me a dance?"

Suddenly overcome by tongue-tied introversion, I adjusted my glasses and, in a moment of weakness, nodded. I was an MVP basketball player in high school and athletic, but in no way a great dancer.

After Xuan left, I was too jittery to make much sense of the new data numbers I'd scribbled down. I was still recovering from my surprise—the fact that he'd asked me to save him a dance, and the fact I'd said yes. I read over the last few lines of data, but my brain was too distracted to concentrate. I needed a few minutes to collect myself.

Something about Xuan made me want to go to the club, and that shocked me. *Go, have fun,* said a little voice in the back of my mind. *That's why you took salsa dance lessons at Salsa Gente – to prepare yourself just for this!* Salsa Gente was a Cuban-style dance school that offered evening classes at the London Nelson Community Center. After I signed up for the trip, I started to do research on the country and quickly learned that Colombians loved to dance. And not your boring two-step repeating dance moves where the guy puts his hand around your waistline and you wrap your arms around his neck and stare adoringly into his eyes while trying not to laugh.

Having two left feet, I decided it was imperative to practice and learn the basics of how to dance salsa, merengue, and bachata before I left California . . . just in case the need should ever arise.

For me, my dancing experience began and ended in high school. School dances were always a torturous night, where you spent hours stepping side-to-side until your feet throbbed. I'd always found the ritual of Winter Formal and Prom to be absurd, but Raylan always insisted we go. I did *not* enjoy the experience.

Holy Saints, Cassie. Focus. Don't think about Raylan or Xuan.

Putting in my ear pods, I quickly thumbed through my phone and pressed play on a classic rock mix. Two minutes into *Wind of Change* by the Scorpions and I was ready to focus again. I needed to use a set of qualitative methods to dive deeper into the data for a better understanding of what the numbers truly meant and their implications.

Three hours later I plopped down in the teacher's vacant desk chair and powered up my laptop. My thoughts only betrayed me a total of five times by flickering to images of Xuan throughout the remaining scientific method process. Mercifully I didn't think about Raylan once.

I had run the experiment a second and then a third time, just to be sure. Pulling up the data, I let out a relieved sigh. This time the numbers were spot on. There must have been an unknown variable that caused an error in my first test. An error that would bother me the rest of the evening. *Holy Saints. What could it have been?*

Checking my watch, I realized it was getting late. It was easy to fixate on work when you enjoyed it—in fact it was what people came to expect of me once they knew me. I was as obsessed with science as a person working on Wall Street was about money and stocks. I'd always seen and interacted with the world in a different way, and science and data just made sense. Dancing, drinking, and nightclubs not so much.

Tapping my pen to the desk, I was tempted to continue working. But if I touched the keyboard again, I knew five more minutes would turn into twenty, which would turn into hours. I'd promised Amanda I'd join up with them after I finished documenting my final lab results, called my mom, and packed for the return flight home. I really did want to celebrate with my classmates, try something new, even if it was out of my comfort zone.

Tick, tock. Tick, tock. Should I stay or should I go . . .

Checking my watch again, I calculated the time. I'd finished later than expected, but I could still meet up with everyone if I hurried to get ready. There was no way Amanda was turning in early on our last night in Colombia. She'd drag her hindquarters to the airport completely hungover if it meant a few extra hours clubbing. I was sure the group had already left their mark up and down the bustling strip of bars and nightclubs, but I could send a quick text and find out where they were headed next. After all, a promise was a promise.

I sent Amanda a quick message. *Where are you guys going to be in the next hour?*

Saving my work, I powered down my computer, cleaned my station, and put everything away, including a few test tubes other insouciant students had left out. When I was finally finished, I plopped my shoes back on and went to lock the doors.

Hurrying back to the dorm, I raced to finish packing. The phone call to my mom could wait.

My excitement increased exponentially as I placed a few pins in my long blonde hair and applied smoky colors to my eyelids and a thin layer of mascara and eyeliner. From showering to slipping on a pair of heels, jeans, and a black tank top, getting ready took a grand total of thirty-four minutes. I was generally very shy and self-contained, but not that night. I wanted to forget the soldier boy who had broken my heart. I wanted to celebrate passing my exams and ending the four-month journey in a foreign country. But even more surprising, a small part of me wanted to see Xuan one last time. Maybe I'd even find the courage to take him up on his offer, even if it was only for one dance.

My phone vibrated. Amanda had finally replied. *We're headed to the Iguana Roja right now.*

Grinning, I grabbed my black blazer and dorm key and called for a rideshare to join Amanda and take part in a night of debauchery.

Chapter Three: The Red Iguana

Twelve hours before the accident
October 14, 2016; El Poblado, Colombia

Young and beautiful crowds filled the myriad bars and clubs in El Poblado, in the heart of Medellín. Amid the hypnotic sound of Latin music, vibrant colors swayed back and forth across a tiny dance floor as I walked into the *Iguana Roja,* or Red Iguana, salsa club. "Cassie, over here!" Amanda, a fun-loving gal pal who knew how to unwind, spotted me and waved me over to the bar.

Bodies were pressed up against each other, dancing reggaeton. I blushed at the picturesque displays of sexual intimacy as I made my way through the tight crowd toward my roommate, who was clinking shot glasses with some tall, random variable sitting next to her.

As soon as I was close, Amanda bounded up to me and hugged me hard. "No lab coat? I almost didn't recognize you." She and I'd been placed together as roommates during our study-abroad program. She was outgoing and charismatic.

Another one of the girls from school stood near the bar. Have I mentioned how much I love women in science or any STEM field? Just not this one. The fiery redhead seemed to be sizing me up like I was her next victim. "You look very . . . professional," she stated.

That wasn't so bad. I just ducked my head and tittered in agreement. "Thanks, Rachel."

"Did you just finish an interview or something?" Rachel continued.

A gaggle of girls in low-cut dresses fake-giggled into their hands and whispered like a pack of hyenas from the elementary school playground.

Slightly flustered and embarrassed, I shrugged my shoulders and felt like a skittish dog ready to bolt. My anxiety over clubbing had escalated exponentially since I'd eyed red Fire-drake sitting next to Amanda. Rachel was known for having a bad attitude and she tried to constantly pick fights with me. Her temper resembled the fire breathing dragon from Tolkien's writings. *But she isn't wrong. Maybe I should've skipped the blazer.*

Amanda eyed Rachel with a look that could kill. "Stop it, Greene! You're just jealous our sexy Ms. Brainiac looks hot enough to be on the cover of a magazine."

"As if." Rachel sounded disgusted.

"Just look at her. With those black-rimmed glasses, she could fulfill every guy's hot-for-librarian fantasy!"

"Yeah right. I bet our lil' perfectionist is still a virgin. She's probably never even made it to second base."

Instead of confirming Rachel's suspicions, I turned to leave.

Amanda reached for my wrist to stop me. "It's fine. She's just jelly that her slinky ass doesn't even look half as good as yours. Just ignore her."

"I really don't think I belong here." I motioned toward the club and Rachel and then looked down at my clothes.

"Rachel's just a diva who loves drama in all forms. Everyone knows it. Don't let her push you around."

"Amanda, I think I should just go. I had to stay late at the lab and I still have a million things to do before tomorrow."

"Don't be so boring! You're nineteen. As your roommate, I order you to loosen up for one night and seize the moment, Cassandra Temperance Steel."

Only my mother used my full name, and that was when she was angry with me. I sometimes wondered why my mom gave me the middle name Temperance. Maybe it was because she wanted me to exercise self-restraint.

Amanda nudged me. "I expected you here sooner. I was beginning to worry you'd bailed."

"I had to run a second and third test. For some reason, there was an error in the data on my first experiment. I did everything the same. I can't figure out the unknown variable, and it's going to drive me insane the rest of the night thinking about it."

"Did you have to use a beaker by any chance?"

"Yeah. I grabbed one from the cabinet."

"Don't go ballistic, but I was in a rush to get back to the dorm and I may have accidentally put two of my used beakers back on the clean shelf. I just wasn't thinking straight when I cleaned up. Honestly, I figured everyone was done for the night."

Could that explain the random anomaly? Did I grab one of the dirty beakers?

"I swear I was going to go first thing in the morning and deal with it."

"It's okay, I'm not mad. I just had to stay late to rerun the data. You should be a little more careful, though. I'm lucky none of the chemicals had a negative reaction when mixed."

"I thought you were going to ditch me," admitted Amanda.

"The thought crossed my mind. But since it wasn't midnight, I couldn't use the excuse that my ride turned into a pumpkin. Besides, a promise is a promise."

"Thanks for coming."

I nodded. "So, where is everyone?"

"Dancing, drinking, the usual. You would know if you ever spent time with me." She gestured across the packed dance floor.

I didn't see Xuan anywhere. "We do spend time together. A lot."

"Yeah, but school and rooming together don't count."

"We took a cable car to the library," I offered.

"Yeah, for research."

"We had dinner last night at Carmen."

"Again, for school."

My mouth almost started watering at the memory of the butter-poached shrimp infused with lulo, a local citrus fruit. The dish I'd ordered was a mélange of flavors. We'd all gone out as a class, along with our professors, to celebrate the end of our semester. I gained at least ten pounds after the five course meal, but I didn't care. Our semester in Colombia was coming to a close, and I deserved some commemorative face-stuffing for all the late nights and hard work.

Amanda called our classmates over to the bar, then placed the shots in front of everyone, excluding Rachel.

The college lab suited me, not the party universe. "Uh, I'll pass," I said impishly.

"Drink up," she sang. "Or I'll be forced to give your shot to Greene."

I still wasn't sure if I wanted to drink tonight. I didn't like to lose control.

Amanda finished hers off. "Don't look so scared," she shouted. "C'mon. I dare you!"

I took one of the shot glasses filled to the brim with liquor and mistakenly put my nose up to the rim. I tipped it back and was surprised to taste licorice—a drink the locals call aguardiente, apparently a Colombian favorite. I'd never been a fan of drinking.

"Oh, Cassie, I can't believe we're going home to California tomorrow. I wish we'd spent more time hanging out. I felt like I never saw you during the day."

I sniped jokingly, "Maybe that's because you should have tried to spend a little more time *in* the lab."

"I know," she said with charming self-assurance. "But not all of us are perfectionists like you."

I didn't say a word, not one. Amanda had traded in her microscope and plant samples for high heels, fake eyelashes, and scandalous outfits, but she always looked amazing and she really was smart . . . even if research wasn't her top priority. Amanda wanted to major in Conservation Science and Forest Wildlife Management. Biology wasn't her favorite.

Truthfully, I liked Amanda. She was a good friend and she always had my back. Secretly I wished I was more carefree like her. She was social and outgoing, and she always forced me out of my comfort zone, which was something I needed at times. Amanda was an absolute believer in charging forward, taking the plunge. Her motto was *Carpe diem.*

Another one of our classmates came to give us parting hugs before she headed back to the dorms. "Thanks for inviting me tonight, but I need to get some sleep. I'll see you ladies on the plane tomorrow. This trip's been amazing. Totally one for the record books."

I was distracted by a familiar face. "I couldn't agree more," I said absentmindedly.

Zhang Xuan walked up to greet me and Amanda and waved to Rachel, who was now a few seats down. In response, the redhead turned up her nose and sneered at him, like a dog baring its canine teeth in warning. We all just ignored her.

"Great, I'm surrounded by two hot brainiacs," teased Amanda as she hugged Xuan by way of greeting.

He stuck his hand out to greet me. "Ms. Steel, I'm glad to see you could make it."

So formal. I wrapped my hand in his and shook it. "Nice to see you, too."

When he released my hand, Amanda motioned him toward the empty bar stool next to me. "Care to join us?"

"Sure, I'd love to."

I sipped from my water glass and then began to sway to the beat of the music that filled the air. When I noticed Xuan watching me, I stopped.

Amanda looked from me to Xuan, as if she was formulating some interesting hypothesis. After the bartender took Amanda's next order, she turned to Xuan. The twinkle in her eyes was absolutely mischievous.

"Xuan, would you be interested in helping me solve a problem?" Amanda asked, a little too sweetly.

Oh no, this couldn't be a good thing.

"Sure, if I can."

Amanda bit her lip to try and hide her smile. "Here's the

thing . . . it's been four months since we've arrived in this country and Cassie hasn't been on the dance floor once. It's our last night here and I refuse to let her leave Colombia without experiencing Latin dancing. What do you say? Do you think you can help me rectify the situation?"

My breath caught in my throat, unsure what to say. Leave it to Amanda to pawn me off like I was a situation to be dealt with.

Xuan sent me a searching look. "Is that true?"

I wanted to die from embarrassment, especially since Xuan had avoided responding to Amanda's pitch.

What did that mean? Does he no longer want to dance with me?

Amanda laughed. "Of course it's true! I did go out almost every night. But this is the first time I've been able to talk lil' Ms. Bookworm into coming out and having a little fun."

I rolled my eyes. "I think you and I have very different definitions of fun."

"Your idea of fun is spending Saturday night obsessing over your research. You're a workaholic, Cass. And for fun you volunteer and raise money on campus for good causes, like the local school you brought all those school supplies for. Your effort is commendable." Amanda reached for my glasses and slipped them off, then gently set them on the bar. "I'm just saying you only live life once, and tonight it won't kill you to have a little fun."

Completely embarrassed, I waved her off. My cheeks were probably blooming with color. For some reason it was hard for me to be complimented, especially in front of others. If there was one thing I hated, it was having the center spotlight. Amanda's comment probably confirmed Xuan's suspicions after catching me in the lab tonight. *He probably thinks I'm the most boring person in the world.*

I tried to quickly change the topic. "I would have come out with you more, I just couldn't leave until I finished my work." That wasn't a complete fib. Truth be told, my mode of operation was to stay late at the lab and take a rideshare to the bars and nightclubs after I finished my studies to pick Amanda up, a safety thing.

"I heard you've been going out every week to the local bars and dance clubs together. I thought you'd both be good dancers," Xuan said.

"I've never been a very good dancer," I said in way of explanation. Our eyes met for a moment before I forced myself to turn away. *Did he only ask me to dance because he thought I was good at it?* I tried to make light of the situation by adding, "I attempted to take a few salsa classes back home before coming on this trip, and I also watched Dirty Dancing: Havana Nights at least ten times. While I'm not quite as clumsy as Elaine from Seinfeld, I'm probably a close runner-up."

Xuan's eyes narrowed speculatively and he frowned. He knew I stayed late at the lab, but for some reason he seemed dumbfounded by this revelation. I guessed because his assumption was incorrect, a wrong mark. *Not a party girl after all.*

Amanda handed him a shot.

"Thanks." He held it up and said, "*Gānbēi,*" which he explained was a toast in Mandarin that meant drink up or finish it.

"*Salud,*" I said with Amanda at the same time as we laughed and clinked our glasses to health in Spanish. Having completed two semesters of foreign language study, I was able to manage with the basics as long as the person I was conversing with spoke slowly and used simple words. However, speaking remained a challenge for me, despite the progress I had made in understanding the language over these past few months.

Xuan ordered a third round of aguardiente, which I took, needing some liquid courage before I could muster the nerve to step out onto the dance floor without feeling like a complete idiot. I knew it was only a matter of time before Amanda forced me on to the dance floor with someone, even if it wasn't who I'd hoped for.

Right on cue, Amanda slumped her arm onto Xuan's shoulder and left it resting there. "So what do you say, Mr. Zhang? Would you be up for dancing with my sweet, adorable roommate, or should I find someone else?" She hadn't forgotten.

"I would love to, but only if she'll have me." A genuine smile curved over Xuan's lips as he turned to me. "Did you save me that dance I requested earlier?"

His gaze was unwavering as he waited for me to answer.

Should I? I smiled and whispered in his ear. "I did, but I should warn you, I have two left feet."

"Then we're *sole* mates!" he exclaimed. I laughed at his wit, but little did I know he was a dashing dancer who was simply attempting to ease my inhibitions and insecurities.

Amanda removed her arm from Xuan's shoulder and patted him on the back. "That's the spirit!" She then cleared her throat and held out her hand to me. "Give me your blazer."

All I had underneath was a tank top. "No, that's okay."

"It's too hot on the dance floor and you've been drinking. You're going to get overheated."

I reluctantly shrugged off my jacket and immediately felt bare. I never wore just tank tops. I always felt uncomfortable with my body, and uncovering my arms left me feeling exposed.

"Now your glasses."

My mouth went dry as I handed them to her. "Busybody."

Smiling, Amanda stood up from her stool and whispered in my ear. "You have nothing to feel insecure about, even if you do turn out to be as bad of a dancer as Julia Louis-Dreyfus. That boy hasn't taken his eyes off you since you arrived. You're a total babe. You should own it."

I tossed all reservations aside as the music changed, and Xuan took my hand, leading the way onto the crowded dance floor. My palm sweated so badly from nerves that I didn't know how he could stand touching me. The moving lights cast strange colored shadows all over the bar. The music was pounding away, inside and outside my head.

I counted the beats and realized the song was bachata, a popular music genre in Colombia, known for its highly romantic lyrics. *Okay, I can do this.* I repeated the basic steps I'd learned in my head. *Side with right foot. Close left foot to right foot. Side with right foot. Tap left foot to right foot, partial weight.* Dancing was like an equation, and once you learned the formula it became easier to master with practice.

Xuan was slightly taller than me, standing close to five-eleven. He was thin but strong, and his muscles were defined, which was easy to see underneath his white T-shirt. Usually five-six, not short, I was five-nine that night, a giraffe-like model with my heels, so my eyes were almost level to his as he gave me a playful grin.

Xuan's hand searched my back until he found a place to touch me where we both felt comfortable. As he pulled me closer, I smelled a masculine leather and Indian patchouli scent that was enough to make me weak in the knees. His body was waging biological warfare on me. Closing my eyes, I inhaled, committing the scent and his touch to memory.

Xuan smiled as I stumbled, like Baby in the beginning of that film *Dirty Dancing*. He put a hand around my waist to keep me from falling headfirst onto the dance floor.

"I'm sorry." I laughed. "Definitely no prima ballerina here."

"In the sake of fairness, you did warn me."

Before long, my feet and body got the hang of the fast rhythm and I relaxed my hand in his. The room began to spin. Xuan's grip on me tightened while my feet collided as if I was on an ice rink.

Our bodies picked up an elemental tempo as he drew me in even closer, until our chests pressed against each other. I must've drunk too much, because my reservations quickly drained away. I had to admit, dancing was fun once I got the rhythm down.

"You're good at this," I said to him. "Perhaps even as good as you are at science."

Xuan stepped closer, tightening his grip. "Not even close," he said in my ear as he spun me in circles across the floor. I felt giddy, like a kid on the Tilt-A-Whirl at an amusement park.

As I peered up at him, something about his smile made me feel undone, like a button that was no longer fastened. It was nice to see him away from his studies. He rarely smiled in the lab. The idea that I might never see him like this again when we returned to school in California haunted me. But I didn't know why.

"La Mordidita" by Ricky Martin came on, and suddenly we were dancing merengue. Thankfully this style of dance was easier and had a distinct beat. I began to count to a simple one-two, one-two as I shifted my weight on each pulsing beat. Xuan held his arm up and I did an underarm turn while he stood in place, keeping the rhythm.

I immersed myself into the pulsing beat of the music and the twists and twirls, to the euphoria brought on by a little too much liquor, and to the sweat sliding down my body as I shifted my hips back and forth across the dance floor. For a moment, I glanced up at Xuan, with his light-brown skin and tousled black hair. His lips curved into a slow, crooked grin. I could feel my throat involuntary swallow in response. Our eyes met and I felt myself melting like M&M'S as I looked into his brown eyes. A wave of heat swept over me.

Without us realizing it, the song had ended and we were suddenly dancing salsa.

"You look stunning tonight."

That was a lie of course. Jeans and a tank top didn't really spell out *stunning*. I hadn't dressed up or had time to do anything special, and so I looked the same as always. "Thank you," I murmured. I smiled but couldn't quite meet his eyes.

Slightly flustered, I accidentally collided with another dancer.

"*Lo siento.*" I quickly apologized to the Colombian girl I'd bumped against.

After the song ended, I pushed through the crowd to return to our table. Right on cue, Amanda brought over another round of shots, before she was stolen away by another partner asking her to dance. With each sip, the warm liquor slid down my throat, providing a much-needed respite from my phobia and social anxiety. It served as my liquid courage, gradually making it easier for me to relax and let go.

"You seem to have quite a high tolerance," observed Xuan.

"Actually, I don't drink a lot, never have. My father collects wine, but besides the occasional wine and cheese tasting, it's not really my thing."

"You don't drink?" he asked.

"Um, I didn't say that. I just don't do it a lot. I think it's been over a year since I did shots, though I've never turned down a strawberry margarita or piña colada with my girlfriends."

"The guys in the dorm all said you went out almost every night with Amanda these past four months. I didn't realize it was just to pick her up."

I didn't know what surprised me more—the fact they'd talked about Amanda and me, or the accusation behind the comment. "I wanted to make sure she got home safely."

"You're a good friend."

"Just an hour ago you thought I was a party girl."

"You're right. I should never have assumed."

"It's okay, Xuan. People don't know me that well. In general, they assume that I drink a lot and party based on who my friends are and my past boyfriend." I didn't want to tell him that I lost interest in drinking socially because my ex turned out to be somewhat of a binge drinker. I didn't like to be around him when he drank. I didn't know Xuan well enough to say that, nor did I want to seem excessively insecure. "But I have the second-highest GPA, second only to you, Mr. Zhang. And I can't beat you if I'm dancing or drinking. But since tonight is our last night here, I thought I'd get out and live a little."

Xuan ordered two waters from a waitress passing by. "I love competition, but I'm curious. Why is it so important to you to outdo me?"

"The master's degree program is expensive. I need to get a scholarship or I probably won't be able to afford school. I don't want to wait to save money. People who wait and say they'll go back don't. Well, that's what I've heard. It's important to me to finish my program."

Despite my confession of wanting to defeat him academically, he genuinely smiled. "I've been watching you at the lab."

"You have?" I felt my cheeks burn.

"Your research paper on the yagé culture's shamanic practices, and their ritual use of their sacred plant, ayahuasca, is remarkable. I've been reading the case reports regarding the use of ayahuasca in the treatment of prostate, brain, ovarian, stomach, and colon cancers. I've heard a lot of oral reports of ayahuasca helping people with cancer among South American communities, but unfortunately, written reports with details and clinical data seem scarce. Your proposed model, based on the molecular and cellular biology of ayahuasca's known active components, was very thorough. I have to admit it's been kind of fun to watch you this semester."

He'd paid attention. "Thank you. It's been a fascinating research project."

"A word of advice . . . you should probably steer clear of poker. I think the card sharks would eat you alive."

"That was random. Why?"

"I could easily decipher the play of emotions across your face as you worked on your labs this semester. I could always tell when you were upset or disappointed or excited just by the look on your face. Honestly, your utter absorption in your work is quite refreshing, but don't ever play poker for money."

How observant. "Ummm, thanks. I'll keep that in mind if I ever decide to go to Vegas on a whim."

The waitress dropped off two waters and I greedily gulped mine down. Putting one of the ice cubes in my mouth, I began to suck. The cold felt refreshing against my tongue.

"Did you finish everything you needed to do at the lab?" Xuan asked.

"I did, but it took me longer than I expected. I encountered an interesting set of data that puzzled me on my first experiment—an unknown variable. I—why are you looking at me like that?"

"I was just thinking that you're adorable and sexy when you talk about your work."

"Those two things don't generally go together."

He laughed. "They do when it comes to you. I love your genius brain," he admitted.

There were a lot of words people used to describe me—surfer girl, tree-hugger, hippie, science geek, nerd, athlete. Never sexy. But he wasn't laughing or teasing me, and so maybe he really was being serious.

"Amanda is right about you," he continued. "You're pretty, smart, and caring. You're like a perfect ten."

Is he trying to flirt with me by scoring me on some arbitrary system of measurement? "I think your rating scale might be broken."

"I guess I'm biased." He laughed. "I'm glad we're in the same class, Cassie."

"Me too." That was the truth. Something about Xuan had pushed me to be better. To be the best I could be.

"To be honest, I think my heart did a literal back flip when I saw you on the plane to Colombia," he admitted.

I didn't know what to say. I remember being happy to see him, but I wouldn't describe my feelings as doing back flips. His was such a bold statement that anything I said in response would probably just sound awkward or embarrassing.

Thankfully he saved me from having to say anything as he asked, "Ready for another dance?"

"You came out unscathed from the first round, are you sure you want to push your luck?"

"Absolutely."

"Then I'm all yours."

"Hmmm. I kinda like the sound of that."

Before I could respond, Xuan's warm hand reached for mine. As our hands touched, I felt an exhilarating shiver run through me . . . or maybe that was just the aguardiente. Whatever the reason, he felt good.

He once again pulled me into the crowd. The room was

flashing red and orange as the crowd screamed with excitement while the Spanish music worked toward some kind of climax.

The music changed, and I instantly recognized the J Balvin song that began. Amanda had been playing "Mi Gente" over and over again the past few weeks in the dorm while I'd been trying to study. Dancing reggaeton was all about feeling the music and the beat. There was really no other secret. You had to move your hips and you had to move your feet. He was in such close proximity to me that his nearness made me feel as if we were enclosed in some tight closet. The contact felt charged with electricity. Xuan's hands trailed over my hips, my ribs. *It's part of the dance.*

This style of music and dance were supposed to make you feel like your body was singing from the skin-to-skin contact.

Toward the end of the song, Rachel appeared out of thin air but I couldn't hear what she said. From the look on her face, she seemed to want to cut in. Her sudden attention on Xuan made sense. After all, why wouldn't she want to dance with him? She might have sneered at him like a rabid dog earlier, but he was energetic and exotic, and he stole the spotlight when it came to dancing. Anyone paying attention could see his strength and grace. He'd even managed to survive my two left feet and make me look like a somewhat fluid dancer.

Xuan whispered something in her ear that sent her stomping away like a two-year-old throwing a tantrum.

One of the servers came over and handed us another shot. "*Tu amiga ordenó estas.*" She then tried to say the sentence again so I would understand. "You friend buy drink," the woman said at last in broken English.

"*Gracias, señorita.*"

"I think you've had enough," Xuan suggested.

I didn't disagree. But drinking made me feel relaxed. And the more I drank, the lighter I felt, as though the weight of my studies had been lifted. Plus, I didn't like to be told what to do on principle. Against my better judgment, I took the shot glass and tipped it back.

Another song came on. My blood pulsed in time to the music, as if I had been crafted just for this. My feet shifted and turned quicker and quicker as I became more confident, as I moved to the rhythm and the bass and the Spanish guitar. I was able to match Xuan's every movement as he led me into a turn and then dipped me. Supporting my lower lumbar with his arm, he tipped my face upward with his free hand. For a moment, I thought he was going to kiss me. His face inches from mine. Electric sensations crackled through me. Then the song ended and he pulled me back to my feet, leaving an intense yearning clawing at my heartstrings.

Time slowed and bled from one song to the next. I felt the full effect of the liquor. My hair clung to the back of my sweaty neck, my legs felt numb and my throat ravaged. The way he touched me made me want to wrap myself around him and hold him.

My heart pounded in a dizzying rush as Xuan pressed his chest against mine. I looked up at his face. For a fraction of a second, the earth felt as though it shifted slightly on its axis, the tectonic plates sliding into position under my feet as I lost balance. It only took me a moment to return to planet Earth, but Xuan had already taken notice.

A burning feeling began to climb up the back of my throat, as though I couldn't get enough air in my lungs.

"Are you all right? Would you like to sit?" Xuan's smile faded as his expression turned serious.

"I think I need some water. Excuse me for a moment." I dropped his hand and walked toward the barista and internally applauded myself for ordering water in Spanish. My face felt hot. The Red Iguana was suddenly too warm and too loud.

"Easy, slow breaths." Xuan pulled up a barstool next to me just as Amanda sauntered up with a new guy she'd met on the dance floor. She ordered another shot for each of us. She was able to converse in almost-perfect Spanish and made quick introductions in the common tongue as she waited for the bartender to pour the drinks.

Amanda's new friend reached over and kissed me on the side of my face. In Colombia, kissing complete strangers on the cheek is a friendly way of greeting. The Spanish culture is warm and friendly. To them, Americans seem kind of ridiculous because they don't hug and kiss friends and parents, or even pick up the phone to call them every day. Family means everything in the Colombian culture, and the way they express it is even more important. I just wasn't used to random men and women kissing me and had taken a few months to become comfortable with the custom.

Amanda handed me a full shot glass.

"Amanda, Cassie's had a lot to drink already tonight, don't you think?" Xuan was like a protective lion, slightly reminding me of my favorite vampire character.

"Don't worry, Cassie's fine!"

"No, she isn't."

"Just one more," pushed Amanda.

Xuan took the shot meant for me and tipped it back before picking up his own and finishing it. "Amanda, that's it. No more. Cassie already looks like she's going to be sick."

Was he upset . . . on my behalf?

Amanda began to analyze me. "How ya feeling, Cass?"

I hated to admit it but Xuan was right. I'd been so busy at the lab that I'd forgotten to eat. Without having had any food for the day, I felt light-headed. "I should probably go."

Amanda looked pouty but she didn't argue as I swayed in my seat.

Xuan reached out his hand and placed it gently on my arm before turning his full attention to me. "I think you need food. There are plenty of late-night restaurants still open if you want to get some air."

My stomach twisted as Amanda eyed us both as if she were suddenly stargazing at a new wonder in the sky. "Ah, great idea. You two should go together," she said, her voice mischievous. "Xuan, will you make sure she gets home okay?"

My stomach twisted in retribution for the alcohol, which did not bode well for the impending future. "Err, that's okay. I can go alone. I feel fine," I protested. I would die from embarrassment if I threw up in front of him.

He stared at me with an amused expression. "I don't think that's a good idea."

"Really, I'll be fine. I can just get a rideshare back to the dorm. There's a blue caseta near where we're staying that serves the best arepas and empanadas late at night. I can just pick up something there."

Xuan smiled a dazzling, natural, all-teeth-showing smile. "If it's okay with you, I'd like to escort you the rest of the evening."

"Really, why?" I asked before I could stop myself.

His lips twitched with a smile before he reached out and combed his fingers through my long hair. "I want to make sure you get home safely. Would you be okay with that, Ms. Steel?"

I considered making a mad dash for the door, but knowing my luck and balance when I drank, I'd trip and break my leg.

As if he guessed what I was thinking, Xuan covered my hand with his and squeezed. He really was a charming gentleman for wanting to make sure I'd arrive back to the dorms safely. I didn't know why I felt hesitant about saying yes, but Raylan and his friends used to tell me I had zero streetwise skills.

Amanda looked genuinely amused. After an awkward silence, she glanced at me with a grin that would've made the Norse god Loki proud. Her body language seemed to be shouting her non-verbalized thoughts—*Don't be an idiot! Let him walk you home.*

I nodded timidly. "Sure. I mean, if you want to." Saying yes would be a giant mistake that was likely to end badly in three possible ways. First, it was highly likely I was going to end up doing something embarrassing. Second, I had a terrible habit of saying stupid things when I drank. Or third, I was probably going to get sick on the way home.

When I turned to look at him, he was leaning against the bar counter to cash out his tab. Saints, he was hot. For some reason, my eyes immediately found his lips. I had only kissed two boys in my life. Scott, when I was six years old, on the playground during first-grade recess, and Raylan, tall, lean, and tattooed, whose wardrobe was made entirely of one color—black—and who was my high school sweetheart before he left to serve in the military. But I didn't want to think about him, not then. Maybe not ever. Out of sight out of mind. Repeat.

Gripping the edge of my seat, I hated to admit it but Amanda was right. Xuan really was easy on the eyes, very good-looking with a capital *V*. I caught myself picturing him leaning over the bar to kiss me. My pulse began to race at the distracting image of his lips finding mine. *Snap out of it Cassie! Why the hell am I thinking about kissing him?* Had to be the liquor.

Xuan finished paying and fixed his posture as he stood up straight. His hand slid to my shoulders to ensure I could stand. I didn't know whether I wanted to swat it away or turn and fall into his arms. *What would he do if I did?*

"It's a pleasant night. Care to walk for a while?" Xuan asked as we staggered out into the starlit street. His tone was matter-of-fact, but he seemed nervous as he stood there waiting for my reply.

The restaurant and dorms were far away. *What would we talk about if we walked that entire time?* My brain was having a nervous lockdown. Besides biology class, what did we have in common? Something in me nagged at my inner consciousness that I'd regret it if I didn't go with him.

I didn't have an excuse not to say yes. "Y-yeah, sure. That sounds nice."

A boyish grin covered his face as he took my arm and helped me down the stairs leading away from the bar. We stepped into the crowded streets, despite the fact my stomach was now full of butterflies.

Chapter Four: The Perfect Gentleman

Nine hours before the accident
October 14, 2016; El Poblado, Colombia

Xuan and I decided to stroll down the streets, past several open markets and large street murals on old buildings. The cool night breeze felt wonderful against my skin.

Xuan kept a casual distance from me as I walked beside him. With a little liquid courage, I'd said yes to walking home with him for no other reason than I wanted to be with him for a while longer. He'd insisted on carrying my bag, probably because I staggered a few times. At one point I had the hiccups. Acid rose from my stomach into my throat. *Please don't get sick. Please don't get sick.*

"How are you feeling?" Xuan handed me an unopened bottle of water he'd purchased from an OXXO gas station outside the Red Iguana.

"I think my stomach's a little irritated with me from all the shots."

"Anything I can do for you?"

"Distract me."

"How?"

"Just keep talking. It seems to help."

As we strolled along the broad pavement, I was vaguely aware of the traffic progressing, ghostlike, along the avenue. I asked him questions about China and his roots just to make conversation.

"I was born in Xi'an, China, but my family moved to Beijing when I was three. My father is from Korea, and my mother is from an island in Southern China."

"What's your father's name?"

"Park Ji-Hoon."

"And your mother's?"

"Zhang Mei."

I put two and two together. "Are your parents divorced?"

"No, why?"

"You kept your mom's last name."

"It's traditional for a married woman to keep her name unchanged without adopting her husband's surname in Chinese culture. Generally, children inherit their father's surname as a norm, but my parents decided to have me take my mother's surname since we were living in China and my father's parents had both passed away when he was young."

I tried to focus on him and keep the spotlight off me in order to maintain control. "Why do you write your name *Zhang Xuan* on papers instead of *Xuan Zhang*?"

"In China, last names appear first because our family name is more important than our own individual name. In many Asian countries you can tell the entire history of a family's ancestry based on their last name."

He didn't seem accustomed to talking so much about himself so I prompted him by asking him questions whenever he seemed to be running out of things to say. When he did talk, our conversations were generally very formal. "When did you come to the US to study?"

"I came here during my sophomore year of high school. I lived with an American host family during the school year and then I returned to China during the summers."

That meant I'd been in school with Xuan for three years before our crazy Urkel-style—nerd times a thousand—science teacher assigned us as lab partners. Sure, I got an A in biology, but physics was grueling. Xuan was brilliant and we worked well together in class. We were always the first ones to finish our labs so we helped each other with other classwork. We had an unspoken agreement. I helped him pass Language Arts and he taught me physics. We never even talked about anything outside of classwork.

Sadly, I realized I knew almost nothing about Xuan. Outside of class and studying left a whole lot of time for him to have another life. What did he do when he wasn't at school, and what was he like?

Xuan took my hand and held it as we passed the La Cocina Coctelería, where people were lining the outdoor patio holding bright-colored cocktails garnished with fruit wedges on the edge of their glasses. His touch was timid at first, but when I didn't object, he grew bolder. I analyzed the way his touch made me feel. Excited—as though I could do fifty somersaults in a row on a gymnastic mat.

"Your mom's in the States now, isn't she?"

"Yeah. She finally moved here last year on a business owner visa that allows her to work."

"How about your dad?"

"He's still back in China, running the family business."

"Saints, that must be hard for her, to be away from him."

Xuan let go of my hand after we passed through the crowd of people on the streets.

"It has been. We have family in San Jose who promised to help her adjust but they live a few hours away. Like most immigrants, leaving her home, language, culture, and family was an act of faith. My aunt and uncle convinced my parents their business would thrive here, but it's been difficult for her to adapt to American life. She's tried to avoid places and people who didn't want her. She's worked hard to fit in by enrolling in ESL classes while maintaining her business. I think she's finally settled into her own skin."

"Do you like living in Santa Cruz?"

"It's the American dream."

I loved this part of getting to know someone, how every piece of new information seemed captivating. Being with Xuan felt so natural. Easy. He wasn't like anyone I'd met before and I couldn't imagine conversing with him ever becoming old, or not wanting to hear what he had to say.

Xuan stopped at a little street vendor cart selling cheap empanadas. There were only two left, an empanada with ground meat and potatoes, and an empanada with ham and queso, and so he purchased both.

"Here, this will tide you over until we get to the restaurant." He handed me a container of ají picante sauce.

We ended up sharing the empanadas so we could try both flavors.

"So Amanda told me you were the one responsible for organizing and collecting the school donations being delivered tomorrow. You're quite the champion of causes."

I nodded. "The university program here has been really amazing in helping me connect with the right people and organizations. I honestly couldn't have done it without señor Nieto or señora Gálvez."

"That's really cool. Do you like to volunteer a lot?" he asked.

"I try to volunteer three to five times a month with different organizations. I used to do more in high school, but it's hard with school right now."

"Any organization in particular?"

"I like Grind Out Hunger, the Boys and Girls Club of Santa Cruz County, and the Ronald McDonald House up at Stanford, but I work with others."

"Doing what?"

"Anything. I like working with animals, children, and the elderly."

"Maybe when we get back, I could go with you sometime?"

"Yeah, that would be nice."

"So what else do you like to do for fun, Ms. Steel?"

"I've always loved kickboxing and lately I've started running. How about you?"

"I don't have much time outside of the lab, but when I do, my friends and I play basketball or go to the beach."

Music flitted out from almost every side street. The weather was warm and pleasant, despite the cool October night breeze.

The city was known as the city of eternal spring and everyone seemed to be outside celebrating something. Or just living. With Xuan by my side, I felt as though I was part of this busy night on the streets and not just an onlooker.

A large group passed us on the street. Once again, he grabbed my hand as he closed the gap between us. This time he interlaced our fingers and held on with firm pressure. He didn't let go.

"So what's been your favorite part of the trip?" Xuan changed the subject almost as though our conversation were a tennis match—he hit the ball in my direction to focus on me, not him any longer.

"Since I was a little girl, I wanted to see the Amazon. I remember picking up a picture book in my kindergarten class with pictures of the rainforest and being fascinated. I wish we could have spent more time down there before heading to the school in Medellín. I've never seen anything like it. How about you? What's your favorite part of the trip?"

"I don't have one."

"C'mon, there must've been something."

"I took a weekend trip to Caño Cristales. I liked seeing the different colors of the river. It was like a liquid rainbow."

Many of the students had spent their time traveling around Colombia on the weekends. No one had a car, but we could hop on a plane for fairly cheap and fly into different areas such as Bogotá, the country's official capital city, or Cali, the salsa-dancing capital of the world. Amanda had even convinced me to fly with her to the seductive, sizzling city of Cartagena. We climbed the fortified walls that had once protected the city from pirate attacks and watched the sunset. The entire city had a Miami-style skyline and, after the sun went down, infatuation seemed to bloom into fever and take hold of the city. At night we could hear the clink of rum bottles and mojito glasses in cafés on almost every street as moonlight picked out the silhouettes of softly swaying couples. We walked for hours along the coastal city streets. Candle flames beckoned from the dimness of nearby baroque churches.

"Who's your favorite scientist?" Xuan asked.

"Definitely Marie Curie. She just made her own way and she didn't apologize for it. Yours?"

"I'd have to go with Sir Isaac Newton."

"Why?"

"Thanks to him, scientists believed they had a chance at unlocking the universe's secrets. He connected the heavens and the Earth with his laws. And his mathematics transcended his time."

I felt a wrinkle form between my eyebrows as I considered his opinion. "I use Newton's laws all the time, but I've never thought about him like that. You're absolutely right."

We continued talking about colliding black holes, dinosaur parts in amber, potentially life-friendly planets, the 30 ft. long giant marine crocodile that had turned up in the Tunisian desert, and the first space-time ripples that were detected. The more we talked about science and mathematics, the more I liked him.

"Do you have a favorite scientific theory?" I asked.

"Probably the Infinite Universe Theory. I grew up a Marvel fan, so I've always been fascinated with the idea of the multiverse."

Xuan suddenly stopped on the sidewalk. "Sorry," he said as he raked his fingers through his black hair, making it stand on end.

I rocked forward slightly on my toes. "What for?" I honestly didn't understand why he was suddenly apologizing. Had I missed something?

"I'm happy to be here with you, Cassie. You just make me a little nervous. And so I've been rambling all night about science. I'm probably boring you to tears."

My heart plummeted a little. *How can he think that? Did I give him that impression somehow?* "Not at all!" I promised.

But he didn't seem convinced. I somehow sensed his full attention was now inquisitively on me.

"Do me a favor. If I start talking about anything related to STEM for the rest of the night, will you stop me, please? I don't want to ruin this." His dark expressive eyes were heartbreakingly sad as he said this.

A knot formed in my throat and my chest constricted as though it had been wrapped and coiled by a boa. "Xuan, you haven't ruined anything. I love talking about science and math with you."

"Really?"

"Really."

My stomach untightened a fraction as I realized I wasn't the only person who was anxious when talking to people about their work and the things they loved. I forced my eyes to meet his and took a deep unwavering breath. "To be honest with you Xuan, you also make me a little nervous." That was hard to admit, but he needed to hear the truth because he didn't seem to believe that he had done anything wrong.

Xuan gazed at me like I was the glowing star of Sirius A, "I do?"

I had no idea how to tell him that this was just another thing we seemed to have in common. Shaking my head, I finally said, "In fact, when we left the Red Iguana, I was so worried about what to say that I was honestly relieved we connected so well. I love science and mathematics. Finding someone who shares my same passion honestly thrills me."

He took a breath as if he meant to speak but decided against it. Straightening his back, we continued walking. My reassurance seemed to have given him the confidence he needed to continue talking.

Outside a closed tienda, someone began playing music on their Bluetooth stereo. Within seconds a spontaneous dance party broke out in the street as people gathered around to dance. The streets of Colombia were beautiful in the day, but at nighttime they came alive. Xuan grabbed my arm and led me into a slow spin. No one seemed to mind as we joined in, but my feet were already blistered and in no shape to continue dancing. After one song, we kept walking. I still needed food.

Xuan cleared his throat before asking, "Do you have a favorite equation?"

"Hmmm . . . ." I paused to think. "I'd probably have to go with one equals zero point 9999999999999999 . . ."

"Really?"

"Yeah. I love how simple yet provocative it is, yet it was the first equation that infuriated me in high school math. I had a hard time grasping the concept, because it seems like there should be some tiny infinitesimal number between the two, and it seemed strange that they would equal each other. But once I understood what an infinitely long decimal expansion like zero point 999 actually means, it became easy to grasp. Math is challenging for a lot of people, including myself, and yet that's what I like about it. The challenge. In a way, the left side of one equals zero point 9999999999999999 represents the beginning of mathematics and the right side represents the mysteries of infinity. It's just beautifully balanced. What about you?"

He didn't even have to think about it. "I like the formula for special relativity because it embodies a whole new way of looking at the world and our reality."

Most people would find our conversation stale, but talking about science with Xuan was like a soothing elixir that made me like him even more. We continued to talk, and I honestly couldn't remember the last time I'd conversed so much. More often than not, I usually felt self-conscious, worried that I would sound uninteresting to the individuals listening. But with Xuan it was different—as though we both spoke the same language. I'd found Xuan handsome before, but now I found him irresistible.

"We're here." Xuan gestured as he held the door open for me. He slid into a vacant wooden bench of the restaurant. "Sit beside me." He patted the bench.

Thankful not to be standing any longer, I slumped down into the seat next to him and removed my pair of heels under the table. The shoes were too tight, too awkward. And now my feet were tender with large blisters.

"Sorry, I hope you don't mind. I'm usually more of a flip-flop kinda gal."

"Not at all."

I looked at the menu in Spanish and immediately felt my head start to spin. My concentration was interrupted by the waiter as he approached the table and took our drink orders. "*¿Quieres una bebida*?"

He ordered us both water and guanabana juice. "So what sounds good?" Xuan asked.

"Everything, really. What do you plan on getting?"

"I think I'll go for an arepa and some yuca frita," I said, remembering how much I loved fried yucca.

"That sounds good."

"The menu says they fill their arepas with different ingredients like chicharrón, cheese, ham, pineapple, and shrimp. All that different meat sounds amazing mixed together."

"Why does that surprise me?"

He glanced up. "Do you have something against meat?"

"Not at all. You just sound like you're ordering for a small army. Besides, you just kinda strike me as more the tofu and healthy food type."

"All that dancing made me hungry. Besides I doubt they serve tofu here, and carbs and fried yucca sound awesome right now."

"I, on the other hand, have to watch my girlish figure."

"So what are you planning to get?"

I looked at the menu, but the words appeared blurry. "I don't know yet. Something with lots of meat and carbs. That fried dish also sounded good. Any advice?"

Xuan laughed before he suggested I order caldo with a yellow arepa to fight off the next day's hangover. Frankly his recommendation sounded good and I was relieved, unsure if I could make any further decisions after a night of indulgence.

"So what gave you the impression I only eat healthy food?"

"You forget I used to go to high school with you. I always saw the containers your mom packed for you. Frankly, I think most of the students were envious based on the crap the kitchen ladies used to serve us."

"Were you jealous?"

"Of course."

"Then maybe we can eat together sometime on campus. I could have my mom pack a few extra dishes."

"I'd like that." *What does it say about me that I want to meet him for lunch after we return home?* A small part of me even considered what it would be like to meet his mom.

The bowls of caldo clattered and sent the hot liquid splashing over the rim of the bowl as our meals were dropped before us.

"Eat," Xuan insisted. "You're looking a bit pale."

I debated telling him not to give me orders. But I ate, and Xuan watched me as I watched others who came and went. He continued to ask me questions about my hobbies and family. I tried to avoid talking about my family too much, but I did tell him about my father forcing me to take martial arts as a child. The agreement was I had to reach a black belt rank if I ever wanted to date a boy, once I became old enough. I hated to admit it, but I'd ended up enjoying it, and that led to me taking kickboxing and boxing classes throughout high school.

It was late by the time we were done, and our time together was ending soon. I wasn't ready for that to happen yet, but Xuan ordered a rideshare to shuttle us back to the dorms. The streets were dark and quiet. It was probably close to four o'clock in the morning. He helped me out of the car and I groaned at the sight of all the stairs.

"Want me to carry you?" he offered.

"Absolutely not. We're not newlyweds," I teased.

He shot back as if on cue. "The year is still young."

"Don't be silly." I was grateful for the darkness because I'm sure my cheeks flushed bright red at Xuan's words. I knew he was joking, but his comment still surprised me.

Focusing my attention on the dreaded staircase, I took off the high heels a second time to make the walk less painful.

Xuan walked me to my dormitory. My feet and legs were

screaming by the time we made it upstairs. My feet felt as though they were going to need an ice bath and a week to recover.

When I fumbled with my keys, he gently took them from me and opened the door to the room. Xuan took my hand, clasping it with his long, manicured fingers, and walked wobbly me over to the bed. The room began spinning despite having something solid on my stomach.

"Sit."

"Woof!" I responded to his human-to-dog-like command. Then, silently, I swore I was never going to drink again.

Xuan laughed, then grabbed a bottle of water from the used minifridge Amanda and I had purchased.

He put the bottle of water by the bed. The chalkiness in my mouth overwhelmed me and I was instantly grateful.

For a moment, I worried that he would make a move on me. But, instead he waited for me to climb in and wrapped the quilt around me as though I was a burrito.

"A little light reading, I see." He eyed my literature collection that included Homer, Hemingway, Dante, and Dickens. "I'm surprised. No Jane Austen?"

"I'm not the kind of girl who swoons over Mr. Darcy. I don't find him to be the impossible romantic hero everyone else makes him out to be. I would take Pierre Curie over him any day. Or Ryan Gosling."

Xuan sat on the edge of my bed. "That's good to know. At least I don't have to compete with Darcy to gain your attention."

"Wh-what . . . .?" I stammered, but stopped, ignoring the unformed question swimming in my brain. I thought he was cute before, but he was even cuter then. And the fact that Xuan had been standing in my room discussing a character from Jane Austen was just one of the many surprises of the night.

As I wet my lips with my tongue, I felt Xuan's eyes on me, causing a sudden heat to flush through my body. I couldn't help but suck on the bottom fold, feeling a surge of desire stir within me.

Xuan leaned in closer, his breath warm on my cheek, causing butterflies to explode in my stomach. He looked like he wanted to touch my lips, so I braced myself.

Instead, he hesitated, his fingers brushing a strand of hair behind my ear. The disappointment was fleeting, but the moment of anticipation had left me unhinged. My pulse raced with desire, and I felt a deep ache inside me as I longed for his touch.

I couldn't deny that I was suddenly aching to learn what Xuan's lips felt like. After a minute, I realized I'd forgotten to breathe and took in an exaggerated gulp of air.

The tip of his nose grazed my cheek as he angled himself even closer. As Xuan's warm breath fanned over my ear, I couldn't help but shiver as goosebumps erupted along my spine. My knees felt instantly weak and I was glad I was sitting down. Considering the effect he was having on me in addition to still being tipsy, I'd probably fall off the bed if he kissed me right now.

"Can I get you anything before I go?" His breath fanned over my ear, sent goosebumps down my spine.

The word *go* quickly sank in. *Does Xuan know what kind of effect he's having on me? Is he just toying with me?*

Discontented, I shook my head. "No, I'm good. Thanks for the food, and for walking me home."

Xuan's gaze softened as he spoke. "I enjoyed spending time with you tonight."

"Me too."

"Well, I guess this is it. I should probably get going," he said, his tone regretful.

For a moment, I held my breath, hoping that he would kiss me. But then I realized it might just be my own desire playing tricks on me. As always, Xuan was every bit as noble as he first appeared to be. Instead of kissing me, he simply said goodnight, leaving me to admit that his manners were impeccable, and that Amanda had been wrong about his intentions towards me.

"Sweet dreams, Cassie," he said, pressing his lips gently to my temple.

I nodded. "Night, Xuan. Sleep well." I swallowed any of the impulsive words that would have asked him to stay.

Xuan grabbed me another water.

I shut my eyes, feeling my mouth grin slightly, and sighed. *Inhale, exhale.*

Exhausted, I didn't take long to fall asleep.

That night as I slept, I dreamed of brown eyes that reminded me of the cusp of autumn, with flecks of deep brown mixed with lighter hues.

The next day, I'd be going home. Little did I know that, as I slept, the universe was already conspiring, like a table full of gossiping women, to help nudge me in the right direction toward my fate . . . or to my death.

Chapter Five: The Other Passenger

The next morning-two hours before the accident
Copacabana area, Colombia
October 15, 2016

Ethanol plus carbon dioxide was like a demon spawn pounding against the frontal lobes of my head from the previous night at the bar.

Somewhere in the city there was a church bell ringing, and—oh, not a bell. That was my phone.

My head pounded and I felt dizzy, like I was spinning in circles on a Tilt-A-Whirl ride. Slowly, I opened an eye to try and find my cell phone. I groaned as I reached for the blue-and-silver-plated device on my nightstand. The spins from alcohol sucked.

"¡Buenos días, señorita Steel!"

It's too early to be that chipper, I thought as I yawned.

"Hola, señor Nieto, buenos días," I replied a little groggily. *Why was my professor contacting me?*

"I hope you don't mind me calling, señorita Steel. La señora Gálvez is indisposed, so I suggested you take her place in delivering the school supplies this morning. I figured I'd ask you before calling any of the other teachers, since you were the one responsible for bringing these donations. You might enjoy seeing some of the beautiful, unique landscapes and meeting the children."

Ringing ears and a splitting headache were minor consequences, but the caldo and aspirin had been lifesavers after we left the Red Iguana. And I did want to see the children. "I'd be happy to help."

"Do you think you'll feel comfortable driving alone? Unfortunately, my very pregnant wife just called. Her water broke and she's headed to the hospital. I won't be able to go with you, but

I'll still meet you at the campus dorms," he apologized. He hadn't anticipated his wife going into labor so soon with their first child.

"I'll be okay."

Señor Nieto's voice was warm, possibly amused, but it was difficult to tell over the phone. He was the male dormitory supervisor and the head of the science program in Medellín. He reminded me of a young grandfatherly type of man even though he wasn't very old. Probably late forties to early fifties. "We've packed three vehicles with supplies so we need an extra driver to help deliver them. Just follow the other vehicles."

"How far away is it?"

"About an hour's drive outside the city. The other drivers and I will meet you outside your dorm in thirty."

Prior to departing California, I posted humanitarian flyers on campus and collected essential medical and school supplies to donate. The medical supplies were delivered during our first week in Colombia to towns located inside the dense Amazonian region. Our class spent four weeks studying tropical ethnobiology in the midst of the lush ecosystem. This involved exploring the interconnections between this field and the surrounding environment. For as long as I could remember, it had been my dream to immerse myself in the biocultural diversity of this environment, learning from the shamans and indigenous groups residing within it. I'd been under the direction of señora Gálvez, who was an experienced field ethnobiologist and an excellent translator.

The supplies I'd collected were for various schools. Students on campus had donated book bags, colored pencils, other writing utensils, world maps, flash cards, and sports equipment such as soccer balls.

"See you in thirty, señor Nieto."

Hurrying to get ready, I threw on a light-blue shirt over a sports bra. Squeezing a white tube of topical cream, I reached down and hurried to blot several bug bites that were furiously itching up and down my leg before throwing on a pair of khaki shorts. I'd tried to keep the pesky little demons away with shields of spray from cans I'd purchased back in the States that promised false hope. I'd lost count of my insect bites collected from the Amazon region in southern Colombia, and I had at least a dozen more from the ecology hike up Salto del Tequendama, and the Arví Park in Medellín. My legs looked as though they had chicken pox with all the red bumps.

After I finished dressing, I logged on to my computer to check in for my flight and then checked my recent messages. Raylan. Again. The prodigal fighter returns.

From: Raylan Thompson
Subject: Please Answer Me
Date: October 14 2016 19:29
To: Cassie Steel

Cass, I really need to hear from you. Why do you keep ignoring me? I've written you a hundred messages! I'm going to deploy with my unit on Tuesday. Middle East for twelve months.

I'm sorry, I'm SOOOOO FREAKIN' SORRY! I don't know what else to say to make you forgive me. I swear to you, it didn't mean anything. I was drunk, and it just happened the one time.

I'm going crazy without you. Please answer me. You are the only one I want. YOU.

I don't know why it's taken me so long to say this, but I love you. I'm in love with you, Cassie. I decided I want to marry you and settle down with you when I return, and I'm sorry it's taken me this long to realize it. There's no one else I want. You're my girl, and I can't believe I'm doing this over email, but since you won't answer me, I need to say this . . .

Cassandra Temperance Steel, will you marry me?

Please answer me!
Love,
Raylan

My ex-boyfriend was dramatic, adventurous, and selfish. At one time I thought I'd do anything to make him happy. I thought I might even love him, but I'd never told him that. He had me under his spell. That was before I found him sleeping with someone else. The three-year enchantment was broken after that. The magic lifted. Finding my boyfriend and a high school friend in bed together was horrific. Made me feel like I wasn't good enough for him, and it took me a while to realize that wasn't true. The aftermath of our breakup left me feeling utterly defeated, and my self-confidence plummeted to unimaginable depths—perhaps as low as the wreckage of a sunken ship or the depths of the Mariana Trench, which is known to be the deepest point in the ocean. It was *that* bad.

The answer to why the equation of 1 + 1 + 1 = 0 was that Raylan didn't want the real me. He only thought he did, and therefore the solution to the problem ended up being a simple subtraction equation.

And now Raylan wants me to marry him? Holy Saints, what was he thinking? After all, I knew I certainly wasn't marriageable material. And deep down he had to know that too if he decided to sleep with someone else.

The problem was it wasn't just Raylan's fault that we broke up before he left to play G.I. Joe. I wasn't exactly a *great* girlfriend, because I was always too focused on my studies and research. There's no excuse for cheating on someone, but despite what he *did*, I was the true bigamist. I'd been in a long-standing relationship with science since I was fourteen years old. I knew what I wanted in my life and that did not equal banshee-screaming babies within the next ten years. Maybe ever. Plus babies meant husbands, and husbands meant boyfriends like my cheating high school sweetheart, who only wanted *sex.* And sex was just not something on my to-try list anytime soon. Something I was in no way ready for. Even thinking about it made me uncomfortable.

I had my life already set and carved in stone and it did not include being a housewife like my mother, Stella. My end goal was *The Lasker Awards* for major contributions to medical science. Admittedly that was a long shot. But my dream was to study ethnobiology and eventually publish findings that would lead to the treatment, cure, and prevention of human diseases, such as cancer. But *The Lasker Awards* were like the *Nobel Prize*—prestigious. I had a vision for a better world, and the only way I was capable of helping to improve society was through my dedication and scientific research. Dealing with mountains of exploding diapers would only hinder my goal.

I grazed over Raylan's message again with absolutely no intention of replying to his declaration of love. As far as I was concerned, I didn't owe him anything, especially not a response to an email proposal sent out of desperation. So I chose silence. Letting him go was the best choice. "Goodbye, Raylan. Stay safe," I whispered.

I tucked an escaped tendril of hair into a messy bun and slipped on sandals before waking my dormmate, Amanda, to tell her where I was going. She waved me off in wordless recognition before falling back into slumber. Even on a good day, Amanda was definitely not a morning person. I learned quickly that it was dangerous to try and rouse her out of bed before noon. Like loss of life dangerous.

I grabbed the knife my father had insisted I bring on my trip from the bedside drawer. He was a Command Sergeant Major in the United States Army and believed in self-protection. Both my parents were respectable people, but they were set in their ways. There was no way I was going to board the plane to a foreign country without a knife and a can of pepper spray packed into my checked bag.

Señor Nieto and two other men—Santiago and Marlon—were waiting downstairs. Marlon's belly was like stacked cheddar rolls while Santiago was the complete opposite. Señor Nieto was the only one who spoke good English. The other two drivers could say a few words and basic sentences, but señor Nieto assured me they were two of his closest friends. He said they were good men and he trusted them with his life.

The utility vehicles were small and packed, which was probably why they needed three drivers. The agency that had arranged the school-supply donations had lent señor Nieto the vehicles to make the journey delivering backpacks and school supplies to children and teachers in need.

I took a minute to get the feel of the vehicle. A few years had passed since I'd driven a stick shift. Finally ready, we pulled away from the dorms and set off into the city on clear roads. It was still early—my return flight didn't leave from Olaya Herrera Airport until 8:30 p.m.

While cruising along the backstreets of Medellín toward the Medellín-Bogotá highway on-ramp, my mind wandered. I replayed the night over and over again in my head. I had never drunk so much alcohol, and I felt embarrassed by how I must have seemed to Xuan, who was nothing but a complete gentleman. *Could he tell I was into him?* Parts of the night were hazy recollections. The more I dissected it like a frog, the more a splitting headache pierced my slush brain. Maybe it was easier to try to forget. Besides, it wasn't like I'd see Xuan much after we returned to the States. Maybe on campus or in a science class, *if* I was lucky.

I checked the speedometer, which was in kilometers per hour versus miles per hour. I was driving more cautiously than I would on any other occasion in the States. Hundreds of motorcycles zoomed by, weaving in and out of traffic.

Leaving the city limits behind, I sat back and listened to the music on the radio as I pressed down on the accelerator. The limit on the two-lane road didn't pass seventy kilometers per hour, which roughly equaled forty miles per hour in the US. The speed wasn't fast, and I felt as though I was driving on a main street in California. But it seemed dangerous to go any faster as the road began to twist and turn like a coiled snake up into the lush, green mountains of the Copacabana area. The news came on, and I heard something about the weather, but I couldn't understand what they were saying in Spanish so I changed the station to one playing music.

I began to feel out of my comfort zone as the sky turned dark. Driving in a storm on a winding road was not what I had expected. The farther we drove, the worse it became. Wind-driven rain blew hard across the mountainside, sweeping rivers of water against the windshield. Another news report bellowed about a storm. The heavy rain was cleaning the juicy splatters of bugs so I could see better. For some reason, the insects were bigger down there, as if they were on steroids.

Up ahead, I noticed red taillights and slowed down, then came to a stop. *Great, probably roadwork.* I was used to the gridlock on the US 101 and SR 17 in California, so a little traffic didn't bother me as long as I arrived back in time to make the plane.

Santiago and Marlon were in the two cars in front of me. Santiago's skinny arm reached out from the window and gave me a thumbs up.

I'd reached out to turn down the radio just as a faint rumbling startled me. I couldn't see anything unusual, but the sound didn't stop, growing louder. Then the ground began to vibrate, sounding as though trees were cracking or boulders were knocking together. I was used to earthquakes in the Golden State, but this was different. The faint, eerie rumbling noise increased, like an oncoming train or—*holy . . . what is that?*

No one else was moving or getting out of their cars. I put the car in park and stayed put.

Then the world exploded.

A wall of slurry water filled the street as mud cascaded down the hillside. My car started to move in a way that wasn't normal in taillight to taillight traffic. I held on and put both hands on the wheel, making sure it was straight. The water flow rapidly filled the street at avalanche speed, lifting my vehicle. A river of mud sent me careening down the street in a sideways motion. Then the boat-ish rocking movement stopped.

Horror-struck, I watched as a barrage of rock and debris streamed down the slope with roaring speed and power. The cars in front of me were in the path of the landslide of rock that swept over the road.

Santiago got out of his car to check on me. "Stay car!" he yelled in broken English, and then dashed to get back inside where it was safe.

I heard the scream form in my throat before I could warn him. Monster-sized boulders tumbled, one by one, down the hillside. Fountains of dirt and mud sprayed up, geysering into the sky, striking the vehicles in front of me. The pressure continued to knock into the driver-side door of my car. I watched in horror as Santiago's and Marlon's vehicles slid closer and closer to the edge of the cliff that was blocked off by orange construction cones. Within seconds, Santiago and Marlon were nowhere to be seen . . . gone.

Before I could see what happened, I felt my head slam into the steering wheel. Mud continued to shove the vehicle forward, a violent thrust meant to send the car down the ravine. *No, no, no,* a little voice begged inside my head. *Not like this.* Then suddenly the car stopped moving. The world seemed to pause, but only for a moment.

A hard thump hit somewhere in the back of the car. My whole body twisted, slamming face-first into the door, as more debris thrashed into the side of the car. Every muscle and tendon roared at the sound of the snap of a bone inside my left arm. My wrist hit something sharp, but what? I could feel sticky blood drip across my leg and the seat. I didn't cry.

Metal groaned. I felt something hard tighten around my right leg from underneath the dashboard as something large slammed the front of the vehicle causing glass to shatter. I was pinned.

The muddy water level continued to rise on the road as the car banged against a small rail. Everything around me was spiraling out of control, but I was safe. Whatever was holding the car in place had saved me from falling into the watery death that awaited me below. The vehicle was little better than a coffin on wheels. Santiago and Marlon were gone. There was no one who could help me. I had to save myself.

I panted through my teeth as I reached forward with my right arm and tried to free myself. My leg didn't budge. I tried again.

I can do this. Don't panic. I have to think. My seat belt was jammed and wouldn't release. I tried to reach for my pocketknife in my left pocket, using my right hand. I gritted my teeth and reached it but accidentally hit my hurt left arm.

Hands shaking, I gripped the blood-smeared knife as my father had taught me. The knife slipped from my grasp and tipped forward, burying itself point-down in the leather seat. *Pull yourself together.* I felt faint from the amount of blood I'd lost, but this was time for Hulk-like adrenaline. I refused to be some helpless character like Princess Andromeda in the Greek myth, or some modern-day damsel in distress like Lois Lane, who required constant rescuing by Superman. I had to be the heroine of my own story.

I cut through the fabric of the seat belt. *Now what?* My leg was stuck. I tried to move my ankle and calf muscle, but my leg wouldn't move. Gritting my teeth, I wiggled and yanked. But short of turning into Aron Ralston in *127 Hours* and cutting off my own leg with a three-inch knife, I wasn't getting free.

Outside, the intense burst of rain had stopped and was now little more than a mist. The murky water trickled instead of flowed. *Maybe the disaster is over.* Then, out of nowhere, I heard my name. "Cassandra!"

I heard it again. *Or am I dreaming?*

Just moving my head sparked agony, but I had to see. To know if I was imagining or hallucinating my name being called.

"Cassandra!"

It was Zhang Xuan. He was standing near a vehicle, in ripped denim jeans and a black shirt. Seeing him was a prayer answered.

"Xuan! Over here!"

He was already running like hell as he made his way toward me. A small path was clear of the major debris that littered the entire highway. He waded knee deep through the mud toward where the vehicle was stuck.

The softness in his eyes when he saw me disappeared within seconds as he began to assess the situation.

"Are you okay?" he asked.

"I've been better."

"I can see that."

"Xuan, what are you doing here?"

"That's kind of a long story. First, let's get you out of here."

He paused before touching my injured arm. His eyes met mine in silent question, still concerned with being polite.

"I can't get my leg free."

His head bowed down below my leg so he could see what it was stuck on. I watched him as his inky hair spilled onto his brow.

"I need a crowbar." His expression was resolute. "Let me go see if I have one."

Xuan reached out and took my face in his hands. I was surprised to see his eyes blazing, his breathing as ragged as my own. "I'll come back. You're going to be okay, Cassie. I promise I will get you out of here."

I nodded.

Then he did something I didn't expect. I opened my mouth to say something but Xuan lowered his mouth to mine. I stiffened as his mouth briefly touched my skin. His gesture was so sudden, a featherlight graze, barely a whisper of a kiss, and yet it was full of longing. I don't know why this took me by surprise, but it did. Then his mouth was on mine, and he pushed his tongue between my lips in passionate desperation.

I swallowed. I'd been kissed before, of course, by Raylan, often enough that I was no stranger to the deed. But when Xuan kissed me it felt right, as though I was home. As though the fortress I'd built around my heart had slowly cracked and was ready to fall. As if this boy in front of me . . . a boy I barely knew . . . held the key.

Next to me, Zhang Xuan looked cool and calm as he pulled

back and studied my face. Rain dripped off his long black eyelashes like tears. And before I could say anything, he turned away and hurried back toward the car he must have borrowed from someone.

I had so many questions. *Whose car is that? Why are you here? How did you find me? Why did you kiss me?* But those questions could wait.

I watched as Xuan quickly moved toward the vehicle, parked far enough away that he was not directly in the path of the mudslide. Up about a half mile ahead, on the opposite side of the road, I saw bright lights pulsing red like an artery as rescue vehicles appeared, their sirens blaring.

Xuan stormed back toward me, stepping over large debris and fragments of earth as he waded through the slush, crowbar in hand.

"People are here to help, Xuan."

"They're too far away. We need to get you out of here. Now."

He took the crowbar and started to pry the area enclosing my leg. I could feel something lift, but my leg still wouldn't budge. His muscles contracted as he worked.

"You know, you're kinda beautiful," I said as I focused on the earthy hues of his eyes. Blood drops splattered everywhere. I tried not to look at my arm or the cuts on my body and instead focused on looking outside. Light was still visible in the sky despite the storm clouds, as streaks of sunlight were scattered off the atmosphere. "I'm serious. You're like an angel."

His eyes flickered "Likewise," he said, his mouth curling in a half-smile.

He grunted through his teeth as he tried to lift the dented metal. Finally something cracked and I could feel my leg slightly loosen. I was almost free.

Xuan's head snapped up.

Instantly he sprang to his feet, whirling toward a sound, a vibration.

"Is that more water?" I asked, panicked.

"We need to hurry."

Crowbar in hand, Xuan quickly moved his body inside the vehicle so the current would not sweep him away. More debris came hurtling toward the vehicle, knocking into the back. Xuan hurried to buckle himself as metal groaned. "We're going down!"

I couldn't help but scream. Xuan reached for my hand and grabbed it tightly.

"Cassie, look at me. It'll be okay. I promise you, we'll make it through this. Together."

I nodded. "Together," I repeated with a shaky voice.

I remember the water. I remember screaming as the vehicle ricocheted forward, then down again, and the guardrail gave way, sending the vehicle toward the edge. Then the metal gave out and we were falling.

Xuan yelled something loudly in Chinese as the car continued to plummet down the side of the mountain. Xuan yelled and the next thing I knew his head was rolling forward, his eyes closed. He was out cold.

Metal and glass cut into my flesh. I remember the tears that rolled down my face, silent and unending as the wrath of the mountain. Everything after that happened so fast that it didn't take long before we hit the bottom.

I remember looking up toward the angry mountain and the sky. There were areas much steeper and sharper that would have surely been a death sentence.

Sometime during the descent, Xuan lost his hold on the crowbar. It must have fallen into the back, but I couldn't reach it while I was pinned. I remember trying to force my leg free. I remember the blare of a horn, and the bright headlights of a second car. After that, darkness embraced me, a darkness that hurt like hell.

Five minutes. An hour. A day. I had no way of knowing how long I was unconscious. At first there was nothing. Time seemed to mean nothing. Then flashes of images from the night before snaked their way into my mind.

School lab.

Bar.

Dancing.

Arepas.

Amanda.

Zhang Xuan.

Falling, falling, falling.

As my eyes gradually but painfully began to open, confusion washed over me. I tried to remember what had happened

Where was I? Why was my head bleeding?

As I put the pieces of the story back together, something was different. I was alone . . . and I had been alone the entire time.

That's not true.

Looking over to the passenger seat, I saw Xuan. *Is this real?* The images of Xuan over the past half hour had vanished completely.

This doesn't make any sense.

Think. I didn't remember driving up the mountain with Xuan. I didn't remember why he was there. I didn't remember Xuan being with me in the car when the guardrail finally gave way. It was like my mind had erased him entirely from the scene of the accident.

But why would I do that? *Because Xuan being there didn't make any sense. This wasn't a fairy tale. Handsome boys don't just magically appear screaming your name the moment you need them.*

Swaying slightly in my seat, I wanted the image of Xuan sitting beside me to just be a manifestation, because that was the only way I could keep him safe and perfect—alive.

"Xuan?" I whispered. My lungs burned as I said his name. The sheer dryness of my mouth was unbearable.

I reached out to touch him, but before I could grab him I passed out. *Maybe he really isn't here.*

When I regained consciousness, my toes and heel were submerged in water that continued to rise. At one point I thought I could see a pale female figure with long ebony hair and black wings in the rearview mirror. I hated Death. She reeked of blood and a rich, earthy, salty smell. I knew she was still a passenger.

Death could go to hell—

My mind continued to play tricks on me. Sometimes I would see an empty seat, and other times I would see Xuan. But it would not let me delete the hero of the story for long.

The sound of coughing seemed to snap me back to reality. Beside me, Xuan was still unconscious, but he was moving.

"Xuan?" *Is this real?* I wanted so badly for my guardian angel's daring rescue attempt to be nothing more than a fantasy—a good dream. But as he coughed again, I knew it wasn't. He was really sitting there next to me in the passenger seat. A knight in shining armor. "Xuan, if you can hear me, you have to wake up. We fell, and now we're stuck. And no one's coming to help us. You have to wake up, because if you don't something worse might happen. If you can hear me, come back to me."

Somehow, the thought of him getting hurt—or worse—terrified me. If Xuan really had come to save me, and he died—I didn't know if I could ever resurface from that. A dagger in the heart would be less painful.

I needed to wake him, but I couldn't seem to hold on. I felt too weak to stay awake for long. I just needed a little more rest. I reached for him and closed my eyes. Grabbing his left hand, I gently enfolded my fingers over his.

The next time I woke, I was more determined. I shifted my body to the right and continued to gently shake Xuan awake.

"Xuan!" I yelled in panic. No reaction. I put my hand in front of his nose and watched his chest. *He's breathing.* His neck and hand were skinned, but he didn't look as though he was bleeding profusely or suffering any severe cuts or life-threatening injuries. At least, none that I could see. Internal bleeding was always a scary danger.

With a sigh of relief, I tried to nudge him again. "You need to wake up for me now, okay? *You* need to get yourself somewhere safe. Please." I interlaced our fingers and squeezed our palms together as I brought his hand to my lips. I fanned my hot breath over the back of his hand before kissing his skin.

Xuan's muscles tensed. The next time I said his name, he let out a low groan.

"Cassie—"

My insides melted with relief at the sound of his voice. It took him a minute to regain full consciousness.

"I'm okay," he whispered.

When he finally opened his eyes, I fought the desire to kiss him.

Once I heard a response and saw his conscious face, I breathed a sigh of relief. My guardian angel was still with me and he was okay.

He eyed the blood splatters on the airbag and dashboard. "And you?"

"I just want to get out of here."

He seemed fully alert now as he began to assess the full situation. My eyes followed his as I began to look around and get my bearings. We were surrounded by a muddy pit of bodies. The ground was a graveyard of metal and smashed-up cars. The school supplies that had been packed on top of the jeep now littered the mountainside. *Santiago and Marlon, where are they?* I looked around for their car, but there were just too many.

"Thankfully you were driving an older, heavier car or I think we might've been smashed to death."

That thought was far from comforting, but he was right. We'd been lucky in so many ways.

"It looks like we went from being stuck on a cliff to being stuck in a ravine," Xuan offered.

I knew I should feel lucky that we'd both pulled through, especially when many others had not likely survived the plummet. But our situation had not improved and the disaster was still not over.

These were the things I knew to be true. The vehicle was stuck at the bottom of a ravine, with water and mud still pouring off the edge of the mountainside. The water level had risen enough to come into the floor of the vehicle. The crowbar was nowhere in sight and I was still pinned. Beyond those facts, there were probably a lot more unknown variables working against us.

We were both science majors. We knew how to calculate the math. The odds of survival were stacked against us—especially me.

"Xuan, we need to hurry."

"I know." In response he wedged himself between the center seats and looked for the crowbar. "Found it!" Then he ducked between my legs and started to examine the metal pinning me in place.

"I can get you out." He sounded determined. "Close the door and roll down the window," Xuan commanded as he tried to roll down the passenger-side window.

I did as I was told. I knew science. I knew that once the water filled the car, the water pressure would force the window against the doorframe, making it impossible to crack it open. Thankfully the vehicle was not automatic and I could roll it down with the handle.

Grunting, Xuan didn't waste time as he got to work. The water continued to rise. Six inches of water.

"Take off your seat belt."

"I already did."

Outside the rain was relentless. Water continued to plunge into the ravine like a waterfall.

He continued to work, prying the metal with the crowbar as the vehicle continued to fill with mud. One foot of water.

Two feet.

Time was critical. We only had a few minutes until the water would rise to the bottom of the driver-side window.

There wasn't much I could do to help. Outside, another car began to do a tumbling barrel roll, flipped through the air and crashed.

At three feet Xuan's usual take-charge manner seemed to slip a bit. The car continued to fill up. Xuan panted and then gritted his teeth, his hands white-knuckled on the crowbar as he tried to free my leg.

His efforts were useless. My leg hadn't budged and time was running out. Icy coldness dug into my muscles and joints from the water. Shivers cascaded all over my body.

This entire time I'd been looking for hope in numbers and equations, but math did not lie. Hope was reserved for faith and miracles. And while I considered myself a Christian, I did not believe I'd be spared. But that didn't mean there still wasn't time to do the right thing.

Suddenly everything made sense. There was really only one solution.

"Xuan, you need to leave me." *Because only one of us is supposed to survive.*

"Cassie, if you don't get out of this car *now*, we won't stand a chance against that water. We'll drown. Not you . . . . *we*, because I'm not going without you!"

I reached for his arm and then began to shove him. "Xuan you need to go!"

"No—" he yelled. "I don't want to hear it. I'm staying."

How can he risk his life for mine? Whether it was courage or stupidity that made him stay, I didn't care. I was grateful, but that didn't change the fact that I wasn't going to make it out of this. The sooner I accepted this, the easier it would be when the time came.

About thirty feet in front of us, another vehicle fell from the cliff, rolled over facedown into the water and muck and then continued to slide.

Xuan's struggle became apparent once the water reached my chest. I felt something budge slightly, but it was not enough. Xuan could no longer see my leg or the area below to guide him.

"Xuan, it's almost time. You need to leave."

He ignored me and put his head under the water to see and feel the submerged area below the steering wheel.

I don't want to die. My mind raced with what-ifs. I knew I was losing control. Denial, shock, bargaining. My mind was on hyperdrive, trying to process the stages of my own grief.

Next burning anger pulsed through my body, immobilizing me. *Why me?*

I almost wished I'd died the same way Santiago and Marlon did—fast. It seemed unfair to survive falling off a mountain only to drown. But I wasn't alone, and drowning would be better if it meant saving Xuan.

I heard something loud and suddenly my leg felt looser.

"Can you move?"

I tried to move. "Not fully."

He went back under to get a look at what he needed to do. While he was under, the water reached my neckline.

I felt myself begin to hyperventilate. I gasped for air as if these would be my last breaths.

Xuan came back up. "We're close. Cassie. I've almost got it."

I nodded. I couldn't speak—I couldn't breathe.

"Cassie, look at me. Look into my eyes. I *will* get you out of here. Hold on as long as you can."

I nodded and focused on his voice of reason. "I trust you."

"I need you to stay calm. You're a surfer, Cassie. You've been submerged in water before. I need you to focus on your breathing and nothing else right now. I need you to imagine a big wave is coming—the biggest you've ever surfed. What would you do to prepare for it?"

He was right. When you surf, you learn breath training because your life depends on it. Literally. "Okay, I can do that."

"Good, now focus."

I didn't know how long I could hold my breath. A minute, maybe? Five if I stayed calm. I remember the first time I was caught in a three-wave hold-down. I thought the nightmare was never going to end. Since then, I'd been in plenty of hold-down situations where I got caught under a set of waves. Each time there was fear, anxiety, and that instinctual need for breath that kicks in. The freaking out, the chaotic kicking and paddling for the surface, all of which does nothing good for the situation. *This is just like that.*

I began to take deep breaths in, expanding my belly and then pulling air into the bottom of my lungs.

While Xuan worked, I tried my best to relax my muscles and mind, but the only way I could do that was by closing my eyes. After twenty breaths, I slowly began to focus on expanding my ribcage to fill my mid-lungs. At forty breaths, I raised my chest and focus on filling my top lungs. Each inhalation and exhalation lasted for four seconds.

I saw Xuan as soon as I opened my eyes again, and I knew there wasn't much time left.

As if sensing the same thing, Xuan turned to look at me. The water was close to reaching my mouth now, and there was still so much I needed to say. "Xuan, if I don't make it, I need you to call my parents," I said quietly. "I need you to tell them—"

"Stop—"

"Tell them that I loved them, and that everything I am is because of how they raised me. I'm sorry for all the crap I put them through growing up but I couldn't have asked for better parents. Tell my father I forgive him for always being away. I know it was his duty and I don't blame him. I only wish we'd had more time together."

"Don't do this, Cassie. Don't make those kinds of goodbyes. Just focus on your breathing, okay honey?"

So much could go wrong. I needed them to know. "Tell my friends I was grateful for them and I'll miss them. Tell them life's too short and to remember to enjoy each moment."

"Shh!"

I didn't listen. I needed him to hear my last words. "Tell Raylan Thompson I forgive him," I said, shaking. Tears filled my eyes.

Xuan's expression turned from panic to agony and desperation, but he kept working. "Don't waste your breath. You'll be able to tell them all yourself when we make it out of here."

Reaching out with my right hand, I grasped the top of the tool he was using. "It's time to stop now."

"No!"

"I wish I could have spent more time with you. Thank you for trying to save me, Xuan. But you need to go. You can still make it."

"I'm not leaving."

There was beauty in his face—and strength, and honor, and loyalty. I knew he would stay and fight until his last breath to try and save me. But it was pointless. "You have to, Xuan. We're both out of time."

"I'm so close, I can still save you!"

"Listen to me! I'm going to die and it's *not* your fault. Whatever happens, do *not* die because of me. Get yourself out. You have to live, even if that means letting me go."

Xuan twisted toward me. His breath felt alien and distant as his fingers caressed my cheek. He brushed his thumb against my lower lip. And then he leaned forward across the center divide and kissed me. When his mouth touched mine, pleasure jolted to my heart, down to my pinned leg. I closed my eyes as he claimed my mouth with his tongue. My entire body went taut and molten in all the right places as he bit my lower lip and then sucked at it. I wanted to dig my fingers into his hair, but that was impossible given my position. I tried to imprint his taste and softness so I could take those memories with me, into the terrifying water.

My instincts came over me with desperate yearning. I kissed him back with everything in me, hoping that this kiss would articulate everything that I couldn't bring myself to say.

When I opened my eyes again, he was still staring at me. His eyes begged me to live and hold on as the water continued to rise. I had about six to ten breaths left before water would enter my lungs.

This was it.

"Xuan, I li—"

My mouth was now fully submerged. I could no longer speak.

Xuan knew what came next and howled. He began to pound away harder and faster than before with the crowbar. I watched his shoulders as adrenaline shot through him.

It was time. The water was about to flood into my nose, suppressing my ability to breathe. I had to make my last intake of oxygen count. I inhaled deeply through my nose and exhaled three times before taking one last breath.

The last thing I saw before I was inundated by the muddy water was the horrified look on Xuan's face. His facial features flared with rage and despair and grief—I would never forget his angelic face.

I let out discreet, minuscule amounts of air through my nose, trying to buy as much time as I could before it was too late . . . praying for a miracle. *Don't panic. Fear is acceptable, panic will only consume energy.*

I couldn't see Xuan. I only felt him as I sat trapped inside the metal tomb. *I can't breathe. I can't see. Was it the French author Arthur Rimbaud who said, "I believe I am in hell, therefore I am"?*

The instinct not to breathe underwater was so strong that it overcame the agony of running out of air. *Stay calm. If my heart rate is twenty-five percent higher than normal, my lung capacity will be dramatically diminished.*

Just then, I felt fingers on my face. Xuan's mouth and lips reached mine, blowing in a small mouthful of air. Xuan must have gone out his window for air and come back in. I felt a hand touch my leg and then pressure as Xuan continued to work to free me.

Don't panic. Don't panic. I tried to imagine I was surfing and fell off my board during a killer set on the Banzai Pipeline on O'ahu's North Shore. In surfing, being fully submerged underwater and unable to come up for air was like being caught in a reef break. Reef breaks are brutal areas in the ocean where machine-like waves form one right after the other. At first, that's what drowning felt like. That image didn't last long.

Half-conscious and enfeebled by oxygen depletion, I knew the water was suffocating me. *I'm going to die,* my mind told me. My body felt tight. I tried to kick my leg loose, trapped like an animal in the wilderness. The clock was running down now. These were my final moments of clarity . . . of my life. Even if Xuan did somehow get my leg loose, I would never make it to the surface. Xuan wasn't going to be able to keep his promise. There would be no escape.

So I prayed . . . not for me but for Xuan. I prayed he would live. He could still make it out, but he was endangering himself by staying. He'd risked his life to help me. Jeopardized his own safety for a girl he really barely knew. He didn't deserve to die like that, a nameless hero.

Knowing I was about to die wasn't a peaceful feeling. I didn't want to accept the fact that life was over. But as the seconds continued to tick by, I knew I was on the verge of losing consciousness. I actually contemplated breathing in the water on purpose, just to get it over with, but that idea felt too horrible to consider.

No—I was a fighter.

So I held on until I reached the breaking point . . . the point where there was too much carbon dioxide in my blood and too little oxygen. I fought against the urge to breathe until I couldn't hold out any longer.

The chemical sensors in my brain triggered an involuntary breath. The spasmodic breath dragged muddy water into my mouth and windpipe. I felt an immediate contraction in the muscles around the larynx. *It won't be long now.* My body thrashed in response so I swallowed more and more water.

I looked up to see sunlight one last time, but I saw none, zilch. The catacombs in my mind opened revealing the ancient tall redwood forests near my home and I felt a sense of peace. My parents and friends were there with me. Even Xuan was standing there. His beautiful eyes held the same look he had right before he kissed me . . . my last kiss. Then darkness began to spread across my eyes and the world blackened at the edges.

There was no bright white light, only darkness, nothing, zip.

There was no more pain.

Finally, I let go.

Chapter Six: The Weight of Water

Copacabana area, Colombia
October 15, 2016

As my guardian angel held me, we drifted together in the black current of a watery death.

I remembered only a long and silent fall and then nothingness as the river and the rocks hurtled toward me while Xuan desperately tried to free me. Then there was nothing.

Fade out. Curtain drops. The End.

I recalled Xuan's voice. "Breathe, Cass. Breathe!"

I could feel his lips pressed against mine . . . and then something hard slammed against my chest, over and over.

The next thing I knew I was spitting up filthy water, gasping for breath. I didn't remember being pulled up. I only knew that my lungs and stomach burned like lava as I vomited up water.

"I've got you."

Xuan's voice grounded me for a second, gentle and deep and worried. His voice was like solid ground and the sound of it kept me from floating away like an untethered kite. I struggled and coughed, unable to catch my breath. My eyes fluttered open. Staring up into that beautiful face etched with determination, I realized that Zhang Xuan had saved me. I was alive, but I couldn't see anything else beyond his face. I'd heard of convergence insufficiency before, but I'd never experienced it first-hand.

He stopped compressions and gazed down at me. Breathless, I clung to him for support, wondering how on earth I'd been lucky enough for him to find me.

"Oh, *xiè tiān xiè dì*—thank heavens! I thought I'd lost you," he half-sobbed. "If anything had happened to you . . . if you were really gone . . . ."

I felt the shudder that ran through him. Each word was soft, like the sound of a lullaby half-remembered.

Suddenly a tree came into focus. My blurred vision cleared. More and more objects converged while I tried to focus on nearby objects. The landscape surrounding us registered slowly but in unison. The ravine appeared to run a minimum of eight or nine football fields, likely longer, and was a total path of chaos. Then it jogged to the west, where we were, to meet up with a narrow track of unpaved road and an old abandoned farm that had only been partially washed out from the mudslide. Nearby a few other survivors stood on the west side.

My body continued to react as I heaved again, as I gagged on more water. I remembered the terrible fear, the silence of death. Then my vision blurred, black shapes swallowed the sky. I'm burning yet freezing. Darkness once again consumed me.

When I regained consciousness, I lay sprawled across a cold dirt road, shaking. I didn't know how much time had passed.

"I'm going to see if someone has a bottle of water."

"Don't leave me," was the first thing I said. Xuan was holding me in his arms and I felt like melted butter. Warm. Safe. I never wanted to move again. How was it possible to feel like that when he was around, despite everything that had just happened?

"Please," I said. My hand curved around his elbow, moving slowly down his arm to his hand. Against great odds, God had spared me. He'd sent Xuan to find me when I desperately needed him . . . and against all odds he'd brought me back to life. Later, when I was finally back at the dorm, I'd thank God properly. If it wasn't for Xuan, I'd be scattered all over this pit, in bits and pieces. Future crow food.

Xuan's fingers tightened around mine. "I'm not going anywhere. When I left you, you ended up going over a cliff. What will happen if you get on a plane, ship, or train without me?"

He was trying to make a joke to make me feel better, but his words didn't brighten my mood. Instead, tears began to fall as I remembered the suffocating feeling of water filling my lungs.

"Hey, you're safe now," he said softly. He placed a gentle finger up to the corner of my eye and wiped away a tear.

"Sorry," I murmured. "I don't usually cry." That was true. I normally wasn't a crier. I didn't cry when my father left us to go overseas. I didn't cry after I caught Raylan cheating on me, or after our breakup. But in the face of dire odds, the bottled-up emotions I'd suppressed during my near-death experience seemed to rise from my belly and into my throat. I did what I could to put a lid on them, but that wasn't easy.

I could hear the smile in his voice as he kissed my forehead. "You have definitely earned the right to have a meltdown. But right now we need to find a way to get to my car. And we need to get away from here as quickly as possible. Then you can cry as much as your heart desires."

I'd forgotten where his car was parked. Dread filled me as I looked up at the Mount Everest-sized mountain before us. Climbing *that* with my leg seemed impossible, even if there was a road, because at some point there would be an incline to reach the top, and that was *if* it even connected to the main highway. I let out a deep sigh, wondering how far back the dirt road went. It could lead us miles in one direction. *Can I even walk miles in the shape I'm in?*

"Okay." Even that little four-letter word burned in the back of my throat. My tears had already been waiting a long time to come out. They could wait a little longer. I silently thanked Xuan for not letting me free-fall into a pit of despair. I promised myself I was going to revert to adult status.

Xuan eyed the dirt track leading west. "You know, in China we would call this a Class Four Highway." He was joking. "Can you stand?"

I nodded. "I think so."

Xuan must have noticed my weakness because he helped me sit upright. Every movement was stiff, but he made sure I was steady before he took off his shirt.

"Is this the part where you take off your clothes and start

ripping them into shreds to bind my wounds?"

"If you wanted me to rip off my clothes, you should've just asked," he said good-humoredly.

I couldn't help but laugh through chattering teeth as he tore the cotton in half, making a sling out of the material for my left arm. My conscience battled against my raging hormones at the sight of his bare skin. Maybe I'd hit my head harder than I thought.

"Ready?" he asked

"Let's do this."

A half-smile cut across his mud-stained face. He stood first and then gave me both hands to try and help me stand. Putting pressure on my right leg was excruciating and I collapsed under the weight.

"This won't do," he said before scooping me up into his arms. "I guess I'm just going to have to carry you back to the car."

A rescue worker approached as Xuan held me on the side of the road-turned-river. I could see the flashing lights of several emergency vehicles parked on the top of the mountain highway. There were no police or other rescue workers nearby that could help us. We were mostly alone except for this man and a few of the other lucky cases that had survived the fall. His vehicle wasn't even a city vehicle, but it looked like it had four-wheel drive. Possibly he was just a local, there to help. He said something in Spanish. *"Por favor ayúdeme, señor. Hay gente atrapada en ese coche de allí, y necesitan ayuda. Parece que están bastante lastimados."*

Neither of us understood what the man was saying. I vowed to brush up on my Spanish when I got back home.

He seemed to be asking for something, but the others just waved him off or shouted at him. Someone even called the man loco. *What did he want that made him sound crazy?*

Then, surprisingly, he changed to English, though it was very basic. "Help. There." He pointed. "Family in car."

Xuan turned slightly, and we both looked to see where the man was pointing. He said something in Chinese that sounded like a swear word, based on his tone. About thirty feet away, a car was tipped completely over onto the roof, but out of the main flood zone.

Xuan turned to face the man and nodded that he understood. I already knew what Xuan was thinking. He was going to help the people trapped in the car. The vehicle wouldn't be too tough to reach—challenging but not impossible. The difficulty would come in getting whoever was in the vehicle out with it tipped over like that. *Why wouldn't anyone else go?* Cowards.

"Xuan, put me down."

He did so gently. I kept myself balanced as I put most of my body weight on my good leg. I could stand, though I was as shaky and wobbly as a newborn deer.

"Uh, what are *you* doing?" Xuan asked. "Stay here."

"I want to help you."

"You're hurt!" Xuan shouted with mixed fury and terror.

A wisp of black hair fell on his brow as he cocked his head. "How can you do this?"

"Because it's the right thing to do."

"Family," the man said and pointed again.

Xuan did not reply to the man. Deep in thought, he rubbed his forehead with his fingers, as if coming to terms with the reality of this seismic event.

I heard the word *family* and slowly took a couple steps forward to assess my ability to balance and hold weight under pressure. I hissed like a cat through my teeth and whimpered at the movement. Then I took a couple more steps. It was painful, but manageable.

"Don't," Xuan ordered.

I turned to him, and he looked even more handsome from that angle.

"Don't what?"

"Don't go. You'll be in worse pain if you do."

"Holy Saints, Xuan. I'll be fine."

"No. You'll get yourself killed . . . again. Stay where you are."

He reached for my arm but I twisted away from him.

"Not a chance. I'm going, Xuan."

His eyes seemed to harden, hot and dark and frustrated. "What about your leg? You shouldn't be putting any weight on it. You can barely stand. You've probably fractured your femur."

A family was trapped in that car, and no one else was there to help them but us. "Normally I'd agree with you, but this isn't a normal situation, Xuan. This is an emergency," I said, determined. "I know I'm hurt, but I can still help you."

Xuan cursed. "It's dangerous. Rocks and debris are still coming down the mountain. You shouldn't live your life so recklessly. The world needs a Cassandra Steel in it." He sounded exasperated.

"I'll survive," I insisted.

"You've lost a lot of blood. And you can't even use your left arm. Are you really going out into that?" He pointed toward the mudslide.

"Yeah. And so are you. The mountain can come down any minute and people are still trapped."

"No."

I could feel the tension between us. It didn't take long to realize that this was about to escalate into a full-blown fight.

"Listen, Xuan, you don't know me very well. I'm hardheaded and stubborn. And I rarely do what I'm told. I know you think you can tell me what to do because you saved me, but there might be children in that car. I'm going. You're not going to stop me, and we're just wasting valuable time by arguing."

The volunteer rescuer waved to Xuan to follow, said something in Spanish, and then changed to English once he realized Xuan didn't fully comprehend. "We hurry!"

Xuan scanned my face, silent. Then sighed. He seemed to be waging some kind of internal debate. He looked me directly in the eye. "Do *not* get hurt. That is an order." His tone was steely. Inflexible. "I'm not giving you permission to injure yourself or die for anyone."

I was taken aback by the strength and power he put behind those words. I nodded slowly. "Fine. Same goes for you."

"Are you worried about me?" he asked, surprised.

"Of course I care about your safety. You saved my life."

"But only because of that, right?"

"Xuan—"

"It's fine. Forget I asked." Xuan kept his eyes locked on me. "Cassie, I don't want you to go back out there. If you get hurt—"

"I won't." I made sure my knife was still in my pocket. And perhaps I was being a bit stupid and wild and reckless from the blood loss, but given the situation, there wasn't much of a choice.

"If I can't change your mind, then stay with me. I don't want to get separated. Whatever we do, we'll do together. If I can't see you, I won't be able to focus and help them. Most importantly, use common sense."

I agreed. Uncoiling my aching shoulders, I limped forward with determination and then followed him.

We passed a few lifeless bodies stuck face down in the earthy muck. I winced as my leg shook. Pushing through the pain, I was still too slow and got farther and farther behind Xuan.

Xuan looked over his shoulder thinking I was right behind him and then halted. His mouth instantly tightened as he turned to face me. I noticed the assessing stare, and the doubt that danced in his eyes, along with a silent question. Without saying anything, Xuan waded back through the mud for me. He gripped my hand and slowly tugged me forward, leading me safely along a pathway behind him.

I had cheated and survived death because of Xuan. His bravery and strength and certainty made me fearless, as though I could do anything with him there. Together we stepped through water and moved around debris. The volunteer reached the driver-side door first and bent down to assess the situation of the tipped over vehicle. He pointed to Xuan to go up alongside the passenger window. The volunteer counted how many passengers were there and held up a finger. *Four.*

Xuan reluctantly let go of my hand. His eyes dipped to my mouth before saying, "Remember your promise."

Wincing as my ankle all the way up to my femur barked in pain, I nodded my head. Xuan moved to the opposite side of the vehicle and began to assess the front passenger.

Lightning flashed overhead. A bolt forked and branched out, white hot, from sky to earth. Suddenly the rain picked up again, as if God were putting a time limit on our amateur rescue mission. Saints, if the rain caused another mudslide, there would be no chance of survival . . . for any of us.

I came up beside the back driver-side door and saw two small hands pushed against the glass. The water wasn't as high in this area, meaning the car wasn't completely submerged as ours had been. I bent down as much as my leg would allow and looked in horror as a small girl peered out the window at me. Next to her I saw a small infant wrapped in a blue bundle with a dinosaur print. The boy was buckled into a car seat. His eyes were closed.

Xuan and the man were preoccupied with helping the parents. I began to gauge the situation and my own limitations. The back door was smashed in. I'd have to crawl into the car and take the kids out through the window. *Am I capable?*

One step at a time. I couldn't use my leg to kick so I'd have to punch through it. I took off my shirt using my right arm, trying to avoid hitting my left. Using my side and just my left fingertips, I tried to wrap the shirt around my right fist. Every movement I made with my left arm was painful, but I didn't have a choice. I punched the glass on the door, but the angle was weird. Nothing happened. *Holy saints, this is bad.* Despite my efforts, I couldn't crack the glass. As I crouched as low as possible and tried again, I realized that this wasn't a scene from a disaster film—it was real life. I wasn't a stuntwoman and I couldn't rely on special effects to save me. Desperately searching for a solution, I reached down into the murky water and felt around until my fingers closed around a sharp rock.

I punched the glass with all my strength. *Third time's a charm.*

Rather than shatter the entire window, the impact concentrated on a tiny area in the window and had created small cracks. I began to hit the window over and over in different areas until it spiderwebbed. Finally, I was able to start pushing through the remaining glass until it fragmented.

I could see Xuan glance toward me when the glass broke. He appeared to be upset, his eyes burning at me. But I was determined, so I ignored him. This wasn't the time for a hyperprotective Edward Cullen or Fifty Shades' Christian Grey, because I was going to need his help to pull me back through once I had secured the girl and her brother.

A few glass pieces remained that the kids could cut themselves on, so I ripped the large shards off with my shirt-covered hand. I knew I was semi-naked, only wearing a sports bra. I didn't care, or at least I tried not to. I knew the notion of feeling embarrassed was stupid since women often exercised in sports bras, but I had always been more conservative. *So much for modesty.*

I heard Xuan shouting orders and gesturing to the nameless man. I wasn't sure he fully comprehended what Xuan was saying but he moved.

When the car emitted a groan that reverberated through my bones like an anguished cry, I swiftly sprang into action without a second thought.

My leg roared and practically collapsed at the weight as I lunged down and landed on my already swollen knee. My shoulder felt as though it was ripping as it curved inward, my chest caving. I quickly overcame the sharp pain as my body released spikes of adrenaline, forcing me to mentally concentrate. Honestly, it was a welcome distraction, but I wasn't worried about my own safety or pushing my body too far to prevent further injury. There were children in the car—my injured leg and arm didn't matter. My life didn't matter.

Adrenaline had the ability to make you feel invincible. I was feeling less than superhero status right now, but I could live with the pain. What I couldn't live with was letting these children die, knowing there was something I could have done to save them.

I slid on to my stomach and slithered like a snake through the broken window. My leg was easier to manage once I was on the ground. Using my upper body strength, I reached into the car, my wrist scraping against glass. I didn't let myself think about the pain. There was no time. The kids were small, they were light. *I can do this.*

"*¿Estás bien*?" I asked the little girl with brown pigtails.

"*Sí,*" she said in a small squeaky voice. "*¿Están bien mis padres y mi hermano?*" She wanted to know if her parents and brother were okay. "*Están bien,*" I assured her. That was a lie. I'd caught a glimpse of the driver, and his condition seemed pretty unstable. But I couldn't tell her that. I wouldn't even know how to translate that into Spanish.

I could hear Xuan's voice muffled with the other guy's Spanish, and a female voice.

As I looked at the infant, a deeper sort of terror spread quickly through me like wildfire. I reached up to feel the crease of his elbow by gently placing my dirty fingers on the inside of his arm. *Please be alive, please.* My bloodied face crumpled in terror and sorrow as I waited. But then the soft, rhythmic beat of the baby's pulse reached my fingertips. He was alive. To confirm this, he woke up and began to scream—a unique decibel of desperation reserved for infants, even though I highly doubted he understood the situation. Babies were just like that. They liked to yell and hear their own voices and see what reaction came from their parents.

"*Estás . . .*" What was the Spanish word for hurt? I racked my brain for the word. Was it *enferma*? No, that meant sick. "*¿Estás herida*?" I finally asked, wondering if the little girl was hurt.

She shook her head. "No."

I stretched my hands out and reached for the strap holding the girl safely in place.

"Soon . . . *Pronto.*" I pointed my finger to her and then held up my hand, connecting my thumb and index into a circle to signal okay or good. Hopefully she understood what I meant. "*Pronto estarás bien.*" I hoped my words made sense. I was trying to tell the little girl that she'd be okay soon.

Again she nodded, confirming she understood.

"I promise," I said in English. "*Te lo prometo.*"

I grabbed the seat belt and unbuckled it. In a heartbeat, both my arms were around the little girl's middle as she fell, slamming into my stomach and knocking the wind from my chest. My ribs screamed in response, and a few tears escaped. But that was the only way to keep her from falling into the broken glass.

I scooted toward the baby. Still holding the little girl across my chest, I sat up and began to assess the situation. The baby's cheeks were dotted with little freckles of refracted light from headlights, like a disco ball. Using both hands, I tried my best to cradle the infant before releasing him from the straps. Taking the baby boy in my arms, I motioned for the girl to stand. Then I began to re-position myself to climb back out through the window.

"Xuan," I called.

"Cassie, are you okay?"

"Yeah. Do you think you can help me? I have both kids."

Xuan hurried to my side and knelt down. "Are you hurt?"

"No more than I already was."

"How are the kids?"

"They're surprisingly okay. How are their parents?"

"I don't know about their dad, but the mom just woke up. She broke her leg. She seems pretty shaken, but all things considered, she's okay. I'm going to release her from her seatbelt when I get back."

"Good."

"So what's your plan?"

"I'm going to hand you the girl first. Once she's okay, I'll hand you the baby. She should be able to hold him while you slide me out."

"Okay."

I helped the girl through the window before moving the baby to my aching left arm. As soon as the girl was free, Xuan picked her up and stood her near the back of the car so she couldn't see the shape her parents were in.

Grimacing, I reached back up through the window to hand Xuan the little boy.

Xuan motioned at the girl and then at the baby and gave dramatic gestures to ask her if she was okay to hold her brother so he could help me. She nodded and took the infant in her arms.

I crawled toward the window and reached my good arm out. Xuan grabbed it and pulled. I twisted my body through the opening. When I was free, he lifted me into his arms and carried me to where the children were standing. Tears soaked the girl's freckled cheeks as she stood there and took in the scene as she held her brother.

Searing pain tried to swallow me whole as Xuan put me down. I didn't let that happen. He held me as I put weight on my leg again and tried to find my balance.

"I got this," I assured him.

He reached out and grasped my chin, forcing me to look at him. I held Xuan's stare and all the words I needed to say to him hung there. I saw the affection in his eyes, too, as he realized I had to make my way alone, back toward safety, for the sake of the children.

My hand paused over Xuan's heart. It was a raging thunderous beat. Reaching down, he brushed his lips against mine before pulling away. "Go," urged Xuan. "I'll be right behind you."

I nodded as I offered him a grim smile. Later, if we somehow survived this, we'd speak then.

I couldn't carry the girl, but she was tall enough to make it through the water without sinking below the surface. I took the baby in my good arm and held her hand. Limping, I held on to the kids with every ounce of strength I possessed, willing my arms and legs not to let go, or to give in, as I made my way across the covered roadway. Adrenaline alone powered me.

Keep going.

When we arrived at the relative safety of the dry portion of the dirt road, I collapsed from dizziness and a sick feeling in the pit of my stomach. Whatever force had rushed through my blood had vanished, leaving only pain behind. We were safe. That's all that mattered.

Hearing voices come closer, I whirled just in time to see the man and Xuan make their way across the water toward us. The man carried the male driver. Behind him, the dark-haired female passenger grasped Xuan's neck.

We were safe, we were alive . . . we had done it.

Overhead, a small, blazing golden light arced from over the clouds. The sun was appearing.

I handed the small baby to his mom once Xuan sat her down next to me. Instantly I felt light-headed. The little girl ran to her father, who had been gently placed on the dry ground, and threw her arms around him. He appeared to be badly injured, but still he grasped his little girl lovingly in his arms. *Exhale.*

I tried to move and failed. I was instant jello. A warm, strong arm slid across my back and held me upright. He pulled me close to his chest. "I'm going to help you sit. I don't want you to move while I go and figure out how to get to our car."

"Okay."

"We're going to do this slowly. Are you ready?"

"I think so."

No matter how gentle Xuan was, the movement was still painful.

The woman Xuan had helped spoke pretty good English. She was able to tell the other rescue worker that Xuan's car was on top of the mountain and it was urgent to get it. It took a minute for everyone to talk and for the woman to translate the conversation. She said there was a side road about half a mile away that would lead to the highway. The rescue worker offered to give Xuan a lift and waved for him to follow.

I stood with the family as they hugged each other tightly. There was no conversation; we all seemed to be silently grappling with the recent brush with death. It was during this time that I discovered the little girl's name: Emilia. She spoke to her father in Spanish and pointed upwards. I followed her gaze and beheld a beautiful sight—a rainbow that spanned the entire spectrum of colors, produced by the refraction and dispersion of light through water droplets in the air. It was a magnificent sight, a symbol of hope and a reminder of God's promise to the world.

Before long, Xuan pulled up in the car. I tried to put pressure on my leg so I could stand, but to no avail. Sensing my distress, Xuan scooped me up effortlessly, almost as if I were a child, and carried me to his car. After gently settling me inside and opening the passenger-side door, Xuan climbed into the driver's seat. I noticed him flinch and asked, "Are you okay?"

He nodded. "I'm just a little sore. We need to get you to the hospital."

"I'm fine, Xuan. Really." I was shaking so hard I thought my bones might snap. That day was by far the worst day of my life, but I was safe and out of harm's way. Because of Xuan, I was alive. Because of him, I was able to laugh.

Still hovering over me, Xuan continued to watch as I violently shivered.

"Cassie," he whispered gently. He reached over to cup my face, his thumb warm on my skin. "You died today. Your heart stopped dead in your chest. You're *not* fine."

"You saved me."

"You may be alive but you're far from unscathed. Your leg's likely fractured and your arm may be broken. Your cuts need to be cleaned. Some may need stitches. You've lost a lot of blood today."

I closed my eyes and focused on my breathing. "But shouldn't we help the others?"

A muscle ticked in his jaw and he pulled his hand back. He looked frustrated, angry. "More rescuers with four-wheel drive vehicles have arrived," he said tightly. "We're leaving. We need to get you to the hospital. And I want to get off this road and put as much distance as possible between us and this mountain before nightfall."

Xuan started the ignition and the engine roared to life. He turned on the heat before reaching over and buckling me safely into the passenger seat. Stretching his arm behind the back seat, he grabbed his Santa Cruz sweatshirt.

"Here, put this on."

Suddenly self-conscious, I realized I was still sitting there in a sports bra. My shirt had been ruined by the glass. "I don't think I can. My arm hurts really badly. I don't want to move it any more than I have to."

"Um, do you want me to help you?"

I took the sweatshirt he offered and draped it over myself like a blanket. Xuan seemed aware of how little his sweatshirt actually covered as he surveyed my bare arms and short shorts.

I must've looked hideous. My cheeks were stained with sweat and tears and smudged mascara. Maybe even gruesome with all the mud and blood caked on like theatrical makeup for a character on the set of a horror or slasher film. Xuan didn't seem to mind or appear too repulsed, at least judging from the way he was staring at me.

"Rest for now. On the way to the hospital I'll call our professor to let him know what happened and ask if he can arrange for clothes to be brought to us."

"You have cell service?"

"Not yet." He began to check our surroundings before announcing we were leaving.

My cell phone was gone—as lost as a needle in a stack of hay—or in this case mud. I wanted to call my mom and Skype my dad just to hear their voices. I wanted to call my best friend Roxy and text Amanda, even though I knew she was already on the plane. Although that was a nice idea, just the thought of talking right now made my head explode.

At some point I'd need to borrow someone's phone so I could at least tell my mom what had happened and why I wasn't on the return flight home. I knew she would start freaking out at the airport if I wasn't there when she went to pick me up.

"Cassie, are you okay?"

"I was just having a mini-panic attack, but I'll be fine."

He studied me for a long beat. Then he nodded, once. I could tell he was still worried about my overall health, but there wasn't much else he could do for me apart from drive.

I tried to crank the heat up to its highest level. "Hey, thank you for today. I wouldn't be alive right now if it weren't for you."

"You're welcome."

Mesmerized, I continue to stare up at Xuan's infuriatingly handsome face. I mean seriously, how could this guy survive a catastrophe and still look like a cover model? I was transfixed. Maybe he was some kind of sexy vampire—not the sparkly kind—and I was under his spell?

Okay, time to get real Cassie. He's too busy driving to notice you gawking. Give yourself another five seconds to look at the man and then let's snap out of this little fantasy and come back to Planet Catastrophe before Xuan thinks you've gone mental.

Back on planet Earth, there were a few things driving me nuts, and I was too weirded out by the sequence of today's events not to ask him a couple of questions outright. I took a deep breath and tried to act nonchalant. "Soooo," I said, perhaps longer and more drawn out than necessary. "Why were you up here?"

He didn't seem to mind the question. "I went to your dorm to take you and Amanda coffee and pastries this morning 'cause I figured you were both nursing massive hangovers. When I got there, Amanda told me you were delivering the school supplies to the kids. I wanted to help so I called señor Nieto. He told me you'd already left and so I just kept packing my suitcase."

"Whose car are we in?"

"It belongs to señora Gálvez. I was watching the news in my room and the subtitles said there were storms and flash flood warnings all over the countryside. I was worried so I called señor Nieto again. When he didn't answer, I just had this terrible feeling. I knew I had to come. So señora Gálvez let me borrow her car and I typed the directions into the GPS."

"You came after me?"

"Yeah, I sort of did."

"I can't believe you risked your life for me. You barely know me. You could've died."

"I don't want to think about what might have happened if I hadn't come."

"I know," I whispered.

We were about five miles down the bumpy, single lane dirt road. The car we were in was not made for this kind of track, so Xuan had to drive extra slowly. My body felt the impact of every thud and hole as we continued cautiously down the path. I didn't want to go to the hospital. I wanted to go back to the dorm, brush my teeth, and go to sleep. I mostly just wanted to take a hot shower and wash off the mud plastered to my skin. But there was no point in arguing. "Whatever you say, Iron Man."

"What?"

"You're like Tony Stark—wickedly smart. And then today you became Iron Man."

Xuan seemed amused as he turned back onto the highway. Before I knew it, we were pulling away from the mountain graveyard and speeding back toward the city, away from the hellish destruction caused by nature's wrath.

Out the window, the storm clouds had finally drifted away to reveal a canvas bathed in hues of orange, like a burning log on a winter's hearth, as though the entire heavens were on fire. The storm had passed and blushing clouds reminded me of cotton candy and the boardwalk back home as the sun cast its golden rays upon the clouds, turning them pink and red. I felt as though I was seeing the world being born again after receiving a second chance at life myself. The setting sun was bright enough to lead us safely back through the narrow, winding roads toward the city.

Chapter Seven: Catalyst

Hospital Universitario de San Vicente Fundación, Colombia
October 15, 2016

"Yes, Stella, for the hundredth time," I said softly and held on to the phone as if it were my lifeline to home. I called my mom by her first name because she didn't like to be called *Mom* or be reminded of her age, despite the fact she was a poster girl for the fifties era, down to the polka-dot dress.

I adjusted my stance as I tried to balance on crutches with the phone in my hand. Once Xuan and I had arrived at the hospital, he helped me put his sweatshirt on. I could barely stand. There weren't any wheelchairs available due to the amount of people coming into the ER, so he had to carry me inside. The waiting room was jam-packed with people in critical condition as more and more ambulances pulled in, and there was only one available seat. Señor Nieto already knew what had happened, thanks to Xuan's phone call, so he was there waiting for our arrival. He went with Xuan to check in and answer questions. My brilliant, take-charge professor had even asked one of the nurses to bring me crutches to hobble around on.

A triage nurse came by to ask Xuan and me questions—which thankfully señor Nieto was there to translate—and gather information about our condition and injuries. She checked our vital signs and then took our temperature, pulse, breathing rate, and blood pressure. This information allowed the triage team to determine the urgency of our situation and the order in which we'd receive care. After the initial medical evaluation, they determined we could both wait. There were many other patients—some whose conditions were likely more acute and required more time-sensitive care. Other patients bypassed the waiting room entirely, having entered via ambulances and quickly been whisked through the ER doors.

"Cassandra, are you even listening."

Oops. "Yes. I'm fine. I have whiplash, and some cuts and bruises. Maybe a broken arm. Other than that, I'm good. Alive." In reality, I was a mess. My racing heart rate reminded me of Edgar Allan Poe's classic The Tell-Tale Heart, but no way would I tell that to my mother. I hated lying even more than I hated spiders. But I was alive and that was what was important. Besides, the lie wouldn't last long. She would find out as soon as I landed in San Francisco and saw the physical state I was in.

"Darling, you and I have a very different definition of fine and in one piece."

I'd omitted other little details, such as the fact I was now on crutches. I had a huge bruise from the steering wheel that covered my chest and more black-and-blue spots across my legs and back. Not to mention my left arm would likely be placed in a cast and the deepest cuts would need to be stitched. But my mother didn't need to know. I was protecting her from the non-PG gory stuff to keep her calm. It worked . . . sort of.

My mother's voice caught my attention momentarily. "Cassandra Temperance, you're my one and only. You could've died today."

I knew that better than anyone. I was still trying not to freak the hell out when the double doors into the hospital room slammed open and several gurneys were wheeled in. Seeing them . . . the blood and dried mud . . . everything rushed back to me. *No, no, no.* I needed to focus on something—*any*thing—to keep my mom from hearing the panic in my voice. From the hospital window, I could see a kaleidoscope of deep purple sky and shimmering lights that flickered in the distance. I concentrated on that and on breathing. "Mom, I love you. I'll be home soon."

"When?"

"I can't fly for at least a week."

"I don't like this. Your classmates are coming home tonight.

You're injured. You're in a foreign country and you shouldn't be by yourself!" she yelled into the receiver. My mother had always been very opinionated, and I could tell she was emotionally jarred and panicked by the sound of her voice over the phone.

"I'm not going to be alone, Mom. Señor Nieto will be here. And Xuan."

"The boy who saved you?"

"Yeah. Señor Nieto said he's already changed his flight schedule. His shoulder separated when he was trying to pull me out of the car, but they were able to reset it here at the hospital. I think we both just need a few days to recover. Besides, señora Gálvez and señor Nieto have offered to let us stay at the dorms. They said the campus will be empty for the next week and the kitchen is fully stocked."

"Is that boy going to be staying with you?"

Of course that's what she cares about. "No, Mom. Xuan has his own dorm room." I started to close my eyes, the last of my energy pouring out of me. I was too tired to have a conversation with my mom about what she considered proper, for the 1.5 billionth time, give or take.

"You said he was nice, right?"

I rubbed my eyes wearily. "Yes, Mom. He's very nice. A complete gentleman." Actually that was another lie. Since we'd arrived at the hospital, Xuan had become distant, just as he was in college . . . cold. He was like a superhero who came to the rescue and then went AWOL. I was dazed and confused, and not in the 1993 stoner-movie sense.

"I don't like this," she repeated. "I'm half tempted to get on a plane and fly down there right now."

"Mom, it'll be fine." I shifted my weight on my crutches. "I'll Skype you every day—twice a day—from my computer, if that makes you feel better."

"And what about Raylan? What would he say about this?"

I let out a long, boisterous sigh. Trust my mom to bring up something I didn't want to talk about in the span of ten minutes on an international call, while at the hospital. I wanted to make my mother proud and happy. No matter what I did, I always fell short of her expectations. Despite winning an academic scholarship out of high school, no number of awards or promotions would be enough in Stella's eyes. Marrying Raylan Thompson would do that.

"Are you ever going to tell me what happened? And why you're not *together* anymore?" Stella asked bluntly.

I could hear her battle-ready voice, which did not bode well for the remainder of this conversation. I grabbed my cup of ice chips and began to chew. "It's really none of your business." And it wasn't. I had to draw the line somewhere.

"Don't ignore me, Cassandra."

My mother could be as prickly as a cactus at times. I could picture her squinted eyebrows set against her tenacious face.

"Can you please drop it?" The very thought of Raylan was causing me to break out in a sweat. I could only imagine how disappointed my mother would be if she knew what a disaster our relationship had turned out to be. Knowing Stella, she'd probably find a way to blame the breakup on me. In my parents' eyes, Raylan was a saint. The only problem with that analogy was saints didn't typically carry guns and sleep around.

I could hear her sigh over the telephone. "And you'll be home next week?"

"Yes, I promise."

Stella asked a dozen more questions about Xuan, hardly any of which I could answer, because I still didn't know that much about my rescuer.

As my mother droned on, I was grateful this was a collect call. I imagined myself hanging up the phone, but instead I simply began watching other patients and staff. A little dazed, I didn't realize she'd stopped talking and was apparently waiting for me to respond.

"Sure, Mom," I said automatically. Apparently, this was the wrong thing to say.

"Cassandra Temperance Steel, are you listening to me?"

"Of course I am, but I gotta go. The doctor just called me," I lied. "I love you, Mom."

Two and a half hours slowly and painfully passed as foreign doctors came and went. The mudslide was all over the news. When señor Nieto came to bring me a change of clothes he'd had someone deliver, I had him ask one of the staff to put the English subtitles on the TV for me so I could understand what was being said as I sat on the hard hospital chair and stared at the images on the television. The report was about the landslide we had just survived. I read the words:

A landslide on a major highway in Colombia has killed at least forty-seven people as tonnes of earth engulfed the main highway leading north from Colombia's second-largest city, Medellín, into the Copacabana area. The mud from the mountainside covered just over two hundred meters and buried nineteen cars and three motorbikes. Dozens of homes near the town have been buried. More than forty people are still missing after the hillside collapsed early this morning following the heaviest rains in the country for decades. Emergency workers and rescue dogs are searching the mud for survivors.

My eyelids felt heavy as the words washed over me. I'd had enough of the disaster, but there wasn't much else to do as I waited for what felt like an eternity. The hospital was crazy with emergencies and medical people with places to be. Doctors and nurses must have known they were in for a long night. They looked as though they were wired on their fourth or fifth cups of coffee as they walked up and down the halls holding freshly poured cups every hour or so. Sirens continued to blare and emergency vehicles pulled up to the front doors of the ER. An older man on a gurney died of a heart attack as the hospital staff performed CPR and shocked his heart with the defibrillator as they raced towards an open operating room. Several more people had come in by ambulance over the last couple of hours. They were strapped to backboards to ensure their necks didn't move. The hallways were filled with the torturous nails-on-chalk wailing reserved for family members when they realized their loved ones were never coming back. I didn't want to see or hear any more, but I couldn't block out the sounds or look away either. Despite the cuts, bruises, and likely fractures, I was fortunate to have survived today's tragedy.

Needing to pee, I found the energy to stand and limp my way to the bathroom. I took the bag of clothes señor Nieto had given me. Inside was a black Adidas shirt, a men's small. There was also a pair of men's shorts. Unfortunately, they were too big. I used a towel to wipe my face and arms clean.

As more bodies were being wheeled in, I felt as though I was a spectator of death—just like the Grim Reaper who'd sat idly in the backseat of my car today, waiting to see what would happen. Every time I saw a shadow move, I was almost certain she was there, prowling these halls just as she'd hovered over the mountain.

"Cassandra Steel," a nurse called with a thick Colombian accent and a roll of the letters on her tongue that made the name almost foreign to my ears.

My pain was palpable as I slowly got up from the chair to follow the nurse. Stiff, I placed my weight on the crutches and passed Xuan in the hallway just before he slipped behind a closed curtain. He didn't look at me. In fact, he hadn't spoken a word to me since he'd brought me into the waiting area. He was silent. Thoroughly, wholeheartedly silent, as if I were invisible. *Have I done or said something wrong to offend him?* Maybe I really did die earlier and I was now a ghost, just like Bruce Willis in *The Sixth Sense.*

Fine. Two could play that game. I planned to give him a supernova of the silent treatment. A lot had happened today and perhaps I was the culprit in some way. But I didn't give a flying bumblebee's butt because I was mad.

The nurse's voice reverberated through the air, its urgent tone amplifying the pounding in my head. Each word she spoke in rapid-fire Spanish intensified my disorientation, making the room spin and my temples throb with increasing intensity. Her hands moved with animated gestures, her eyes filled with anticipation, as if she held the key to a world of understanding just beyond my reach.

Thankfully, señor Nieto knocked before anything else was said. "There you are. I thought I'd check in."

"Señor, the nurse said something in Spanish, but I didn't fully understand."

"I'll ask her to repeat it." He turned to the nurse and they exchanged a few words. "She asked you to please take a seat and be still so she can look at you."

"Thank you." The nurse used a blood pressure cuff to take my systolic and diastolic measurements.

"How are your wife and baby?" I asked señor Nieto.

"They're both perfect. Healthy."

"I'm happy for you."

"Truthfully, I can't stop looking at my beautiful baby girl. My wife and I didn't think we'd ever have kids. The doctors told us it wasn't possible. I couldn't have asked God for a more perfect miracle. I just hope that at my age, I can give my daughter the world."

"You will. I've seen the way you run the lab. You have the energy of a twenty-year-old."

The nurse asked a few general questions, with señor Nieto there to translate as she began to assess, treat, and care for my wounds.

"*Señorita,* the doctor was going to come meet with my wife and me. I need to get back to my girls. Will you be okay if I leave you alone?"

"Of course. You should definitely go." The birth of a child was a big deal. I didn't want to make him feel obligated or to ruin his moment by asking him to stay because of my rusty Spanish.

"I'll leave you my cell phone. It will be easier for you to talk with the nurse if you open the translate app. When you and Xuan are ready, I'll drive you back to the dorms."

"Thank you," I said again. "I'm so happy for you and your wife."

"Gracias."

I licked my lips. They were still dry, even after the three bags of fluid they'd given me through an IV to help replace what I'd lost due to vomiting up the dirty water.

"*Señorita, ¿todavía se siente deshidratada*?"

I only understood the words miss and dehydrated, and only because the Spanish version sounded similar to the English word. I think *siente* meant to feel. Yes, I was still thirsty—and everything in my body hurt like hell when I moved. I typed my response in the app, and then read the words. "*Sí. Sedienta y adolorida.*" I told her I was thirsty and sore. Now how did I tell her I was hurting? I typed it into my translation app. *"Me duele mucho."*

They'd left the stupid needle inside me so they could connect a bag of heaven knows what into my bloodstream. This time the nurse gave me a painkiller through the IV along with another bag of liquid goo. The pain didn't take long to stop as I lay back and watched the slow drip of feel-good juice through the tube. Numb, tingly, I hadn't felt that good since I could remember. *More please.*

I wanted Xuan to sit beside me and hold my hand while the nurse injected me with something that stung in order to deaden the areas being worked on. I hated needles. I tried to hide my arm under a thin blanket so I didn't have to look at or see the IV. That was a selfish thought, needing him. I knew he was getting looked at as well, and he had his own injuries. *Maybe I should find him and go sit with him or offer to hold his hand. Men are always trying to put on a fearless face.*

I needed to get a blood transfusion. Not to mention my left arm had been placed in a cast and the deepest cuts had to be stitched, while the others were protected by butterfly bandages. The most severe diagnoses were a concussion, fractured ribs, a simple fracture in my femur, and a sprained ankle. I would definitely be keeping the crutches.

The nurses and doctors at the Hospital Universitario de San Vicente Fundación took care of me, and after a few hours I was pretty well patched up, like a female version of the Frankenstein monster. Another doctor would come talk to me about my head injury before I could be released.

After another half hour, Dr. Avalos, a neurologist, came in and read my CT scan. Dr. Avalos had studied English at an ESL program in New York and he could easily talk without a translator.

"Señorita Steel, because the brain is complex, every brain injury is different. Some symptoms may appear right away. Others may not show up for days or weeks after the concussion."

"So what do you recommend?"

The doctor gazed at me, assessing. "Get sleep at night and rest during the day. Try to avoid visual and sensory stimuli, strenuous physical or mental tasks, and activities such as exercising or working on the computer. I heard from your other doctor that you canceled your flight tonight?"

There was a knock at the door and I felt my heart race as Xuan entered the room evasively. "Sorry to interrupt, Doctor. Señor Nieto said for me to wait here."

I turned so fast I almost pulled a muscle and scowled at his sudden appearance. *What the hell?* Dr. Avalos looked at me as if to confirm Xuan's presence was okay. *Is it okay for him to be in here? Yes. No. Yes.* I hadn't forgotten how much of a jerk he'd been since we'd arrived.

I ignored Xuan and answered the doctor's interrupted question. "Yeah, we missed our plane. I called and changed my flight to next week."

"Good," he continued as Xuan took a seat near my bed. "An airplane flight shortly after a concussion could make symptoms worse. I'm glad you were able to change your flight."

"Do you have someone to watch after you tonight? And for the next week while you are in Colombia?"

"No, not really. My roommate went home tonight."

"Sometimes a head injury makes it difficult for people to recognize or acknowledge they're having problems," said Dr. Avalos. "It may be helpful to enlist the support of someone to help with recognizing symptoms. Head injuries are not to be taken lightly. Not at all."

Xuan's eyes met mine. "I'll stay with her."

I wanted to yell at him to mind his own business, but I was too shocked. He hadn't talked to me since we arrived at the hospital, but now he was volunteering to take care of me? *Why now?* I closed my eyes and slid my throbbing head into my hands, holding it steady. The room was spinning.

"You faced a lot of trauma today, and you've sustained multiple injuries. Unfortunately, with a concussion it's important to avoid medications that cause drowsiness or other side effects—pain pills or sleeping pills or muscle relaxants. We'll prescribe Tylenol and a low dose of pain medication. If you become confused at any time on the pain medication, stop taking it. Eat a light diet, especially if you're feeling nauseated."

"Doctor, it's been a long day. I'm tired and I want to go back to the dorms." I stared down at my shoes. Exhausted was a better word for how I felt.

"It's fine to sleep after a concussion so long as someone wakes you up every two hours. They need to make sure you can be easily awakened and aren't showing symptoms of a worsening condition. Any questions?"

"Can't I just set my alarm?" I suddenly felt guilty.

"You have a serious head injury, señorita Steel. You may not hear your alarm. Or you might not be able to wake yourself up from it. I don't advise that."

I nodded. "Right. I get it. Can I go now?"

"Be sure to schedule follow-up appointments with your own doctor once you arrive back in the States. It's very important."

After five hours and counting, we were both released under the care of señor Nieto, who was kind enough to leave his wife and newborn daughter to drive us across town. Señor Nieto had been running back and forth between different wings in the hospital and had helped translate most of our hospital visit. Technically, Xuan and I were not underage and should have been able to check ourselves out, but the government required señor Nieto to sign a waiver saying he'd take responsibility for us since we were foreigners.

We hadn't eaten dinner, so señor Nieto picked up food for us along the way back to the dorms. That was one of his gestures of apology. He blamed himself for sending me in his stead to deliver the school supplies.

"You're both lucky to be alive."

He was right. *Who knew a scenic, humanitarian drive could turn into a life-or-death major event?*

"Señor, is there any news about Santiago and Marlon?" I asked. I'd been too afraid to ask before. I was hopeful they'd been rescued by the search team.

"Uh, they didn't make it."

An awful brew of guilt and sadness continued to eat at me. They'd died because they were trying to deliver school supplies. Xuan stared at me with some unreadable emotion, worsening the tension in my gut.

"I'm sorry, señor. Santiago was coming to check on me during the chaos," I said. "He tried to warn me."

"It's me who should apologize, señorita Steel. I never thought I was putting you in any kind of danger or I wouldn't have asked you to go. I'm sorry. Truly."

Señor Nieto's usually bright and expressive eyes were dim. In the convex mirror, I could see him pinch the bridge of his nose. He was quietly crying.

I squeezed his shoulder. Today he'd welcomed his daughter into the world and, within that same hour, he found out he'd lost two of his best friends. "I wanted to go, señor. It wasn't your fault." It wasn't anyone's fault.

Xuan looked sternly at me. I shifted uncomfortably in the back seat under his scrutiny and resisted the urge to tell him to shove it. Out the window, I could hear the sound of stray dogs barking, while the deafening music from the car echoed around the street. The sky was a blanket of generous black velvet that made me think of my bed. More than anything, I wanted to sleep.

Señor Nieto gave a small smile that didn't quite reach his eyes. He reached behind and handed Xuan a pair of large binoculars. "There's a comet tonight that will be visible in the Northern Hemisphere," he explained. "According to the news, it's been visible for several months, but weather conditions and light pollution in the city have hindered people's ability to observe it. Medellin being a big city, it's often challenging to see the night sky due to light pollution. However, tonight is expected to be clear since it rained earlier. The news station mentioned that the comet should be as bright as the full moon. I know you're both interested in science, so if you're not too tired you should watch for it. They suggest that the best viewing time will be during the pre-dawn hours or late evening when the sky is dark. They suggested looking for it around midnight until about two in the morning because there's less interference from sunlight and the city lights, making the comet more visible against the dark sky."

"What about you, señor? Don't you need these to see it?"

"My comet was already born today."

"Thank you, señor."

Xuan had been silent in the car during the entire trip, but he thanked señor Nieto for the ride once the car pulled up in front of the dorms.

Señor Nieto extended his hand towards Xuan, a grateful smile on his face. "Thank you, señor Zhang, for saving her. You were incredibly brave," he expressed warmly. Glancing at us through his rearview mirror, he continued with earnestness, "If you need anything tonight, don't hesitate to reach out. I'm just a phone call away."

Xuan bowed his head slightly. "You're welcome." He handed me my crutches and helped me out of the car then turned and was already striding toward the dorms as señor Nieto drove away.

I called after him. "Hey, wait up!"

He turned to look at me.

"What's up with you?" I asked as I caught up to him on the crutches. "You don't talk to me at the hospital and only spoke to señor Nieto about canceling your flight, and then you tell the doctor you'll take care of me. Hello? You didn't even ask me."

Xuan studied my face.

I went on, my voice strained. "Why won't you talk to me? It's like you're trying to push me away."

He blinked at me, surprised by my outburst. Finally, after ignoring me for hours, Xuan sighed. "Sorry, Cassie. I needed time to think and process what happened today."

"You seem mad."

"I'm not mad."

"No?" I gestured accusingly at him. I needed to curb my mood before I turned around and bit his head off.

He adopted a serious face. "And you seem to suffer from extreme altruism . . . or do you just have a death wish?" I could hear passion under the cold detachment of his strained voice as he unzipped the jacket señor Nieto must have given him at the hospital and slung it over his uninjured shoulder.

"It wasn't safe for you either. You wanted to help those people as much as I did. There were *children* trapped in that car. A family."

"That's different."

"How?" I massaged my neck.

His face fell and his mouth pressed into a sharp line. "You walked back into harm's way like it was a walk in the park. You should have stayed by the car and let us go."

I folded my arms, my anger spiking. "Holy saints, Xuan. They needed help."

"We would've handled it."

I suddenly remembered the kids' faces as I broke through that glass to get the boy out. I remembered the relief on his sister's face as she looked at me—like she knew everything was going to be okay. "Maybe. But there were kids in that car and time was *not* on our side."

"You were already injured, Cassie. Your actions were reckless!"

"Please stop yelling," I said in a pained whisper. My head was beginning to throb and my usual tolerance was gone. I didn't want to fight. "I know what happened today. But just because I was hurt didn't mean I should sit on the sidelines. You risked your life twice today, both times for strangers." He didn't say anything as I continued to push. "That mountain could have come down again at any time."

"I know that. That's why I'm irritated." His voice was cool. "You promised me you'd be careful and you got hurt. Again." His expression was guarded, unreadable.

A mix of unholy emotions coursed through my veins. "I'm sorry," I said. And I was sorry that he was upset, but that didn't mean what I had done was wrong.

"Me too."

Did he mean it?

" . . . . but I thought I'd lost you, Cass."

My cheeks felt as though they were burning. "What?" Holy saints, I felt confused. This boy was seriously giving me whiplash. Why did he care so much?

But he just said, "Look . . . I'm sorry, okay?"

Xuan began to pace up and down in front of me and rake his fingers through his hair. I could tell he was preoccupied, lost in thought . . . annoyed. But so was I. I couldn't quite understand the way he was talking. *What am I to him? This doesn't make sense. It's not like we really knew each other outside of class. Truthfully we weren't even friends back in the States.*

"I just need you to understand," he began. "I know I've been avoiding you these past hours, but I was beside myself with worry." He stopped in front of me and then wrapped an arm around my waist to pull me close.

Too stunned to speak, I took a surprise breath. *Was he really that concerned about me?*

He glanced up and met my eyes. "Ms. Steel, truce? You didn't deserve the way I treated you at the hospital. I know you're in a lot of pain. Would you allow me to make up for my poor behavior with you this evening?"

I cocked my aching head. "Pray tell, how do you plan to do that?"

"Please. Come. Come watch the comet with me."

"I've never looked through a telescope before," I admitted.

"It'll be a memorable experience, I promise."

I needed a bath and clothes that fit. We both did. But having company would be nice, and the comet would surely be a beautiful sight if I could stay awake. But I would also be following doctor's orders. "I'd be honored, Mr. Zhang." I tried to match his polite etiquette. "It's already late. Should we meet up in a few hours? Let's say just before midnight?"

Relief flashed across his face before he checked his watch. "Sounds great. I'll meet you at your room."

I checked my wrist but remembered my watch had fallen off in the accident. "What time is it?"

"It's already nine."

I had every intention of taking a nap, but only for an hour, maybe two. Xuan would be at my dorm, so I wasn't worried about falling into a deep sleep. If I slept through the alarm, he would be there. Doctor's orders.

As if sensing my apprehension, he asked, "Cassie, do you plan on sleeping?"

I'd always been self-reliant and somewhat reserved. But when you almost die and your doctor tells you to do something, you do it. "Yes," I answered truthfully. "Just for a little bit."

"I can come over in an hour or two."

"I'm okay. It's going to take me a while to shower and dress with these crutches. I'll set my alarm in the dorm. If it makes you feel better, you can come by around eleven. If I don't answer, you can come in. I'll leave the door unlocked in case you need to wake me."

"Can I help you up the stairs?"

He had already done so much for me today. "No, really, I'm fine," I insisted.

"Don't argue," he said sternly, his voice unwavering, as he reached out his hand.

Our eyes locked, his filled with the glimmer of stars, as my pale fingers gracefully reached out to meet his.

With heavy feet and a heavier chest, I began the climb. This wasn't my first time on crutches. I was decent at using them, even with one arm broken. But going up stairs proved to be a challenge.

Xuan helped steady me while carrying the boxes of food señor Nieto had purchased in his left hand. I was too exhausted to eat. The only thing I wanted at that moment was my fluffy pillow.

Xuan held the door to my room open, and I thanked him for the millionth time that day.

"See you soon," he said as we prepared to go our separate ways. "And remember, no somersaults while I'm away."

"Zero gymnastic moves. Got it."

He turned to leave. The girls' and boys' dorms were separate, with the stairs leading to the girls' rooms on the left. Xuan's room was up a different flight of stairs and to the right. I watched him walk down the stairs and didn't tear my gaze away until he was out of sight.

The room felt achingly empty as I opened the door. A slight draft from the bedroom window I'd left open that morning kissed my face and sent chills down my spine.

Amanda and my other classmates had already departed for the airport. Maybe they were clueless about the mudslide madness. I didn't know. They were probably flying over the Caribbean Sea right about now. Amanda probably freaked out when I didn't return in time to make it to the airport.

It was all I could do to keep from collapsing as I entered, groaning. Painfully, I dropped into the corner chair so I could undress. I slowly removed with one hand the large, borrowed shirt señor Nieto had gotten for me

The ensuing task was going to be more difficult, so I gave myself a minute to rest first. Trying to keep my mind off the accident, I looked out from my dorm window. The city night was alive as the starry sky swept over the city that never slept. The streets shimmered with the glow of the bright, yellow streetlamps. Huge university buildings stood opposite the dorms. Some windows gave out white and yellow lights, but others were pitch black. Hazy clouds enveloped the moon, creating its own realm of perpetual darkness. The faint glow of Earth's satellite colored the entire city in white and grey.

Next I needed to get my shorts off before I could lie down on my clean sheets and bedspread. Taking a deep breath, I leaned forward, causing my ribs to ache. One leg at a time, I scooted, lifted, pulled, and slid my shorts until they were off.

Exhausted, I grabbed my crutches and hopped over to the bed. The bath could wait.

The sensation of collapsing onto my soft pile of pillows would have been almost heavenly if it weren't for the throbbing ache all over my body. My pain was off the charts, physically and mentally. The agony was everywhere, seeping into the marrow of my bones. The pain medicine the hospital had given me must have worn off.

My final thought, before exhaustion slammed down on me and blackness swallowed me whole, was that there was a lot more to Xuan than I had realized. He'd saved me from drowning. He was protective of me, though I didn't understand why. But I intended to find out.

Chapter Eight: A View from Above

Medellín, Colombia—Student Housing
October 15, 2016

An hour later the alarm began to chime, but I hit the snooze button on the weathered alarm clock. *Twenty minutes more,* my body and mind craved . . . begged.

By the time I climbed out of bed, it was almost 10:30 in the evening. I had slept longer than intended, but I was awake. After soaking in the tub, I found myself in a chair, book in hand, my fingers wrinkled from the water as I sat in a bathrobe, waiting for my skin to dry.

My long, blonde hair was still wet and uncombed when I heard a loud knock at the door. *Holy saints, is he already here?* "Just a minute," I yelled. "Well, maybe a little longer than that."

"Take your time," he yelled back.

My heart jumped into a gallop as I hurried to get ready, but the crutches made it nearly impossible to go very fast. A white, layered summer dress would suffice. As I looked in the mirror at the featured lace patchwork and tiered ruffles, I saw the white bandage on my swollen head. My face was as puffy as a jumbo marshmallow, and peppered bruises showed under the spaghetti straps. The garment featured a tie back, but a large bruise covered the low back. *Lovely.* Note to self – avoid looking at the mirror for a week—maybe two.

Wincing, I hobbled at a snail's pace to open the door. Pain accompanied each and every step.

Xuan was leaning carelessly against the hallway wall, dressed in a monochromatic three-piece outfit. He was wearing slim fit bottoms, a white T-shirt, and an unbuttoned topcoat. He held a leather duffel bag on the side of his good shoulder and a bright-green suitcase had been deposited next to him.

"Going somewhere?" I asked.

"I told the doctor at the hospital I'd stay with you. I'm your new roomie," he said mischievously with a Shakespearean Puck-style grin.

I narrowed my eyes at him, processing this new development. If Amanda were here, she would call it Fate and tell me to go with the flow of the universe. Our connection was out of my control—or so it seemed. In retrospect, it was Kismet.

With the utmost respect, Xuan patiently stood outside my dorm room, seeking my permission before crossing its threshold. His demeanor exuded the essence of a true gentleman, displaying his courteous nature in every gesture. Leaning casually against the wall, he remained there, allowing me the time and space to come to my own decision.

My head started pounding. "Xuan, you don't have to. I can set the alarm. I'll be—"

"Cassie . . . what we went through today, that was a lot. It's just us. There's no one else here. I'll take care of you and keep you safe until we return to Santa Cruz."

I was alone in a foreign country. We both were. And we had both sustained injuries. Maybe it would be better for him to stay. Then we could look after each other.

Xuan seemed to carefully watch my reaction.

I felt Xuan's intense gaze as he carefully observed my reaction. In the midst of the whirlwind of improbable events that had unfolded over the past twenty-four hours, the most unforeseen twist was the sudden realization that Zhang Xuan would be sharing the same room as me, for the next week. So much for parading around in my bra and underwear.

I moved aside and let him enter as a small, vulnerable part of my heart swelled. I decided to be brave. "I'm going to finish getting ready. Amanda's old bed is yours. Use whatever you need. Give me just a minute."

He passed into the bedroom and then placed his suitcase on

the empty bed along with his computer bag. Then he sat patiently and waited.

I placed my hairbrush on the countertop and met my weary gaze in the mirror. The signs of exhaustion were etched on my face, highlighted by dark circles resembling those of a raccoon. I knew deep down that no amount of makeup could conceal the fatigue. With a resolute sigh, I declared that I was done.

Xuan jumped up from the bed. "Ready?" he asked while moving to stand by the door to my—*our* bedroom.

"Yeah. So where are we going?" I asked.

"To the roof."

Stairs. Great.

"Here, let me carry you."

"That's okay. I'm just going to go slow." I silently cursed the building designer for not putting in an elevator.

"At least let me carry your bag for you," he offered.

"You don't have to do that."

"You don't know the way I was raised." He grabbed my bag before I could object.

The pain was stronger this time as I climbed the Mount Everest of dormitory stairs on crutches. The pain med was not doing its job. S-1 -o-w-1 -y, I followed him up to the tenth floor, counting the steps, one by one. He held out his arm to help balance me as I walked like an injured trooper on a mission. Everything felt swollen. Everything *was* swollen.

My eyes lost focus for a moment when the dizziness from the climb hit me. His hand moved to cup the back of my neck. Somehow his touch was exactly what I needed.

"Cassie, are you okay?"

Does looking like the Bride of Frankenstein count as okay? Instead I replied, "Yeah, I'm good."

Xuan turned the doorknob, revealing the entrance to the rooftop. It was a place I had never ventured before, holding a sense of mystery and anticipation. Stepping out, I was greeted by a spacious yet intimate sanctuary above the bustling city. The air carried a cool, humid embrace, adding a touch of freshness to the atmosphere. As I gazed out, the metropolis sprawled before me, its vastness resembling the intricate lines on the palm of someone's hand. It felt as though I stood at the very edge of its vibrant pulse, connected to the heartbeat of the bustling city.

On a small bamboo coffee table, binoculars, a steaming pot of tea, two delicate cups, and a vibrant red box of cookies were carefully arranged. Colorful banana chairs beckoned us to relax and enjoy the view. Adjacent to it, a towering telescope stood tall, its lens focused on the expansive Northern Hemisphere, providing a captivating vantage point overlooking the city.

"Did you do all this?"

"I found the chairs in the student lounge. The telescope was in one of the astronomy rooms downstairs."

My eyes shifted towards the steaming pot of tea, and a smile spread across his face. "I thought we'd celebrate being alive tonight," he said, his voice laced with excitement. "Nothing beats a good bottle of wine, but considering our antics of the day, tea seems like the perfect choice."

"Tea it is, then," I replied, feeling a warmth in my heart as we settled into the cozy banana chairs. "When did you even have time to get this?"

"I had the tea, found the teapot in the kitchen. And the cookies? A gift for the trip from my mother."

Xuan gracefully settled into the chair across from me, his eyes gleaming with warmth. He reached for the teapot, skillfully pouring the fragrant tea into our cups, his movements steady and deliberate. As he handed me a cup, our fingertips brushed, sending a tingle of electricity through my veins.

With a gentle smile, Xuan raised his cup, and I followed suit. "To living."

"To living," I echoed as we clinked the tiny ceramic cups. I took a single sip of the green tea leaves steeped in water.

"Thank you, Xuan. This is very generous."

Xuan leaned back in his chair, his eyes fixed on me with

curiosity. "Well, do you like the tea?"

The delicate fragrance of the green tea enveloped my senses as I took another sip. "It's perfect." He was alarmingly handsome, with his eyes reflecting the brilliance of the sky.

A hint of a smile played on Xuan's lips as he noticed my gaze. "You're staring at me. Is something wrong?" he asked, a touch of amusement in his voice.

Heat rushed to my face and I quickly averted my eyes, feeling a mix of embarrassment and intrigue. "No, nothing's wrong," I murmured, my voice tinged with a hint of shyness. "It's just . . . you have a way of drawing people in, Xuan."

"I'd give anything to know what you're thinking right now."

"I was thinking about how little I know you, really. At school, you seem to be a reserved person. Or is that just your alter ego, like Clark Kent?"

He laughed. "That's the second time you've compared me to a DC or Marvel character."

"Seems fitting."

"Do you like comics?"

"I've always been a huge fan of Joss Whedon's writing. I grew up on *Buffy, Dollhouse,* and *Firefly*. I wouldn't be the same person I am today without my female idols as a teenager, my school-age idols. And male heroes? Amazing! Just like you were today."

"I'm not a hero, Cassie. There's nothing wild or gallant about me. I work hard. My friends call me stolid, which isn't like your typical superheroes. I'm protective over the things I care about."

I looked quizzically at him. "And I am one of those things?"

"Yes."

I couldn't help but be swept away by the sheer certainty in his reply. "It's weird. I know we attended high school together and now we have the same classes, but I still felt like I barely knew you. Then I was stuck, trapped. I thought I was going to die. And you were there, like one of my graphic novel characters come to life."

"Hmmm, well, what would you like to know about me?"

"Everything."

"So ask."

I plagued him with questions about his parents and family, about growing up in China.

"Did you always want to be a scientist?"

"I've always loved science. When I was younger, I wanted to be an astronaut."

"Why do I have the sense that there's more to the story?"

He smiled. "Because there's always more to the story."

"And how did you fall in love with science?"

He shook the hair out of his face. "My parents both work in science. My father's a physicist and my mother's a chemist. I majored in biochemistry and physics because they chose those fields of study for me. I haven't yet decided which path to pursue for my Ph.D. program. Either way, my parents will be pleased once I receive my doctorate in science, though my mom wanted me to go into medicine to become a doctor."

"They chose for you?"

"My parents have always been utterly devoted to my success. They ultimately want to ensure I'll be more prosperous than them, more financially secure. They've always pushed me to achieve high standards."

"Sounds tiring."

"They're just thinking about my future welfare. As their only child, it's expected that I'll either inherit their biotech company once I finish my studies or venture into starting my own company here. I'll help my family expand their Eastern pharmaceutical business into the United States once I graduate. Eastern medicine has become very popular in parts of the States."

I looked at him silently for a long moment. "What would you have chosen to study? If you had a choice, I mean. Are you following your heart or doing what your parents want you to do?"

"I love science, but instead of physics or chemistry, I probably would have pursued my Ph.D. in Astronomy and Astrophysics."

"Wow. Those would've been interesting fields to study."

Sadness was etched on his face. "They would've been. I've always loved studying the planets and the stars."

I studied the sky. "So between you and me, are you really okay with allowing your family to choose your career and future for you?"

"It's complicated. I've always obeyed my parents and honored my elders. In China, children have no authority over their own lives. Our family provides us with a sense of identity and a strong network of support. Decisions are typically made for us. I'm not saying that to complain, just so that you can understand. The younger generations are always at the receiving end of family decisions. We grow up with a great respect for our elders."

I didn't know much about him, or China, or Chinese culture, but when Xuan talked about his dedication toward his family, the word *honor* came to mind. In a way, I wished I felt like that towards my own parents.

"I feel like my parents and I have completely different outlooks on life," I admitted. "According to them, my future involves marrying someone like Raylan and settling down as a housewife. But honestly, that's just not something I can see myself doing. As much as I love my parents, I don't think I could handle living the life they want for me. Their idea of happiness just doesn't align with mine."

"When you talk about happiness and your family, I can't help but notice the differences between our cultures," Xuan said.

"What do you mean?"

"You're American. Your entire childhood and education have always taught you independence." He went on to explain that Western civilization is more individualistic, with a focus on finding the meaning of life in the present moment, with self as the center of the universe, which is seen as given and divine. Meanwhile, Eastern cultures prioritize interdependence and view life as a collective effort, where the greater good is more important than individual success.

I didn't really know what to say. I'd never thought about how unalike we were, especially because we were alike in so many of the ways that mattered. Sometimes I felt mystified by the magnitude and reach of culture—how it lingers under the surface, sneaking its way into just about every aspect of our daily lives. "I've always loved learning about history and world cultures. I never really thought about how different our cultures are."

"They are." He nodded in agreement. "We come from two completely different worlds, each with its own rich tapestry of culture and philosophy. Chinese civilization draws deeply from the wisdom of Confucianism, Mahayana Buddhism, and Taoism, while Western civilization finds its foundations in Greek and Roman philosophy, as well as Christianity."

There was a moment of profound silence as our gazes locked, bridging the vast expanse of space, history, and philosophy that spanned the nearly six thousand miles between us.

"I've been wanting to visit China for some time now. And even though our cultures may seem vastly different, I think they both have their own unique beauty," I replied.

"Where would you want to go?"

"I definitely want to see the Terracotta Army, and the Forbidden City. It would also be cool to hike part of the Great Wall, depending on if I'm in good shape. Studying in college has turned me into a couch potato."

Xuan smiled warmly, "If you do decide to go, let me know. I'd be happy to go with you and show you around—I mean as a guide. Getting around can be tricky if you don't know the language, and I'd love to introduce you to my family and show you the city."

I couldn't ignore the intense curiosity that welled up inside me, a strong yearning to know more about him and his country of birth. "I'd like that."

He stared at me for a long moment and I could have sworn that his whole face changed—became softer, more reflective, before he quietly said, "For what it's worth, I don't care that we're different. Not one bit. And I'm happy you're not marrying

Raylan . . . I mean if that's not what makes you happy."

As a stray strand of hair caressed my face, Xuan's hand instinctively reached out, gently sweeping it behind my ear. A tender smile graced his lips as he leaned closer, his eyes filled with anticipation. "So, what else would you like to know about me?" he asked, as if reading my mind.

"Family seems to be a very important part of your life," I remarked.

"Absolutely! For me, family and home are the two most crucial components of my life."

"Are you close to your grandparents?"

"When I was growing up, my parents worked away from home; they traveled back and forth between China and Korea for research studies, so my maternal grandparents played a significant role in raising me. Quality family time was scarce. As per Chinese tradition, the elders in our family are highly respected and regarded as the source of wisdom and spirituality. I've always been close to my grandparents and I respect their decisions. We consult our elders on important decisions, and as they age, it's our duty to care for them. And as an only child, I'll be expected to care for my parents as they age. We do not send our elderly, especially our parents, to an aged-care facility like you guys do in America. That's considered shameful in my country."

I thought of my grandfather, who had lived for several years in the veterans' home. He and my father were not on speaking terms.

"Are you close to your family?" he asked.

I didn't really want to dive deeper into the complexities of my relatives with Xuan. "We see each other for holidays."

"What about your parents?"

"I love my parents, but we're not the same." The word *different* was an understatement. Polar opposites was more like it. I changed the topic back to Xuan's family. "So where do your grandparents live?"

"My household includes three generations living together."

"And that's common?"

"Most Chinese families have three to five generations living under the same roof. But that's a lot of deep family and culture talk for one night. Let's talk about something different," Xuan suggested. His smile was genuine this time.

"Okay, what would you like to talk about?"

There was a slight breeze, and the sudden urge to lean into his warmth was staggering, but there was an invisible line between us I couldn't explain or cross.

"You asked me how I fell in love with science. How about you? What made you decide to study ethnobiology?"

Strangely, if someone had asked me about my life plan a week ago, I would've told them about my perfectly mapped-out timetable to go to UC Berkeley, get my Ph.D., and go live in the rainforest. I thought my love for science was all I needed. None of those plans would have included a boyfriend, and certainly not a husband. I wanted to forsake the idea of love and live nun-like in my own lab somewhere in the rainforest. But after a big day like today, when Xuan saved me from a total, catastrophic implosion, it all seemed so distant. I wanted to live. To experience life outside of the lab.

"Cassie?"

"Sorry, I was just lost in thought. When I was about six, my parents watched a movie called *Medicine Man.* The main actor, Sean Connery, lives in the Amazon jungle in Brazil with a native tribe for six years, and then he possibly discovers a cure for cancer. I remember seeing the Amazon in the video, and I thought to myself, wow, I want to study plants and cures for diseases. I want to help people who are sick. I remember seeing the film and wanting to do that, to study ethnobiology and anthropology."

Leaning forward, Xuan carefully placed his cup on the table before turning his gaze towards the woman in front of him. "You know," he said, his tone thoughtful, "I find you utterly fascinating."

Perking up at his words, I replied with a raised eyebrow, "Is that so?"

Xuan nodded earnestly, his eyes meeting mine as he continued, "It's not often that I come across someone who is not only strikingly beautiful but also has such an intriguing mind."

In my complete embarrassment, my cheeks were probably blooming with color. The word *beautiful* wasn't something I've ever thought about myself. Cute maybe, if I was being kind. Beautiful was a word used for girls like my best friends, Roxy and Sky. A word used for Amanda and other girls with long legs and runway model curves. Girls with long eyelashes and luscious lips that made you want to bite on them. Girls with a nice beach tan and flawless skin. But not me. I was none of those things.

"Thank you," I said shyly. Xuan must have noticed, because his smile was absolutely bewitching in response.

Xuan laid his hand on my arm. Being this close to him felt peculiar—like a déjà vu presence, despite having little contact with each other and barely speaking over these past few years.

Xuan looked up to the sky and then turned toward me, already on his feet as he straightened up. "Come on. Let's check out the telescope."

CHAPTER NINE: WRITTEN IN THE STARS

Medellín, Colombia—Student Housing
October 15, 2016

Xuan helped me stand from the banana chair, his grip warm, comforting even, as I slowly moved to peer over the edge at the shimmering city lights below. Meanwhile, he adjusted the lens. This was like being in the front row at a movie theater on opening night, waiting for the curtains draped over the sky to shift, to announce the start of the movie and the promise of starlight and wonder laid across a pure-black velvet theater screen of the night.

As I waited for Xuan to locate the comet through the telescope, I marveled at the gentle, twinkling stars that adorned the night sky like scattered fairy lights. The world around me seemed quiet with anticipation, as if the streets had been taken over by an army of shushing librarians.

Xuan positioned the telescope. "It's visible! Come here, come look."

He took my hand and pulled me toward him. Then I saw it—like a glittering needle threading the sky. "Wow. That's amazing."

Inside the lens, I saw a blue gas mixed into a curved yellow dust tail trailing behind the green object. "I see two tails."

I stepped back from the telescope, giving Xuan his turn to immerse himself in the celestial beauty. His eyes were once again fixated on the celestial spectacle, as if he were communing with the cosmos itself. "You see," he began, his voice filled with awe, "comets are like giant cosmic snowballs of frozen gas, rock, and dust orbiting the sun. They give birth to a magnificent tail that stretches across millions of miles, trailing behind them as they journey through space."

As Xuan spoke, his words carried a sense of wonder and reverence. "The intense heat of the sun causes the ice within the comet to melt, releasing copious amounts of water and gas that burst forth, breaking through the icy facade and liberating fragments of trapped debris. It is truly a sight to behold, a dance of cosmic forces."

I listened intently, captivated by his explanation, my own sense of awe growing with each passing moment. The universe, with its intricate workings, held secrets and wonders beyond imagination. And in that moment, standing beside Xuan, I couldn't help but feel a deep connection to something much greater than ourselves.

"Did you see the comet's green glow?" Xuan asked. "It's a bit like the northern lights but a bit different too."

I nodded. "What causes that?"

"It's created when ultraviolet light from the sun interacts with diatomic carbon molecules—two carbon atoms in a single molecule—in the comet."

I looked sideways at Xuan. He was smiling as he looked up into the mysteries of the universe—a cosmic cocktail, blended together with the past and present. Xuan waved at me to come look again.

"I can't see it anymore. I think it moved."

"In the telescope, comets can appear to move slowly against the backdrop of stars," he explained, his voice tinged with excitement. "Their movement is a result of their orbit around the sun, combined with the Earth's own motion. It's like witnessing a celestial dance as the comet gracefully traverses its path, leaving a mesmerizing trail of light in its wake."

I watched in awe as Xuan carefully tracked the comet's movement across the vast darkness, and then repositioned the telescope. "Here you go."

The ion and dust tails seemed to be pointing away from the crackling fire of the sun. Looking more closely, one tail was gray mixed with yellow and white and the second was blue fading into teal. The color change was softer than melting wax. A bright green coma glowed around the center. I felt as though I was seeing magic for the first time as the warmth from our great star heated up the comet, causing it to spew dust and gasses into a giant glowing head larger than most planets.

The comet's magnificence and grandeur stirred me, much like a transcendent piece of music that envelops one's soul. "I've never seen a comet before," I confessed, my voice filled with a mix of wonder and emotion.

I could feel a tear form in my eye. I blinked it away. *Bello, pulchram, bela, hermoso, yafah, ómorfi, Meilì.* I could express the concept of beauty in numerous languages, but none of them truly captured the essence of my feelings as I gazed at the comet. It was a sight of indescribable beauty, as if musical notes had been sketched across the canvas of the night sky. I would never forget the comet—similar to Xuan, exciting, rare, and stunning.

"It's the most beautiful thing I've ever seen," Xuan whispered.

I looked at Xuan, but instead of looking at the sky, Xuan was staring at me. He stood, his hands jammed into his pockets, as he quickly turned his gaze to wander over the peaceful metropolis.

My heart began to race. Holy Saints. Oh, Holy Saints. *I think I like him.*

The chilly wind blew slightly, causing my loose hair to fly across my face. He reached out and brushed it back, almost absentmindedly. "You don't have a jacket?" He frowned as he shrugged off his own and draped it over my shoulders.

"Thank you." A quick flashback of a date with Raylan on the Santa Cruz boardwalk haunted me. It was cold one night, and I'd forgotten to take a sweater. I asked him if I could wear his jacket. His response was "But then I'll be cold." That was a sign of who came first in our relationship. And it wasn't me. It was obvious he hadn't learned chivalry from his dad . . . or any role model, for that matter.

Xuan gently pulled me into his arms and wrapped his arm

around my shoulder, keeping the wind at bay.

"Xuan."

He turned toward me. His eyes took me in—all of me.

"Xuan, there's something else I want to ask you," I said.

"Ask me anything. I'll tell you."

"Why . . ."

Patiently, he waited.

"Why did you kiss me today?"

His eyebrows lifted in surprise, followed by a resigned expression as he shook his head. "You might not recall due to shock, but you kissed me back."

"But then at the hospital, you wouldn't talk to me. You ignored me. You went from being so direct to being shy and quiet. I thought you were mad at me."

Xuan stared at me for what felt like an eternity. His gaze was intense. "A lot happened today, and I just needed to process it, okay? I didn't know what to say or how to say it, especially to you."

"I know today was crazy, but *you* kissed me. And then you ignored me. Was I that bad?" Something inside me longed to be desired . . . to be listened to and accepted without judgment.

"Of course not!" His voice was loud and exasperated.

"Then why?" I thought about his lips and how surprisingly soft they were. Maybe it was simply that he'd caught me by surprise, but I'd replayed the kiss a hundred times in my head since that afternoon. I liked it. I liked it a lot, which had confused me even more at the hospital.

Xuan stood tall, his eyes cast down at the ground, as if searching for an answer within the cracks of the pavement. His hands rested on the roof overhang, folded tightly over each other in a gesture of nervous anticipation. "Regarding the kiss," he said, his voice laced with uncertainty, "what should I do?"

I was taken aback by his sudden question, my mind reeling with confusion. "What do you mean?" I asked, trying to gain a clearer understanding of his intentions.

Xuan took a deep breath, his voice soft and barely above a whisper as he continued, "Should I apologize for kissing you? Or would you rather hear my true feelings?"

The weight of his question hung heavily in the air, like an unyielding fog refusing to dissipate. My heart raced as I remained silent, struggling to process his words. I found myself unsure of how to respond.

The tension between us was palpable, like a rubber band pulled taut, ready to snap at any moment.

Xuan let out a resigned sigh. "Hmm, I guess I have my answer," he said, his voice heavy with disappointment.

"I didn't say anything," I whispered, my voice barely audible.

Xuan removed his arm from my shoulder, his posture deflating as he took a step back. "I'm sorry for kissing you," he said, his eyes filled with regret, "but I've thought of doing that a hundred times. It's a very strange thing to be in love."

Love? Did he just say that he was in love with me? The realization hit me like a lightning bolt, electrifying my senses and sending shivers down my spine. My mind was a blur of conflicting emotions—confusion, excitement, and fear—all
mingling together like colors on a canvas.

Xuan's words hung in the air between us, a fragile thread that threatened to snap at any moment. I didn't know what to say or how to react, but one thing was clear—everything had changed in that moment.

"Qīn'ài de," he said with a hint of longing in his voice, his gaze fixed on the ground. His broad shoulders, usually held with confidence, were now slumped in defeat. "Why are you avoiding my eyes? Look at me."

As I lifted my head to meet his gaze, I was taken aback by the intensity of his stare. It left me feeling a little breathless, unsure of what to say or do next. "What does that mean?" I asked.

"The closest translation in Chinese is *honey* or *dear*."

I found myself taken aback by his sudden use of an endearing term. The intensity in his words left me slightly breathless.

"Xuan, I don't know what to say. You barely know me," I said, trying to make sense of the sudden shift in our dynamic.

"I know enough about your heart," he replied, his eyes never leaving mine. Before I could say anything, he continued, his words carrying a sense of purpose and conviction. "And I am enchanted by you, like an astronomer enthralled by the beauty of a starry sky or a painter captivated by the colors on their palette."

As he leaned forward, I found myself not at all afraid of the emotions stirring within me, as Xuan brought his hands up to tenderly grasp my chin, forcing me to look at him.

Every time we touched, an energy drew us together. I felt as though a magnetic force was shoving me closer and closer. I tried to resist my emotions and growing feelings toward him, but resistance was hopeless.

Then he leaned forward and pressed his lips against mine, the touch soft and fleeting. It was a delicate graze, yet I couldn't help but be drawn in, unable to break away. In that singular moment, the world around us faded into insignificance. All that mattered was him, and the warmth that radiated from his touch. It felt as if he had unlocked a hidden part of me, a facet I had concealed for far too long. Our kiss transported me beyond the confines of time and place, the roof and the foreign land melting away. The comet and the mudslide became distant memories, momentarily eclipsed by the intensity of our connection. In that instant, I even forgot my own name, until I heard it being whispered from his lips.

"Cassie," he said, pulling away.

I wanted this—dreamed of it, but now that it was happening, I didn't know how I'd ever want anything else. I wanted more. I wanted him. As he held my gaze, I realized that I had never felt more alive. And I knew, deep down, that this was only the beginning of our journey together.

I stepped closer, wrapped both arms around him.

"Cassie, do you—"

"Shh, don't talk. Just kiss me."

So he did.

Xuan kissed me gently, carefully, trying not to hurt me or touch any of my cuts or injuries. Even with the dwindling light of the comet in the background, my eyes were on him, and his on mine, and both of us were breathing, watching each other. I didn't know whether we were kissing for five minutes or an hour, but I couldn't let go, because it felt so good to be held by him. *Exhale.*

Xuan withdrew his mouth from mine, then traced a path down my cheek. "Cassie, are you sure? If you want me to stop, tell me now," he whispered.

Completely enchanted, I said nothing.

Relieved, he bowed his head and kissed my mouth again, his lips against my lips, brushing them lightly. This time it was sweet, slow, savoring. Patient. That light touch sent shivers through my spine. This was nothing like I'd ever experienced. This was passion, and it was hot, just like fire. And just as dangerous.

In high school, I remember reading poetry by John Keats, Percy Shelley, Pablo Neruda, and William Blake and not understanding their romantic odes and verse. But right now, in this moment, I was a poet, and I think I finally understood all the words and lines they'd written. Tonight the world was full of poetry.

He cupped my cheek, and this time I gave his tongue a small opening and it found mine. He took advantage of the moment. A pulse of energy zapped through my body, like electricity. I'd never known anything as right as that moment.

As Xuan pulled back, a hint of nervousness flickered in his eyes. I felt a rush of heat bloom across my cheeks that betrayed the intensity of the moment. His arms encircling me trembled slightly, mirroring the rapid pace of his heartbeat against my chest. In that instant, I could sense the unmistakable reciprocation of emotions. What I felt, he felt too, a hundredfold.

"*Wǒ wèi nǐ fēng kuáng,*" he whispered.

I would later learn that this meant he was crazy about me.

I had never believed in true love, that there is one right person for everyone. Love is just high levels of dopamine and norepinephrine released into your brain, making you feel euphoric and giddy. But that day had been one of the most terrifying, beautiful, and romantic times of my life, enough to *almost* prove me wrong. Dying and being rescued, the comet, Xuan kissing me—these were the kinds of moments you remember all your life. Those that made me want to reconsider the possibilities. *Maybe true love exists after all.*

As I pondered the dynamics of love, Newton's laws and equations came to mind. It was an unusual connection, but suddenly the concept of love made sense through the lens of physics.

It occurred to me that when two people connect, their interactions are subject to the same fundamental laws that govern physical objects. For every action, there is an equal and opposite reaction, as described by Newton's Third Law of Motion. This was the basis of physics, and human behavior seemed to follow the same pattern. If one person makes a choice, the other will respond with an equal and opposite reaction.

I couldn't help but wonder if this was the essence of love—the Law of Force in action. It seemed to me that the forces at play in a relationship were not so different from the forces that move the stars and planets.

Xuan took my hand and led me back to the banana chairs. "Ms. Steel—"

"Cassie," I corrected him.

"Cassie, let me ask you something."

Our eyes were so close together, I could still see a tint of the comet's tail in his irises.

"Okay."

"You didn't say anything when I confessed my feelings toward you?"

"I didn't know what to say," I said honestly. Still, I had to admit I was drawn to him. He'd danced into my life when I'd least expected it, in the most unlikely of ways. "I like you. But I've only been in one relationship, and that ended very badly and not long ago."

Suddenly I thought of Raylan, and despite all the emotions I was currently feeling, I couldn't help but feel a little sad, betrayed. *How can I be heartbroken and happy all at the same time?*

He lowered his voice, his chest rising and falling as he took several deep breaths. "Let me ask you something else. Did you feel something when I kissed you?"

I found my gaze drawn to the pulse at the base of his throat and I wanted to kiss him there. Surprised to find my voice steady, I admitted, "Yes. But I'm not ready to be with anyone else. I was with him for a long time."

Something like agony ripped in his eyes, the most human and unsure expression I'd ever seen him make. He'd always been so confident in the lab and during our study groups.

Xuan collapsed back in his chair with a sigh, distancing himself slightly from me. "I never met Raylan but I remember seeing you two together in school. What was he like?"

I glanced toward him in surprise but said nothing.

"If you'd rather not answer, we can change the subject," he offered. "I'm sure it wouldn't change my opinion of him anyway."

Curiosity piqued, I asked, "And what is your impression of him?"

"I don't like him."

I couldn't help but laugh. "Why do you say that?"

His response was firm and resolute. "Because you don't like him, and he hurt you."

"Very perceptive, detective."

"Why'd you two break up?"

"We were together for a few years in high school." What I didn't say was that I wasn't important to him, like some figure in the background of an old picture, half faded away.

"That's not really an explanation," he pointed out.

"Well, as soon as high school ended, Raylan left for basic training and I began to take credits at the University of California. He was my high school sweetheart. I worked hard in college and took on extra classes to distract myself. By the middle of my freshman year in college, Raylan received leave but things between us were strained. He wanted to do things I just wasn't ready for. He was already different and he hadn't even left for overseas yet. Over Memorial Day weekend, he went camping with a few of his friends, and I think he may have hooked up with one of the girls we knew back in high school, but he said he didn't. I decided to believe him. We tried to make things work, but I caught him with someone else, and we finally ended it right before I came here. I don't think relationships that are based on lies can last. Not in the long term."

"Did you plan on marrying him?"

I shook my head. "I'm only nineteen. Before the cheating incident, I said I'd wait for him while he was stationed overseas. I have my own plans, though. I want to graduate with my master's degree before I ever consider marriage, and he always said he wanted to finish serving in the military before he considered marriage. My work and my studies are important to me. I want to see and explore a little more of the world before I settle down. But the idea was there, that one day we would end up together."

"Raylan's an idiot," he said in a whisper that couldn't quite disguise the hoarseness in his voice. "One day when he grows up, he'll realize what he's lost."

"I doubt that. And he's gone now. He's leaving in a few days to serve his first combat tour."

"Trust me."

"This is the second time in less than twenty-four hours you've asked me to trust you. I'm starting to feel like I'm in a James Bond movie."

"That's worked out pretty well so far, considering the events of the last twenty-four hours."

Laughter bubbled up from somewhere deep inside me, the type of laughter that came with the giddiness of infatuation.

"I'm sorry he hurt you." Xuan failed miserably to hide his disappointment. "Do you still want to be in a relationship with him?"

I still felt betrayed by Raylan, but I made myself say, "No. I thought I meant more to him, but I guess I was wrong. It took being an entire continent away from him to realize the truth."

"Which is what?"

"Raylan might've been my first serious relationship, but I'm not a doormat. He was a coward. The moment I caught him chasing another fantasy of what could be, I felt this light switch turn on. All of a sudden, I simply didn't care. It was as if all those years had simply disappeared with the turning of that switch. As if my feelings were a shadow, or a monster hiding under the bed, revealed to be nothing more than a figment of my own imagination once the truth was illuminated. There are some truths that, while others might accept, some can never get over. For me, cheating is unforgivable in a relationship. Our breakup was hard, but it was for the best. And there was no magic in the world that would change my mind about taking him back." *Not even a marriage proposal or a strong love potion or Cupid's arrow could convince me otherwise.*

"What did your friends think?"

"Everyone expected me to fall apart. Instead I just felt empty. I honestly couldn't stand their pity. So I came here to get away—and heal."

"I bet you're really angry with him. You guys were together for a long time."

"I was. But the more I think about it and analyze it, it seems like something bigger—like a phantom dark energy was repelling us, like bug spray. I don't think we were ever meant to be together, and the acceleration of the Big Rip just increased over time. I think it was bound to happen eventually, I just wish it didn't end the way it did."

"That sounds an awful lot like Fate."

"No," I said matter-of-factly. "It's just science."

"In the car you said something . . . you wanted me to tell him you forgave him."

"I thought I was going to die."

"You must still care about him if he was one of the last people you thought about."

I could hear Xuan's unspoken question lingering between us. "He does mean something to me still, but probably not in the way you think."

He nodded. "Do you still plan to forgive him?"

"Raylan hasn't exactly had an easy life. I wanted to put his mind at ease so he wouldn't feel guilty for my death. I've been following Elizabeth Gilbert's advice from her novel. I've tried sending Raylan some love and light every time I think about him, which is better than stabbing a small voodoo-doll look-alike with a thousand pins at night. Forgiving him, so he could move on and not blame himself, was my last act of mercy. Life's too short to hold grudges. I learned that yesterday. I forgive Raylan, and I wish him the best."

"I won't ever do anything to hurt you, Cass."

I nodded as I looked at him. In my heart, I believed him . . . or at least I wanted to believe what he said was true. But people never mean to truly hurt the people they care about. It just happens.

"Do you think you could ever give me a chance?" he asked. "Could you possibly ever want a relationship with me?"

"Yes. But I just need time to allow myself closure, so I can move on."

"So you don't want to be in a relationship with me right now, but you would consider it in the future?"

I could sense the imaginary lines between us were blurring. We weren't professional acquaintances or friends . . . but there was something else there. Something I couldn't explain. "Would you be mad at me if I said yes?"

"Not at all. I'm just planning my strategy for when we get back to the States. I planned to ask you out when we get stateside, but I'll wait until you're ready. You don't need to answer me now . . . or ever. You could show up on my doorstep one day, finally ready to give me a chance to let me take you out, and I'd still want you."

"What if I'm not worth the wait?"

"Trust me, you are. You're exactly the person I thought you were, from the first moment we met. And there's no way you could ever be a better fit for me."

He gently touched my cheek, turned my face toward him. This all seemed so fast, but that moment held the promise of something exciting and new.

"Xuan, you can't know that. What if it takes a year or longer for me to be ready?"

"Cassie, I haven't had many relationships. I've only been out with a few girls my parents tried to set me up with. There was someone I did care about back in China, and I know it's painful to lose your first love. But what I feel toward you is more than that. I'll wait for you as long as it takes. Months, or years . . . or a lifetime."

I looked up at this beautiful man who'd rescued me, and I believed him. The way I felt about Xuan was different. I could sense it too, whatever it was he was feeling. There are a few times in your life when your instincts are screaming from every fiber of your being, and telling you to do something, even if it defies logic and scientific reason. Despite the complications, when this happens, you give in to it, to the idea. Its phantom presence was unseen, but it was there, something small but present . . . like a pebble under the water, the idea of something more, something better.

I chewed the bottom of my lip. "Are you going to kiss me again?"

"Would you like me to?"

"More than anything."

His arm slipped around my waist and he held me tightly to him as his smooth lips slowly moved against mine. I liked this—liked being kissed by him. After a while, my breathing turned uneven, but I couldn't look away from him. Not even as he pulled away.

Staring at Xuan, I felt for the first time since I'd arrived that I was finally beginning to understand the reason I'd come . . . and it wasn't for science, or school credit, or to escape my breakup. There was another force at work here, something I'd been trying to deny.

But this thought was so large and complex that I suddenly felt very tired. My head was thick and hazy like morning fog.

"Come sit with me." He took my hand and gently pulled me toward him.

I melted against him like ice cream on a hot summer day as I curled up beside him on his banana chair. He reached over and grabbed a blanket from the dorm room and placed it over us. We were shrouded with a cover and snuggled up together in our own private world.

Comfortable, I nuzzled up against Xuan, eyes closed, my head on his shoulder.

"Tired?" he asked.

"Yes. I think I've had enough adventure for one day." I yawned sleepily.

"Let yourself rest, Cassie." He touched his fingers lightly on my hand. "It's the best way to heal."

Interlocking his fingers with mine our entwined hands rested on his leg. My eyes were already drifting closed. I heard the faint sound of his voice as he sang in Chinese, something that sounded like a lullaby.

"What are you singing?" I whispered. I could still feel the fantom touch of his lips as they lingered on mine.

"A lullaby my mother used to sing to me. Now go to sleep."

I shook my head, trying to clear my blurry vision so I could stay awake. Cuddled next to Xuan, I could feel the warmth of his body, and his fingers were soft around mine. My heart felt like I had leapt from a cliff and was still waiting for the net below to catch me.

A weight pressed on my eyelids. It was impossible to stay awake as they became heavier, so I finally closed them. Blackness swallowed me up.

I barely heard Xuan's song. Beneath the dark, his voice faded. In its stead, I could have sworn I heard the rushing of water. A flash of white lightning, the crunching of metal, and the distant, hollow screams of faces I could not see all filled the starless void.

I looked up from the dark ravine just as the black haired Grim Reappear appeared, her head now angled, as if inviting me to join her. The ravine only seemed to grow wider, as if the rising water was going to devour the entire world in darkness. Alone, I was suddenly back in the vehicle, plummeting towards the rocky ground. There was no escape.

Out of dreams of blood and mud and glass, I awoke terrified. I tried not to wince at the pain that shot through my arm and leg. I was so disoriented and dizzy that, at first, I didn't know where I was.

"Cassie!" Someone was soothingly shaking me awake.

I shook my mind clear and opened my eyes. It was Xuan. He was there with me. *It was a dream. Just a dream.*

"Are you okay? You were having a bad dream."

I tried to swallow, but found my mouth was dry and leaden. Xuan switched on the night lamp so that the room was bathed in dim light. Somehow I was in my room, but I didn't remember walking down the stairs.

The alarm clock illuminated the time. It was 3:05 in the morning. "I'm sorry, I didn't mean to wake you." I lay on the bed, tucked like a child beneath the covers, my hair plastered to my face in panic and sweat. "I was having a nightmare."

Xuan gazed down at me with concern as he brushed away my tears.

"What did you dream about?"

I stared into the abyss that had filled my dreams. "I was still trapped in the car. You weren't there, and the water had just passed my neck. I was about to go under."

Xuan leaned down. He brought me into his chest in a full embrace. "You made it out. You're here, you're alive," he soothed.

"Thank you for saving me." When I finally could swallow, I tasted mud on my tongue. It was so real.

Xuan sat on the side of my bed. He was shirtless with black pajama bottoms. He pulled me toward him, but he didn't kiss me. Instead, he flattened our palms against each other, causing me to shiver.

"Are you cold?"

"No." He was close, close enough that I could feel warmth coming off his body, the smell of Dolce & Gabbana. "I was just scared. Every time I close my eyes, I see the car filling up and I'm about to go under."

"It's just a nightmare. You're safe, here, with me."

I stared up at him in wonder, memorizing the lines and angles of his face as the light of the lamp hit his skin. "Xuan, will you stay with me? Just for tonight? "Please? I know you'd probably rather be—"

"Nowhere else," he said without skipping a beat. "There's nowhere else I'd rather be." He looked down at me and then pulled my hand slowly to his mouth. He kissed the back of my hand in an old-fashioned gesture.

"Are you sure?"

"Yes, of course I'll stay with you, Cassie."

I threw back the covers and he crawled into the single bed with me, sliding underneath the blanket until we were facing each other in sudden intimacy.

"What are you thinking?" I asked.

Xuan glanced away briefly before facing me again. "I was thinking about what would have happened had you never been in the accident this morning."

"I wouldn't have a concussion or stitches and broken body parts," I declared.

Xuan laughed before growing serious again. "But do you think I'd be here now if that hadn't happened?"

"I don't know," I said at last. "I'd like to think so, though."

"Me too. My mom and grandma used to tell me people were

destined for one another."

"That's a romantic idea that young girls grow up hearing in the US as well. That there's a prince out there meant just for them, and a fairytale ending. I guess part of me still wants to believe in the possibility."

Xuan nodded. His skin felt hot and his breathing sounded rapid. After a few minutes, Xuan pulled back a little and planted a small kiss on my lips. "Shut your eyes and try to picture your favorite place, somewhere you've been where you feel calm and relaxed."

I closed my eyes and pictured the massive ancient forest back home. The bark is a reddish-brown color, and the towering trees that grow very close together create a natural cathedral, a dense forest that seems almost impenetrable. Gazing up, I was awe struck by the sheer size and majesty of the redwood trees. The bark is thick and rough, with deep grooves that run vertically up the trunk. I watched as the sun broke through the spaced between the branches, lighting up a dirt path ahead. The forest was alive with color—the vibrant green of ferns, the soft pink of wildflowers, and the deep emerald of moss that covered rocks and trees. I felt like I was walking through a fairy tale. I could almost feel the crackling of twigs and leaves beneath my feet. The forest floor is covered in a thick layer of needles, and the quiet of the forest is occasionally broken by the sound of bluebirds singing or the rustling of leaves as a gentle breeze blows through the trees. As I walked deeper into the forest, the trees grew taller and taller until their tops were lost in the misty sky. The trunks of the trees were massive, and the bark was thick and gnarled, with deep grooves that twisted around the trunk like veins. I ran my hand along the rough bark, feeling the texture of the wood. Take a deep breath, I could feel a sense of tranquility and peacefulness that is hard to find in other places. *The forest is my happy place.* I did not see images of the accident or female Death Angel again.

Xuan tucked his arm underneath my neck. "Now sleep. I'm here, and you're safe. I'm not going anywhere."

"Promise?"

"I promise. *Yǒu yuán qiān lǐ lái xiāng huì.*"

"What does that mean?" I muttered sleepily, my eyelids refusing to open.

"It means that even from thousands of miles away, Fate has intervened," he said softly and wrapped his arm around me.

Lying under the sheet with the oscillating fan rattling in the background to help with the humidity and heat of night, I found myself hoping and praying that the whole thing was real.

His voice was distant, an ethereal part of my dreams, as I finally slipped into darkness. The last thought that went through my mind before falling into obscurity was that love might just be a chemical reaction but that doesn't make it any less meaningful and real. And that maybe, just maybe, I'd been wrong. But that was still too early in the history of *us* to tell. We were just at the beginning of our story.

Part Two: A Twist of Fate

Three years later . . .

Chapter Ten: Waiting

San Francisco, California
May 1, 2019

It was a day that began with optimism. A day that started like any other. I got up, slid my pink fluffy slippers on, and tiptoed out of my bedroom, careful not to wake my mom, who was likely still sleeping. Downstairs, I started the coffee pot, and the familiar sound of bubbling liquid filled the kitchen. Trying to wake up, I stood there and sipped a cup of joe with far too much creamer. The fragrant notes of roasted coffee beans mingled with the creamy decadence of the added sweetness. The coffee had done its part, infusing me with a renewed sense of energy and purpose. After I had my fill of caffeine, I dressed and sat on the porch, waiting for Xuan to pick me up. I couldn't possibly know it then, but this was the beginning of a day that would change my world as I knew it.

I spotted Xuan's blue Mercedes-Benz as it turned down the lane and curved around and opened into a sweeping, brick driveway. His father, Ji-Hoon, had purchased the vehicle for him after graduation. Ji-Hoon had gotten into trouble with his tourist visa ten years ago. He had overstayed by a month and was having a hard time reentering the country. Apparently, Homeland Security doesn't like it when you overstay your visa. His mother, Mei, traveled back and forth a lot. She came to visit her son in high school and decided she liked California so much that she hoped to settle in the Golden State permanently once her husband's visa was approved. Due to China's changing social and economic context, it was actually common for married couples to have a *Liang tou hun*, or two-sided marriage. They were both devoted to their work and accustomed to being apart for extended periods of time.

Xuan was on his iPhone as he put the car in park. After getting out, he walked around to open the passenger-side door for me. He looked sexy in his black suit jacket with a plain gray T-shirt underneath, and a faded pair of blue jeans. Turning, he beamed at me and hurried to wrap up his call in Chinese.

"Morning, my beautiful fiancée." He regarded me intently before bending down to kiss me.

To me, Xuan looked like a Chinese god or a heroic warrior. From the inside out, he was as radiant as the sun god Helios . . . and he was mine.

"Morning, handsome." My heart was already pounding in my chest like a galloping racehorse. Sometimes the word *fiancée* still felt strange, as though it was a magical word, brimming with possibilities. I remembered it took a while for me to start dating Xuan after we returned from Colombia. There had been an adjustment period. At first, I didn't see Xuan. But Fate kept forcing us together, like the planets trailing the sun. Xuan took a few months to get up the courage to ask me out on a date. But I was partly to blame since I'd told him in Colombia that I wasn't ready for a relationship yet. He waited for me and my broken heart and ego to heal. He waited. And soon I'd be waiting for him in more ways than I ever imagined.

When he finally asked me out, I said yes. After that our relationship progressed with a dreamlike intensity. When we were apart, we longed for the sight of each other—when we were together, we wished for more time. We met for lunch on campus between our classes, we studied together and talked on the phone at night before bed. Before very long we'd fallen in love.

Xuan took my hand and ushered me inside with subtle haste. "We need to get going. There's an accident on Highway 1."

Xuan and I had been on the road for three hours, mostly stuck in morning traffic, but we were nearly to the golden city of San Francisco. The roads were no longer damp from yesterday's rainstorm.

As I peered out the window, I saw the long narrow bay intruding into the coastal plain across the Bay Area.

"I wish we were still in Sorrento," admitted Xuan.

I was sitting cross-legged in the passenger's seat, the window down, the salty ocean air from the Bay Area filling the car and lifting my hair around my temples. I loved the briny smell that remained in the air after a storm.

San Francisco was a microclimate, meaning you could literally drive over the Golden Gate Bridge and suddenly go from 50 degrees and fog to 70 and sunny. Frowning, I replied, "So do I." May was supposed to be the best month in Sorrento.

Xuan had graduated with his master's degree at the end of the fall semester, but his father was denied a visa at the embassy and couldn't attend graduation. Ji-Hoon booked two tickets to Italy as a graduation gift to make up for not being able to come to America. The tickets were a second long-distance graduation present. I'd agreed to take spring semester off so we could go on vacation together and resume classes in summer. We were happy and in love.

I was still pursuing my master's degree. I had several grants, which had helped cut the cost for the program. My goal was to teach and pay off my student loans while working as an intern at a biology lab. We'd decided to go during spring because Xuan would be starting his Ph.D. program in the fall semester, though he had yet to decide where he wanted to study. He'd received acceptance letters to UC Berkeley, Stanford, John Hopkins, Yale, and Duke. Wherever he'd go, there was no question that we would end up together.

Italy was like one giant living museum that came alive with music and art. There was no other city in the world like Rome, as I thought of the domes and basilicas. We'd spent nearly a month exploring the Northern Italian cities of Milan, Venice, and Tuscany, before traveling to the Roman-era ruins in the golden Eternal City, and then down to the Amalfi Coast.

We had taken a tour of the Colosseum and St. Peter's Basilica. I touched sand and dirt from the floor of the Roman Colosseum, where thousands of gladiators had spilled their blood, and was instantly sucked into a different time in the past, like Claire Fraser on the TV series Outlander.

We walked to the Trevi Fountain from our hotel and made a wish. We ate gelato outside the Pantheon and visited the Vatican. I would never forget looking up in awe at the breathtaking ceiling of the Sistine Chapel.

Going to Italy had always been my dream, one I was happy to share with Xuan. Together, we tasted wine near the volcanic soils of Mount Vesuvius and saw the bodies frozen in time at the ruins of Pompeii. We'd stayed in Rome for a week before traveling down to Sorrento and Positano. But the most memorable part of the trip was when Xuan got down on one knee and proposed to me under the old tree at Cloister of San Francesco. That was one of the happiest days of my life, the start of a whole new chapter in our lives.

I gazed lovingly over to the driver's seat, watching my fiancé intently. Xuan looked like a cross between the actors Nam Joo-hyuk and Song Joong-ki from my favorite K-Pop shows. I absolutely loved watching Korean dramas. The wind coming in from the window caused Xuan's jet-black hair to dance gracefully across his forehead. He caught me staring at him and smiled, trying to be positive and reassuring despite the fact we were on the way to see a specialist at the hospital. Xuan had been sick since returning from Italy.

"Ice cream after?" Xuan asked.

"You know my sweet tooth. If we were in Italy, we would have already eaten gelato twice by now."

Suddenly the car swerved. I opened my eyes to notice we were between lanes.

"Whoa. You okay?" I reached over to place my hand on Xuan's leg.

"Sorry," he said.

"What happened?"

"I just felt a little light-headed."

"Want me to drive?"

Xuan's brown eyes met mine. "I'm all right, *qīn'ài de*."

I felt the warmth of Xuan's skin as his strong hand took hold of mine. Knots conjured in my stomach. Looking down at his bare skin, I realized how pale his complexion was, which was odd because he helped his mom, Mei, in their sunlit garden almost daily. Compared to Xuan, my skin color was almost an olive-like complexion from my time spent surfing and playing beach volleyball.

"I want today to be over," I admitted. Learning the doctor had asked Xuan to come in instead of giving him his results over the phone had been unsettling.

"Thanks for coming, Cassie. I need you here with me. I know I've lived in the States for years, but I've never needed to go to urgent care or the hospital for anything serious. American doctors are different from the ones back home. I'm nervous."

"We're engaged. Of course I wanted to come."

"I know. I just wanted to say that having you with me has meant everything to me. I hope you know that."

"I do." The past few months had been busy for both of us, but together, we made it work.

His expression went serious. "I can't wait until we're married and you're officially mine."

That made me smile. "Good, because I don't ever plan on letting you go."

"Ditto."

Xuan glared at my bare feet, one of which touched his leg. "Why do you have so many Band-Aids on your toes and heels, *bǎobèi*?"

Xuan often called me *bǎobèi*, which was similar to "babe" in Chinese and used as a term of endearment. He also called me *tián xīn*, and *qīn'ài de*, which was "dear," and darling.

"My mom doesn't do barefoot. So I've been wearing platform heels for the past week while I've been trying on wedding dresses. Hello, blisters. A few have even started to pop and ooze Ninja Turtles style."

"Graphic."

"Disturbingly."

"You could always wear sandals for the wedding."

"I think I'd give my mom a heart attack."

"She'll survive."

"It would certainly give her something to complain about for the next ten years."

"Don't tell her then. Have Roxy stash a pair of flip-flops in her bag, and then after your mom sees you put the heels on, you can switch out your shoes."

Honestly, I almost found it funny—flattering, even. "I'm not going to show up to our wedding in flip flops."

He turned to look at me for a brief second. I loved the way he looked at me with such tenderness and care, like I was the most precious thing in the world. "Why? I don't care. You could come wrapped in a white sheet and you'd still be the most beautiful thing I'd ever seen. I want you to be comfortable—happy. I don't want you to say your vows in pain."

His words had touched me deeply, sending a fluttering sensation through my heart. "Thanks. That means a lot to me, Xuan."

His eyes softened. "When we're done at the hospital, we should go into Chinatown for a traditional Chinese foot massage."

"What's a—" I started to ask.

"It consists of a foot bath followed by an intense massage on various pressure points in the feet, ankles, and legs. Foot massage and foot reflexology have been practiced for centuries. They're really popular in China for reducing stress and aiding digestion. Every week when my father and I would shop at the night markets, we would stop in for a thirty-minute foot massage."

"Sounds nice."

"We'll both get one after we finish eating dim sum. I've been craving authentic Chinese food." The section of the San Francisco city known as Chinatown was supposed to be the oldest in the US. I wondered if it would resemble an actual city in China. Mei had found an herbalist there she frequented quite often.

"I'm always up for dumplings," I said enthusiastically.

Xuan exited the freeway. We were close to reaching the inner city. Shortly after the Mercedes was off the freeway, we pulled into the parking structure of a building the size of a grand hotel. Nearby, the arches of the Golden Gate Bridge reflected off the hospital's glass windows.

Xuan stepped out of the vehicle just as a nearby clock tower chimed noon. A crowd of businessmen and women, all dressed in tailored suits, swarmed the streets as they hurried to beat the lunchtime rush hour. For a few seconds, I was disoriented by the bustling, New York-style stampede. Xuan seemed to take no notice as he moved to open the car door for me. The city was much too loud and much too crowded.

I was only two steps out of the car when Xuan pulled me into his arms. Public displays of affection made me uncomfortable. That day was different. I couldn't explain it, but it felt as though there was something bigger than us at work. I didn't know this visit would be something life-changing.

"Kiss me," he said against my lips. Those two little words won me over as I parted my mouth. His lips were immediately against mine. In that moment, nothing else mattered. The world could have fallen away and I wouldn't have noticed. I felt a rush of emotion that made me want to hold him close and never let go.

If I were a superhero like one of the characters in my favorite childhood comics and I could choose a power, I'd choose to possess the ability to stop time. The world felt as though it was spinning clockwise. Its axis was like a ticking clock that I couldn't stop. I had no control, like drowning in the mudslide. The time was too short, and the world in its present form was passing away with each second, leading up to the moment we would walk through those tall glass doors. And little did we know that our lives would change, time after time, until it was too late to go back to our safe world.

"Come," he said. Taking my hand, he led me through the glass doors.

We entered the lobby of the medical center. I squeezed his hand, hoping to feel security overcome my intense hatred of hospitals, which somehow still reminded me of my near-death experience in Colombia.

The waiting room smelled so thickly of chemicals that nausea began to twist and turn in my stomach. Xuan and I stood in a short line, waiting to check in for his appointment.

"Insurance card?" The front desk helper was a little cranky. She probably didn't like her job.

"I'm an international student. I don't think my university insurance will cover this. My plan only works at the campus doctor's office." He showed her the card just in case.

The secretary glanced up from her desk. We were just more anonymous faces, another sick patient file to bill. "We don't accept that here. Without insurance, the cost will be five hundred fifty dollars for today's visit. That will include meeting with the specialist and the labs that need to be completed."

That seemed like a lot of money for one visit. Xuan fiddled with his wallet, trying to find his credit card.

I beat him to it, pulled out my debit card from my pocket and handed it to the secretary.

Xuan's lips pulled into a tight line. "*Bǎobèi*, I don't want you to pay for this. My father already offered to pay since I'm still in school."

"It's okay, Xuan. Your father paid for my ticket to Italy. It's the least I can do. Besides, we're going to be married soon." Truthfully, he paid ninety percent of the time. He rarely allowed me to pay for anything when we went out. He'd already secured a paid research technician position with his bachelor's degree. International students were allowed to work legally in the USA after they completed a degree. They were given hours called Curricular Practical Training—CPT, which were authorized work experience hours in their field of study, so that experiential learning could physically take place. This meant that Xuan didn't require a visa to work for a year, and he could be employed in the US before we were married and started the Green Card process. Once Xuan had secured a job, he was issued a new I-20, and a Certificate of Eligibility for Nonimmigrant Student Status. But the company Xuan was working for didn't offer insurance for temporary employees, which meant Xuan's CPT hours excluded him. That wasn't his dream job, but he was happy finding a company that would allow him to work as an international student while he completed his schooling.

"Fine, but I'm paying for dinner later."

The lady took the card and hurried to process the payment. Then we waited for his name to be called. Chair to chair, I could feel Xuan's breath on my neck. Leaning in, he whispered, "I love you," in my ear.

About thirty minutes later, the nurse came out to take Xuan back to the examination room. Xuan stood politely, his expression unreadable. He looked like his usual perfect-and-collected self as he turned toward me, but I could tell there was something different about him, something off, under the surface of his calm mask. His hands were steady and his expression somber. "*Bǎobèi*, I was actually wondering if I could go into the exam room alone." He regarded me intently. "I have a few questions, and I would like to talk to the doctor in private, okay?"

I was not okay with that, and I felt a little hurt that Xuan didn't want me to go with him. "Sure." I shrugged and gestured for him to go.

Before he exited the waiting room, he turned and looked back at me.

"I'm not leaving," I reassured him.

"I hope not. It would take a long time to walk home . . . or a very expensive cab."

Xuan always made jokes when he was trying to make light of a situation. There was no reason not to feel optimistic, but I was crazy scared. I didn't dare tell him my true feelings then.

Finding myself feeling utterly alone and bored, I took a seat, confident that whatever bug or virus Xuan had caught, the doctors would cure.

Xuan had been sick since we returned from Italy. He had a prolonged cough, wheezing, and shortness of breath, slight chest pain, difficulty swallowing, and severe fatigue. Xuan's mom made him chew candied ginger, a proven anti-nausea ancient remedy. Mei also gave Xuan valerian root to chew for pain and a mixture of Chinese herbs.

I had heard stories where medical cases turned to Eastern medicine as a last resort, when modern doctors could no longer provide an answer or a prescription that did the trick. Despite what some people think, Eastern medicine is complex, and sometimes preferable to Western medicine. At the heart of many Eastern practices is the concept that life and medicine are one. Healing is approached through harmony of body, mind, and spirit. Mei wasn't a fan of Western medicine or the doctors who treated their patients like a statistic.

Looking around at other people who were waiting, I felt out of my comfort zone. I was so not dressed for the occasion. I was wearing bell-bottoms, flip-flops, and a plaid, long-sleeved Quiksilver shirt. The others around me were in a suit, a dress, and one wore a miniskirt with an immodest designer shirt. Compared to them, I looked like a flower child of the 1960s. I wished Xuan and I could go back in time to a freewheeling era of love and peace. But we were Gen Z, with a future of high-tech promise ahead of us in the twenty-first century.

Minutes seemed like hours. As time passed, I felt myself grow more and more restless. Over an hour and a half had passed since Xuan was taken back into the room. As I looked at the clock, the seconds seemed to be ticking away at a sluggish rate. This was one of those times when life was painstakingly drawn out, each and every second.

Slowly, another hour on the clock passed by. Then another.

Xuan still hadn't come out. Just past 4:00 p.m., my phone began to vibrate. It was my best friend.

"Hi, Roxy."

"Cass, I just stopped by your house and your mom told me you were at a hospital in San Francisco. Is everything okay? We were supposed to go shopping today."

I could sense Roxy's disappointment. "I left you a voicemail about canceling."

"You know I never check my voicemails. The majority of people who leave me voicemails these days are salesmen, or my parents, neither of which I really care to talk to."

Roxy was right. The way we communicated now was different from how our parents communicated even a decade ago. "Sorry, Roxy. Xuan and I are up here seeing a specialist."

"What's going on?" she asked impatiently, her tone full of concern.

"Xuan's been really sick since we got home."

"Well, if he needs any blood work done, tell him I would be happy to stick him."

Roxy was a phlebotomist, a profession she seemed to enjoy a little *too* much. "Wow, you really are a professional vampire."

"A modern-day, licensed one. Besides, it's what I do best."

"Thanks for the offer, but I think the hospital has it covered."

"It must be serious if he's at the hospital. Did he catch something in Italy?"

"I don't know, maybe."

"Well, I hope he feels better."

"Thanks. I'll tell him you called."

"I've got to go, but if you need anything, call me. Otherwise, I'll see you two young lovebirds at the bonfire."

What do I do now? After I hung up, I mindlessly began flipping through pages of a magazine. I turned to a page advertising wedding and gift registry items from Macy's. Our wedding date was five months away. Because of my college schedule, my old-fashioned, wedding-obsessed mom, aka Weddingmomzilla, had been hounding me with details. October could not come soon enough.

I closed my eyes for a moment, and when I did, I found myself in a happy place. The color palette for our fall wedding came to mind. Mediterranean deep browns and rich reds were the lively pops of color in my chosen wedding theme. Vibrant red roses and other floral pieces would decorate the aisle, which led down to a gypsy-style tent where Xuan and I would someday soon, say our wedding vows. We had chosen an outdoor, forested area for the wedding and reception.

For the evening wedding reception, I saw white-and-copper table settings sprinkled with fall tea-light holders for a touch of romance. The cake and other decor would be placed out against the woodsy wilderness setting. I could picture myself and Xuan dancing under burlap and lace and Chinese lanterns, string lights shining as brightly as little stars. I was walking down the aisle to meet my groom.

All of a sudden, I felt a tap on my shoulder. "Cassie, are you ready to go?" Xuan asked.

I hadn't realized Xuan was standing over me. "Yeah, I didn't see you come out."

"Were you sleeping?"

I smiled. "I drifted off."

I noticed that Xuan was no longer wearing his black suit jacket. He looked uncomfortable, as though he was sweating. His gray shirt was stuck to his body and his hair was plastered to his neck.

It was half past six. *What took over six hours to diagnose?*

"What happened? You were gone for a super long time."

"The doctor wanted to run more tests on me." His voice was husky and laced with tension.

"Well, what's the verdict? Bronchitis, pneumonia, strep?"

"I won't know anything for a few days, maybe longer."

"It shouldn't take that long. What about the earlier tests?" I asked skeptically.

"Let's get out of here. I don't want to be in this place another minute," Xuan said quietly. His fingers were trembling.

I stood up, allowing Xuan to lead the way. His pace exiting the building was a lot more rushed than when he'd come through the hospital's main entrance. The setting sun was sinking rapidly. Glowing blood-orange hues bled into the sky, melding with the darker purples and wispy clouds, the colors reflected in the deep, still waters of the bay.

Reaching for Xuan's arm, I retracted my hand at the sight of the gauze bandage. An additional, smaller bandage had been placed on his neck. I paused for a moment, but Xuan took no notice and continued his quick pace. Jogging to catch up to him, I felt an eerie vibe about his manner that reminded me of his distant behavior after the devastating mudslide. I felt scared—like when the car was filling up with water and I lost control. It was like that.

Chapter Eleven: The Long Night

UC San Francisco Hospital, California
May 1, 2019

As we drove down the highway, the beauty of the midday sun that had welcomed us on the drive in had now vanished behind the densely wooded hills. A familiar darkness greeted us. Xuan didn't want to stay in San Francisco, so we continued home. There was no Chinatown for dinner, nor did we stop and savor lovely foot massages.

I twirled the ring Xuan had given me. It was a vintage-inspired round sapphire halo, surrounded by brilliant round white stones. Diamonds were overrated. I was heavily involved with Invisible Children and Amnesty International in high school, and the last thing I ever wanted was a blood diamond. I loved my ring, but I also would've been happy with something much simpler, more traditional, like they do in China. In Asia, most couples had simple bands. I didn't care what my ring looked like. It could've been a fifty-cent knockoff from a vending machine and it wouldn't have mattered. I just wanted to be married to him.

Looking down at my hands, I tried to keep my eyes from making contact with Xuan. I observed him from the corner of my eye. His eyebrows were naturally full, and he had beautiful arches on his symmetrical face that was radiating a deadly brooding silence. He hadn't spoken since we got into the car, except for a few words in Mandarin.

Xuan focused on driving. The Beatles song "Let It Be" played on the radio, but I didn't feel like singing. I mustered up the courage to break the silence.

"Xuan, talk to me. What happened?"

Xuan tightened his hold on the steering wheel. The question

caused him to accelerate so quickly that I was thrown back in my seat. He didn't answer my question. Instead, he appeared deep in thought.

"Xuan, please."

Suddenly he turned off the road. As he pulled off, he began to hit the brakes. The car lurched forward, dust rising up in plumes as we skidded on the dirt shoulder beside the highway. The Mercedes was not meant for off-roading like my jeep, and the traction on his tires was not the same in the dirt. Coming to an abrupt stop, Xuan whirled toward me, as if to say something, but he hesitated.

He got out of the car and slammed the door, his expression one of anguish. Seething, Xuan clenched both hands in his hair. I'd never seen him like this. His look was absolutely miserable. He was barely holding on to his self-control.

I listened to his steady footsteps fade, felt my muscles tugging my back, as if warning me not to move or get out of the vehicle. I sat and waited . . . and waited. Each minute that passed was agonizing. I finally opened the door and slowly stepped out of the vehicle. He stood with his back facing me.

Xuan picked up a large rock and threw it as hard as he could into an open field.

"Xuan, please talk to me," I whispered. This was the man I loved, and I was being shut out of his world. "You're starting to scare me."

Xuan turned to face me. His autumn-brown-and-gold eyes were wide, cold and distant. The look on his beautiful, tortured face in that moment would forever be etched into the back of my mind.

"It's bad, Cassie. Really bad. There's something I haven't told you," he said, his voice trembling with apprehension.

My heart sank, sensing the gravity of his words. "What is it?" I asked, my voice barely a whisper, filled with concern.

"During my last appointment in Santa Cruz, the doctor listened to my list of symptoms and conducted some preliminary blood work," he began, his voice heavy with worry. "He expressed concern about my elevated white blood cell count. He suspected it might be an infection and started me on antibiotics. But it didn't help. The doctor recommended further tests, which is why I decided to go to San Francisco to see a specialist. It seems the regular clinic doesn't have the necessary equipment."

My mind raced, trying to comprehend the implications of his words. The weight of uncertainty hung in the air, as if time stood still, and the future suddenly felt uncertain.

"Why didn't you let me go in to see the doctor with you?"

"Because I was afraid of what they might say. I know you're scared of doctors and needles. I just didn't want us both to be frightened, not until—"

"Until what?

"I expected it to be some kind of Italian superbug. The right antibiotic and it would be gone, right? I'm young. I was healthy."

"What do you mean *was*?"

Xuan's eyes met mine. "The doctor at the hospital ran a combination of several tests on me, including a thoracentesis and a chest X-ray before and after the thoracentesis."

"What's a thoracentesis?"

"They took a needle and placed it through the skin and muscles of my chest wall into the space around the lungs, called the pleural space."

"What does that mean? What were they looking for?"

"It means, Cassie, he thinks I may have . . ." Xuan paused and let out a deep exaggerated exhale. "Lung cancer."

I couldn't breathe. I couldn't move or think. I couldn't even swallow the knot in my throat. I might actually cry. Cancer. The big C. This couldn't be happening. "And what did the test show?"

"I still have to wait for the results."

"So maybe it's nothing?" I was trying not to be a pessimist.

"I think we need to be prepared for the worst, based on what the first doctor found. The specialist's job was to confirm it. There has to be a reason why my white blood cell count is off."

"That's insane!" I practically yelled. "You're so young. It has to be a mistake. The doctors can be wrong. I've never heard of anyone in their twenties having lung cancer. How could you have lung cancer?" I asked defensively, choking back an exasperated sob.

"Cassie, it might be rare for someone my age, but that doesn't change the fact that it could be true. I may have cancer."

I closed my eyes, feeling momentarily light-headed. I felt my heart race. Breathing suddenly became hard, really hard, as if I'd just finished running a marathon. "This can't be happening. You don't even smoke."

I knew I should be strong for him, but I was lost. That morning I'd woken up to a pot of brewing coffee and a plate full of optimism about our trip to the hospital. I hadn't seen this coming. I never expected cancer.

The news was overwhelming . . . for both of us. I searched Xuan's golden-brown eyes and watched as he tried to repress his fear and devastation. I had never seen him like this.

That felt like the darkest hour of my life, and there wasn't enough time for my mind to sort everything out. "It's going to be okay," I said.

I reflexively took Xuan in my arms, tried to comfort him, like winter clinging to summer's grave. Raw, unrelenting feelings won against my self-restraint. My eyes brimmed over and dripped salty tears.

"*Qīn'ài de,* please don't cry," he whispered, not letting go of me.

I asked the question I was most afraid of hearing the answer to. "But there's treatment, isn't there? Either way."

"We didn't even begin to talk about possible treatments yet. I need to schedule an appointment to get more tests done so we can create a plan if it's confirmed."

"How soon?"

"I don't know."

We stood there, silent. I think we were both in shock,

unprepared to cope with this new reality. I wanted to build a wall of denial as long as the Great Wall of China and safely hide behind it.

"Let's go home," said Xuan. "I need to talk to my mom." Xuan turned as if to leave, but I continued to hold on to him, reluctant to let go.

"Cassie, I'm just getting in the car." His tone was placating, as if he were reassuring a child.

I relinquished my grasp on him, but I didn't want to. I felt like Alice sliding down the dark rabbit hole . . . I didn't want to go.

Once in the car, Xuan mechanically reached over for my seat belt and pulled it around me to fasten it when I didn't move to do it myself.

The engine started. I laid my head on Xuan's shoulder, needing to touch him. Despair curled up like a boa constrictor around the pain in my stomach such as I'd never experienced before. I tried to think positive thoughts, but I was too overwhelmed with the "What ifs".

The moment Xuan said that six-letter word—that he might have cancer—every part of our future changed. I sat there, wishing for the clock to rewind so I could recede into the past and go back to the way things were just a few hours, days, months ago. The horrifying memory of that night would live on to haunt me forever—the beginning of the end.

My brain felt as though it was swimming in thick and gooey mud, sucking me down like in the mudslide when Xuan rescued me. But, I pondered, *what if I can't save him?* I shut my eyes and it was dark. I didn't remember falling asleep.

Chapter Twelve: New Divide

West Cliff Drive, Santa Cruz, California
May 2, 2019

Blood and tubes. As I made it to the end of the hallway, I could see a sign outside the door. Zhang Xuan. I put my hand on the door to open it. The sound of steady rhythmic beeps and air being delivered by a ventilator reached my ears.

"Xuan," I muttered. Then everything went bright white, cold.

It must have just been a horrible dream. *A dream. It's only a bad dream.*

Hadn't I been with Xuan? I must have drifted to sleep in the car on the way home, because when I woke, I found myself in the comfort of my own bed. Mentally exhausted, I wanted to fall back to sleep, but outside, a beautiful sailor's dawn was breaking, and the sunlight and heat made it hard to sleep.

The smell of pancakes, bacon, and eggs wafted in the air. After getting dressed, I hurried downstairs. My mother had put on a pot of Colombian coffee from the beans señor Nieto had sent us from Café San Alberto. The coffee had a luscious, sweet aromatic note, reminiscent of caramel and a soft dark-chocolate flavor. Señor Nieto had sent a family picture taken at the café. I couldn't believe how much his daughter had grown.

"Well, thank you, Mei. I'll let her know. Bye now."

"Why were you on the phone with Xuan's mom?" I asked as I began to smother my banana pancakes in blueberry syrup.

"Sweetie, Mei told me about what happened yesterday at the hospital in San Francisco."

My breathing picked up. I could no longer deny that yesterday had in fact happened. "It wasn't just a bad dream," I said quietly.

"No, Cassandra, it wasn't," Stella confirmed.

My watery eyes filled to the brim as fear struck an internal chord like the sad notes of a violin. In shock, I felt sick, so I leaned on my mom for support in the kitchen, allowing her to lead me to the living room couch to sit down.

Stella ran her fingers gently through my hair as she tried to comfort me. But it wasn't my mother's touch that I needed—it was someone else's.

"How did I get home last night?"

"Xuan carried you up to your bedroom before he went home. You had a panic attack and passed out from hysteria."

My chest ached. "I should've been there." *I should have stayed awake. How could I let him go home alone? I should have been there for him when he told his mom.* A single word crossed my mind. *Selfish.* If I had a single, universal turn-back-the-time free pass, I would have used it on the previous night.

"Actually Mei said Xuan was more concerned about you."

That was pretty typical, considering it was Xuan. He always put me first, just further confirmation of my need for a do-over card.

"Honey, what happened?"

I managed to tell my mom the story in spurts. "He still has to get a few test results back. There's still hope, Mom."

I needed to see Xuan. I needed the comfort of his voice, and to tell him how sorry I was for how I acted, for leaving him to face this alone. Most of all, I needed this all to be some horrible nightmare. Standing, I grabbed my keys hanging by the door.

"Cassandra Temperance Steel, where do you think you're going?"

I hated it when she used my full name. "I need to be with him."

"Honey, I know you want to be with your fiancé. But right now, Mei needs some alone time with her son. They need to have time to contact his father and to process this. I understand that need as a mother. You need to be patient—have patience and temperance."

"Oh." Stella was right. I put the keys down and headed back

upstairs to my room.

If I'd had a bottle of wine, I'd have opened it. I could have used a little escapism right then. Maybe even something a little stronger. Instead, I sat down at my desk. On my laptop, I began to research and familiarize myself with Xuan's initial diagnosis. Navigating from the terminology of a "thoracic oncologist" to the intricacies of 'biomarker testing' felt similar to learning a foreign language. I looked up information on getting another opinion. The possibility of Xuan's lung cancer diagnosis had sent me reeling into a new world, one where I felt I didn't belong. But I would be an apt pupil.

Just before the fourth podcast ended, my cell phone vibrated. *Unknown caller.* I answered.

"Hello?" I said into the phone.

"Hi. Is this Cassandra Steel?"

"Yes. Who's this?"

"This is Pastor Clark from Twin Lakes Baptist Church."

I silently wanted to curse my mom for having her pastor call. I wasn't ready to talk to someone else about Xuan.

"Xuan called me this morning. He told me what was going on and that he was worried about you. He thought I might be able to help."

"Oh, Xuan called?" I asked, feeling surprised. Xuan had always emphasized that he was a spiritual person with a strong connection to his ancestors. According to him, Confucianism, Taoism, and Buddhism were the three pillars of Chinese society. These three philosophies have influenced society alongside each other, changed each other, and at times blended together. Given his beliefs, it was surprising that he would reach out to a Christian pastor from my childhood church.

"Yes. We talked for over an hour."

"Xuan's Buddhist."

"Yes, I know that."

"So he told you what was going on?" I asked. My stomach tightened. I couldn't bring myself to say *cancer* right then. The word felt dirty on the tip of my tongue.

"He told me," Pastor Clark assured me. "I'm sure Xuan's diagnosis is hard to grasp."

"It is."

We talked for a while longer, and he tried his best to offer me comfort. Despite his efforts, I still felt like I was in a dark abyss, akin to the one in *Dante's Inferno*, but I thanked him for his kind words nonetheless.

"Cassie, I understand this is a challenging time for you. Whenever you need someone to talk to, I'm here for you. Don't forget that feeling grief and anger doesn't make you weak. It makes you human."

"I'll try to remember that. Thank you, Pastor Clark. Goodbye," I said before hanging up the phone.

The thought of talking about Xuan's diagnosis was unbearable, but maybe someday I could.

I felt trapped in a never-ending nightmare, like the character in Groundhog Day who relives the same dreadful day over and over again. But this was no movie; it was real life. And it was all wrong.

Chapter Thirteen: June Ward's Kitchen

West Cliff Drive, Santa Cruz, California
May 3, 2019

"Hey, Cassie, you awake?"

I groaned at the sound of my name being called. My body and cognition were in total overload. Basically, just like when a computer gets a virus or crashes, I was in total system shut down, drastically limiting my ability to process my life. Sleepily, I opened my eyes and saw the bedroom was now shrouded in a comfortable darkness. The Friday sunshine was already gone.

"Dude, your mom said you've been asleep for hours."

My two best friends, Roxy and Sky, stood staring down at me. I could see Roxy's dark-brown hair, red flames bursting from her head like an erupting firework shell. Sky had dirty-blonde hair with highlights framing her face and sea-green eyes. She wore her hair with a natural long wave.

Feeling slightly annoyed at being awoken, I muttered a low go away.

"But it's eight PM. We're supposed to meet Xuan and his friends at the bonfire for Nick's birthday." I'd always liked him, Raylan's baby brother, with three years between them. They could pass for twins, minus tattoos and Nick's blond hair and lankier build. Their other brother was also in the military, but he didn't look anything like them.

I remembered the plans that Xuan and I had made with our friends for the birthday party, but that seemed light-years ago.

Sky and Roxy would both be anxious to get down to the beach and meet up with everyone to celebrate. Xuan's college friends would also be there. His friends were from South Korea, China, and Taiwan, and I loved them . . . a lot.

Xuan's and my social circles had taken a while to blend because of the cultural differences and language barriers, but once they did, we all became inseparable. Nick had even been planning to visit Beom in Seoul the next year around the same time we'd be on our honeymoon. We planned to visit Xuan's family in China.

"Are you even listening?" Sky asked.

"What?" I looked up at their gaping faces.

Sky and Roxy both continued to stare at me.

"We said we would wait for you, but you need to take a shower and run a comb through your hair," remarked Roxy.

"Roxy is nicely telling you that you're a hot mess. Now get up," Sky commanded. "We're not leaving you here alone in la-la land."

In truth, I was in the complete opposite of la-la land. If LA had been swallowed by hell and the cast of *La La Land* had turned out to be evil manifested or a horror film, then Sky would've been closer to being right.

I grabbed a bra, jeans, and underwear and headed for the bathroom. I turned on the water and forced myself into a hot shower that was too damn hot. I turned off the water and dried off with a towel before coming out of the bathroom.

"I don't want to go." I sat back down on my bed.

Roxy flipped on the mosaic overhead light and then threw me a Jim Morrison and the Doors T-shirt.

"Too bad. You're going," said Roxy. "C'mon, Cassie. Xuan already told us what's going on. I know things are hard right now, but you have to get out of bed. Nothing is certain yet, and Xuan wants to be with you. He made us promise we would make you come."

I nodded and slowly sat up. My hair was still wet, so I plaited my waist-length mane back into a simple braid, then followed Roxy and Sky out of my bedroom, down the stairs, and into the kitchen, where my mom had just finished baking fresh cookies.

I could sense my mother's instant disapproval. Her mood had changed as quickly as a cup of dried noodles into hot one-minute ramen. Sky was wearing an LGBT-pride midriff, and Roxy was wearing a politically graphic tank top with the word *Ineptocracy* and the definition under it, about the government's inability to lead.

"Where are your shoes, girls? Your feet are black with dirt. Aren't you worried about stepping on something sharp?"

"Not really," admitted Roxy.

Stella's mouth set into a hard line. I used her distraction to take out my phone and found that Xuan had written two messages.

The first read *Were Sky and Roxy able to bring you back to the land of the living?* The second read *I know the last few days have been hard, but try to have fun tonight. I love you.*

Something in my chest softened as I quickly sent back a reply. Roxy and Sky had attempted to make light conversation with Stella, but their efforts fell flat like deflated balloons. I smiled gratefully at my friends' attempt, but the lines on my mother's face deepened into a frown, casting a shadow over the room. My parents stood in stark contrast to Xuan's family and the parents of my friends. Stella, my devoted stay-at-home mom, and Richard, my father serving as a Command Sergeant Major in the U.S. Army overseas, embodied a different era. His role demanded hands-on leadership, and he believed it was his duty to dive headfirst into dangerous operations. I once overheard him confiding in my uncle, boasting about going on as many as two or three combat missions day and night. They seemed trapped in the mindset of the 1950s, adhering rigidly to conservative values and embracing predefined roles. My mom, with her prim dresses and functional, short hairstyle reminiscent of the women from that bygone era, embodied the essence of their time. They both clung fiercely to the beliefs and attitudes of that period, and their antiquated notions regarding relationships had strained our own connection over the past few years.

Prior to my engagement, my father harbored a strong dislike for Xuan, his disapproval radiating through every conversation we had. It was palpable in his tone of voice and the way he mentioned Xuan's name during phone calls and video chats, as if it left a bitter taste in his mouth. Despite Xuan's heroic act of saving me during our time in Colombia, he never showed genuine interest in Xuan or our relationship. Every time I enthusiastically shared stories of our dates, extolled Xuan's brilliance, or proclaimed that he understood me better than anyone else, my father would invariably bring up Raylan.

And when the news of our engagement finally emerged, the situation spiraled out of control like a tornado tearing through our lives. Fueled by my father's deep-rooted opposition to interracial marriage, my parents launched a relentless campaign to dissuade me from marrying Xuan, their efforts becoming a tempest that threatened to upend our lives. It took all my strength to resist snapping at him, fully aware of the unfairness and prejudice behind his stance. But one day, the mounting tension exploded like an A-bomb, leaving a massive rift between us—a divide spanning from the width of the Rio Grande to the expanse of the Great Rift Valley. It changed nothing. My father had tunnel vision. To him, it didn't matter if a person's skin was yellow, brown, or black; he only saw a white military man in my future, someone like Raylan Thompson. I couldn't help but think to myself, time and time again, if he only knew the truth about Raylan, the real Raylan.

Initially, my mother stood by my father, bound by the vows of marriage. And so the rift between my parents and I, an ever-widening gorge, echoed the pain that tore at the seams of our once-tight-knit family. The harmony we had once cherished seemed like a distant memory, fading like an old photograph weathered by time.

After my return from Italy, where our engagement was announced, the already gaping chasm between my parents seemed to stretch wider, like a bottomless abyss devouring any flicker of understanding or acceptance. Their differences, once mere cracks in the foundation of our relationship, now threatened to crumble the very walls that held us together. I still loved my parents—will always love them, but I would not give up Xuan for them, even if that meant I had to lose them. Deep in my mind and soul, I knew without a doubt that Xuan was the one for me. My unwavering belief in our connection fortified me, and I stood strong, united in my conviction that Xuan and I were meant to be together, even if it meant standing against my own family. I knew deep within me that our bond was unbreakable, like a diamond forged in the pressures of adversity. And though the storms of familial discord howled and raged, I clung to the belief that love had the power to heal even the deepest wounds and bridge the widest divides. Because love, like a beacon of hope, had the power to illuminate our path, and guide us all through the darkness of uncertainty.

One evening, my mother cunningly prepared my favorite dinner—a trap disguised as a gesture of love—and subtly voiced her doubts about marrying Xuan due to our differing cultures. "Sometimes," she said with a weary sigh, "differences like culture and religion only make marriage more difficult than it already is." In an attempt to sway me, she urged me to watch the film "Guess Who's Coming to Dinner." However, I retorted, reminding her that we lived in a different century, where love should conquer all boundaries. Frustrated and disheartened, I started finding excuses to stay away from home as much as possible, not only because of my parents' disapproval of my relationship but also because of the growing sense of disillusionment I felt towards my own family. Little did I know then that some things, like racism, have a stubborn resistance to change. As tensions escalated, I reached a breaking point and threatened to move out with Roxy, severing all ties with my parents. It was a desperate plea for them to understand and accept my love for Xuan. Unexpectedly, my mother began to reconsider. Loneliness crept into her heart, a result of years spent as a military wife, separated from loved ones. I was her only child, and the thought of losing me weighed heavily on her.

Gradually, she started to warm up to the idea of having a Chinese son-in-law. Xuan, ever the gentleman, charmed my mother, drawing her back from the shadows of doubt. Stella witnessed his unwavering respect and the way he treated me with tenderness, and that became her measuring stick of approval. She gradually came to realize that she had been wrong—that love knows no color or cultural boundaries. It embraces the beauty of diversity, weaving a tapestry of understanding and growth. Her heart softened, however, our relationship remained strained, scarred by the battles we had fought and the wounds inflicted by our conflicting beliefs. In hindsight, my mother should have supported me throughout the journey, from the beginning. And although the wounds of the past remained, a glimmer of acceptance and reconciliation flickered in the distance as we moved forward.

As for my father, he remained distant, a ghostly figure hovering at the edges of my life. He hadn't been physically present for years, but his presence loomed large in his refusal to bless our union. Despite the emotional void he left behind, I had to find the strength to carry on without his approval. Love doesn't always conform to societal expectations or fit neatly into predetermined boxes. It is a force that transcends boundaries and defies the narrow confines of prejudice.

"What are you watching, Mrs. Steel?" asked Roxy as the sound of my mom's favorite soap opera blasted from the television in the living room. If it were up to Stella, Ward and June Cleaver's world of milk and cookies would still be playing.

Unlike my friends, my parents were exactly like the Cleavers. Our house even came complete with a porch and a white picket fence. Growing up, I had the biggest collection of Barbies out of all my friends. Dad wore a suit when he wasn't in uniform. I don't think I ever saw my mom without an apron. And our house always smelled like a bakery, just like today.

"I had to run errands earlier so I recorded *Days of Our Lives.*"

"I think my grandmother watches that," Sky chimed in. They'd finally succeeded in finding common ground with my mom, who was all too happy to talk about her favorite soap opera.

"That wouldn't surprise me. It's been on for over fifty years. My mother-in-law was the one who got me hooked on the show," Stella admitted.

"You know what the best part of a soap opera is?" I asked sarcastically. "You can watch a few episodes and then not see the show again for six months to a year, but the exact same plot will still not be wrapped up."

Stella looked absolutely offended. Before my mom could recover herself to ask questions about our night, I hurried to usher my friends outside. Xuan was probably waiting at the bonfire, so I led the way out the door. Roxy had driven Sky to my place in her old 1968 GMC pickup truck, but she didn't like taking it to the beach because of parking.

We piled into my black Jeep Wrangler Unlimited. The hardtop was stowed away in the garage, and the night wind brought a howl that was sharp and high-pitched, like a baby crying, only this sound wasn't from any human baby. I paused to listen as the nearby coyote continued to howl before I started the engine. Coyotes were often to be found in the hills and forests surrounding Santa Cruz.

"Cassie, c'mon," urged Roxy.

Moments later, our trio headed toward the glimmering lights of the Santa Cruz Boardwalk, a perfect escape—or so I thought.

Chapter Fourteen: The Boardwalk

Santa Cruz Beach Boardwalk, California
May 3, 2019

Ever since I was little, I'd spent many unforgettable summers at the Santa Cruz beach area. For a little money, I could sip a Cherry Pepsi and ride the rides all night. The best gyro I'd ever eaten was eaten there. And there was nothing like riding the Giant Dipper, the classic wood roller coaster built in 1924. This place held many happy memories for me of s'mores, bonfires, and sandcastles. My friends and I have played hundreds of games of beach volleyball here.

Finding parking on a Friday night was near impossible, so I let Roxy and Sky out at the entrance and went to find what I could. I finally located a spot where I could parallel park and then set off past the whirling neon lights of the Ferris wheel and toward the beach. I recognized old acquaintances from my high school graduating class hanging out on the beach, many celebrating the beginning of summer by eating cotton candy and pitching coins into fish bowls for prizes.

"Cassie, is that you?"

I turned to face a girl I hadn't seen since high school: Ashley Haws. Ashley stood at about five foot four and still weighed about a hundred pounds. She was blonde, the kind from a bottle, and had obviously undergone surgery for breast implants. In high school, she was known for two things: her pom-poms and her tendency to pretend and create false identities in order to engage in deceptive online romances with college boys. And when Roxy came out as bisexual, her locker got tagged in the girls' locker room. We all suspected it was Ashley or one of her friends, but there was no way to prove it. Needless to say, engaging in a conversation with someone like Ashley was not at the top of my agenda for the evening.

"It's nice to see you," I said and continued walking.

"Hey, wait up," she called.

I smiled my best fake smile, and ignored the uneasy feeling crawling up my spine as I turned back around.

"So are you still with that Asian guy?" asked Ashley. The smell of liquor and cigarettes lingered heavily on her breath.

I paused. "His name is Xuan, remember? You went to the same school as him."

Brett, another school acquaintance, came up behind Ashley and wrapped his arms around her from behind. He then took his hands and began to move them upward until he was touching his girlfriend's melon-sized boobs. Stella had always warned me about men who seemed to have eight arms like an octopus and were always trying to grope their girlfriends. Some men really were loquacious monsters with monosyllabic tentacles. The next thing he did was so unfathomable, with way too much PDA, that I felt ill at ease and turned to leave. I face-palmed internally.

"Don't walk away. I asked you a question," the girl pressed. "Well, are you?"

"Why do you want to know?" I asked.

"Just wondering. We were both surprised to hear the news about Italy."

"How did you find out?" I asked.

"People talk."

I kept my voice calm as I said, "If you heard about our trip and the news of our engagement, then you already know I'm still with Xuan."

"Chinese people are rude and sexist. Why would you want to be with a Chinaman when you could be with your own kind?" asked Brett. The ex-prom king looked like he'd gained some weight since his football days. Despite his years playing varsity and winning plenty of school trophies, he was the human equivalent of a participation award.

"My own kind?"

"American."

Ashley smirked at Brett's comment. I wished I had a witty comeback, but I was too mortified. "I never knew you were that big of an asshole to actually say something like that."

Ashley smiled drunkenly and snorted to Brett. "Cassie must be sick with yellow fever."

Holy Saints, are they really this ignorant? I knew the comment was about his skin color, since Asians were typically described as yellow. I clenched my fists, restraining myself.

Brett looked at his girlfriend. "Of course she does. Why else would she fall for some Chink?"

My blood boiled. I wanted to kick this guy in the nuts.

I took a deep breath. Then another. "You're both pathetic," I said, my voice filled with disappointment. I decided to take the high road. I turned to walk away.

"Isn't Xuan a foreign exchange student? Green-card marriage. Tell *Slant Eyes* to go back to China."

Although I had heard stories of Asian-Americans facing racial prejudice, I had never personally witnessed it outside of the context of my own family's drama. These types of insults came from their parents, peers, or resistance to accept anything different from the norm. The words were meant to get a rise out of me. Their tactic worked. Their remarks had tapped into a deep reservoir of emotions. *Walk away. Just walk away. Don't let them win.*

"We all just thought you could do better," Brett replied.

I exaggerated my laugh out loud so he would catch the mockery behind it. "What? Someone like *you*, Brett? You're right, I can absolutely do better than someone like you. And I did. I found Xuan." I had won the jackpot, but they would never understand that.

"You would be lucky to have someone like me," he countered.

"You? An out-of-shape college dropout still living with mommy?" I instantly regretted that I'd resorted to fighting back. "Apparently my standards are much higher than Ashley's."

"No one wanted Raylan's sloppy seconds, so you ended up with kung-fu boy? Is that it?"

I was speechless.

"You were always just a spoiled know-it-all," slurred Brett. And then his mouth began to spew a string of expletives directed toward me. "If you weren't such an uptight bitch back then, I might have given you a chance after Raylan left you—you know, out of pity."

"Wow, what a perceptive bigot," I replied. I was on a roll. "I was single back then, not desperate. You know, I used to envy the people who hadn't met you. I guess much hasn't changed, because I still do."

"Dating me would've been the highlight of your life."

I laughed out loud for dramatic effect. "If you were the highlight—that mythical light at the end of the tunnel—I would have gladly turned back around and sought refuge in a nunnery."

"Watch your mouth," warned Ashley.

I looked at the two former classmates standing before me. "You two deserve each other." *Make your departure. Now.*

"You think you're better than us?" asked Ashley.

"No. But Xuan is. Xuan is better than you *and* your man-child." *Good. I should walk on by, perfect time to just go.*

Ashley raised her hand as if to slap me. But then I heard a voice call out from a short distance. "Back off, Ashley. Don't touch her!"

Raylan came running up, shirtless and covered in sand, probably from a game of beach volleyball. *When did he get back to the states?* The last time I'd seen him he was dressed in the U.S. Army standardized military greens. Now he just looked so casual. He was tall and fit, likely from his time serving in the military. He had tattoos that sank into the side of his neck and down his back and arms. Raylan had a history of jumping into the middle of fights and breaking them up in school. Most people cowered like a beaten dog at the complete dominance in his gaze, but I'd never been one of them.

"What's going on?" he asked.

I tried not to laugh when he puffed out his chest like a giant peacock.

"Just talkin'," said Ashley, a little too innocently.

I shook my head and grinned. "Since we're *just talking*, don't insult Xuan again. Got it?"

Ashley looked as if she were a viper, coiling up and ready to strike. Raylan seemed to be able to sense the change in tension. He stepped in front of me, blocking me from danger. I tried to ignore Raylan's presence as he stood there.

Truthfully I was a little annoyed he'd come to the rescue. I was not a damsel in distress, and I did *not* want to be rescued—not that night, and certainly not by him. I was honestly just relieved Xuan hadn't been there to hear any of the insults targeting his race. But I was surprised he hadn't come to find me when Roxy and Sky arrived. *Strange. Maybe he hasn't arrived yet.*

"Whatever you're thinking of doing—don't do it," said Raylan. "You'll have to get through me to touch her. My advice is that you both turn and walk away. Go enjoy the night before this gets ugly."

Brett lost his balance and stumbled a few steps forward. Unable to keep his mouth shut, he moved his lips to make another comment. "What was it even like being with one of them? I can't imagine you were satisfied. After all, Asians are so small." He put up his thumb and finger to indicate an inch.

Something strange, like adrenaline, pumped through my veins like a welcome drug. I halted and turned to face Brett, my braid swaying. As I stared at him, I fantasized about spontaneous human combustion, or using my scientific knowledge to burn this guy to a crisp. *Oh, if looks could kill.*

Raylan's voice was weary. "Dude, that's not cool. You shouldn't say crap like that."

Brett waved off Raylan's warning and continued on like a broken record. "Plus how can they even see through their small eyes? You think your kids will have slanted eyes?"

Lunging forward, I pulled up my fist in the last moment before he could realize I was going to hit him and aimed. Bone crunched as I connected with his face just above his cheek. Thick blood trickled from one of his nostrils.

Brett swore and staggered back. His eyes looked stunned as he yelled another cuss word. Swaying, he moved to attack and raised his hand to deal a backhanded blow to my face.

Raylan moved to block him, but he wasn't fast enough. I struck again before Brett could land a punch. This time, I hit him in the throat and then pulled a *Miss Congeniality* and elbowed him in the solar plexus, all while repeating in my mind, *solar plexus, instep, nose, and groin.* The combination was a little excessive and it knocked him out cold.

"Crap, Cassie!" Raylan exclaimed.

"He'll live, unfortunately," I said. I had never been in a fight, but my father had insisted I take karate lessons to be self-reliant and safer. So from the time I was seven, I'd taken martial arts.

Ashley screamed and sobbed in drunken hysterics. "Why is he bleeding? What have you done you crazy b—"

"He's bleeding because he's an idiot and he deserved it," I replied.

Raylan looked at me. "People don't just start bleeding because of idiocy. I think you broke his nose." To his credit, if he was smirking, he was doing it on the inside.

Good. "He's lucky it was just his nose." I should have ignored him, but I wouldn't allow anyone to threaten or insult my family and that included Xuan. I was ferociously protective of him.

"Cass, he was drunk."

"Holy Saints, Raylan. I'm not going to apologize. He got what he deserved." Violence is rarely the right answer, but I couldn't just let it go.

Raylan reset Brett's nose and made sure he regained consciousness before he ran to catch up with me. Several onlookers waved to me from the beach, but I wasn't in the mood for exchanging words with anyone else.

Music from the Beach Boys blasted from crackling speakers.

The smell of typical boardwalk greasy foods and cinnamon twists rose steadily in the night air.

"Hey, hold up for a minute," said Raylan.

"What?" I continued walking.

"Cassie, stop!"

I turned to face Raylan. Ever since he joined the military, his normal light-brown, shaggy hair had been traded in for a clean new buzz cut.

His expression was neutral when he asked, "You okay?" Raylan went to put his hand on my shoulder. For a moment, I looked up into his blue eyes, a place where I'd once felt safe. I was reminded of bluish steel and a midwinter sky.

That was too friendly a gesture in an unkind history. I flinched away, not wanting to be touched by him. "I can take care of myself, Private Thompson." And that was that.

Raylan dropped his hand in response. "It's actually Corporal Thompson now. It may even be Sergeant soon, based on my commander's recommendation."

"Great. Well, you can drop the white-knight complex, Corporal."

"Why'd you let them get to you? You've never cared what people say or think."

"I don't care what people say about me, but I couldn't let them say those things about Xuan," I said defensively.

"Cassie, you could have gotten hurt."

"So? Why do you care?"

"They were drunk and looking for a fight." Raylan's face was grave, disapproving. "You kicked a man already down. Brett's probably going to feel like less of a man after he wakes up and realizes he got knocked out by a girl."

"It's not my job to make him feel like a man," I pointed out. "Besides, no one can make Brett something he's not."

"Why are you acting stupid? You're better than that."

"You have no right to lecture me on ethics, Raylan. I didn't ask for your help, nor did I need it."

"That's not what I meant, Cassie."

What could I say? That night I didn't want to be the bigger person. "Look, I've just been so worried about things lately. I lost my head." That was the truth. "I know I should have walked away, but I couldn't." *And a part of me didn't want to.*

"What have you been worried about? The moon and the planets?"

He always used to say my head was stuck in the clouds, or some dusty old book. I knew he was being sarcastic. But it was bad timing to make a joke.

"No, about doctors and . . ." I paused. "Never mind. I don't owe you an explanation." I didn't want to talk to Raylan about Xuan or what was going on. "Why are you here?"

"I came home. For you."

Right on cue, a female came up and wrapped her slender, tanned arm around Raylan. The first thing I noticed was the girl's watercolor sleeve tattoo, which was pretty damn cool. Her mermaid-colored hair fell below her neckline, a pastel periwinkle tint of blues and purples mixed in with her platinum locks. She was absolutely gorgeous and so different from me with my typical surfer-girl look.

"Emma, can you give us a second?" Raylan asked.

The girl slid her hands down across his torso and then reached around to make Raylan look at her. She grabbed his face and drew it closer to her own before kissing him. She ran her pierced tongue over his lips and then winked at him with a seductive smile before leaving.

"Yeah, it totally looks like you came back for me."

Raylan waited for Emma to leave before saying anything. "She isn't really my type. We're just having fun."

"Does she know that?"

"If you had met my mother, you would understand why."

"Holy Saints, Raylan. No, I wouldn't. You're using your drug-addict mother who abandoned you as an excuse for how you think of and treat women. Someday you need to make the choice to be a better man than your father and stop demeaning women because of your mother. Your brother has moved on with his life and so should you." *TMI. Misplaced anger. I regret saying such mean stuff to him. It isn't fair, and it's a low blow. I want to apologize, but I can't. I won't.*

Roxy came running toward Raylan and me before he could respond. "There you are!" She sounded surprised. "I've been looking everywhere for you. Why haven't you joined us?"

"Sorry, I just got caught up."

Roxy eyed Raylan suspiciously before asking, "Is everything okay?"

"Yeah. I'll be there in a minute. I just need to finish this . . . this conversation."

Roxy looked uncertain. "Are you sure? Do you want me to stay with you?"

"No, it's okay," I assured her. "I'll be there in a few."

I waited for Roxy to be out of earshot before I said anything. "Raylan, thank you for trying to help tonight. I wish you the best in life, but I don't want to see you or talk to you tonight or ever again. I'm sorry. I've moved on. I'm engaged to a wonderful guy and I'm happy. I hope one day you can be as well."

"You don't think we can be friends?"

"I'm sure we could be but I truly don't want to be. I know I'll see you around since we still hang around a lot of the same people, but I think it would be best for everyone if we just ignored each other during those little group get-togethers and tried to forget."

"Cassie, I—"

"Sorry, Raylan." I cut him off. "My fiancé is probably wondering what happened to me. Goodbye. Take care."

I didn't look behind me to see if Raylan was following me as I headed toward the water where a respectable bonfire raged. A lot of random fires and groups sprawled out across the beach.

"Isn't this fun?" Amanda asked with a large grin, obviously unaware of what had happened.

I looked around. The night was still young. "Lots of fun," I absent-mindedly agreed. "Where's Xuan?"

"He isn't here."

"Xuan's late?" I asked. "He's never late."

"No, he isn't coming. Nick and Beom went to pick him up but he said he's ill."

I reached into my pocket and dialed Xuan. No answer.

Roxy came up next to Amanda. "You guys meet Raylan's new girl?"

"She isn't his girlfriend. He changes girls every week," said Amanda.

That didn't surprise me. He was broken, lost.

"Emma isn't dating him?" Roxy asked. "Sure looked like it."

"No way. Raylan doesn't date. He just messes around."

The fact Amanda knew all this was a revelation. *Does she like him?*

Nick walked toward us with a blonde-headed, clingy Sky hanging on to his waist. "Hey, Cassie!" *I like him. It's not his fault Raylan was unfaithful and betrayed me.*

"Officer Thompson! Happy Birthday." I hugged him and gave the dedicated local policeman a friendly kiss on the cheek.

Beer in hand, Raylan went to stand next his brother. Emma was nowhere in sight.

"Beom and I stopped at Xuan's house when I got off work but he couldn't make it," Nick said. "He wanted me to assure you that he's fine and that you should stay here and have fun at the bonfire."

If Xuan was fine, he would be here. I knew where my heart wanted to be, so I told Nick Happy Birthday, promised him a belated gift, and found rides for Sky and Roxy. I knew they would want to stay until the crowds at the boardwalk were thin, everything closed up for the night, the pile of bonfire wood diminished and the fiery mass was no more.

"Let me walk you back to your vehicle," offered Raylan.

"Nah, I'll pass." He seemed to be on a mission to reconcile with me.

"Cassie, it's not safe. Brett may see you."

"No, thanks. I can take care of myself." I began hiking back toward my jeep alone.

I didn't turn around to see the dutiful outline that stayed far enough back that he could blend in with shadows and other groups, didn't see the shadowy figure standing and watching until I safely got into my jeep and pulled away, tugging his broken heart along the way.

I wasn't looking.

Chapter Fifteen: Coughing Colors

Seabright, Santa Cruz, California
May 3, 2019

The wind chimes danced lazily through the spring winds at Xuan's house, the sound of the ringing chimes more pleasing than any nightingale's chant. Everywhere throughout the yard flowers were in bloom. Like many people in the area, Xuan tried to grow his own fruits and vegetables in the backyard. But he said the climate was different from China, so many of his favorite vegetables wouldn't grow here. When his mother came to America, she bought the small, pale-yellow house Xuan's host family had lived in during his high school years. I liked the location on the hills of the Santa Cruz Valley. Once married, the plan was for her to go back to China and leave the house to us, a wedding present surrounded by Mother Nature.

Mei's red MINI Cooper wasn't in the driveway, which meant Xuan was home alone. I knocked on the front door, covered in the shadows of tall redwood trees.

"Xuan?" I said, trying to announce my presence.

No answer. Odd vibe. I turned the handle of the door. It opened. Mei's fluffy Persian cat, Chairman Meow—named in honor of the Chinese leader, Chairman Mao—lay stretched out on his back near the cool stone in front of the fireplace, likely waiting for belly rubs. The Chairman's tail was fluffier than a raccoon's and the size of at least three or four normal tails put together. The tail had an odd black stripe running up the middle. The bottom of his feet were partly black, making him look as though he'd just stepped into an inkpot. The tricolored cat did not have the typical smooshy face of a Persian. He gave a little owl-like hoot, demanding my attention as I entered.

The lights in the living room were off so I removed my shoes and put house slippers on before heading upstairs. I found Xuan sitting at his desk, scribbling something down on paper, his back to the bedroom door. His room was magical, like something out of a Pottery Barn catalog.

I leaned up against the doorjamb. "Hey, handsome, want some company?"

Xuan turned his dark eyes toward me, and I was greeted by his smile, which seemed more like bravado than happiness. A square face, dark eyebrows, and high, angular cheekbones stared back at me. He was clad in faded jeans and a long-sleeved blue Santa Cruz shirt, probably to keep the chilling wind at bay.

"Hey, love."

"How are you feeling?" I asked.

Xuan looked distracted. "My whole body feels like a truck hit me. Twice."

"Anything I can get for you?"

"Just you being here makes me feel better, *qīn'ài de*."

I loved it when he called me sweetheart in Chinese. "I didn't mean to just barge in, but the door was unlocked and—"

He interrupted. "This is your home too. You don't have to apologize for coming to see me. We're going to be married soon."

I felt comforted by his words. *Home.*

"Tea?" I asked.

Standing from his desk chair, he said, "That would be great. My aunt just sent us a few new boxes of tea leaves from Beijing."

I gave a slight smile. His mom hated the American and English version of tea bags. Set on making tea, I gave Xuan my arm and slowly helped him downstairs to the living room couch. I made my way toward the kitchen to brew a pot of hot water.

In the kitchen, a pan of a thick "Mei's home cure" greeted me, a mixture of anise seed, licorice root, and wild black-cherry bark in a covered pot of water. I'd watched her make this recipe before and I knew Mei would later add fresh thyme and raw honey. This remedy was an herbal cough syrup, probably meant to soothe

Xuan's throat and help prevent him from coughing.

Emerging from the kitchen, I brought him the hot cup. He stood to receive it and almost fell over.

"Whoa, are you okay?"

"I'm fine, just a bit light-headed."

I watched him as he sat on the very edge of the couch and took the cup from my hands. He seemed to be grasping it for warmth before finally, shakily, raising it to his lips.

"Cassie," he said, and for one of the first times in three years I couldn't read his voice. It was low, rough. "I don't like you seeing me sick. Maybe it'd be better if you went home."

"Let me take care of you. In sickness and in health, remember?" I said in protest.

"We haven't exchanged those vows yet." Xuan raised his free hand and placed it gently on the side of my cheek. "You're off the hook."

But I had no intention of leaving. Real love wasn't just a euphoric feeling. It was a deliberate choice, every day, to love the person I was with—for better or worse, in sickness and in health, for richer and poorer, until the end of time. "Think of it as practice."

I saw the open doubt on Xuan's face. "You don't have to—"

"I *want* to take care of you, the same way you always care for me." It was as simple as that. Moving closer to him, I couldn't stop myself from reaching for him. "What can I do?"

"*Qīn'ài de,* I think I need to sleep. But you're welcome to stay with me if you want."

Back in the bedroom, he fumbled through his dresser drawers. "Here, take this," Xuan threw me one of his long, white shirts to wear.

"Turn around," I said with a bashful smile.

Ever the gentleman, he closed his eyes and turned completely around as if to make a point that he wouldn't peek. I loved wearing his clothes. His fragrance in my breath and all over me made me comfortable.

After I was finished, he changed out of his jeans and into long blue-and-white pajama bottoms. Once he was decent, he joined me under the covers, lying beside me.

"You're always so beautiful," Xuan said, looking into my eyes.

I felt my face warm.

"You're blushing."

I had no doubt my cheeks had turned the color of blood-red anemones. I watched his body as he moved to get snug and felt heat in my neck and breasts. He gently put his arm around my shoulder and tucked my body toward him. I could hear his breathing quicken, followed by the sound of coughing.

Xuan's teeth chattered uncontrollably. I reached for the end of the bed to grab another handmade quilt from his grandmother. Despite the May warmth, we had two thick blankets on top of us in order to keep his body warm. After a while, Xuan stopped shaking. Cradled in my fiancé's arms, I felt my eyelids grow heavier. Trying to keep my eyes open proved to be a losing battle with each minute that passed. Giving one last look at Xuan, I finally allowed my eyes to close. "Goodnight, babe. I love you."

"I love you too, *qīn'ài de*," Xuan muttered.

Chapter Sixteen: The Legend of the CowherdAnd Weaver Fairy

Seabright, Santa Cruz, California
3:00 a.m. on May 4, 2019

Night swept across the sky like a soft blanket. Several bright lights blinked like bright white stars across the city. I was standing on top of the college astronomy tower, looking out at the dazzling city sights in the background and observing the sky. Xuan stood beside his telescope, identifying some new constellations. He was looking north, in the direction of Polaris, trying to identify Draco. He'd picked me up from my house, flowers in hand, along with a picnic basket, blanket, telescope, and bottle of white wine packed in the back seat of his car.

He was charming, and I was irrevocably in love with the out-of-the-ordinary man before me . . . the man who had dared to show me the stars. We were polar opposites but I could feel my heart being tugged into Xuan's gravitational pull. I understood then that something was stirring within me, had been since the night on the roof in Colombia. What I was feeling wasn't just brain chemistry and the release of oxytocin – it was something more. And to deny that was like denying a portion of my soul. Love was like a metaphor or the expression of an artist, and I was being carried by love like a strong wind. I already loved him more than there were stars in the universe, and that thought absolutely terrified me.

As my eyes fluttered open, a faint glow from the moon filtered through the curtains, casting deep shadows across the walls and floor, creating an ethereal atmosphere. I reached out for Xuan, hoping to feel his warmth, but he was MIA, and the sheets had already grown cold. The memory of our first date replayed in my mind, a dream that felt like reality. Love was never part of my plan, but once I was with Xuan, I was powerless to resist. My emotions for him were indescribable, like the verses of a romantic poem. We were as different as day and night, in body and culture, yet we were drawn to each other like apple pie and vanilla ice cream, or peanut butter and jam. Like puzzle pieces, we fit together with some places smooth and others rough, jagged, creating a masterpiece of colors blending together imperfectly but perfectly.

As I got up to find Xuan, the old floorboards creaked beneath my feet, amplifying the eeriness of the early morning hour. A cool breeze wafted in from the slightly open window, carrying the fragrance of blooming flowers and fresh dew, a sign that May had arrived. The world seemed still, with only the hoot of an owl and the occasional car passing by as reminders of its motion.

"Xuan?" I called out, my voice barely above a whisper.

"In here," he replied from behind the closed bathroom door.

"Can I come in?"

"Sure."

Xuan was hovering over the toilet in his bathroom. Without saying anything, I sat behind him and slowly ran my hand over his back, hoping to comfort him.

Xuan continued to cough and vomit, more than once. As I stood there, my hand poised to flush the toilet, something caught my eye—a vivid red color swirling amidst the watery mess. Pools of blood mingled with the vomit, creating a haunting image that sent chills down my spine.

"Xuan," I whispered, my voice barely audible, yet laced with deep concern and fear. The sound of my plea hung in the air, carrying the weight of worry and uncertainty. But before he could respond, a wave of dry heaves seized him. The violent spasms wracked his body as he coughed desperately, each cough punctuated by crimson splatters that painted the pristine white of the porcelain. He was coughing up blood.

My mind raced with fear, like a startled deer caught in the blinding headlights of a speeding car, as I contemplated the possibility of a serious disease, *not* a virus. "How long's this been going on?"

"A week."

There was no more denying it—reality. Xuan had cancer. I swallowed hard as the moment dragged on in silence. Sweet Mother of mercy, the way he looked broke my heart.

"Talk to me," he whispered. "Distract me."

I racked my brain for something to say, anything that would bring a smile to his face. And then it came to me, "I was dreaming," I said. "Of our first official date."

"I remember. You wore a light-pink shirt and white shorts. Even your toenails were a light shade of peachy pink."

His reminiscence caught me off guard. I didn't even remember what I had worn that night. But Xuan's attention to detail made my heart flutter.

Xuan continued. "I didn't think you noticed me," he said.

"You mean the night of the comet?"

"No, in high school. After we graduated, I thought I missed my chance. Then I remember seeing you on the plane with me, headed to Colombia, and I recall thinking, *now's the time to tell her how you feel. Don't be an idiot or it'll be too late."*

"Raylan and I weren't technically together on that trip," I said.

"I know. And every day we were in Colombia, I wished I could muster the courage to go talk to you. Or that you would notice me and start a conversation with me."

"So why didn't you?" I asked.

"You know how some people feel about Asians. We would've been more popular if we'd been an alien species. Most of our class treated my friends and me like the plague. Or they ignored us unless they needed homework help. At least that's the way it was in high school. I just figured college would be more of the same."

"I'm sorry people can be so cruel. It shouldn't be that way."

In a society that can sometimes be as putrid and decayed as the gills of a weathered old mushroom, the acceptance of interracial relationships is often met with resistance by individuals like my father, Ashley, and Brett. It's an unfortunate truth that many people are quick to judge and slow to understand, clinging to narrow-minded views and unwarranted prejudices. Despite the events that unfolded at the Boardwalk earlier, I made a deliberate decision to withhold the details of my encounter with Brett and Ashley from Xuan. I knew that sharing that information would only cause him pain.

Our relationship was already considered unconventional, and I didn't want to add any more fuel to the fire. To me, the color of a person's skin held no weight in my heart; I was colorblind and loved Xuan for who he was.

"No matter, because my wish came true when you signed up for the study-abroad trip to Colombia."

"I guess fate really does have a way of working its magic."

"Fate was kind back then."

"Hopefully it will be again."

"I knew it was only a matter of time before our paths crossed after high school. I finally got my chance when Amanda put us together at the dance club. I knew it then."

"Knew what?" I asked.

"That our lives were never meant to just be passing ships in the sea of night. We are soul mates, a powerful connection."

I had known on top of the astronomy tower that what I had felt for Raylan wasn't love. I had cared about him greatly. But what I felt about Xuan only happened once in a lifetime on a molecular level. Some might call it true love. But it wasn't just that. It was something more, like somewhere across the icy, ancient sky our names had been written, fused together like hydrogen and fuel or helium and carbon.

"Think you can make it back to the bed?" I asked.

"I need to shower first and brush my teeth."

"Here, let me help you." His eyes widened, but he made no move to stop me as I reached up and gripped the front of his shirt. He obliged by raising his arms. Touching his chest, I felt him draw in a breath.

I turned on the water so it could start to get warm and handed him his toothbrush. Lovingly, he gazed up at me. His need for me was reflected in my own need for him. Allowing me to care for him made me feel strong, desired, and loved—loved by this captivating man who wanted nothing more than to lay the world at my feet. When the shower was ready, I held out my hand to him. "Come."

He yanked the rest of his clothes off and left them in a pile on the floor.

Thankfully, Xuan could not hear my thundering heart over the steady stream of water as it flowed from cold to lukewarm. "I'll wait for you."

He stood in the cascade, letting it run down over his face. The hot water filled the small space with steam and hints of sandalwood and lemon soap. Mechanically, I picked up his clothes and began to fold them, before going to get a fresh pair from his dresser.

After a few minutes, the shower stopped running. I froze. He wrapped a towel around his waist before stepping out from the curtain. His hair was soaked, and the damp towel stuck to him.

Xuan leaned against the wall for support as he brushed his teeth, but this seemed to drain a lot of energy from him. His chest was rising and falling rapidly, as if he was on the verge of collapsing.

"Think you can make it to the bed?"

"I'll manage."

We made our way to the mattress where I softly patted his hair dry with a second towel.

Wordless, Xuan entwined his hands into my hair and began to undo the braid. Handfuls of strands cupped my face as he gently grabbed for me. The genteelness was gone, replaced by a fierce need. Sitting close together, I could feel the solidity and warmth of him. I ached to touch the arch of his back, his torso. But he felt hot, too hot.

"All I can think about is kissing you," he whispered.

"I could kiss you all night. But if we started, I wouldn't be able to stop," I whispered. I gently ran my palm down his bare chest, his stomach, to the top of the towel. He reached for me and held me against his body, his heart. His hand slid up the back of my shirt. Shaking fingers danced across my skin.

"Fine by me." Xuan leaned in, but then he began to cough again.

"It's okay." I kissed him gently in the groove of his collarbone. Then I put my hands on Xuan's shoulders and I stood up. "You need to rest. Put these on." I handed him a new pajama set and socks to keep his feet warm.

I shut my eyes and waited as he took the stack from me and finished dressing. There were frantic gestures to dry himself. When he was finished, he reached up and grabbed my wrist. I clutched at him, desperately wanting to touch him, to tumble over that edge like it was some great cliff.

"Now, lie down." Our roles shifted. I was in alpha mode, the way he typically was with me—like in Colombia, during and after the mudslide.

Xuan obeyed. Beside me, I could feel the muscles in his body tighten. He was feverish and I was feverishly longing—needing him like I needed oxygen to breathe. But this wasn't the moment to give in to desire. There would be more time. There had to be.

I wanted to get his mind off being sick, and I needed to get my mind off the warmth that was turning into fire across my skin—desire. So I asked him to tell me one of his stories, or a tale he grew up hearing.

"What do you want to hear?" he asked.

"Anything."

"What about a story from China? I heard this one when I was a child. It was called the *Legend of the Cowherd and Weaver Fairy*."

"Sure," I said.

He smiled as he sank backward into the pillows. Chairman Meow came into the room, purring as he jumped onto the bed and curled up between us for story time. The cat had the personality of a king, demanding attention as he saw fit.

There once was a young and poor but kind-hearted cowherd called Niulang who had an old ox. The ox was actually once the god of cattle but had been downgraded, as he had violated the law of heaven. Niulang once saved the ox when it was sick. In order to show its gratitude, the old ox helped Niulang get acquainted with Zhinü, who was a fairy and the seventh daughter of a goddess and the Jade Emperor. When Zhinü escaped from her boring life in heaven to look for fun on earth, she met Niulang and soon fell in love with him. The two got married without the knowledge of the goddess. Niulang and Zhinü lived a happy life together. Niulang worked in the field while Zhinü did weaving at home. After a few years passed, they had two children, one boy and one girl. However the Goddess of Heaven, Zhinü's mother, found out that Zhinü, a fairy girl, had married a mere mortal. The goddess was furious and sent celestial soldiers to bring Zhinü back. Niulang was very upset when he found his wife had been taken back to heaven.

Then his ox asked Niulang to kill it and put on its hide so he would be able to go up to heaven to find his wife. Crying bitterly, he killed the ox, put on the skin, and carried his two beloved children off to heaven to find Zhinü.

Just before he caught up with Zhinü, the Goddess of Heaven took out her hairpin and created a huge river between them, and they were separated forever by the river that later became known as the Milky Way. Heartbroken, he and his children could only weep bitterly. However their love moved all the magpies to take pity on them, and they flew up into heaven to form a bridge over the river so Niulang and Zhinü could meet on the magpie bridge. The goddess was also moved by their love, so she allowed them a meeting on the magpie bridge on that day every year, which is the seventh day of the seventh lunar month.

In my heart I wept for the ox that sacrificed his own life for love and for the star-crossed lovers who painted the night sky.

"You know how I feel about you, don't you?" Xuan asked quietly.

I met his stare. "You love me," I whispered.

"More than anything."

Heart thundering, I lifted myself onto my elbows. "I feel the same. You mean *everything* to me." I breathed and he exhaled deeply.

"I know."

"I have never said those words to anyone before you. I mean, like, romantically."

"Really?" he asked.

"Why the surprise?"

"I thought you and Raylan . . ."

"No. I might have one day after he returned, but back then I was still too young, and I needed more time, for a lot of things. I might have thought I loved him, but I never told him."

"Did he love you?"

"I think he did, in his own way. But he never told me when we were together, not until we'd broken up and I was in Colombia. I think he finally said it in desperation."

"He called you in Colombia?"

"It was through an email."

"You guys were together for a long time." Xuan grabbed my hand, pressed a kiss against my skin. "Why do you think you put it off?"

"Who knows? Maybe I was just waiting for you."

There was a flicker of joy in the dark. For that moment we let ourselves forget the past days. Peaceful silence descended as Xuan relaxed into my arms and eventually fell asleep from exhaustion.

In the hours that followed, I stayed awake, my eyes fixed upon him. I was prepared to ward off any lurking monsters and keep them at bay while he peacefully slept.

My mind drifted as he lay there, and I couldn't help but wonder not if, but when, death would separate me from Xuan. Even if it was sixty years from now, at a ripe old age, someday we would both die. Death was inevitable. *Will death be cruel like the goddess from the story, creating a huge gulf between our souls?* Would we be separated forever by the river of time, or heaven, or would we one day be able to find our way back to each other in some other life?

I stared into the dark night and prayed for a fairy-tale ending. I whispered to myself, "Xuan and Cassie lived happily ever after."

Chapter Seventeen: The Ticking Clock

West Cliff, Santa Cruz, California
May 17, 2019

Despite the captivating sight of Carpobrotus edulis and California poppies blanketing the hillside, I found myself too distracted to fully appreciate the vibrant foliage or watch my steps. Inadvertently, I stepped on a blooming ice plant, my mind consumed by thoughts of Xuan and his upcoming test results. *I hate waiting. The complete opposite of temperance.* The dampness from the morning ocean fog seeped through my blue jeans and oversized hooded white lamb cardigan. My attire wasn't warm. A shiver spread into my bones as I looked out over the ocean at West Cliff and the rising sun. I had always loved the ocean—all of it. The water, the waves, the marine life, the warm sand. The constant ebb and flow of life. I loved surfing and the hot summer days spent on the beach with my friends and Xuan. I loved the sunsets where you could see pods of dolphins jumping freely in the waves and nights when the water looked like a giant mirror reflecting the stars.

Easy, graceful steps sounded in the dirt as several twigs snapped. I'd developed a keen awareness of Xuan's presence, like the ability to sense rain before a downpour. He stood inches away, close enough that his warm breath made the small hairs stand on the back of my neck.

For a moment we both stayed still, watching, pretending the world was still full of possibilities. The beach was bathed in the first light of a sailor's dawn, and the foamy crests of waves crashed against the rocks and sand. The area was serene in the morning. The only sound I could hear, besides Xuan's breath, was the cry of hungry gulls. In a few hours, the entire coast would be bathed in the sounds of surfers, children playing and laughing as they jumped over waves, and the melody of ice cream vans as they attracted sunburned patrons the color of fresh cooked lobster.

Xuan let out a deep sigh as he stood with his white Adidas shoes crossed in front of him. He was wearing jeans and a light-blue shirt that looked flawless with his wet black hair and skin tone. He could have easily passed for a male model.

"Tell me," I finally said.

"The doctor we saw in San Francisco called me late last night. That's why I asked you to meet me first thing. I didn't want to tell you over the phone."

"What's the verdict? The results? Is it—"

"Not great."

A long two weeks had passed while we anxiously waited to hear the results. We didn't have much to say as we waited, so we went about our normal days and lives . . . waiting, pretending, hoping.

"And?"

"Confirmed. Cancerous cells. The tests validated the doctor's suspicion."

The moment I saw the blood, I'd sensed the prognosis would be grim. Still, hearing this was difficult. For just a few weeks, I had believed there was still hope.

I didn't know anything about lung cancer. "I just don't understand. You're so young. And you don't even smoke." I tried to mentally rationalize his diagnosis. But there was no such thing as reasoning with cancer.

"When I was young, I lived in close proximity to the factories where the air in China was heavily polluted. In addition to that, I spent several years in computer bars where smoking was permitted, and my grandfather happened to be a smoker. I've been around it, but I've never smoked myself due to personal preference, and I've always strived to maintain a healthy lifestyle. The fact is you don't have to smoke to get lung cancer. Even individuals who lead a health-conscious life can become sick. But I don't think my cancer was caused by smoking."

"What do you mean?"

"I guess I have some kind of mutation, like a Ninja Turtle. I'm not really sure if that means it was always inside me or if it was changed by some environmental factor. That's a moot point."

I shut my eyes. I could picture Xuan sitting in a dimly lit computer bar, engrossed in a game of League of Legends. The sound of clicking keyboards and animated chatter filled the air, mingling with the glow of computer screens illuminating his focused face.

"The doctor said there were signs. I just didn't know what my body was telling me. I was stupid. I had all the warning signs of cancer. I just never really registered it. I ignored all the symptoms. In truth, I'm so young that I didn't know I was supposed to even be looking."

"Tell me, how bad is it?"

"The prognosis doesn't seem good, Cassie."

I could feel a lump forming in the back of my throat. "Has it spread?"

"I don't know. I have to go in for biomarker testing. I felt like I was listening to the diagnosis from a third person POV, not comprehending details. After I heard that I had cancer, everything just sounded distant, like blah, blah, blah. I wasn't able to register anything else. I just couldn't—can't believe it. He wants to start treatment right away."

How is this possible? I had seen signs. Spreading purple-and-yellow blotches had been scattered on the surface of his skin like a disease. I should have begged Xuan to go to the doctor sooner.

I had noticed the bruises months before we left for Italy. But Xuan had always been athletic. And he played basketball with his Chinese and Korean friends at least once a week at the college gym, where he could have gotten hit. So I'd shrugged off seeing strange skin changes and tiredness and chalked it up to jet lag. He'd been extremely tired after returning from Italy, but that was common with changing time zones and messing up one's internal clock. Still, his fatigue lingered, even after he rested. I'd finally convinced Xuan to go to urgent care. There were probably other signs I missed. *I should have paid more attention. What do I know? I'm not a cancer doctor. All of this is surreal, like in the films. Worse, we're the main characters.*

"This is my fault. I should have—"

"No, I'm not going to let you blame yourself for this. It's not your fault, Cass." His voice was soft but implacable.

"We have to fight this," I whispered. Time was important. "So how soon can you start treatment? People beat cancer. It's the twenty-first century. One neighbor lady in her forties had breast cancer. After radiation and no chemo, she survived. During radiation, she worked, jogged, and lived her life. She's alive and well as I speak."

"Yes, but lung cancer and breast cancer are different. There are treatment options once all the biomarker testing comes back, and the results of a few more tests. But the doctor has to schedule treatment right away. He said we would meet again in the next two or three weeks."

"Weeks?" Xuan and I had a very different definition of what right away meant.

"Weeks," he confirmed. "There's still a lot to discuss before I agree to anything."

"I can cancel my classes for summer. They're just starting."

"I don't want you to. I know that might sound harsh, but your studies are important. And I don't want to think about what you might be giving up or postponing your future career because of this. Can you understand that?"

I groped for the right words. "If it's what you want."

Xuan slipped an arm around my shoulder and pulled me toward him. That was the only time I'd ever heard him cry about his initial diagnosis. I didn't know what I could say. We held each other wordlessly, both of us trying to convince each other that everything was going to be okay until our sobs began to subside.

The sound of crashing waves had always been soothing, like an orchestrated symphony, but not today. I stood despairingly in the California sunshine, wanting to feel warmth permeate my being. But there was only the coldness of the coastal bay seeping deep into my bones. The ocean, adorned with opals, aquamarines, and cerulean hues, presented a breathtaking sight. Yet, in that moment, I found myself momentarily detached from its beauty, lost in a state of emptiness as I stared, desperately trying to absorb something that evoked no feeling within me

I couldn't help but wonder . . . why him? The entire situation felt surreal, as though we had suddenly been cast as romantic leads trapped in a nightmarish horror film, navigating an unforeseen and treacherous plot. And to make matters worse, we were the protagonists, navigating a story we never anticipated.

There was no way of knowing what was written in the stars. I couldn't help but wonder how our story would end.

There was no way of knowing what was written in the stars. I couldn't help but wonder how our story would end.

Chapter Eighteen: The Turning Page

West Cliff Drive, Santa Cruz, California
May 25, 2019

It was a cold coastal morning, despite the fact it was the end of May. The wind's whip and snap of the long white curtains drew my attention as I sat facing my mother in a single oversized lounge chair.

"Mei called me," Stella announced. "The results from Xuan's lung biopsy came back."

Why had Mei called my mom? They weren't close. And why was my mother now telling me the news about his test and not Xuan? I rubbed my eyes and felt as though sandpaper had been scraped over my eyelids from all the crying I'd done over the past few days. "And?"

"Mei was crying on the phone, so I didn't understand everything she was saying, but the results aren't good. He's at a Stage III. The doctor they met with said Xuan's probably had cancer for a long time now. It's just gone undetected. His family in China pooled together money for the treatment, but Mei said he refused."

The word *refused* was like a sharp, pointed dagger stabbing me in the heart. *He isn't going to do chemo or radiation?* I didn't know. That didn't make sense. His parents had the means. "How can money be a factor when we're talking about his life?"

"You may not want to hear this, Cassandra, but treating cancer is expensive. A lot of patients choose not to undergo treatment or fill prescriptions because of the cost. He doesn't want to be a financial burden on his family."

How can he be so altruistic? How could he make this decision alone? And worse, what if he doesn't change his mind? I just couldn't understand. This was not the time to be selfless.

"Xuan hasn't told me anything about this," I mumbled. I hadn't seen him for almost a week. Even though we loved each other, we both needed time to process everything.

Stella took my hand and swiped her short hair behind her ear, revealing an ever-present pearl earring. *She swerves into stoic mode, void of drama, probably learned from my father.* "The prognosis of lung cancer in later stages isn't good. The numbers show the odds of survival are not good." There was a lack of emotion. *Maybe she is concealing her emotions for my benefit.* I sensed she'd done some research on cancer, as I had by now. "Stage III lung cancer patients have a poor survival rate. Lung cancer kills nearly sixty percent of those diagnosed within a year. It sounds like he's made up his mind—"

"Great." I cut her off. "Thanks for reducing the love of my life to a statistic," I snapped. *Did she really have to use the word poor when talking about Xuan's chance of survival?* "Looks like you've done your homework, huh?" *Why do I lash out at my mom? Maybe I strike like a poisonous snake because my anger is all over the map. She is here, an easy target. But that's not an excuse.*

"I'm sorry, Cassie. That wasn't my intention." Her voice sounded hurt. "Mei said the doctors believe Xuan has only a few years left, even with treatment. It will just depend on how fast the cancer spreads."

The time stamp was also news. "You're saying he could live three years, maybe even more, and he's settling for less?" Stella couldn't possibly understand the river of misery now coursing through me. "Why would he do that, give up time?"

Stella looked at me empathetically, and I saw the certainty in her eyes as she said, "Because in the end, he will still die, and he's decided to accept that. Not everyone who has cancer chooses to have treatment. It's not about the months and years, Cassie. It's about his expected quality of life during that time."

"We can still have years together . . . . get married . . . ."

"No, sweetie, there isn't going to be a wedding," she said. "I'm really sorry, hun."

My parents had never wanted me to marry Xuan. They had both made that clear after we got back from Italy.

"I know you don't want to hear this, Cassandra, but this . . . .Xuan isn't your responsibility. You're not married yet."

I got up and took a step toward the door leading outside, away from my mother. "Of course he is, Mom. Whether we're married or not, I love him. A piece of paper won't change how I feel about him. Who's going to take care of him, if not me? Whose responsibility is he?"

"His family's."

"Xuan *is* my family, Mom. He's sick, and he needs my help. And I'm going to be there for him."

I opened the patio door and ran outside as quickly as my feet could carry me before my mom could say anything else. I couldn't help but brood over Xuan's refusal to undergo treatment, and the time that had been stolen from us.

After taking a moment to catch my breath, I made my way into the garage. It had been years since my father had hung an old punching bag there. The worn-out bag, weighing approximately a hundred pounds and filled with sand, stood as a testament to past workouts and untapped emotions. Feeling the need for a release, a way to channel my tension and aggression, I cranked up the stereo and blasted Metallica. The heavy riffs and pounding drums reverberated in my ears, drowning out any other noise.

I put on my old faded gloves, slightly staggered my feet, and began to go to work with a series of punching combinations. I focused on positioning my knuckles, finding the angle that delivered the hardest blow. Each punch was a fiery combination of wrath. A helpless anger simmered in me like boiling water, directed at various targets—my mother, the doctors, cancer, even God. And in that mix of emotions, there was also a tinge of resentment towards Xuan, who didn't tell me himself about his decision. So I took off the teapot top and punched and kicked through the heat as I opened the lid on those boiling emotions.

There were no feel-good endorphins that day. By the time I was finished, the anger I'd felt had turned into steam and began to dissipate safely into the ether of tiredness.

Later, alone in my bedroom, I sifted through memories, ignoring the stale and bland colors of my life. The vivid colors were memories with him—such as Latin dancing, and Xuan saving me from the mudslide in Colombia, where he first kissed me. Looking back, I remembered being scared, knowing I was about to die. Between being rescued and seeing the comet, that was one of the most romantic days of my life.

There had been many nights since then that held weight in my memory. Like staying up and talking all night, tailgating at college football games, taking camping trips during the summer, hiking the redwood forest, discovering the romantic cities of Italy, spending long nights at the beach, or watching the sun disappear into the ocean. The little moments meant the most.

There was no denying that Xuan and I were different in many ways but it had always been surprisingly easy to overlook our obvious differences. And we did. I honestly loved everything about him—how he held doors for other people, let others cut in line at the grocery store if they had fewer items than he did, and generally went out of his way to accommodate others and pay them consideration in matters big and small. Xuan was completely chivalrous, a rare form of gentleman in today's world. The list went on and on.

Every moment we'd been together since then had been seared into my memory like a branding iron. But my favorite recollection was the day Xuan proposed in Italy. *But now . . . Maybe Stella is right. No* I dos. *No us. No future.*

Hot liquid tears fell against my pillow. I didn't hear Xuan's car as he drove up to the house, didn't hear him as he knocked on the door, didn't hear his voice as he spoke to Stella, or as he made his way up the stairs toward my bedroom and entered, or as he stood there quietly in the doorframe and watched me.

Reaching for my box of tissues, I finally saw him. Like a

frightened cat, he slowly came out of hiding and came to sit on my bed next to me. I didn't know how long he'd been standing there, watching me cry my eyes out like a child. His sudden appearance surprised me, especially since my mom must have let him in, knowing he would end up here, in my bedroom. Stella had a strict no boys in the bedroom policy, even after Xuan and I were engaged, a rule Xuan had completely respected for the past three years . . . until today.

He reached over to kiss me on the forehead and whispered in my ear, "*Bǎobèi,* it's okay. Everything's going to be okay."

"Did you read my mind?" I asked. "I was just thinking about you and now you're here like Mary Poppins."

"I'm sorry. I wish I had a spoonful of sugar for you."

"I don't need sugar. I just need you." *Inhale. Exhale.* "No wedding? No treatment? When were you going to tell me your plans?"

His face said it all. He was heartbroken. "I was planning to. I needed to think and sort out how I was going to tell you. I didn't find out my mom called Stella until I got home an hour ago. I'm sorry about how you found out. I wanted to be the one to tell you my decision."

"I already know your decision, but I don't accept it."

"I'm sorry. I know this must be hard."

Xuan put his finger up to my right eye and wiped away an oncoming tear. I was sure my eyes had dark circles under them, and my nose was running. Not exactly the picture of a model. "Real attractive, right?"

Xuan slipped off my shoes and covered me with a comforter. "In the day, you're beautiful, but in the evening, I think you're extra beautiful."

I began crying into the soft material.

He said, "It's okay. Everything will be okay. Don't cry."

"No, it won't."

"You're right. It won't be."

"You and Mei met with the doctors again?"

"We did."

"And?"

"I have some kind of mutation. EG . . . . exon . . . . something 19. I don't remember exactly. They want me to meet with a cancer specialist to talk about starting drugs and treatment right away."

In that moment, I wanted to believe that we would fight against all odds. And we'd do it together. "So there's treatment."

Xuan looked at me with cold, distant eyes. "Does it matter? I'm still going to die."

And there it was . . . .the awful reality of Xuan's cancer was in front of us.

"Of course it matters!" I said furiously. "You can go through chemo or radiation."

"Cassie, I don't know if I want to. The cancer is terminal, so I need time to think about what *I* want."

"Isn't it worth it if treatment will give you more time?"

"I want to live the way I want with whatever time is left for me. I want to die the way I want, not hooked up to machines and sick in a hospital."

I pictured my mother's old oak grandfather chime clock in the family room. I believed the countdown of death started from the day a person was born, a clock ticking away in an encircling twelve-hour clockwise motion. Then suddenly the human body reached the peak of its existence, some unknown and unidentified midpoint of its life. At that moment, the clock would begin to tick counterclockwise, counting down to the moment of some eternal darkness that no one really understood. The chimes set at thirty-minute intervals were like a mocking reminder that time was not something that could be controlled.

Unknowingly, the clock of this story had already begun its countdown. Death was not the opposite of life—it was just a part of it. And a pendulum inside Xuan had already begun to count down each second until the day he would die, mechanically moving back and forth, with the hour hand already winding down from twelve.

Terminal cancer. The term felt dirty. I refused to accept Xuan's death sentence. I would never accept that he would be gone from my world. This was the beginning of the end, and the countdown had already begun.

Swallowing hard, I took off my Fitbit watch. It was a somber reminder that time was not on our side, that there was no escaping this nightmare. Tick tock. Tick tock.

Xuan crawled into the bed, whispered more soothing words in my ear as if he were comforting a small child afraid of the dark. At some point my body stopped shaking and exhaustion pulled me down into its heavy currents of troubled waters. I drifted into a dreamless black sleep.

I woke up to a strange sound and realized the sun was setting. For a moment, I thought the roaring Santa Cruz winds outside had woken me. But lying next to me, Xuan had his arm around my torso, and loud, lion-like snores were coming from him. I'd fallen asleep lying next to the love of my life, though I was somewhat surprised Stella hadn't come in to yell at us or give a thirty-minute lecture on observing the proprieties—a small gift.

Slowly the sleeping lion opened his eyes. His arm tightened around me.

"Tell me a story," I whispered.

"What kind?" he asked. "Another one from China?"

"The one where you tell me that everything is going to be okay. And that whatever happens, we're going to face it together."

"But, *qīn'ài de,* it's not going to be okay. You know I'm going to die, right? There isn't a cure that will save me. No cure for this cancer."

"I know." I could feel my chest constrict with guilt for what I was about to do. This would be the most selfish thing I had ever done. "Xuan, I need something from you. But I don't know how to ask."

He studied my face for a long moment, speculating. "If it was in my power, I would give you all the beauty in the galaxy."

"If that's true, then will you take the treatment for me? I know I'm being selfish, but I want you as long as I can have you."

"Cassie, I don't want the treatment. It can't save me."

"Xuan, please," I whispered. "I need more time. We can start over. We can go to the beach every day and surf. We can go sky-diving, bungee jumping, or cliff diving. We can go to those fancy plays you like. We can go anywhere you want. Please don't give up yet," I begged. "At least meet with the doctors and discuss different treatment options."

"Cassie, if I do treatment, I'm most likely going to be too sick to want to do any of those things. It may only prolong my life for a short time. And leaving my parents with an enormous amount of debt because of medical bills is not what I want. How can I do that to them?"

"They love you, Xuan. There's no price tag on your life."

"What would you do if you were me?"

"I would fight!" I shouted.

"I've been trying to accept my fate, and I think you need to as well."

Does Xuan not love me enough to fight for his life? I immediately hated myself for thinking that. "I'm not ready to let you go yet," I said angrily. I couldn't help it. Unlike Xuan, I wasn't good at hiding my emotions.

"Okay." Xuan looked up at me. "You beat me this round. You win. I'll try it. But I'm only doing this for you. No promises that I'll finish treatment."

A lump began to build in my throat. Treatment was not what Xuan wanted, and his answer only made me feel small and guilty. His words should have comforted me. That he would try, for me. But they didn't. Xuan did love me enough to get treatment. But maybe I should have loved him enough to respect and accept his decision.

Chapter Nineteen: Treatment Plan

Dominican Hospital, California
June 5, 2019

Mary & Richard Solari Cancer Center at the Dominican Hospital on Mission Drive held a revered reputation as one of California's finest medical facilities. It was renowned for its exceptional cancer care, offering cutting-edge treatments and a dedicated team of specialists. Their cancer team did more testing on Xuan and reconfirmed the dreaded diagnosis of lung cancer.

In the end, Xuan agreed to enter the treatment plan they proposed, and Mei had scheduled the first appointment available at the center.

Now, Mei sat with Xuan in the patient admitting room, filling out long insurance forms and questions. As nervous as if I were the patient, I couldn't sit in a chair waiting to hear about the plan. I paced the floor. I collected brochures. I gathered info about his illness—possible treatments, the meds the doctor might recommend, and even a cookbook with recipes that might help with nausea and other symptoms. I decided to think of cancer like a boxing opponent, and I planned on being right beside Xuan in the ring, fighting. My goal was to fight alongside him, until the end.

A nurse came to collect us. "Follow me." We were all escorted to another area. The nurse pointed toward a room and indicated for Xuan to sit so she could take his blood pressure.

"That's not fair," Xuan exclaimed.

"What isn't?" the nurse asked.

"To take a guy's blood pressure while his girlfriend is sitting in the room."

"Why, because she's going to scold you and force you to go on a diet?"

"No. Because, she always makes it rise. Just look at her . . . she's beautiful. Every time she's in the room, my heart goes into triple overdrive. We've been together almost three years. I'm surprised I'm not dying of a cardiac related disease by now."

The nurse could tell he was flirting, and even she had to laugh. Xuan was being sweet, but also incredibly funny.

"The doctor will be in shortly to visit with you," she said once she finished.

Besides the examining table, there was only one chair, so I let Mei take the weight off her feet.

For a heartbeat the urge to sit beside Xuan hit me, but I resisted the feeling. Xuan was uneasy about being here. He needed space, so I stood in the corner.

An energetic force swept into the room, personified in the form of Dr. Alexander Hutchinson. This taller, older gentleman with salt-and-pepper hair exuded an aura of wisdom and vitality, akin to a cherished book brimming with life's experiences.

His introduction carried a soothing tone that instantly captured one's complete focus. "Hello, I'm Dr. Alexander Hutchinson," he began, his voice beckoning undivided attention. "I'm here to discuss your cancer and the targeted therapy we plan on using. As you may already know, the gene testing conducted at the San Francisco hospital has identified an EGFR mutation. Our treatment approach aims to specifically target these proteins, effectively halting the growth of cancer cells."

"I was told about the mutation. I don't really understand what it means," Xuan muttered.

Dr. Hutchinson's explanation of the treatment was delivered with a reassuring tone, carefully avoiding any hint of condescension towards Xuan. Recognizing our scientific background, he tailored his language to keep Xuan at ease, despite the unsettling nature of the news.

"Xuan, my boy, your diagnosis is adenocarcinoma with the EGFR exon 19 mutation," Dr. Hutchinson began, his voice composed and gentle. "The epidermal growth factor receptor, or

EGFR, is a well-known biomarker. When this receptor undergoes mutation on the surface of specific cancer cells, it triggers signals that promote their growth and unfortunate spread. The good news—we have a targeted cancer treatment called osimertinib that can specifically address these mutated proteins, effectively halting the growth of cancer cells. It's been successful, but it's not a cure. But it can indeed help you to manage the disease and delaying the onset of severe symptoms."

"No chemo or radiation?" Xuan sounded relieved.

"Well, osimertinib is the preferred treatment for patients with an EGFR 19 mutation. I won't sugarcoat the outcome. In time, cancer learns a way around these treatments, which is called acquired resistance. There may come a time for chemo if your cancer spreads. But right now, let's focus on osimertinib, which is a daily pill."

"Is coughing up blood normal?" I asked. Images of the red stuff after his coughing fit still haunted me.

"Hmm. Xuan most likely experienced symptoms during the early stages of the disease, such as fatigue, mild shortness of breath, or upper back and chest pain. But those signs often progress to coughing up blood, such as he experienced."

"And no matter what, I'm going to die?" Xuan asked.

"Unfortunately, lung cancer with EGFR mutations is often not diagnosed until the disease is at Stage III or IV. In your case, the cancer hasn't spread to other organs in your body. You're currently at Stage III. Remember, the treatment isn't a magic bullet, but it's aimed at managing the spread and relieving symptoms."

"How much time do I have?"

Dr. Hutchinson steepled his fingertips. "It's important to understand that predictions don't mean much. Too much lies outside the realm of medical knowledge."

"Do I have six months?"

"Yes, of course."

"A year?"

The doctor set aside his clipboard. He must have realized Xuan would continue to press him, needing answers, reassurance that treatment was indeed worth it. "I think it's reasonable to say yes, I think you have at least a year. Maybe longer, with treatment."

"Two or three?"

Dr. Hutchinson hesitated. "It's definitely possible. But a lot of what happens next comes down to you and your specific genetics, your attitude, and how your body responds to the medication."

Xuan seemed to settle into the adjustable examination table. He had advanced cancer and there was no known cure. He would never make it to his thirties. Maybe twenty-five, if he was lucky. But he sat in perfect stillness, hands clasped together, like a monk in meditation.

"Give me a moment," said Dr. Hutchinson. He left the room for a brief moment and then brought in a second chair for me.

"What does the pill cost?" Xuan finally asked.

"I don't have those numbers for you. That would be best to discuss with your insurance."

"I doubt my student insurance is going to cover this."

I didn't care about the cost. But I knew Xuan would care, *a lot.* He loved his family more than life itself, and to be a liability wasn't his idea of a doable plan. The cost to keep him alive was important to him, and his mother did not have insurance in the United States. He didn't want his parents to pay the price for prolonging the inevitable.

Xuan pulled out his phone and searched Google. He had to ask for the correct spelling of the drug. He wanted more real information about how much of a financial burden he would be to his parents. Money was a big concern. Possibly a deal breaker.

"Several sites—it's around five hundred dollars a day! That's fifteen thousand a month! How could I let my parents pay that much for me?"

Fifteen thousand dollars. I gasped, appalled. I staggered to the chair and collapsed into it. *He'll never agree to that.*

Xuan opened his mouth and closed it again, in shock. The

atmosphere in the room plunged from friendly and informative to frigid with mathematical figures and calculations.

I sat with my elbows on my knees, my face buried in my hands. Saints, I knew cancer treatment was expensive, but I never imagined it was *that* expensive. That was too much. Ironically, I didn't know if I could live with myself, knowing my parents were working day and night to keep me alive. That would be a huge financial responsibility. I just couldn't imagine allowing it, month after month. Sadly, I wondered how many people died every year because of the cost of medication in the United States. In a way, it seemed like pharmaceutical companies were getting away with murder.

"We have money," Mei interjected, her words cutting through Xuan's objections regarding accepting financial assistance for his treatment. The concern and determination in her voice were palpable as she continued, "Let us handle this. We are not destitute. Your father and I will take care of the financial aspect. Your only focus should be on getting better." Mei's fatigue weighed heavily on her, evident in the thickened accent that emerged. She must have realized this, because she switched to Chinese, and began to reassure and persuade her son. Her tone carried a motherly warmth and concern as she tried to convince him.

Dr. Hutchinson chimed in, almost like an intervention, to encourage us to forget the bills. This wasn't about money. It was about doing what was necessary—anything in order to survive, well, longer. Too bad big pharmaceutical companies didn't feel the same way—that it was about a person's individual care and well-being, and not about dollar signs. "Xuan, more patients are living much longer, tolerating treatment much better, and seeing longer life expectancy after diagnosis of Stage III and IV lung cancer. Life expectancy is more promising than ever. But make no mistake, the response to the drug is different for everyone."

Xuan was still scowling, his annoyance palpable.

"Are the side effects of osimertinib different from chemo?" I asked.

The doctor nodded. "Every person is different. Some patients will experience dry skin, tiredness, or pain in the joints, bones, or muscles, as well as appetite changes. Xuan can always contact us if he has side effects. We'll adjust the dose as needed and monitor his progress."

A profound silence enveloped the room, as if time itself held its breath. Xuan's gaze shifted between his mother, myself, and finally, he locked eyes with the doctor. "Let's do it," he said.

A sigh of relief escaped me. I'd been holding my breath without realizing it. I possibly had several years left with him, which was more time than I'd thought I had that morning.

In the corner, Mei had been holding her stomach—in fear, I was sure. She began to cry happy tears when Xuan finally agreed.

After the doctor left the room, Mei's hand trembled as she grasped her phone, her fingertips navigating the familiar numbers that linked her to her husband and their family members in China and Korea. It was late at night in Asian countries, but each call served as a lifeline—a lifeline that bridged the distance and brought them together in a powerful show of unity and unwavering support. Tears streamed down Mei's face as she struggled to steady her voice, conveying the news that would shape their collective journey. With every word spoken, a resolute determination echoed through the phone lines, reaffirming their commitment to face this battle as a family.

After a few minutes of conversation, Mei excused herself, saying, "I'll be back in a few minutes." She quietly slipped out of the room, seeking the solace and refuge of her own thoughts. In the hallway, I could see her leaning against the wall, her body slumped under the weight of worries and the immeasurable love she held for her son. The burden she carried, both literal and metaphorical, was palpable. Yet, her unwavering determination shone through as a testament to the resilience of a mother's love.

The future had suddenly opened up to us again. *Three years. That was still enough time, wasn't it? We could still get married and start a family.*

The countdown on Xuan's life stalled the moment he agreed to take the pill. As if a cosmic hand helped push pause on the circular clock of mortality. The hour hand rested at eleven. The ticking had stopped for now, but life was like a great spinning wheel. Sooner or later, it would start turning again.

After we met several of the medical team members and completing additional paperwork, we were free to go. Mei left us to go to the pharmacy with several prescription forms.

He visibly exhaled, his relief palpable. "I'm so glad I don't have to stay," he replied, intertwining his fingers with mine as we made our way across the parking lot. With a playful tone, he tried to lighten the mood, "I mean, I was half expecting them to strap me to a table and shout, 'It's alive!' like I was their very own Frankenstein creation. I even imagined them plotting to keep me here as their favorite lab rat. But lucky me, I get to escape and head home instead. It's a win-win! Can you believe it?"

"I'm glad you don't have to stay," I said, my voice filled with genuine relief. "Thank you for doing this, Xuan. I know it's a lot of money, but it means the world to me. Having you right where you belong, with us, is everything I could ask for."

"Anything for the girl I love. Speaking of which, what do you want to do tonight?" he asked.

"Watch a movie. How about you?"

"I want to take my girlfriend on a date tonight." Xuan seemed to have had a weight lifted off of his shoulders. His renewed spirit filled the air.

"You sound almost happy."

"I *am* happy. I'm alive. You're alive. That makes today a great day. That's enough."

"Are you sure you want to go out tonight?"

"I don't know how I'm going to feel after I start taking those pills," he admitted.

"But aren't you tired?"

"I haven't begun treatment. After all, it's your birthday tomorrow. And you gave me the will to live again."

I'd completely forgotten my own birthday with everything going on. Truthfully, I'd never liked the awkward twenty-four-hour spotlight focus. "We don't have to celebrate my birthday."

"Of course we do, Cassie," Xuan replied, his voice filled with a mix of sincerity and tenderness. His words hung in the air, carrying the weight of the newfound reality they were facing. "Since I found out I have lung cancer, everything has shifted. The world seems different, and nothing feels quite normal anymore." His gaze softened as he looked into her eyes, searching for understanding and connection.

"But you know what?" he continued, a spark of determination igniting in his voice. "Despite the challenges we're facing, I want to spend tonight celebrating your life."

I lifted my head, not just from the words but from the unspoken plea behind his request. For one more evening, he wanted to be like any other average, ordinary couple. "Okay, what did you have in mind?"

"How about dressing up for your birthday and going to dinner on the Wharf?"

"We haven't gone out to dinner in a long time. It might be fun."

"Might be?" he asked.

My stomach rumbled. "Are you sure you're feeling up to it?"

"Trust me, I'm up for it."

"Okay." Skeptical, I kissed him on the cheek. "So where do you want to eat?"

"Let's eat at either *Riva Fish House* on the Wharf or a pho restaurant. Fish or oxtail soup," he said enthusiastic. "Which sounds good to you?"

"I didn't realize oxtail ever sounded appealing," I teased.

"You don't know what you're missing."

"Uh, I'll take your word for it. I'm not a huge fan of Vietnamese food. Not a fan at all."

He reached over and took my hand, his skin warm and soft against mine. "It's settled then. Let's go to *Riva Fish House* for your birthday dinner."

A fuzzy warm feeling threatens to explode inside my chest at the thought of Xuan wanting to celebrate my birthday despite everything going on. I love this man. "Sounds perfect."

"Hey Cassie, one more thing about tonight. Promise me that when we go out, we won't talk about doctors, or hospitals, or treatment. For the next four hours, I do *not* want to worry about being sick. I want to have one more night with you, eating dinner and talking about anything besides my disease. Can you do that for me?"

"Yes. I promise."

Leaving the hospital in the dust like the ending of a good Western film felt good, but by morning, sick bays and medical jargons would become our new reality, and there would be no escape.

Xuan would pick me up for dinner, so we went our separate ways. That gave me just under two hours to transform myself into Cinderella for the unforgettable night ahead.

Part Three: A Journey of Two Souls

Chapter Twenty: Sunset on the Wharf

31 Municipal Wharf, Santa Cruz, California
June 5, 2019

Hello, wharf! I watched the server at *Riva Fish House* remove half-eaten plates of oyster shooters, crab cakes, steamed mussels, and calamari, which were all meant to be appetizers, from our dinner table.

Xuan had opted to sit at a table closest to the waterfront. I eyed a sparkly bag that he'd carried in from the car. Even with everything going on, he was still the classic old-fashioned romantic I fell in love with. Xuan had always been thoughtful and sensitive. I didn't have to worry about any fake-alpha machismo crap from him. But there was the catlike distancing, from time to time, when obstacles faced him and us.

The Riva's waiter replaced the side dishes with two bowls of clam chowder and a hot plate of prawns and snapper Florentine, along with a plate of lemon-drizzled shark.

Xuan sat across from me. His smile was radiant. His delicate features were beautiful enough to rival Adonis or any of the ancient gods of myth. He had completely bewitched my soul. Apollo would've likely been jealous of Xuan and turned him into a pig, as Ares had done to Adonis when he won Aphrodite's favor.

No matter what, he was almost always dressed in some sort of suit, dress shirt, or men's blazer. That night he wore a blue blazer with gray suspenders. I had showered and put on a mauve-colored A-line floor-length tulle dress that was impractical with lace beading and elegant sequins. The dress had a thigh-high slit up the front. I wanted to dress up, just as Xuan had asked.

"Babe, I don't know if I can eat any more, I'm already so full of appetizers." Three seagulls were lined up, staring hungrily at me from outside the window. Taking a fry from my plate, I stuck it through an opening in the bottom windowpane.

"It's okay. Just eat what you can," he assured me.

The waiter brought over a huge plate of lobster. Xuan used the cracker to dig into the shell. I was happy to see him eating so much. He seemed content. But then again, he was always cheery when food was in front of him.

I sighed. "I may not be able to get out of this dress later if I eat another bite! Scissors may be involved."

"Sounds enticing. Let me know if you require any assistance."

For a moment, I could barely focus as I gaped at him, at the thought now sizzling through my mind. Only the room full of people kept me from thinking too much about that offer. But there was an ache there I couldn't control.

Xuan's voice broke this moment of reverie, and I couldn't help but blush. "You know, in China it's customary to order an even number of dishes, because an odd number is usually only ordered at a funeral meal."

"What?" I asked with a sensuous laugh.

Xuan leaned both of his elbows on the table and put his fingers together. "Yeah. We have all kinds of traditions."

"I would love to go someday."

"You will."

I forced myself to remain numb and tried not to think of China and all the things Xuan and I would have done together on our honeymoon. After all, I had promised Xuan that dinner would be perfect.

The waiter returned just in time. "Anything else I can get for you this evening?"

"I would like to look at your cocktails and wine list."

"Very good, sir," the waiter said as he handed over a menu.

He scanned the list. "The lady will have a Coral Reef, and I would like to order a Wharf Rat."

The waiter took his leave to place the order. I loved pineapple, mango, and orange juice. The drink Xuan ordered me sounded amazing.

"What's in the Wharf Rat?" I asked.

"Bulleit bourbon, sweet vermouth, and a dash of bitters."

"Sounds good," I said. "Despite the name."

Xuan reached under the table and then handed me a present wrapped in paper with light blue and ornately interlocked silver lines, with a matching ribbon and a bow. He was like the Martha Stewart of wrapping gifts. "Happy twenty-second birthday, *bǎobèi.*"

He'd made me a photo book using Shutterfly. I opened the album and began to flip through over one hundred pages from our trip together in Italy. The last few sheets were dedicated to Xuan's proposal.

"This is beautiful. I absolutely love it." I was immediately in his lap, kissing him, my hands around Xuan's neck. "Thank you."

Xuan appeared completely at ease in his surroundings, despite the stares people were giving us. *Let them stare.*

I returned to my seat just as the waiter returned with our alcoholic beverages.

Xuan said, "I think you should go shopping, or to the beach, or to a movie with your friends tomorrow. You have a lot going on with finishing your master's degree this year. It's important for you to celebrate your birthday."

"My friends are all busy," I lied. The next day was his first round of treatment, and I wasn't going to leave him. Unlike Xuan, I had plenty of years and birthdays ahead of me.

For a while, Xuan and I dawdled over our drinks while trying to finish as much as we could of our large meal without being sick.

"Xuan, do you ever wonder why things happen the way they do?" I asked.

He put down his glass and leaned across the table toward me.

"Sometimes. But Buddhist teachings have taught me to believe that everything happens for a reason. Everything you do, say, think, and feel makes imprints inside you. Nothing happens by accident. A coincidence is just an effect in which we cannot see the connecting cause."

The waiter returned, and this time I ordered the South Pacific Margarita, which was made with pineapple and coconut. Xuan, on the other hand, ordered a rum-based drink called Release the Kraken, which was also made with pineapple.

When the waiter left, I asked Xuan, "Have you ever wondered about God? Or religions other than your own?"

"Most of my family is Buddhist. Growing up, every year my grandparents on my mother's side organized a *chaoshan jinxiang*—what I think you know as a *pilgrimage.* We'd go to the city's most important religious site, Miaofengshan, or the Mountain of the Wondrous Peak, which is considered one of the five holy mountains that match cardinal directions in geomancy. They still go yearly to pay their respects to the mountain and to present incense. Honestly, I've only stepped foot into one church in my life, and that was with my *nǎi nai.*"

I knew *nǎi nai* meant "grandmother" in Chinese.

"You did?" I asked, a little surprised. He'd never mentioned that.

"Yeah," he nodded. "I used to spend weekends at her house. She had a lot of paintings of Jesus, and a beautiful jade rosary. When I was young, she took me to a Catholic church, and I remember watching her as she asked God for several things and lit prayer candles. Nǎi nai believed a church was a place where dreams were realized. She told me to tell God my wishes and He would grant them. I remember what I said to her when she told me to make a wish." Xuan offered an indulgent half smile. "Where is God, huh? Look around us. Look at all the bad things that happen in this world. God isn't a genie, and a church isn't a place for wishes to be granted. It's a place for the lonely, sick, weak, and broken. It's a place people go to not feel alone. But my *năi nai* still went back, every Sunday."

I continued watching Xuan, not quite sure where this conversation was going. I patiently waited for him to make his point.

"I didn't make any wishes that day. I had never made a wish or spoken to God until the night of the mudslide. But I remember, in Colombia, looking out onto the road and seeing your vehicle trapped, and silently I prayed. *I'll believe in you. So please . . . . save her. If you let her live, I'll happily give up the rest of the time I have left alive. Take me and let Cassie live.*"

I blinked several times as I mulled over the words he'd just admitted. "Are you saying you think this *thing* is happening to you because I survived?"

"No, not at all. And to answer your question, I didn't become a devout Catholic after the Colombia incident. However, surprisingly, I have grown closer to *your* God. I think it started when He helped me through the mudslide and allowed for your rescue, knowing full well that I'm a Buddhist."

"Do you believe you will meet Buddha or some higher power when you die?"

"I believe that when we die, we're reborn. Maybe we get the choice, I don't know. But if there's a next life after this one, make sure to come find me," he said with a wink.

"Would you really want to be with me again?" I asked playfully. "What if I'm a bug?"

"Then I'm sure you'd be a cute one."

"Don't make fun of me."

Xuan looked at me seriously. "Cassie, I will choose you every time, in every life. And if there's a price to pay for my choice, then I'll gladly pay it for the rest of eternity. Even if you come back as an insect, or a man-eating crocodile. Even if you come back human and you're disfigured, or sick, it won't matter because I will always choose you."

My throat was suddenly tight. That was the most beautiful thing anyone had ever said to me. I suddenly wanted to pull his face to mine and kiss him, but we were still in the restaurant.

Damn self-control. Instead, I reached over and stroked a thumb over his cheekbone, marveling at him—the words and his beauty.

"So what do you believe?" His tone was thoughtful.

"I think God steps in more than we realize. And I think there's a reason for things, though it's not always clear why. Besides, I have to believe right now."

"Believe in what?"

"Miracles."

"Cassie, I was already given a miracle three years ago, in Colombia, when you didn't die. I don't think I'll get two in my lifetime."

"I have to believe it's possible, Xuan."

"I'm just happy that you love me despite the fact I believe in something different, and you've never asked me to change."

I reached over and squeezed his hand. "I love you exactly the way you are." Xuan was the only one who had ever touched my heart. Which would always be his. I didn't care that we were from different cultures and religions.

"I think you and I have always tried to be open-minded toward each other and I love you for that. It's not easy for a lot of people to commit their lives to someone so different," said Xuan.

Xuan grabbed a bite of one of his prawns with his fork and held it out to me.

I took it.

"Good choice on picking where to eat. I love this place." "I'm glad."

Although the road ahead was uncertain and scary, I felt relaxed. "If we have time, can we walk down to the end of the wharf and see the sea lions?" I asked.

"Of course."

We lingered over our drinks and food, talking and laughing with ease. By the time we were ready to leave the restaurant, the sun was beginning to set and warm colors illuminated the white sails of several boats on the ocean. The boardwalk and wharf still bustled with life. But as night approached, a younger crowd would come out and the beach would stay alive with bonfires until dawn, when surfers would claim their waves.

Several people stared at us as we passed by.

"What do they keep ogling?" I asked. I often wondered if it was because Xuan wasn't white. Closet racism was everywhere, a fact I knew too well. Some people, strangers, acted like they were open to interracial relationships. Then, *bam!* The truth would hit me like an asteroid, as they'd whisper or come out and say it in big, shouty capital letters.

"They keep looking at you."

"Me? Why?"

"Don't you know how dazzling you look?" He offered his arm to me as we left the restaurant. "All these men keep wishing you were the one on their arm tonight."

I was vaguely aware of all who gawked at us . . . at me. My shoes echoed like the sound of horse hooves on the wooden pier as we made our way towards the end of it. With each step, I could feel the blisters forming on my feet, a painful reminder of the discomfort that comes with fashion. Unable to bear it any longer, I slipped off my shoes and walked barefoot, feeling the rough wood under my toes. Xuan, ever the gentleman, took my heels from my hand and held them in his opposite hand. He laced his fingers through mine, a gesture of solidarity and love. As we walked together, the sun began to set, casting a warm orange glow across the horizon. The light illuminated the sea, making it sparkle like a thousand diamonds. The waves danced in rhythm, cresting and crashing against the shore.

As we reached the end of the pier, I couldn't resist the urge to lean over the wharf railing and observe the fat sea lions lounging on the platforms below. One of them, in particular, caught my attention. He kept trying to jump onto the raised boards but kept slipping off, as if his blubber was made of slippery butter. I couldn't help but chuckle at the sight.

I looked up from the sea lions and saw Xuan, who was not staring at the sea creatures but instead looking at me. His mouth was inches away, and I instinctively stretched up to kiss him. My lips brushed his and he automatically opened his mouth to kiss me . . . really kiss me. My entire body felt as though it had been ignited. The pull was there, like a magnet. Forehead to chin, and soul to soul, we stood there amid the coastal breeze and lashing waves. I didn't care about onlookers.

As we pulled away from our embrace, Xuan ran his fingers through my unbound hair, sending shivers down my spine. There was an unspoken understanding between us, a promise to continue this intimate moment later.

"I want to give you the world, Cassie," he said, his voice filled with passion.

"No one can have the whole world. Not even Alexander the Great," I replied, a hint of playfulness in my voice.

"I find you adorable when you begin to reference history, especially during a moment like this."

"At least I didn't reference a comic book," I quipped, feeling a smile tugging at the corners of my lips. "Did I ruin the moment?"

Xuan smiled, his eyes filled with warmth. "That's not possible. And I realize I could never truly give you the entire world, nor has anyone ever owned the entire world, but I will give you everything in my power to give."

"I know," I said. I understood exactly what he meant. Xuan had agreed to undergo treatment despite the financial evils, all because he wanted to make me happy. I couldn't help but wonder if he'd ever resent me for it later on or blame me. But I didn't want to think about that. Not then. Not that night.

Shifting, I brought my arms up around his neck and then leaned forward to once again kiss him.

I closed my eyes. And in that moment, when our lips touched, I felt little sparks, like lightning crawling across my skin, giving me goosebumps. Xuan's lips moved beneath mine. One of his arms tightened around me, while he placed his other hand on my shoulder blade and slowly began to move down the length of my back, gently pushing me toward him as if we were the only two people standing on the pier. I gasped a little as he kissed me in a pleading, almost-urgent manner. His proximity was overwhelming, exhilarating, as my fingers curled in his hair. I was one hundred percent irrevocably in love and the feeling was more wonderful and powerful than I could have ever imagined.

As we stood there, the world around us faded into insignificance, as if it were melting away. It was just the two of us, locked in an embrace, with the distant barks of sea lions below serving as our only witnesses. The taste of him on my tongue was like a potent elixir, intoxicating me and anchoring me to the present moment. His breath, warm and gentle, caressed my skin, and I could feel the rhythm of his heartbeat reverberating against my chest.

In the stillness of that night, I sensed that this kiss held the promise of something extraordinary, an enchanting beginning to an unknown journey. With unwavering resolve, I made a decision, my heart filled with anticipation and curiosity, eager to discover where this singular moment might lead us.

"Xuan," I said, my voice low and sultry. "Let's take a drive. There are secluded beaches we can walk along."

"Sure, sounds like a plan," he replied, a smile spreading across his face as he took my hand and purse, clearly excited to spend more time with me.

The fierce orange rays grew fainter by the second, lighting up the sea and the crest of dancing waves. The evening was still and quiet, and as we walked towards the parking lot, I couldn't help but feel a little nervous and giddy at the same time. I knew there were plenty of remote beaches nearby at this time of night, but I wanted to find the perfect spot for us. Xuan didn't seem to mind where we went, he was just happy to be with me. Without hesitation, Xuan handed me the keys to his car and I got behind the wheel.

Thankfully he remained blissfully unaware of my not so honorable intentions.

Chapter Twenty-One: Celestial Convergence

Santa Cruz Coast, California
June 5, 2019

When we arrived at the secluded beach, our footsteps traced a path in the sand as we strolled together, our hands intertwined. The vast expanse of the shoreline stretched before us, an untouched canvas awaiting our presence. Despite the big C hanging over us—the world—and this moment, were ours, and nothing else mattered.

Scanning the blanket of stars overhead, I tried to find the courage to tell Xuan my intentions for bringing him here. "Xuan I want—"

Stealing the moment, Xuan's lips, warm and tender like silk, met mine in a stolen kiss that stirred a blaze within me. The touch of his mouth against my skin awakened a dormant heat, coursing through my body like liquid fire, finding solace in the depths of my bones.

As our connection deepened, his hands ventured along the contours of my figure, delicately tracing the path where fabric met flesh. Each caress, gentle yet electric, served as a catalyst, fueling the flames of passion that danced between us. With every tender stroke, the intensity grew, heightening my senses and evoking an intoxicating mix of pleasure and anticipation.

Lost in the magic of the moment, a soft, breathless sound escaped my lips, a testament to the overwhelming sensations that enveloped me. It was as if the world around us ceased to exist, and all that mattered was the symphony of our entwined bodies, harmonizing with the gentle rhythm of the waves lapping at the shore as we surrendered to our desires.

"Xuan," I whispered, my voice filled with longing, "I want you to make love to me."

"Cassie, we don't have to do this just because I'm sick."

"I'm ready. I don't want to wait any longer. Do you . . ." It was an invitation and an unfinished question, one I didn't know how to ask.

He held my gaze. I felt completely vulnerable as the words hung there in the space between us . . . as if the offer were dangling on the edge of some cliff.

"Believe me, I want to." His answering smile was tender, hesitant. "Cassie, are you sure? We aren't married."

I didn't need to think twice about my decision. I had wanted to wait until we were wed. But since we were blindsided by his disease, I knew there might not be a wedding, as my mom had said. I wanted Xuan while he was still on earth, coherent and full of life, not a shadow. I wanted to give myself to him for the first time before his cancer took over or he became weak. "Xuan, I am in love with you. I want this with you, if you'll have me."

"Of course I want you."

"Then I'm yours."

"Cassie, I want you to be sure—"

"I've never been more sure." I spread my hands over his chest. "I want you tonight. Here. Now."

Xuan looked nervously around.

My voice was soft, sensual. "There's no one here but us. You and me. Just the two of us."

I reached up. My fingers slowly began to unfasten each button of his shirt. Xuan raised his eyebrows, but he let me undress him as he dragged a sensual finger down my skin. I wasn't sure he was breathing as I unlatched the buckle on his belt and unzipped his pants. Xuan reached down and slowly pulled off his pants and boxers and then tossed them into the sand.

My mouth went dry at the sight of him. He was the most beautiful man I'd ever seen . . . and he was mine.

"Here, help me with my dress." I turned so he could unzip the back.

His lips brushed up the tip of my shoulder blade and then the side of my neck. "Come take a swim with me," he said. "I'll wait for you in the water."

He turned his back as I took several deep, calming breaths. *Don't be a coward.* I tried not to feel shy as I took off my own clothes. I looked down at my naked body and tried to fight the urge to hide myself behind anything, including my hands or a piece of clothing. I felt as though I was standing in front of a crowd of thousands, their full attention and spotlight on me. *Breathe,* I told myself. *It's just you and him. You're just nervous.*

I held my head up as I stepped into the icy tides. The cool water of the Pacific was a thousand sharp kisses along my skin. Then I saw Xuan as he made his way toward me. Everything was leached of color, his black hair turned silver by the moonlight.

Every cell of my body calmed at the sight of him, knowing that he loved me as much as I loved him, unconditionally. The deep adoration I carried in my heart was beyond comprehension.

Despite the cold, a rush of heat flashed across my skin as I waded out into the quiet, ageless water, toward him even with the push and pull from the waves. The low waves broke around us as I stood in waist-deep water. I hoped my face looked bold and unflinching, the complete opposite of how I felt. I'd been raised to be private . . . prim and proper. Now my brain was uncertain, fighting a war between what I had been taught and the rush of emotions sending chills down my entire body.

"Cassie, what's wrong? You're shaking."

"I'm just nervous."

"It's all right." He intertwined his fingers with mine beneath the ocean surface. "We don't have to do this."

I tucked my hair behind my shoulder. "I want to. I just don't know what to expect."

"Neither do I. We'll figure it out together."

I took a deep, shuddering breath and met his gaze.

"Can I touch you?" he asked.

The dark ocean water was kissed with silvery starlight. The night was too dark to see our reflection or anything below the surface of the frigid waters. I nodded, not wanting my voice to betray my confidence. I stood paralyzed, my heart and blood pounding, as I waited for him to touch my bare skin.

Xuan shuddered the tiniest bit as he reached out and put a hand on my shoulder, slightly above my collarbone. He made broad, light circles over my bare skin. He slowly dragged a delicate finger down my arms and body, tracing the intricate contours of my form. Like an artist's brush on a canvas, he followed every movement I made, every subtle flicker of muscle beneath the water's surface. His finger became a conduit, bridging the gap between our souls as he explored the landscape of my skin, leaving a trail of electric tingles in its wake.

His breath came rougher now as his gaze lingered on my breasts and a phantom wind hissed in our ears. My mouth parted slightly, my breathing shallow. I traced my tongue over his lips as I stroked his back. He tasted like the sea as his tongue flicked against where my lips had been.

Picking up my legs, I wrapped myself around his waist, my arms around his neck. He lifted me and slowly began to carry me up out of the water and onto the wet sand.

I braced myself on my elbows as he laid me down. He could see all of me now, the water no longer covering me like a blanket. I took my hands and tried to cover myself. *Be bold. Let go. Let go.*

Xuan grabbed my hand and held it. "Cassie, it's me. You don't ever have to hide yourself from me. You are absolutely perfect the way you are."

I lifted my mouth to the curve of his neck and then his collarbone. A flicker of fear and relief shone beneath Xuan's glazed lust each time my lips connected against his skin. His body was so tense that I thought his muscles would snap, but his hands were gentle as he stroked his fingertips over the apex of my thigh.

Desire twisted and turned inside me as he opened my legs and knelt between them. I knew there was nowhere to hide under his powerful gaze. My entire body was fully revealed to him. For a minute, Xuan didn't move. We just gazed softly at each other—what some would call soul searching. He took my hand in his and held it.

"You're mine." His hand slid up the plane of my torso while he lowered himself over me, his hips nestling against mine.

Yes, I thought. I had been his since Colombia, and he had been mine from the start. I gasped a little at the touch, as his body fit across mine. My breathing was ragged and savage as he leaned down to kiss me, waiting for me to respond. "I love you. I'm yours," I said.

"Are you sure?" he asked again.

"Yes, I'm sure."

Slowly, he eased into me, and a low moan sounded in his throat as I shifted my hips to draw him in. I felt pain, like ripping off the seal of an unopened bottle. But my whole body tingled, electrified, and I arched slightly against him.

Xuan kissed me again and I lost myself in the exquisite sensation of his slow, deliberate movements.

Mother have mercy, it hurts. I winced a little and Xuan immediately stopped moving. Concern filled his eyes as he looked at me intently. "Cassie, tell me if I'm hurting you."

"Just keep going slowly."

"Breathe."

I did. I started by taking a few deep, slow inhales through the pain. He occasionally stopped to let me adjust before he continued to gently move again. After a while our bodies began to come together in alignment, our breathing synchronized. It was an exquisite dance of pain and pleasure, a dichotomy that both bewildered and enthralled me. Despite the discomfort, there was an undeniable undercurrent of ecstasy, weaving its way through the fabric of my being.

Eventually, we found solace in the rhythm of our breaths, allowing the intimacy of the moment to unfold at its own pace.

With each passing moment, the pain subsided, giving way to an ever-increasing sense of pleasure. As the intensity softened, my initial shyness and hesitation dissolved into a passionate yearning that emanated from the depths of my being. In that moment, there was nothing I wanted more than him, nothing I desired more than the culmination of our desires. It was as if something primal in me ignited, and I craved him with every fiber of my being.

Without conscious thought, that primal desire took over my body, moving my hips. My eyes drifted closed. A low moan slipped out of me as we drifted in a rhythm synced to the waves, as we'd danced in Colombia.

Xuan's teeth grazed over my nipple, followed by his tongue. My fingers dug into his shoulders as I buried my face into his wind-kissed neckline. The hardness of him pushed against me a little faster now. My hips bucked, grinding myself against him to ease the building ache and tension between my legs.

Xuan groaned, his smile nothing short of wicked and alive as he pulled away to run a broad hand from my throat down to my thighs.

I felt my body shudder with each drive of his hips. I hadn't known what to expect but I definitely did not expect this. Every breath and touch was synchronized as natural energy flowed through us. The rhythm pushed me higher, faster. Oh saints, yes. I want more.

Release crested within me as I let go. I was vaguely aware as Xuan said my name, as he also let go, his fingers digging into my hips. It was as if our souls had traversed the ages, intimately acquainted from a distant lifetime. Our connection transcended the physical realm, intertwining our minds and souls in a cosmic dance. Time slowed down until we both reached a soul-shattering climax, completely synced with each other. And in that moment, our bodies intertwined like two comets colliding in the sky.

Xuan stilled, then collapsed, sinking to the sand beside me as he cradled me in his arms. He'd claimed me, just as I'd claimed him.

"Are you okay?" He ran his thumb over the back of my hand. "Did it hurt?

"I'm fine," I reassured him, a mixture of tears and laughter escaping my lips.

His brows flicked up and he looked worried. "Did it hurt?"

"It did at first," I responded, my voice tinged with honesty. "But trust me, the pleasure outweighed the pain."

Gently, my fingertips brushed against the contours of Xuan's face, savoring the softness and warmth that radiated from his skin. In this moment, everything I had yearned for, everything I had dared to dream of, became a tangible reality. With him, it felt like coming home, like finding the missing piece of my soul.

Under the breathtaking canopy of stars, we shared an intimacy that transcended the ordinary. This was not the typical backdrop of teenage fumbles in cramped spaces or hasty encounters fueled by lust. And not with Raylan, who didn't respect my innocence—or me. No, in Xuan, I had found perfection itself.

I was covered in sand, but this place and moment was better than I'd ever imagined. I looked at Xuan, his body bathed in moonlight, and saw wonder and love in his eyes. That sacred night had shown me that there was still beauty in the world. "Xuan, it was perfect. Being with you in this moment is everything I've ever wanted. More than I ever expected it could be. I had no idea that being with someone could be so incredible."

For a while, we lay tangled in each other as if we were the only two souls in the galaxy. I could hear the notes of the music in the ocean as he squeezed my hand. "Happy birthday, Cassie."

"Thank you. It certainly was one for the records."

Turning over onto his side, Xuan began tracing his fingers through the wet sand, creating intricate patterns and shapes. "In China, we have a saying—*yīwǎngqíngshēn*—which means to be deeply attached to a person." His fingers wrote Chinese symbols that I didn't recognize. "And then there is *sīshǒu zhōngshēng*, which means *to be together forever*."

Forever sounded nice. Perfect, actually. I knew that, without a speck of doubt, that I would love Xuan even when the world was nothing more than ash and whispers of dust between the stars. I never imagined the force of love would consume me, like a black hole.

Another wave crashed on barnacled rocks, parting around us. My entire body felt tired. I yawned. But no, I didn't want to give in to my exhaustion. Time was speeding up. This moment of perfection was slipping through my hands too fast. I wanted more of him. I wasn't ready for this night to be over.

"*Qīn'ài de,* no matter what happens tomorrow, and in the coming months, I will love you. My soul is so deeply connected to yours that I can no longer see any future or existence without you in it. Everyone is destined to return to dust and shadow, and one day even the sun will die from the depletion in hydrogen, but my love for you will never fade. It will go on forever. It will endure as the sun. And even after then, I will love you . . . across space and time and into my next life, I will search for you. I will always be looking for you. I will love you until my last breath, in any and all lifetimes to come."

I knew that one day I would die, that we were all doomed to oblivion. But I wasn't ready for that day to be near. I wasn't even ready to begin contemplating that possibility. My eyes gleamed as I reached over with my arm to grip his hand. "You'd better find your way back to me, because I'll be waiting."

"I *will* find you in the next life and every life after that. I promise."

"I'd rather you stay with me in this one."

"So would I, *qīn'ài de,*" he whispered and then reached for my hand. "Stay with me tonight." As if he knew exactly what I was thinking, he whispered in my ear, "My mom's gone for the entire weekend to Portland on business."

I agreed. I felt like Cinderella, running to escape the chime of midnight—or in this case the break of dawn and the coming sunrise, when Xuan would take his first dose of osimertinib. But the night wasn't over yet, not by a long shot. The stroke of twelve was still far off. However this clock was much different. Xuan's life depended on medicine, not some carriage that would turn into a pumpkin after the magic had faded.

Starlight stained our skin with muted silver as we dressed. The outline of our etched bodies in the wet sand slowly washed away with the tide. Two shadows, meshed into one, walked along the curved coastline toward the staircase that would lead to the parking lot and a new beginning.

Together.

CHAPTER TWENTY-TWO: THE VISITOR

Dominican Hospital, California
June 15, 2019

Mei drove Xuan to the cancer center for his follow-up appointment. Almost two weeks had passed since he'd started the pill, and he was already feeling the side effects. Mei had more questions about the drug, but she needed to head straight to work after the appointment. I knew I'd be finished with classes in time and offered to give Xuan a ride home.

Respecting their privacy, I'd been waiting in the cafeteria with my nose in Ayn Rand's *The Fountainhead* for the past half hour. The time following Xuan's lung cancer diagnosis seemed like a blur of confusion. More doctor appointments than I cared to count. Xuan spent a lot of his time on WeChat, talking to his family in China and Korea, who were fifteen hours ahead of us due to the difference in time zones. Our conversations with friends had also taken a heavy toll, as we navigated through difficult discussions about the reality of the situation. My mind was a whirlpool of information and tangled emotions, and it felt as though we had been thrust into a new world, filled with lurking monsters that we had never anticipated.

When I looked up from my book and saw the last person in the world I wanted to see standing there, in front of me, I snapped with harsh words. "I thought I was clear. I don't want to see you."

Raylan smiled. "I saw you sitting here alone and thought I'd come say hello."

"Hello. And now goodbye." *Stay away from me.*

Raylan took a seat across from me. "I thought about what you said at the beach last time I saw you, and I think you should reconsider."

"Absolutely not," I said, wholly focused on my task of reading.

He blew out an agitated breath "You don't even know what it is I'm referring to."

"It doesn't matter. I'm not interested in anything you have to say so please leave."

"I can't. Not yet."

"Can't or won't?"

"I still have a few things left to say to you. And then I'll go."

I closed my book, set my hands on the table, and interlaced my fingers. "Like what?"

"I came back here for you. I realized you were the best thing to ever happen to me, and I know what I did was wrong, but I've changed."

I couldn't believe he had the audacity, the ignorance, to say this to me. "I'm with Xuan. I told you before I've moved on. And from the look of things, you've done the same. Moved on with Gemma."

"Emma."

"Does it really matter? Gemma, Emma, who's next?"

"Did you miss me while I was away?" asked Raylan, completely off topic.

"Of course I did. I missed you a lot at first. I couldn't stop thinking about you when I first went to Colombia. But you broke my heart, Raylan. Things changed, and eventually I stopped missing you. I found distance made my heart grow stronger, indifferent."

"I know what I did," Raylan said quietly, his face pained. "I know I hurt you. It was wrong for me to push you. I knew you weren't ready, and I'm sorry."

"It doesn't matter anymore."

"You're right, it doesn't." Raylan's tall frame was still. "Cassie, I know you've moved on. I'm happy for you. In fact, I met him the other day."

I angled my head. "Care to explain that?"

"Your fiancé and I had a long heart-to-heart."

I opened my mouth and then shut it. Xuan hadn't said anything. This could just be a clever lie to get me to trust him.

"Do you love him?" asked Raylan.

"More than anything." Just the thought of him lit a spark of warmth in my heart.

"Is he good to you?"

"Xuan saved my life."

"Why? Because you were so broken and hurt after I left you?"

I let out a loud sigh. "No. Because of what happened in Colombia."

"What are you talking about?"

He didn't know. The fact my father hadn't told him didn't surprise me. "I was trapped in a mudslide, and he risked his life to save mine." Then I told him everything that had happened.

Shock spread across Raylan's face. "I'm sorry. I had no idea, Cass. No one ever said anything to me." He took a deep breath. "I should've been there when you needed me. It's my fault. If I hadn't joined the Army—"

My throat ached. "I don't blame you for joining the military, Raylan. I even promised you I would wait for you to come home. It was you who didn't want to wait for me. You were old enough to make the decision to go to war, and you were an adult when you decided to cheat on me because I wasn't ready to have sex. You needed more and you found someone who could give that to you."

"I was never in love with her."

"You were never in love with me either," I reminded him.

"I am in love with you, Cassie. I just realized it too late. And you can deny it all you want, but I know you felt the same way."

"I once thought I was in love with you. But what I felt then was not even an atom or fraction of the gravitational pull I feel for Xuan now. He is my isomorphism, my one and only. And there will never be anyone else." *Xuan is my beginning, middle, and end. No room for Raylan. Repeat to self as needed.*

His shoulders sagged. "I don't know what isomorphism

means, but I do know what I did, and I'm not here to seek your forgiveness. Scout's honor."

"I already forgave you, Raylan, long ago."

"You did? When?"

"I prayed for you when I thought I was going to die. I was trapped in the car, and I told Xuan that if I didn't make it to tell you I forgave you. I prayed that you could one day forgive your mother. You need to let go of your own past or you'll end up alone."

He paused for a drawn-out, too-tense minute. "Oh."

"Even though we're not together, I still want you to be happy."

"Happiness is not the same as forgiveness."

"You're right, it's not. But I did forgive you for everything that happened between us."

"You really did?" He seemed shocked. His eyes were empty as he asked, "Do I deserve it?"

No and yes. "I guess that's not for me to decide anymore."

"You were always the optimist."

I didn't know whether this comment was a good thing or not. As soon as Xuan and I returned home, my plan was to surrender to the living room sofa, like a dignified couch potato, while I attempted to process everything that had transpired these past few weeks, including this conversation. "Why are you even here at the hospital?" I asked. It didn't make sense that Raylan was here. People don't randomly show up to cancer clinics. It seemed a little too CIA operative or stalkerish that he would know where to find us.

He sighed. "I know what's going on. Nick told me. I'm sorry." There was something different about his voice, but I couldn't place it. He sounded detached. Maybe it was grief I was hearing, even though that didn't make sense and wasn't logical.

"You know what exactly?"

"I know about Xuan's cancer. Nick told me first, but Xuan confirmed it when I met him last week. He told me he was scheduled for treatment today, so I came to see him."

This caught my attention. His words opened up a floodgate of questions. Stunned and reeling, I leaned forward against the table for support. "You're here to see Xuan?"

"Yeah."

"Why did you even meet with my fiancé in the first place?"

"Your father asked me to."

We sat there in silence for a minute. I knew he was waiting for my reaction but I couldn't talk. I shook my head, my throat tightening to the point of pain, my eyes stinging. Finally I said, "You're an idiot."

"I've never claimed to be otherwise. I'm sure you already know he isn't too fond of the idea of you dating someone like him."

I should have seemed surprised but I wasn't. I used to worship my father like the Romans did the planets. I thought the world of him. But after I started dating Xuan my opinion of him changed.

"Like him?"

"Yes. But you have to know that until you said *fiancé* at the boardwalk, I had no idea you were engaged. You have to believe me. I would never have come back to Santa Cruz if I'd known you guys were getting married."

"Why should I believe you, Raylan?"

"Because your father only said you guys were dating and it was nothing serious."

Of course my father had conveniently left that part out, the fact that we were engaged, along with the fact that Xuan had risked his life to save me in Colombia. That felt like the ultimate betrayal. "So you thought it was okay to come back here, thinking I had a boyfriend, but me being engaged crosses the line?"

"I see them as separate. If you guys were just dating, then maybe I still stood a chance."

"You never stood a chance. Not against him," I declared, my voice steady and resolute. I locked eyes with him, a silent challenge passing between us. "I said yes to marrying someone who is not just good, kind, and honorable, but who completes me in a way no one else can. I am in love with Xuan. And I will marry him. With or without my father's consent."

"Why are you mad at me? This was your father's idea."

"So what exactly is it that my dear old dad doesn't like about Xuan? Is it because he's Asian?" I asked with a hint of temper again.

"You already know the answer to that question."

I didn't need confirmation. The words struck true even without his spelling it out. My father was locked into his prejudices. Any attempt to change his opinion of Xuan would be pointless—now or in the future. "So what are you, my father's lapdog?" I practically bit out each word. I knew I was being snarky toward him, but I couldn't help myself. "So you came here to try to break up my relationship, because my father *asked* you to?" In the back of my mind I knew I had just forgiven Raylan less than an hour ago for our history, and I should try to just let it go. But I was angry at him and my dad for conspiring to ruin my love life.

"I came because I wanted to. But he *is* my commanding officer, and I *do* have to obey him."

I could feel my jaw clench. *Coward.* "Go fetch." I rose from my chair and began to walk away. I tried to swallow down my nausea, disgust, and hatred. My father wasn't impressed by the announcement of our engagement in Italy, but I never thought he was capable of something like this.

"Cassie, wait!"

"Raylan, I don't even want to look at you right now. I had no idea you were this big of a coward."

"I'm not!"

"Yes, you are! You said you have to obey my father because he's ranked higher than you. But I'm pretty sure that doesn't mean you have to obey personal commands. You made the choice to listen to him, Raylan. This is on you too."

I'd forgotten that we weren't alone in the cafeteria until I heard some people chuckle as they watched us, clearly entertained. One couple laughed outright and others looked away, obviously embarrassed at our little drama display.

Raylan stood from the table, stretched out his freakishly long arm and grabbed my wrist. "Cassie, calm down. People are watching."

I didn't give a flying saucer if people were watching. He spoke in an authoritative way that made me want to tell him to shove it, and scream at the top of my lungs. My anger had boiled over at this point, but I was able to talk myself into enough composure not to yell. "Let go of my arm *now* or they're going to really get a scene."

"Cassie, just chill out!"

I felt my chest constrict as if a boa was wrapped around it, squeezing.

"Are you okay?" Raylan asked.

Does being thoroughly mortified by my father and ex-boyfriend's actions count as okay? "Raylan, the next time you touch me, or try to go near my fiancé, I won't hesitate."

"I'll let you go, just don't leave. Please." He immediately dropped his hand.

I relaxed just a little, even though I was anything but okay.

A few of the hospital staff stopped and looked over at us to see what was going on. If there wasn't such an audience, I probably would have slapped him.

"Cassie, I didn't come here to fight with you," he whispered, in an obvious attempt to avoid a further scene. "I wanted to see you and tell you I met Xuan the other day because I thought you should hear it from me. I came here to tell you that I didn't want to, but after a few rounds of drinks, I did end up liking him. He's funny and intelligent. And he isn't a wuss."

"Great. I'm so happy to have the approval of my ex-boyfriend. But that still doesn't answer my question. Why did you come to the hospital to see Xuan?"

Raylan held up a bag. "I brought him some magazines—you know, like an olive branch."

"Xuan's only here for a doctor's appointment."

"Oh. I thought he would have to stay overnight."

"No, not this time. It's just an in and out visit."

"I didn't know. I've never done this before, okay? I guess I'm really bad at this whole peace offering thing, but I wanted to come—to try."

"Raylan, I understand you were trying to be thoughtful. It was a nice gesture. But I really don't want you coming around him anymore. Cancer is stressful enough, and having my ex show up during Xuan's treatments will probably make things worse. I just want Xuan to focus on getting better. Please understand and leave us alone."

Raylan's face was suddenly serious again. "I know things must be difficult for you right now. But I want you to know I'm here for you if you need anything."

I weighed his expression and realized he meant it. "Thanks, but I think you're the last person on the planet I would ask for help," I said a little too sharply. Somehow, being near Raylan was bringing out the worst in me, and I hated it. I could easily chalk it up to stress and grief. *Or maybe my attitude toward him means I haven't really forgiven Raylan . . . or forgotten.* I wanted to radiate peace and sunshine, not spit fireballs like a Super Mario Brothers character.

"You're probably right, but the offer's there." He dropped his grip. "Before you storm off, I just want to say one more thing."

"I think you've said enough."

"Please."

I hesitated before cracking open a warning eye. "You have one minute."

"Cassie, we've been through a lot together and nothing will change that. I'm afraid that because of Xuan's diagnosis, you won't be able to smile again."

"I appreciate that, Raylan, really. But you lost the right to worry about those things a long time ago."

"I know that. But, Cassie, we have choices."

"Oh? And you think you're the right choice for me?"

"No. Well, maybe when—"

"Sorry, time's up. This conversation is over."

"But I want to be friends with you."

"But that's not what I want." That was the truth. Raylan had held my heart in his hands and destroyed it, like a clay pigeon being shot by a twelve-gauge shotgun. *Friends? No.* I had no intention of being friends with my ex, even if it had been years since we were together.

"Why? Your fiancé said he doesn't mind, not if it would make you happy. He said he trusted you and wanted whatever you did."

I had to turn away. I had no words for how angry I felt. How dare he talk to Xuan without me knowing? Burning Cosmos, I hated him. I hated my father. I even hated myself a little.

There were only two suitable options on how to respond—start shouting or walk away. I turned back and faced the tall figure of my past. To his country, this figure stood for honor, glory, and his call to duty. "Goodbye, Raylan." I didn't wait for him to answer before striding off. This was the second time I'd walked away from him. This time, he didn't follow.

Seabright, Santa Cruz, California
June 15, 2019

The blinds had been drawn to shut out the bright afternoon sunlight in Xuan's bedroom. Xuan lay curled in a fetal position on his bed, the blankets closed around him. I wanted to confront him about not telling me about Raylan, but he'd been withdrawn and depressed since returning from the hospital. So I held my feelings in and climbed into bed next to him. He was exhausted and wanted to sleep. I stayed there in the silence and listened to him breathe in and out, watching as the sunlight began to fade. I still couldn't believe that Raylan had somehow weaseled his way into Xuan's life, thanks to my father.

Xuan slept restlessly. I placed my palm against his chest, felt it rise and fall. I don't know how long I lay there, awake, staring at the ceiling, watching over him. Occasionally he called out to me, as if I was there inside his dream. "Cassie." My name was a rasp on his lips.

Just over two weeks had passed since Xuan began taking the pills, and the side effects were taking hold. We'd all been hopeful because osimertinib's side effects weren't supposed to be as strong as chemo. But still, Xuan had gotten sick. His back and muscles were also in pain. I'd watched him hover over the toilet for hours, puking his guts out over the weekend. I couldn't help but wonder if this was what the next few years would hold.

A loud knock resonated at the door. I gently removed Xuan's arm from my waist and nearly tumbled over the side of the bed. Before heading downstairs to see who it was, I hastily slipped on Xuan's sweatshirt, its fabric enveloping me in his familiar scent—a captivating blend of Dolce & Gabbana fused with a cedar-scented soap. I spotted a crumpled piece of paper on the floor by the trash can. Curious, I picked it up and then hurried downstairs to get the door. A UPS delivery waited.

I grabbed the package and almost a week's worth of mail from the mailbox on the porch.

The parcel had Xuan's name on it but there was a second name I didn't expect under the sender—it was from my father. I sat on the couch and turned it over and over again, wishing I knew what he'd sent Xuan. *What's my father up to? Hasn't he done enough by sending Raylan here?* Finally I placed the package on the coffee table. I continued to stare at it, not knowing what to think, and that made me nervous.

As I sifted through the mail, an odd postcard stood out. On the front was an American flag. The back contained a simple sentence: "*Return back to your country, Rat Eyes.*" The sender read *God.*

My stomach twisted. I felt an ache inside me grow in anger. Prejudice and hatred were poisonous and all-consuming, spreading like a cancer every day. *But who would do something like this?*

There was only one possible explanation, and the thought

wasn't comforting. Whoever the sender was, he probably knew Xuan. My initial thought was my ex. But that didn't make sense, even if he did want Xuan out of the picture. Raylan was many things, but he was not prejudiced or heartless. *Could it be another soldier boy in my father's fan club who was sent here?* Brett's name also crossed my mind, but there was no way to prove any of it.

I was at a crossroads as to what to do next. The question of the hour was *Should I show Xuan?* There was no threat that could be perceived as criminal, but this was a hate crime. My fiancé already had too much to worry about, and he wasn't feeling well. Still, I didn't know what to do.

I pulled out my phone and placed an order on Amazon for one of those porch cameras. But I couldn't stop thinking about the postcard. It made me feel dark inside.

As a distraction, I opened the paper I'd found in Xuan's room and began to read. The words sent a second punch of misery through my chest. In essence, it was a bucket list, often written by people with a terminal disease. That was a sobering wake-up call that Xuan wasn't going to be able to complete everything on his list in this lifetime.

My Life's Wishes and Regrets

Top Wish List
Get married
Be a father
Return to China one last time

Other Wishes/Regrets
~~Drink wine at the base of Mount Vesuvius and hike up the volcano~~
~~Visit the ruins of Pompeii and the Herculaneum~~
~~Gaze up at Michelangelo's paintings in the Sistine Chapel~~
~~Visit the Colosseum, the Roman Forum, and Palatine hill~~
~~Visit Positano and the Amalfi Coast~~
~~Take a tour of the catacombs and ride a bike on the Appian Way~~

~~*Eat pizza in Naples*~~
~~*Visit the Pantheon*~~
~~*Take a gondola ride in Venice*~~
~~*Eat gelato at nighttime at the Trevi Fountain and walk up the Spanish Steps*~~
~~*Drink wine in Tuscany and take a cooking lesson*~~
~~*Visit the Greek temples at Paestum and eat at a buffalo mozzarella farm*~~
~~*Propose to Cassie*~~
Skydive
Bungee jump
Cliff diving
Exotic car racing
Test drive a Ferrari
~~*Hike to the Hollywood sign*~~
Discover something
~~*Kayak through a cave*~~
Kayak Emerald Bay in South Lake Tahoe
Visit Burney Falls
~~*Invite a homeless person for a restaurant dinner*~~
~~*Join a disaster relief effort*~~
Invent a cocktail
Scuba dive in the Caribbean
~~*Pay off a stranger's Christmas layaway gifts*~~
Learn archery
~~*Swim with dolphins*~~
Fly in a hot-air balloon
Take Mom to drink wine at Buena Vista in Sonoma County
Make my own pasta
Ride an elephant in Thailand
~~*Raise $10,000 for a charity*~~
~~*Visit the Amazon rain forest in Colombia*~~
Make a difference in someone's life
Paraglide over the ocean
~~*Bring candy, stuffed animals, and games to hospitalized children*~~
Bike at Henry Cowell Redwoods State Park

Take a trip to Snaefellsjökull glacier in Iceland
~~*Walk the Great Wall of China*~~
~~*Meditate in the Temple of Heaven*~~
~~*Take black and white nature photos*~~
~~*Graduate with master's degree*~~
Graduate with my Ph.D.
~~*Eat an entirely plant-based diet for one month*~~
Visit the Terracotta Army
Fly a kite
Go to the Day of the Dead in Mexico
~~*Become fluent in English*~~
Take helicopter or flying lessons
Visit Petra, Jordan
Renovate Mom's garden
~~*Learn how to play an instrument*~~
Visit the K-T boundary
Visit the Buddhist ruins at Sri Lanka
~~*Swim under a waterfall*~~
Visit Machu Picchu and stand before the thirteen towers of Chankillo
Make Christmas cookies and drive around to look at lights in Scotts Valley
Help Cassie make amends with her father
Watch The Nutcracker ballet
~~*Learn how to code*~~
Adopt a family rescue pet with Cassie
Take Cassie to Tiananmen Square
Discover a new star or astronomical object
See coral spawning on the Great Barrier Reef
Write a love letter
~~*Learn to surf*~~
Spend New Year's in New York
~~*Visit Niagara Falls*~~
Dive with sharks
Learn a magic trick
~~*Visit Disneyland/Disney World*~~
Release a lantern at a lantern festival—or water lantern festival

Ride a Harley
Be an aid worker in a third-world country
Compete in an IRONMAN Triathlon
Make a short film
~~*Live in a foreign country and study abroad*~~
Visit the Taj Mahal
Learn to snowboard
Stay a night at an ice hotel
~~*Make an acrylic pour painting from a cup with Cassie*~~
Meet the Dalai Lama
~~*Go whale watching*~~
Dive under the ice sheets of Antarctica
~~*Carve Cassie's name and mine into a tree*~~
See the northern lights
~~*Stargaze in Yosemite*~~
White water raft
Visit Crater Lake, Oregon
Hike waterfalls in Oregon, including Multnomah Falls
Try kiteboarding in Hood River, Oregon
Hike/swim in blue pool, Oregon
Hike up the Newberry and Three Sisters volcanoes near Bend
See a NASA launch up close
~~*Explore a castle*~~
See the Compact Muon Solenoid at the Large Hadron Collider
Ride a camel in Egypt to Giza
~~*Make someone laugh during their chemotherapy session*~~
Sponsor a child
Win a Nobel Prize
See a comet again
Leave this world a better place
Set foot on all seven continents

My fingers were slick with salty tears that slipped down my cheeks.

"Cassie ... Cassie, where are you?" Xuan's voice sounded sleepy, hazy.

"I'll be right there!"

Despite my miserable mood, I stuffed the list in my pocket and grabbed the package before going back upstairs.

"Who's the box from?" Xuan asked curiously.

Is that a slight smile on his face? I stopped in the doorway just as Xuan began to cough. The sound was thick and mucousy, and it lasted for a while, unabated. I wanted to tell him about the postcard, but I couldn't find the right words. He still looked so tired and pale. In the end I don't know if I made the right choice, but I made the humane choice and buried the postcard in my bag, keeping it from Xuan for the moment. Some burdens were meant to be shared—others borne alone. I would stop by the police station first thing in the morning to see what they said and go from there.

"I think it's from my father." I reached down to give it to him. My hair swung forward as I bent over him. He reached up and tucked the lock behind my ear before taking the box. "Knowing him, it's probably explosives," I warned.

I felt inexpressibly weary as Xuan carefully opened the package. Neither of us knew what to expect from my father.

Xuan looked at me. "It's boxes of tea from the Middle East. The note says they help with nausea."

"It's probably tea from where he's currently stationed. That was unusually kind of him. Must be poison."

"Cassie, your father's a very honorable man. You two used to be very close."

I didn't dare peer inward to the angry, churning sea inside me at the mention of my father, the memory of our fight. Xuan was gentle, quiet, and kind. His was a different sort of strength, yes, but not what my father would've chosen for me. He didn't understand how I felt and why I'd chosen Xuan. "We were, until he disapproved of you," I said.

"He may not exactly earn the Father of the Year award, but he's still your father."

I thought back to the last fight I had with my father before he left to go overseas again. The argument seemed not so long ago. I remembered the harsh words.

"Cassie, I forbid it. You are going to stop seeing that Chinese boy!"

"His name is Xuan, and I think I'm in love with him."

"No."

"You don't even know him, Dad. Just give him a chance."

"I don't want to get to know him," said my father. "That boy came to our house when you were at class and asked for permission to date you. I didn't even know you'd been seeing him!" He bellowed angrily.

"What did you say to him?" I asked.

"I told him the truth. That he wasn't good enough to date my daughter. I told him I was worried about my daughter's future and I hoped he would be as well."

"That's why he decided to stop seeing me today. It's because of you," I whispered.

I could hear Xuan's words in the back of my mind. "We're from two different worlds, Cassie. We can't keep pretending it doesn't matter." I couldn't believe those cold, heartless words had come out of him. He had always been so sure. I reached for Xuan's hand, looked him in the eye, and said, "All of that – our differences – only matters if we let it." His response had been, "Your father will never accept me."

My father looked almost triumphant and I could tell he was relieved by this news.

"This is your fault!" I yelled. "I'm not one of your soldiers, Dad, and you have no right to interfere in my love life. I'm over eighteen, and I will date or love whomever I choose, with or without your consent."

My father's face was angry, and I could tell that I had hurt him.

"I can't agree to this," he said.

"I don't care," I replied. "Unlike Xuan, I'm not asking for your permission or approval." I got my keys and ran out the door to find Xuan. No one could break us apart, not even my father. And if Command Sergeant Major Steel couldn't accept that, then there would be no place for him in my life.

"Maybe you should forgive him," suggested Xuan. "No man

is ever good enough for a father's daughter. If we had a daughter, I would think the same way."

If only Xuan knew the extent of the fight, he would likely think differently.

Xuan rubbed his hand between my shoulder blades to try to comfort me just as my pocket began to vibrate.

It was a text from Roxy. *Hi, a bunch of us are going to the movies and dinner tonight. You two should come.*

I hurried to text back. *Thanks for the invite, but Xuan isn't feeling well. I'm going to stay with him tonight.*

I put my phone on silent. I'd been blowing off Roxy, Sky, and Amanda for a while. I could hang out with them anytime. Seeing my friends just didn't seem like a top priority right now.

"Who was that?" Xuan asked.

"Roxy."

"What did she want?"

"She just wanted to know how you were feeling." Another lie.

"That was nice of her."

"Yeah, it was."

"You should do something with her tomorrow."

"Maybe." But I had no intention of hanging out with Roxy. I had something else more important to think about. A plan was beginning to form in my mind as I reached into the pocket of my jeans and felt the crumpled paper with Xuan's last wishes inside my jeans. I didn't want to live with regret if something happened to Xuan. We couldn't waste any more time. We had to start living, as if each day was our last—together or apart. Roxy would still be alive in five or ten years. Xuan wouldn't be.

The mean-spirited, unpredictable cancer beast had changed all of our lives. There were unspoken details of our life before cancer. Now, only the stark reality of life after cancer remained. I was acutely aware that, regardless of the treatment's outcome, we were bound in a race against time. A relentless clock, damnably ticking away, measured the fleeting seconds of Xuan's life. Its insistent rhythm served as a reminder of our finite journey. Though it may have momentarily paused, the clock would invariably resume its steady wind down toward zero.

Chapter Twenty-Three: Coffee on Pacific Avenue

Seabright, Santa Cruz, California
July 4, 2019

The soft morning light filtered through the window, casting a warm and gentle glow in the room. With a tender voice, Xuan greeted me, "Good morning, beautiful."

"Morning," I responded sleepily.

This week marked a crucial turning point in Xuan's battle against cancer, a point of no return. Almost a month had gone by since he began treatment, and his body wasn't tolerating the wicked anti-cancer pills very well. "How are you feeling today?" I asked.

"Two point five on a one-to-ten scale. One is a zombie," he admitted with a chuckle.

"Better than yesterday, at least."

Mei and I formed a caregiving tag team, working in tandem to take turns at the house. For the past three weeks, I had spent the night at Xuan's place while Mei worked. However, during the day, Mei dedicated her time to being with her son, while I attended summer classes and completed my homework. Our lives became a delicate balancing act, and we were constantly juggling our schedules, even though Xuan insisted he was fine to stay home by himself.

Sometimes I'd walk in from a day of classes and see Mei and Xuan both sleeping. Or they would often do a Korean face mask together, which made me smile. I remembered doing something similar with Stella after my father was deployed, plastering a green mud mask on our faces and placing refrigerated cucumber slices on our eyes.

I sat up in bed and stretched. "Should I make us some breakfast?"

"Actually, before you get up, I thought you should know that Raylan stopped by. He brought us donut holes." He held a white bag.

"Suck-up."

Xuan smiled. "Honestly I think he's a little afraid of you and that right hook."

"Good."

Raylan had made it a habit to stop by the house a couple of times when I was at school. They seemed to get along. I guess it was good Xuan had another guy friend, even though it was Raylan. "Is he still here?"

"Yeah. I'm teaching him to play League of Legends on the computer."

"Okay. I'll stay out of the way of cyberworld. I have an essay due by midnight, so I can head back home and work on that."

"You don't have to leave just because he's here. Stay."

"Fine. A cup of joe from the kitchen and then I'm on it upstairs."

Two hours had passed before I found myself back in the kitchen, craving another cup of coffee. The moment the boys caught sight of me, their voices hushed into silence, piquing my skepticism. "What's going on?" I asked, unable to ignore the mischievous grins adorning their faces. "You two have the same guilty expression as a pair of kids trying to keep a secret." There was no doubt in my mind that they were up to something.

"Raylan and you are going out this afternoon. I've asked him to take you."

"Absolutely not," I said in protest.

Sadness seemed to flicker in Raylan's eyes, but he said nothing. He was like a gigantic beanstalk as he stood towering over the couch, wearing the size thirteen house slippers Mei had purchase just for him, since the guest ones didn't fit.

"You need to. It would be good for you to get out of here for a few hours," Xuan insisted.

"I haven't left because I'm busy with school."

"It's more than that and you know it. Your friends have all invited you places and you haven't seen any of them since I started taking that stupid pill."

Xuan had told me several times to get out and do something over the weekends. The only time I had left his house was to go to school, the library, one of Xuan's appointments, or home to shower and grab more clothes. Amanda had invited me to dinner, and Roxy and Sky had invited me to a movie. But the idea of watching others live life seemed too long and too painful. And I couldn't stomach dinner. My friends must have switched tactics and begun texting him to extend the invitation, keeping him in the loop.

"This is where I want to be," I said stubbornly.

"Go out with Raylan. Just for an hour."

I exchanged a bewildered look with Xuan. I didn't detect a hint of subconscious jealousy, perhaps because he knew Raylan, my past high school sweetheart, was just that—my past. But it was still weird for him to suggest I hang out with my ex.

When I didn't answer, Raylan began to urge me to go. "Cass, let's go get a late lunch. I promise you, I'll be the perfect gentleman."

I arched an eyebrow in response. "What for?"

"Because I'm hungry and need to eat something."

"Hmmmm," I said. "But I'm not."

"Coffee, then? Or a Jamba Juice?"

I fixed my burning stare on Raylan. "Why?" I realized he was not going to give up. I couldn't help but think he was up to something.

"You should go," Xuan pressed before Raylan could try to offer a dignified response. "For me." He laid a hand on my stiff shoulder, drawing my attention from where I watched Raylan with catlike eyes.

Not on my wish list. "Raylan, can you excuse us for a moment? I need to talk to my fiancé. Alone."

He straightened up. His face had gone tight-jawed. He seemed disappointed but was trying not to show it. "Sure. I'll go check out the backyard. Xuan was telling me about his landscaping ideas."

"Thanks." I waited for Raylan to grab his shoes and exit before eyeing Xuan. "I don't want to hang out with him." I tried to keep my voice steady, but it was nearly impossible. "My father sent him here to try to break us up."

"I know. Raylan told me everything."

"So why are you telling me to go?"

"Because he's sorry."

"And that means he earns your forgiveness? Or mine?"

"I know you both have a history. But he's here, trying to apologize to you. Just give him a chance."

"Xuan, I think he's still in love with me."

"Of course he is."

"And that doesn't bother you?" I asked.

"Not at all. You're my girl and I trust you completely, Cassie. I would never doubt you. And I think you need this. For closure. Forgiveness will bring you peace."

"Do you trust him?"

"It's not *him* I trust. It's *you*."

Ah, so I'm right. The trust factor is real. Most guys would be jealous and overly protective in situations like this. But not Xuan. He knew I would never do anything to hurt him or betray his trust, and I knew he would also never cheat on me. I'd learned that broken trust was like a small piece of chocolate. If you put it in your pocket, the chocolate would melt and become messy. If you tried to put the chocolate in the fridge, it could possibly be saved to eat later, but the shape would never return to its original form. What I had with Xuan was refreshing, even though I'd withheld the truth from him about the hate mail and the extent of my argument with my father.

"Cassie, I don't blame him for his feelings toward you. Just like I predicted three years ago in Colombia, Raylan finally realized what he lost. I'm just thankful he was there to protect you at the beach that night when I couldn't be. You didn't tell me about Brett and Ashley. You could've been hurt. I can tell by that behavior he's a good guy."

Ah, maybe that's what this is about. Xuan wasn't there to protect me. He was sick that night and couldn't defend me at the boardwalk. Nobody wants to be sick, to die young. He trusts me, loves me, wants to keep me safe.

"I took care of myself," I said stubbornly.

"You did. And so can I for a few hours." From the determination in his voice, I knew he'd already calculated all my creative possible retorts and excuses.

"I don't want to leave you."

"I'll be fine," he promised. "You can't always be here to take care of me. I'm going to get sick—a lot worse. You're going to have to accept that. You can't stop living because of me."

"I know that."

"Just try to have fun, Cassie."

I rolled my eyes, but I knew he'd just won the argument. I didn't want to go with Raylan, but there was nothing I wouldn't do for Xuan. We were bonded. I knew there was no need to fall into a trap of worrying about Raylan breaking us up. "Fine, but just coffee. I have a lot of work to do and I could use the caffeine."

Xuan kissed me and then left to let the Army dog back in. He seemed ecstatic about the news. Coffee was going to be oh-so awkward but maybe I could finally get a few straight answers out of Raylan.

For several heartbeats, I just stared at my ex. "I have a lot of work to finish for school. I can't be gone for long. I can spare an hour, at most."

"Well, I wasn't planning a trip to the amusement park."

Oh, if looks could kill. I glared at him, reminding him he just got what he wanted so it would be a good idea to keep mum.

"Sorry, that was a joke," said Raylan. "Agreed. One coffee."

"Agreed," said Xuan.

"Meet me at 4:30 at Verve Coffee on Pacific Avenue," I said to Raylan.

Raylan nodded and then patted Xuan on the arm before grabbing his computer and keys to leave. He hurried to change back into his shoes and then placed the slippers Mei had given him in the foyer shoe organizer.

"I trust you." Xuan ran his fingers over the scar on my wrist from Colombia. "Go home and get ready. I'm not going anywhere."

"Fine," I grumbled.

Xuan handed me my favorite pair of khaki Birkenstock sandals. "Enjoy your not-fighting," Xuan crooned. His amusement was apparent.

I felt guilty about leaving Xuan in order to hang out and have coffee, even though it was his idea. The situation just felt so weird. I felt as if there was a wall growing between Xuan's world of cancer and doctors and my own. Cancer made us live in two separate worlds, despite the fact we were both suffering and feeling the full weight of his diagnosis.

Verve Coffee on Pacific Avenue
July 4, 2019

I followed the hostess through the mom-and-pop shop decorated in driftwood and colorful paintings by my favorite contemporary artist, Elliott Bliss. Elliott is a Santa Cruz local. His craft is painting, but he's also noted for his designs using pens. He'd been featured on *RAW Natural Born Artist* and *Santa Cruz Local.* Elliott is known for his visual art pieces inspired by local Santa Cruz spots and the Bay area and he has some really cool murals around the city. He often paints people and nature, such as the forest and ocean. I bought his painting of the SC Lighthouse a couple of years ago and hung it in my bedroom. I even had one of his greyscales of the seascape, and a custom piece that he did for me on the redwoods. I like to follow him on social media to see his new designs. I'm always in the market for a new piece of art.

The café was full. People lined the bar, waiting for the barista to hand them their orders. I chose a table outside and immediately pulled out my phone to check the time. I found myself searching for Bay Area schedules announcing parades, fireworks, concerts, watermelon-eating contests, and all manner of quintessential American fun as I waited . . . and waited.

But I was not in the festive spirit. In fact, my mood was now as sour as lees in wine. When I went home to change, I'd discovered a second postcard. This one had been delivered to my house, which was a small mercy. The front was titled *Natural Color* and was a picture of newly fallen snow. On the back, the racial message was full of undiluted venom that was not worth repeating. *God's blizzard* was the sender. Again, there was no proof of who had sent the letter. Anyone could hate or send mail. But the fact the aggressor knew both our home addresses was hard to ignore, and made me even more agitated as I sat and waited for my ex.

Reluctantly, I had agreed to coffee because I'd get my caffeine fix and our little soiree would be brief. However, coffee was only brief when a person was not late. Personally, I decided I'd rather be stung by a swarm of jellyfish than be here.

Raylan was twenty-three minutes late. So by the time he pulled up on his motorcycle, I was more than irritated. Being late was not unusual for Raylan. Lateness had always been one of his least charming traits. *I should've gone with the Jamba Juice option.*

Raylan reminded me of a twenty-first-century James Dean knockoff as he walked toward the outdoor table I was seated at. He was wearing all black and leather. How he was wearing leather and a jacket in July was beyond me.

He seemed to be trying to decide where to sit. He settled on the seat across from me, where we fell into an uncomfortable silence for about a minute. "Why do you look so gloomy?" he finally asked, as if he didn't know the answer.

"What?"

"You look unhappy to be here, ma'am," he said.

"This wasn't exactly my idea. And don't call me ma'am."

His shoulders shrugged, but his eyes didn't. "Should I call you Professor Steel instead? Or *my* sexy teacher?"

"No. I'm not a teacher yet and I'm not *your* teacher. Or *your* anything for that matter."

"Always so hostile. Did you know that anger is really just redirected sexual attraction?"

"What? Who told you that?"

"My therapist."

"Wonderful. And with remarks like that, how could you possibly wonder why I feel uneasy about being here with you, Raylan?"

"That was a joke."

"Saints, Raylan. It wasn't funny."

He casually shrugged off his jacket, and in doing so, he unveiled his inked arms. Raylan's tattoos appeared more pronounced than ever, as if he had recently added a few new masterpieces to his ever-growing collection. He was wearing his normally tight-fitting clothes, a simple black short-sleeved shirt and jeans. I hardly ever saw him in anything but black shirts—a Johnny Cash thing, I thought—but it wasn't my intention to analyze his attire. He was history. *I won't let him back into my heart. Not a chance. Keep my distance.*

"Maybe you should go page your shrink. You probably need to have a discussion about having coffee with your ex and making inappropriate comments about sexual attraction."

"You don't want to have coffee with me?"

Ding, ding, ding. Ladies and gentlemen, we have a winner! "I'm not thrilled to be here," I affirmed. Maybe he would take my directness as a sign to give up. "And if you weren't late, we would have already gotten coffee and gone our separate ways by now."

"You can leave. I'm not forcing you to be here."

"I'm not doing this for you. I'm here for Xuan." I let out a deep sigh of remorse. "Sorry. That was rude of me. I just have a lot going on. I wasn't expecting to leave Xuan today, especially to go have coffee with you."

"Gotcha. But Cassie, maybe you should try to be more positive. *I'm* trying to be. What was it you used to say? Positive like a proton?"

"I'm glad you're so buoyant. When your fiancée or future wife becomes ill, or is diagnosed with cancer, you can call me and tell me how weightless you feel. I'll even buy you a cup of java for old times' sake."

"I've been around death, Cassie." From the gleam in his expressive eyes and the frown that tugged on his mouth, I knew he was telling the truth. "I've lost five men and two women in the field. And I lost someone important to me. That loss nearly killed me."

"Death is different when it's someone you love."

"I may not have been in love with any of the people who died, but they were my brothers and sisters in uniform."

I didn't dare to ask about whom he'd lost. "Sorry, Raylan. I just wish I could make things easier for him. The other day, I found a list he'd made—a bucket list of things he wanted to do before he . . . . he's gone."

A careful nod. "Dying's like that. It takes a while to decide how to deal with everything it brings. He's trying to decide how he wants to spend his remaining time. What he wants. The costs."

"Even though there are a lot of things that have been checked off, there are still so many left. I don't see it as possible to complete them all."

"It's a cool idea, like in the movie. I've had a lot of friends in the military start one. Give me an example of one from his list."

"Ride a camel in Egypt and visit the pyramids."

"That would be cool. Are there others on the list that are easier to do, or that you can do in Cali or near here?"

"There are some around here. And there are a few up in the Pacific Northwest, near Oregon and Washington." I recalled some from the list.

White water raft
Visit Crater Lake, Oregon
Hike waterfalls in Oregon, including Multnomah Falls
Try kiteboarding in Hood River, Oregon
Hike/swim in Blue Pool, Oregon
Hike up the Newberry and Three Sisters volcanoes near Bend.

"Those seem more doable. Everyone should make a list like that. Start with the ones that are easier, that you know he can accomplish, and do as many of those as you can. Who knows? It could make you both happier."

The server came by to take our order. I asked for a Dead Eye—a cup of American-style drip coffee with three shots of espresso—and requested our order to go.

"What will you be having, handsome?" The waitress winked at Raylan.

"A large coffee, ma'am. Black, like my dark and tormented soul."

His comment wasn't funny, but the server let out a flirtatious laugh, faker than her orange spray tan, and rushed the order to the barista. She hurried to bring the order back to our table, despite the crowd inside. I suspected the girl had written her phone number on his cup of coffee. When she left to tend to other customers, I turned his cup slightly. Sure enough, there was a number written in bubbly pen across the side of his java cup, followed by a heart. For all the girl knew, we were together. But she still tried to flirt with him and tried to sneak him her number. And she wasn't the only one paying attention to him.

"Those girls are staring at you," I pointed out.

"I guess they can't help finding me stunningly attractive."

I rolled my eyes. "Wow, still conceited, I see. Ever heard of modesty being an appealing trait?" He was definitely not Xuan.

Raylan took no notice of the girls staring at him. "I am *not* full of myself, and I've *never* competed for any woman's attention."

"You're like the male version of Kylie Jenner or Paris Hilton. How are you and Xuan even friends? You're complete opposites."

"You're right, we are. But Xuan's a good guy. And I want us to be even better friends. I know he isn't going to live long, but I think it's important we all try to be in high spirits and optimistic as long as he's around."

"I've known you for years, Mr. Dark and Gloomy. You've never been an optimist. You're kind of like a vampire out of a fantasy novel."

"Do I have superpowers?"

I rolled my eyes again. "No, you're more like Lestat de Lioncourt from *Interview with the Vampire*."

"How so?" he asked.

"Read it, Einstein."

"You know I hate reading. Just tell me."

"Okay. You're afraid of being alone. You lure women to you during twilight hours. Then you seduce them before you drain the life out of them and kill them." Vampire Raylan suited him.

"You always say the most charming things to me." He took a sip of his coffee.

"My blunt honesty was one of the many reasons you liked me back in high school, before you joined the military."

"I always found your personality and honesty refreshing. You've never been like other girls. You deserved better back then. And I know I already said this to you at the hospital, but I'm sorry. I should never have left you."

"So why did you really become a soldier? You never gave me a straight answer when we were dating."

"Cassie, why dredge the past?"

"I'm just curious. You're the one who won't let it rest."

"Fine. It was actually your father who inspired me to join the military. He taught me that serving my country isn't just a job, it's a calling. And it's not for everyone."

"See? Was that so hard to answer?" I asked.

"I guess not. That was a long time ago. I just don't see why it's important anymore."

"So how did my father get his claws sunk into you?"

"He saved my life. Your father's a hero."

"What? How?"

"I can't really talk about it. It's classified."

I wanted to push, but I knew I couldn't. "Do you ever regret becoming a soldier? Sometimes I think my father may have pushed you into joining."

He seemed to relax a little at this question and the change in topic. "For me, signing up was easy right after high school because they offered to pay for my education and I received a monthly salary. I felt that I was protecting people—making a difference. The challenge for me was to say goodbye to my baby brother, Nick, and you. I hated leaving him there with my mom and dad, but it was for the best."

"How are your parents?" I asked.

"I don't want to talk about them either."

"You're the one who brought me here to talk. It's a simple question, especially since you seem so close to mine."

"Your idea of simplicity is my version of pure torture. You know I don't like to talk about my family. But fine," he caved. "My father is still a drunk, good-for-nothing d-bag living on the streets. And my mother killed herself from a heroin overdose last year while I was in Iraq. The money I sent home for the burial was pissed away on hookers and booze by my uncle and anger-driven father. Nick didn't have the heart to tell me until after I returned. I'm not even sure our other brother knows."

"Really?"

"I haven't spoken to Jace in years. He pretty much abandoned our family as soon as he turned eighteen and was able to sign up for the Marines."

"I'm so sorry, Raylan." Something told me Raylan had enough demons to bear so I backed off . . . sort of. But I tried another tactic. "Nick seems to be doing okay for himself."

"My youngest brother became a cop and Jace and I became soldiers because we were all trying to deal with our past in some way. Nick told me on his birthday that he's been considering going into the military so he can afford school. He wants to go into pharmacy school, but it's very expensive. Your father thinks it's a good idea. He's talked to a few people about Nick."

"You seem closer to my father than I am. My mom and I are lucky if he'll even call home once a month."

"Command Sergeant Major Steel was always more of a father to me than my own. He inspired me. But Cassie, you know he's—"

"He's what?"

"He doesn't believe his daughter should be in a romantic relationship with a man from a different race. Maybe it's the way he was raised. I don't know."

I clenched my jaw and ignored that last comment. My father loved all of the men and women who served with him, but that didn't mean my father wanted me to marry just anyone. Ever since I was in high school, he'd made it clear what he expected his future son-in-law to be like—down to his skin color and military uniform.

When it comes to me, my father is a closet racist—I knew it. Raylan knows it. Xuan must sense it. Why am I shocked? Inhale. Exhale. Will he ever change his mind? I can only wish for my dad to lose the tunnel vision, to see what I see.

"Raylan, why did you become friends with Xuan?"

"At first, I did it as a favor to your father. I wanted to know that you ended up with a decent guy, so I asked Xuan out for a round of drinks. But the more I got to know him, the more I realized how much I genuinely liked him. I'm happy Xuan found you and loved you when I couldn't, and I'm sorry you have to go through all of this now. Being with Xuan, you always come first to him. Still do, even through cancer. That's the way you deserve to be loved. I could've never given you that. I may not believe in happily ever after, but you both deserve so much more."

Silence fell between us. There were no words left to say.

"Raylan, thank you for today. I think we've both matured. I really needed this. Needed to clear the air."

"Did you just say thank you? How did those words taste in your mouth?"

"Like vinegar."

"Can I ask you why you hate me so much?"

I found myself saying quietly, "I don't hate you."

He nodded and crossed his arms. "But you're always mad at me. Why?"

I blew out a breath. "I'm not."

"You are."

"I am not!" I yelled louder than I meant to. A couple of girls turned to look at our table. "I'm sorry if it seems that I'm angry toward you, but a lot of that anger is from what's going on with Xuan."

"Then why are you always so unreceptive toward me?"

"Our history," I admitted. "But if you genuinely like Xuan and want to be friends with him, I get it. Understand, though, that I *am* committed to him."

"I know that. I've seen it in both your eyes."

"If you're not going to try to break us apart like my father wanted, then maybe we can try to be friends. *Maybe.* No promises."

He seemed to perk up in delight. "How long can you stay?" he asked.

"Not much longer. Maybe next time you won't be late."

"Next time?"

"As long as Xuan's okay with it." I knew he probably would be. After all, he's the one who threw us together in this petri dish-like experiment. But so far the results were inconclusive. I wanted to take a while to test out this hypothesis.

"I think your fiancé and I reached an understanding. I told him the truth."

"Which is what, exactly?"

"When I returned home from basic and saw my family, I realized I had to let you go. Coming back home was like looking through a window, observing a life I used to know. Those few months away had transformed me in ways I couldn't fully grasp. It was as if I had gained a fresh perspective on life. I realized that I could never be with you, so I cheated on you. I did it so you would let me go and move on because you deserved better. I cared about you more than anything—and I still do, but we were always very different. You were the best person I knew. Being with me would have changed you, without meaning to, just like my father ruined his entire family. My mother's dead because of him—I refuse to do that to you. There were dark times when I was overseas, times that made me think I was more like my father than I ever realized. The only thing that got me through was thinking about you. You've always been an inspiration to me, and I want you to know that I never stopped caring about you. Never. But the worst thing you could ever have done was to end up being with me. I'm just happy that you moved on and you've found someone to give you the stars. You belong with Xuan, not me. I would have destroyed you, Cassie. You got your prince. As for me, I was always more of a slimy swamp toad."

His words sounded like one of those breakup lines—"It's not you. It's me." Somehow, in Raylan's twisted mind, that must've made sense. But there was no point in trying to dissect the situation anymore. Instead of anger, I felt consolation for finally hearing the truth. I was *not* the same fragile, brokenhearted girl I was in high school. Instead I was able to find amity with our past, just as Xuan had wanted. Somehow he'd known that I needed this.

"Well so much for to-go coffees, huh? We didn't go."

We continued talking about lighter topics until we finished our second cup of coffee. My father's orders were aborted and the hatchet was officially buried. Did I still hate him? Yes and no. I hadn't forgotten any of the terrible things he'd done to me, but that didn't mean I couldn't try and give him the benefit of the doubt just this once. I wouldn't call us friends, not yet. But that day we managed to form a rudimentary alliance. So the answer to the question I posed was no then. I didn't hate him. At least not entirely. That day I finally got to see the vulnerable side of Raylan. And even though I didn't agree with his choices, I was able to understand him better. Maybe—and that was a big maybe—there was even a chance we could be friends someday.

Seabright, Santa Cruz, California
July 4, 2019

Xuan was in bed when we got back to the house.

"Well, how was it?" Xuan asked.

"Close to torture, just like I predicted." I walked up to him and kissed him.

"You came back alive, so at least you two didn't kill each other." Xuan smiled. "Did you guys at least bring me a coffee or a pastry?"

"I brought something even better," said Raylan. He pulled up a chair and sat next to Xuan's bedside. He took out a new deck of cards and began to deal.

"You know, Raylan, I like you, but cards are not nearly as appetizing or satisfying as food. Especially when you're being starved to death from all the puking."

"What happened to the donuts I brought you this morning?"

"They're in my stomach—or were."

"I'll surprise you next time," promised Raylan.

"Bring me another dozen donut holes, or a churro from the boardwalk, and you'll be forgiven."

I shook my head sternly. "Xuan, you know that fried foods are likely to make you sick. You're not supposed to eat a lot of added sugar."

"I've been throwing up no matter what I eat, so I might as well eat something I enjoy."

"Maybe Mei can make you steamed dumplings," I suggested.

"Dude, call me on dumpling day and I'll be here!"

"I will ... but only if you bring me something sweet next time."

Unceremoniously, I walked over and grabbed my book and computer from the chair and a blanket near my backpack. I slumped onto one of the oversized cushioned chairs on the opposite side of Raylan and began to read the assigned text for school. The room was a little noisy, but I didn't mind the distraction.

"Speaking of good food, what about good exercise?" asked Raylan. "My brother and I are going on a three-week trip in September to Oregon to stretch our legs in nature. We decided to drive and hit the waterfalls—Crater Lake and Silver Falls, and then Multnomah Falls after a stop in Portland. We may even head up to Hood River. Want to come?" Raylan smirked and clapped Xuan on the shoulder. "This is strictly a guys-only trip."

Xuan's eyes beamed, filled with yearning. "I . . . I don't know if I can. I *want* to go. That's on my list of things I want to do. But I don't know when I'll have to do appointments and tests," he said gravely.

My spine stiffened slightly. Not at the words but at Xuan, and the sadness I knew he must have felt. I'd seen him at the top of his game in Colombia. Then, like a soldier, he was forced to face an enemy that was sneaky and frightening. One that could take him out any minute, hour, day, month, or year.

"If you want to go, we'll work around your schedule," replied Raylan.

Xuan said nothing for a minute as he processed the offer. He then mastered the strain and longing in his voice enough to say, "Thank you. But you and Nick have plans. I don't want to ruin them." He sighed.

Raylan's cobalt eyes held Xuan's for a moment, his hand gently resting on his shoulder. He reassured him that he understood, and I found myself believing him, especially after our coffee outing. Raylan might not be an angel, far from it, but he was trying to do something nice for Xuan, because of the bucket list I'd shared with him earlier.

Raylan and Xuan played California Speed and Jiǎn Hóng Diǎn, which in English was translated as "Pick Up Red Spots." The sound of *Avengers: Endgame* played in the background on the TV screen. Even though not everything was perfect, I felt content. Raylan wasn't there to cause a problem in our relationship, as my father had ultimately hoped for. I prayed I was right about that.

For Xuan, having a friend like Raylan to spend time with brought him happiness and companionship. It made me realize the value of cherishing even the smallest and seemingly insignificant moments. Those ordinary occasions, the shared laughter, and the simple adventures would be the ones he'd likely treasure the most in the long run. I couldn't help but revisit Xuan's wish list, and memories flooded in of the inspiring stories I had heard about children with terminal illnesses who had the opportunity to experience the enchantment of Disneyland or meet their cherished idols. I wanted to transform Xuan's dreams into tangible moments. I understood that it wasn't in my power to cure Xuan, but what I wanted more than anything was to grant him his last wishes. Sure, the pills with side effects would gain him months, maybe years, but he was still dying. He'd told Raylan he couldn't go, but why in hell shouldn't he travel? That would be good medicine.

"Xuan, I think you should go to Oregon with the guys."

"But my doctors—"

"Will still be here when you get back. Go. Fly back if you need to meet with them or if you're not feeling well."

"I want to, but it's not just that."

"Then what is it?"

"I don't want to weigh anyone else down with my cancer and treatments. I don't want anyone to make sacrifices because of me. I don't know how I'm going to feel."

"It's not a sacrifice. You're our bro and we want to go on this trip with you. If we have to drop you off at an airport, we will. But hopefully that won't happen."

Raylan's kindness stunned me in a way I hadn't expected.

Xuan turned to him. "I'd really like to go. I may just have to fly back here for a day and then return. I'll talk to my doctor."

Cards in hand, Raylan threw Xuan a grin from across the table. "We'll make it work. We're flexible. We can leave in August or September. So when you're ready, call us and Nick and I will come over to plan out everything."

That was a good lie. Raylan and Nick hadn't planned a road trip, and it would probably be hard for Nick to take that long off from his job at the police station. He was doing this for Xuan, because I'd told him some of the things Xuan had put on his bucket list. And that meant more to me than Raylan would ever know. He was a good man, though maybe not a great boyfriend. *Redemption?* I contemplated. Sometimes people rise above their past, sometimes not. And sometimes the people you least expect it from—like Raylan and my father—have a way of surprising you in the end.

Chapter Twenty-Four: When September Ends

Natural Bridges State Beach, California
September 24, 2019

I *watched as Xuan's lifeless body was placed into a freshly dug hole in the ground, surrounded by a meadow. The town beyond looked different, old.*

Terrified, I suddenly woke up and immediately reached for Xuan. But he wasn't there. I curled my body into my piled-up bohemian style duvet, which had bold blues, rich reds, and gold oranges, with white detailing and multi-print patterns. The vibrant earthy colors made my room look like a Gypsy or hippie room. I tried to snuggle even deeper into five large pillows that were strategically placed around my head and body for comfort. *What can I say, I really like pillows and soft things.*

Pulling my duvet cover over my head, I took a few soothing breaths. That nightmare wasn't the first, nor would it be the last. I'd been plagued with bad dreams over the past few months, ever since Xuan was diagnosed with lung cancer, but the previous night was the first time I'd seen his grave. Saints, I couldn't stop seeing it—his death.

Xuan had just returned from his guys' trip to Oregon and Washington. They left on the twenty-second of August and returned on the sixteenth of September. Nick wasn't able to stay the entire trip because of work, so Beom flew out and took his place. They camped several nights, but they also stayed in hotels to let Xuan rest and stay warm. Xuan had caught a cold and hadn't been well enough for visitors, not even me. He was on strict bed rest. The trip had taken a lot out of him. He was still recovering almost a week later.

The entire time Xuan was away, I missed him. But I knew I didn't have the right to be selfish with him, even though our time together was limited. It was important for him to have time with friends, check off items from his bucket list, and explore the beauty the Pacific Northwest had to offer. Xuan wasn't aware I had seen his list. Raylan, Nick, and Beom had wittingly helped check off six items on his list in that short period of time.

I stayed with Stella while he was away. She liked the company. I'd been moving between the two houses since Xuan's diagnosis—something we didn't do before he was sick. We had both wanted to wait to move in with each other until we were married. Cancer changed that. His illness made me feel afraid, as if something was going to happen to him when I wasn't there, so most nights I would stay with Xuan and be there as much as I could for the time that remained.

Five more hate letters had been delivered during this time—three to my house, two to Xuan's house. Mei had called me to tell me about the letter she found during Xuan's absence. It was almost too much for her.

The cameras from Amazon I'd had Xuan install picked up an old Honda Civic as it made a sloppy three-point turn and stopped in front of the house—no taillights. A figure in a black hood jumped out and ran up to the mailbox, but it was too dark to make out much else. The figure turned and took off up the drive, spewing gravel. We went to the police station with the mail and the video. Mei didn't want to ruin Xuan's trip so she decided it was best to keep it from him.

More nightmares had haunted me nightly since the hate mail was delivered. They didn't stop even after Xuan returned. One night I even dreamed there was someone at my window. But when I woke up and looked outside, there was no one there. It was hard to shake that feeling of being watched, so I'd taken up running as a way to relieve my anxiety. I wasn't the type of person that liked to medicate my feelings. Rather, I craved all the happy endorphins my body could produce right then.

The memory of this last dream stayed with me, refusing to let me sleep. The initial tightness and panic had eased, but sleep remained elusive. After a while, I decided it was futile to lie in bed any longer. I threw on a pair of yoga pants and a thick hoodie before jumping in my jeep and heading to the beach. My iPhone wouldn't connect to my jeep because the auxiliary cord had stopped working, so I tried to find a radio station. Instead of music, the airwaves were abuzz with news about the ongoing impeachment inquiry against the president. Changing the channel, I tuned into NPR and listened intently to the updates on the Hong Kong protests that had erupted in June. The radio echoed with reports of hundreds of thousands of people flooding the streets, united in their opposition to the extradition bill.

By the time I arrived at the Natural Bridges State Beach, an icy wind had picked up. Thankfully, finding parking wasn't an issue, but that was because it was still early. The landscape was shrouded in a thick veil of clouds, indicating that they would persist for some time. The unmistakable signs of autumn were evident as a crisp and biting cold permeated the air, and my breath curled in front of me like a lizard's tongue. Despite the gust of frigid air off the water, I didn't want to go back home.

I set off at a brisk jog, the rhythmic pounding of my footsteps echoing in the quietness of the morning. Despite the warmth provided by my thick sweatshirt, the damp cold managed to seep through the fabric, chilling me to the bone.

I headed east of the beach and passed Moore Creek, which flowed through the area, forming freshwater wetlands and a salt marsh before it reached the sea. The loneliness I felt during the past night's dream swooped back so easily—its familiar, heavy weight pressed down on my shoulders like an extra twenty-five-pound dumbbell. Pushing through the fatigue that had settled in my muscles, I decided to increase my pace. I was willing to accept the burden that came with knowing that one day I'd wake up and my nightmare would be reality. I knew I was going to have to watch Xuan die.

Nine miles in, I paused to rest a few minutes and catch my breath before I set off again toward a different area where I was going to meet Xuan. The burning in my legs was painful, but the pain felt so good and took away the nightmares. So I kept going, and going.

By the time I reached the cliffs, I was gasping for breath, my head throbbing with each beat of my heart. My sweat turned cold as soon as I stopped jogging, causing an involuntary shiver to run through my body. I gazed out at the wind-whipped waves, their crests crashing against the shore, while the stubborn clouds engaged in a battle with the struggling sun. Despite the sun's valiant efforts, the persistent chill in the air dissuaded any hopes of warmth. It was still too cold for Xuan, and I couldn't take the risk of him getting sick again. With a shiver, I reached for my phone, and checked the weather forecast for the upcoming days. The ocean temperatures were projected to drop starting in October, and the realization hit me hard—I couldn't wait until next year to bring him. None of us could predict how Xuan would feel a year from now, and it became clear that this was a now-or-possibly-never situation.

Pulling up the seven-day report, I realized that postponing our plans was necessary. I quickly composed a text message to Xuan, conveying the change of plans.

Hey, we need to postpone a couple of days. The weather isn't cooperating.

Xuan replied, Are you finally going to tell me what you were planning?

A mischievous grin played on my lips as I typed back, Nope, not a chance. I guess you'll just have to wait and see.

Cliff Diving at the Cove
September 30, 2019

It was a pleasantly warm Monday afternoon, with the

temperature hovering around 70 degrees—a rare occurrence for the coastal region in late September. Standing alone in the shadows, I positioned myself at the beginning of the marked trail that would lead us toward the cliff. I'd been disappointed to discover that Xuan wasn't waiting for me.

A text came in, from Xuan. *Sorry, I'm running late.*

I smiled and quickly texted him back. *Just remember to wear something reflective.*

What? He wrote back. A moment later, he added *OMG! I just got your joke. Sorry again for the hold up, I'll be there soon.*

This time I was more serious as I shot him a quick reminder. *Make sure you wear a hat and a lot of sunscreen.*

Finally a twig snapped in the near distance and I could sense Xuan approaching. He had a certain rhythm to his steps that I recognized. Turning around, I could see Xuan making his way toward my location. I hadn't seen him much since he returned from his trip. My heart immediately began to flutter out of control at the sight of him—as it usually did.

As Xuan drew near, I noticed his dark hair looked as if a bird had been nesting there. He must have had a rough night, but it was mostly hidden by a St. Louis Cardinals baseball cap. He liked the team because of his two favorite players—Yadier Molina, and the young rookie, Tommy Edman. He was also excited about the arrival of Paul Goldschmidt, who had been traded by the Arizona Diamondbacks.

"Hey." He bent down to kiss my forehead, and I could smell the sunscreen on his skin.

Xuan cocked one of his eyebrows defiantly. "I had to go find reflectors," he stated, a playful smile tugging at his lips. "Actually, I was helping my mom with her organic garden while you were in class this morning."

"Are you sure you shouldn't be taking it easy? You were exhausted after your trip."

"I want to help while I can," he replied.

I nodded, understanding his desire to make the most of his

time. "That makes sense."

"So what are we doing here, Cass?"

"Cliff diving, just as you wanted. Are you up for this?" I asked.

His eyes lit up in excitement. "I've always wanted to cliff dive."

Xuan fell into step beside me as we walked along the winding dirt path toward the edge. Doing something normal with Xuan felt good. I could sense his energy and feel his excitement.

As we approached the ocean cliff, my boot caught on a bundle of intertwined weeds and I lost my balance. Thankfully Xuan caught my arm before I fell to the ground and embarrassed myself.

"Are you all right?" He looked down at me attentively. "Be careful and watch your step. The grass and weeds are overgrown in these areas."

I nodded in acknowledgment, relieved that I hadn't stumbled and face-planted. "Are you sure you're ready for this?" I asked. "The water's going to be cold."

"I can hardly wait."

With anticipation building, I removed my windbreaker and began to undress, preparing myself for the coming plunge. The water would only be about fifty to fifty-eight degrees. We'd spent enough time surfing and hanging out at the beach to be accustomed to that. The cold didn't really faze us after all these years. I'd packed our wet suits to put on over our bathing suits.

As Xuan undressed, my fingertips traced a path up his torso, tracing the steady rhythm of his rising and falling chest. Drawing him closer, I wrapped my arms around him, our embrace tight and unyielding, our lips converging in a fervent kiss.

"What are you up to?" he inquired, his voice brimming with curiosity.

"Just savoring a final moment, in case I have a heart attack on the way down," I retorted playfully. Heights had never been my cup of tea. It wasn't that I was necessarily scared of them; they simply didn't resonate with me.

The next time he kissed me was on the mouth. The kiss was lingering and gentle.

After a few minutes, Xuan's excitement became palpable as he asked, "Are you ready?"

Nodding, I experienced a mixture of anticipation and nervousness coursing through me. "Let's do this."

Approaching the precipice, our gazes locked onto the vast expanse of the Pacific sprawled beneath us. It was in that moment that the adrenaline surged through our veins. We had to be attuned to the ebb and flow of the tide, waiting for the perfect moment. When the right swell approached, we would take the plunge.

As we waited for a decent set of waves, the wind picked up slightly, but Xuan didn't seem to mind. Rather, he leaned into the gentle breeze hitting his face. Some days he'd been too sick to even sit up. Other days he endured the osimertinib pills just fine. But today, in this fleeting moment, he defied the limitations. Today, he was alive. He was free.

As the next swell surged forward, gathering momentum, Xuan drew in a deep breath and initiated the countdown. "Three . . . two . . . one."

We flung our bodies over the edge, surrendering to the exhilarating sensation of freefall. The world around us blurred as we descended, weightless and untethered. In that moment, everything else faded into insignificance. We were fully present, alive, and unfettered as birds in flight with beautiful wings. Our ecstatic shouts filled the air as we spiraled downward, our descent reaching speeds of approximately twenty miles per hour. And then, in an instant, everything stopped. It only took seconds for our bodies to plunge beneath the surface of the ocean. It was a feeling of pure elation and control, unlike the mudslide that had taken me down.

Xuan emerged from the water, his head breaking through the surface about ten feet away. He let out a triumphant shout, his voice brimming with exhilaration. I couldn't help but join in, matching his enthusiasm. My heart continued to race, the surge of adrenaline coursing through my veins in intense waves. It felt as though the rush would stay with me for hours, if not days.

Xuan swam over to me, imitating the Jaws theme music. "Dun dun, duuunnn duuunnn."

"No way! Not now, while we're in the ocean!"

He pressed his upper body up against mine. "Aren't you just being jaw-matic?"

"Not funny." I giggled like a schoolgirl. "I don't want to end up shark food, so we should probably get moving."

"Just a little longer," he begged.

"Fine, but just a few minutes."

It didn't take long for the initial warmth and excitement to dissipate. The thrilling sensation from the jump started to fade as the icy temperature penetrated my skin, causing goosebumps to appear on my arms and a shiver to course through my body.

"Brrr, it's a little cold!" I exclaimed.

"Here, let me warm you," Xuan whispered.

Underneath the surface of the water, I could feel his hands slide down from my back to my waist.

"Is it working?" he asked, a smile playing at the corners of his lips.

His touch was indeed warming me from within. "My lips are cold too. Perhaps you should warm them," I playfully retorted.

"Hmm, is that so?" His voice became a tender caress as he leaned closer, his mouth slightly parted to avoid any intrusion of seawater.

The taste of salt and seawater mingled on his lips, and as we kissed, the same flavors danced upon my tongue. I could kiss him every day for the rest of my life and that still wouldn't be enough. Like a fish out of water, I'd been hooked and caught and there was no going back.

"Okay, time's up," I said, reluctantly pulling back from his touch.

"That was only a minute," he protested.

"The water's freezing, Xuan."

"You don't have to treat me like a sick kid."

"I know. It's not that."

"Then what's the rush? We're in wet suits. We've surfed in colder temperatures before."

Xuan needed to change into warm clothes before he caught a common cold that could jeopardize his weakened immune system. The only way to continue these outings and adventures was by keeping him healthy. "We need to get warm and stay well or we can't do what I have planned for Wednesday. Which was supposed to be a surprise."

"What? What could upstage this?"

"Next up . . . skydiving!" I exclaimed with excitement. "We'll need to leave for Watsonville pretty early on Wednesday. And assuming our parachutes do their job and we survive the freefall, I thought it would be a blast to visit the Monterey Bay Aquarium afterward. And guess what? I've already made a hotel reservation."

"You booked a hotel?"

"I did," I replied, a smile playing on my lips. "Oh, and by the way, Amanda and I are going lingerie shopping tomorrow before we leave on our trip. You know . . .just in case you're not tired."

"Are you trying to kill me?" Xuan asked with a sarcastic laugh.

"Not funny."

He found my hand underwater and pulled it upward, past the surface. Both our hands were now out of water as he wove his fingers through mine. "You're right, I'm sorry. That was a stupid thing for me to say."

"It was," I agreed. I couldn't help but examine how our hands fit perfectly together, like a long-married husband and wife. *If only.*

"Cassie, can I ask you something?"

"Anything."

"I wrote a list of things I wanted to do—before the end. I was angry. Once I realized that most of the things on that list weren't realistic, I crumpled it up and tossed it. The next morning, I changed my mind. But when I went to retrieve the paper, it was gone."

"Vanished?" I asked innocently.

"Maybe that list made it somewhere else. Did it?"

"Your bucket list is in safe hands," I confessed.

"I had a feeling it was you, but I couldn't be certain until today when you surprised me with cliff diving."

"You guessed correctly."

"Thank you," he whispered, his voice brimming with gratitude. "Thank you so much for orchestrating all of this for me. Did you also ask the Thompson brothers to arrange the camping trip?"

"Nope. That was entirely Raylan's idea." I wouldn't take credit for one of Raylan's redeeming moments.

"But he wouldn't have known about all those places on my list without a little help."

"It's what you wanted," I reminded him.

"But I never thought it was possible. I was so focused on dying that I forgot I should be living."

I wasn't sure which would last longer, Xuan or his dreams. But I would do whatever I could to grant him those last requests, to satiate him with happy memories before the end.

I don't want you to feel obligated. Like you have to try to complete my list."

"I know. I just don't want you to have any regrets, Xuan."

"Just being with you is enough."

I leaned in and grazed the tip of my nose playfully along the side of his cheek. Together, we had dared to live, to dream, and in this shared experience, we fully embraced the present—the here and now. We were both alive and together, and that made today a beautiful thing.

Chapter Twenty-Five: The Happily Ever Present

Yosemite Chapel, Yosemite National Park, California
October 19, 2019

"Keep your eyes on the road," Xuan yelled over the music. "A deer might run out in front of the car. Or we might hit a patch of black ice as we ascend to a higher elevation."

I was blasting "Tiny Dancer" from the speaker as we followed the GPS toward our next stop in Yosemite National Park . . . an old church. At the heart of the valley stood soaring mountains nearly thirteen thousand feet high, already encumbered with ice and snow as winter quickly approached.

Xuan and I had decided to take a trip together in honor of our one-thousand-day anniversary. We ate Korean barbecue, shared a decadent cake, and then drove three and a half hours to Yosemite. I'd never heard of such an occasion. But in Seoul, where Ji-Hoon was born and raised, there was almost a monthly holiday devoted to romance. We wore similar outfits, which Xuan said was common for couples in Asian countries. Three years was a big deal, especially when we didn't know how many more we'd have. I'd never been to Yosemite, but I'd read several itineraries and reviews, all suggesting we spend at least three days sightseeing. I booked a cabin for five nights—the perfect nature getaway.

We spent the first two days visiting the Three Brothers, the Leaning Tower, Mirror Lake, Ribbon Fall, the California Tunnel Tree at the sequoia tree orchard, and El Cap, where we hiked the short half-mile stroll to Bridalveil Fall. Thankfully the path to the waterfall was flat and easy for Xuan to traverse. The waterfall's spray soaked our clothes as we drew closer. We spotted a few deer and one moose on the flat, short walk. We also went to Sugar Pine Railroad and rode the four-mile excursion through towering trees.

The days were packed with sightseeing and driving. We rotated playing our personal music favorites between stops. I loved classic rock and chose artists like Jimi Hendrix, Bob Dylan, Tom Petty, Aerosmith, Zeppelin, and the Scorpions. Xuan loved old American jazz and blues with a little pop, so he would play more Miles Davis, Engelbert Humperdinck, Bill Evans, Duke Ellington, and Frank Sinatra. We had successfully checked off almost everything on our to-do list, but it took from sunrise to sunset and a lot of driving in between.

Today was our third and final day in the park. We had already seen Cathedral Spires and Royal Arches this morning. By midday, we made it to Yosemite Chapel. It was warm now, warmer than it had been since we'd arrived on Thursday, almost muggy under the October clouds as the sun shone directly overhead. Xuan took off his jacket, baring his slender frame. Despite the weight loss caused by his ongoing treatment, there were still faint hints of definition in his muscles, subtly visible through his fitted light-blue shirt. He caught me gawking at him and smiled. I wanted to pull off my own hoodie and knot it around my waist, but I wasn't about to go into a church with nothing more than a tank top on.

"What are our plans for tomorrow?" Xuan asked. He looked tired, winded.

"I thought tomorrow we might spend locked away in the comfort of our cabin, resting and relaxing. Soaking in the hot tub, among other things."

"This trip's been amazing, but vegging out for a day sounds nice." Xuan needed the rest. The trip had been arduous, even though he would deny it. We'd just gotten back from the 1000 Lights Water Lantern Festival in Long Beach less than a week before our trip to Yosemite. Another item from Xuan's bucket list checked off.

His warm, light touch on my back never failed to make my heart pound erratically as he led the way across the lawn. The chapel was the oldest structure in the valley. The trees that framed it had begun to change color into the yellows and oranges of fall. The building itself was small and intimate. I'd always loved to visit old churches and historic graveyards, especially back east. But standing in front of the church made me think of marriage, and I stopped.

Xuan stared, bewildered by my agonized expression. "What are you thinking about *bǎobèi*?" he asked quietly.

"Nothing, I'm just deep in thought."

"I wish I could read your mind."

I was glad he couldn't but I wouldn't lie to him. "I was thinking about us . . . about our wedding."

A different pained expression filled his face as he looked at the church and then, finally, understanding. "As you must have read, marrying you was on the top of my wish list—still is."

"Then why can't we?"

"You *will* get married, Cassie. Just not to me."

"I don't want anyone else, Xuan. Only you."

"I'm not going to marry you simply to make you a widow." He turned and began to walk away from me.

I felt the blow like a punch to my gut. I hurried after him till I was close beside. "You're being selfish. I'm going to be either a widow or a girlfriend of someone who's passed. Technically, I'll be a widow either way. The title doesn't make this situation any less heartbreaking."

"I wanted marriage with you too, and a child who would be raised in our home. As you know, my top three bucket-list wishes were marrying you, having a child, and returning to China one last time to see my family. But things changed, didn't they?" Xuan seemed to feel justified.

I believed him. The stark honesty in those brown autumn eyes was confirmation that he'd weighed the idea carefully, and had truly come to the conclusion that his cancer changed things.

"Marriage is possible. You just refuse to," I replied with a little more acid than I intended.

"You *are* serious."

"Holy Saints, Xuan, of course I am! I know how this story ends and yet I'm standing here telling you that I want this more than anything, Xuan."

"I cannot let you sacrifice yourself in that way for me, Cassie."

That was his problem. He now saw our marriage as a sacrifice. My throat tightened to the point of pain. "Sacrifice?" I held up my hand, reminding him of the engagement ring that still sat on my finger from our time in Italy. "Xuan, I am in love with you. I *want* to marry you. Love is as strong as, if not stronger than, death, and cancer hasn't changed how I feel about you. Besides, we all have expiration dates. None of us get out alive, not in this world."

He frowned at me. "I don't want to argue with you so let's not talk about this now. I just want to enjoy this trip." Pleading saturated his voice. "The last couple of days have been perfect. Let's not ruin it."

Tears burned my eyes but I controlled myself and kept them from slipping free. He was right. Arguing just wasted energy and he was already tired. I didn't have an answer that might convince him otherwise. His mind was made up on the subject. I tried to smile in agreement but my grin was forced as I continued on.

Xuan watched me carefully, his mouth a tight line. He understood me enough to realize my tone and unconvincing smile were fake. "We can just head back to the car if you want, Cass. We don't have to go inside."

My throat bobbed and I swallowed before nodding toward the church. "We're already here. Might as well check it out."

Xuan paused another moment and then led the way. A haze of buttery sunshine shone on the church, as if calling to us in welcome. As we went inside, the bells in the tower were ringing.

Words of marriage and what *could be* and *should be* hung heavily in the air. We walked in silence the remainder of the afternoon.

Taft Point, Yosemite National Park, California
October 19, 2019

After several hours, the light that filtered through the Sierras transformed the mountains, shifting first to an olive color and then to purple and blue tones. Several stops and quick hikes had taken up most of the afternoon. The Sierra Nevada mountain range appeared rugged as the divine light displayed its dramatic and alluring forms. A clearly marked foot trail with a small wooden marker pointed in the direction we needed to go. The first snow of autumn was light and melted within a few hours.

I pulled over to park on the narrow shoulder and stepped out of the jeep. We checked our backpacks and water supplies before starting up the trail. We were 3,500 feet above Yosemite Valley, and it was late in the day. We picked up our pace, my eagerness growing with every step, to make it to the ridge by sunset.

Xuan watched me with cautious eyes as we stepped out toward the ledge, where the dome offered 360-degree views to both El Capitan and Half Dome. At Taft Point, Xuan withdrew his camera to capture the jaw-dropping view and then took pictures of me. He seemed at ease, comfortable, as he took a seat on the cliff's edge. John Muir described the area as fateful, pervaded with divine light, every landscape glows like a countenance hallowed in eternal repose. The natural beauty was alluring, a must-see.

While we sat on the ledge, our disagreement about getting married seemed to fade away as we looked out at the serenely beautiful horizon with rich and varied hues of vibrant reds, oranges, blues, and purples. When I looked at Xuan, his eyes—the color of butterscotch with the orange sunset reflected—watched me, not the view.

"Are you all right, *bǎobèi*?" he asked.

"Fine," I responded, which in girl language typically meant the opposite.

"I'm sorry about earlier."

Something tight in my chest eased. "Me too. I do understand your reasoning. I'm just disappointed."

"Do you, though?"

"Yes and no." I paused. I inched closer and rested my head on his shoulder. I began to trace the contours of his forearm with my fingertips.

"It's not because I don't love you—it's because I do. I'm not a poet. And I don't really have the words to describe how I feel. But I want you to know I have never loved anyone like I love you. More than Darcy loved Elizabeth or Heathcliff loved Cathy. I just don't want to make you a widow."

"I never really understood why Brontë is considered to be a romance writer. We were required to read *Wuthering Heights* in high school and I always believed that her novel showcased the bleakest aspects of human nature. The story provided readers with a small yet unforgettable glimpse into the depths of human cruelty. Personally, I never considered the story romantic because the love shared between Cathy and Heathcliff was fatal, not just for themselves but for those around them. Their souls were incompatible, and they were a toxic pairing. Despite their love, passion, jealousy, and desire for connection, they were unable to recognize this fact."

"I was never a fan of Victorian romance novels."

"It was never one of my favorites. It's often viewed as one of the great romance novels of all time, but I think it represents something darker: the fatal, selfish side of love, obsession, and abuse. To this day, I have not encountered a more accurate depiction of how love can become selfish."

"Why do you say that?" Xuan asked.

"Because I think you have to love someone in the way that I love you to truly understand what love means . . . and to understand how wrong the story is. My soul and yours are the same in a way that Catherine and Heathcliff's could never be. Widow or not, I will never stop loving you, Xuan. You have mesmerized me. My very soul has been entangled completely by you over these past three years. If Brontë or Austen could write the greatest love story of all time they'd write our story. And whether you marry me or not, how I feel about you will never change."

"After I'm gone, it's okay to love again, Cassie. I want you to know that. I want you to find someone who will love you the way you deserve. I want you to find happiness again. To get married and have rug rats. To have a future."

"There will never be another for me," I said. I was certain of it.

"You're still so young. You have so much life ahead of you, and I wish I could be there to see it. But I won't always be here. You can't forget to live after I'm gone. I want you to find someone else. To be happy and live your life. To find beauty."

"Why?" I asked.

"Because if our situations were reversed, wouldn't you want the same for me?"

"Yes, I would want that more than anything. But why are you telling me this now? It sounds like you're saying goodbye."

"Because death will be a bittersweet farewell. The pain and suffering will end for me, but will continue for you. The doctors say I have years but we never know when it's our time. Lightning might strike me down any moment, killing me instantly. So it's important to me that you hear this now, Cass. When I'm gone—and that day *will* come—you'll have to continue existing in this world. The hardest thing to do is to live, especially after your heart breaks. Give yourself time to grieve. And if there are days where you find yourself unable to get out of bed, or get dressed, and you can't do it for yourself, do it for me. And when the time is right, it's okay if you move on. To find someone who makes you happy. I'll still be with you—waiting for you to join me in the next life," he said with his hand on my heart.

His eyes were soft, penitent, as I studied his face, studied the plea behind his eyes. But I couldn't make those promises. "I'll try."

He kissed the top of my head, tugged me closer to him. "That's all I could ever ask for."

We both fell silent. Through soft tears we sat, awestruck at the fading sunset. There was something magical about watching the sunset fade over Half Dome. We stayed there, hand in hand, in silence as the night fell in an azul-colored bath over the valley.

"Let's get going," I finally said. "We have one final destination before we head back to the cabin."

"Sure."

We made our way back toward the jeep with headlamps and started the engine.

Driving along the path, I moved at a slower speed to watch out for deer and other nocturnal animals. Half Dome rose directly behind the bend in the road, but it was hard to view in the dark. The whole valley became colder with the onset of night. Xuan had insisted on not missing Glacier Point to stargaze when we'd researched the area. We were miles from city lights, and the sky and area were completely bathed in purest black.

Once we arrived at our destination, Xuan stared into the distance as if mapping out what he wanted to see. He'd brought along his star chart and set up his telescope to look for constellations and planetary neighbors. Xuan told stories about the star and planet patterns and the heroic Greek and Roman legends they'd been named after. His mood had suddenly changed to excitement—like a young schoolboy who'd just entered FAO Schwarz, in New York City, for the first time.

The brilliant stars in the nighttime sky were like dancers performing in a ballet as they took their positions and shone brightly against the stage of heaven. Jupiter and Saturn appeared in the west. The waxing moon passed between the two gas giants. Xuan pointed his telescope from south to southwest and used the moon to find them. Jupiter was very bright, thirteen times brighter than Saturn, so he was able to find them easily.

As we sat together, wrapped up in a blanket before God and the brilliant night sky, Xuan turned toward me. "I know what you're thinking, *bǎobèi*." His voice was soft.

"No you don't."

His skin on my hands was warm. "If you had the choice to marry me, even knowing everything that you do—knowing that in a week, I may be gone—would you still want to?"

There was a pained, delicate ache in my voice as I responded. "Yes. I dream about it all the time," I admitted. After his diagnosis, I hadn't burdened him with that knowledge. But I still held a secret wish in my heart, that someday . . .

I looked at his hand clasping mine. Three years ago, on October 15, 2016, the brilliant blue blaze of the comet had crossed the vastness of our world in Colombia. I could see it, almost as if we were back there, standing on the roof of the dorms as we looked over the city together. We didn't know it then, but our life together was just beginning.

The Romans and Greeks believed that the appearance of comets, meteors, and meteor showers was portentous. They were signs that something good or bad had happened . . . or was about to happen. For me, that was the moment I fell in love with Xuan. That was the promise of a future filled with love . . . and beauty . . . and brilliance. That future began and ended with Xuan.

Xuan and I sat on the stretched-out blanket under the black-velvet night, our souls weaving together, spinning a tale of beauty and brilliance, despite the setbacks cancer had brought on. We didn't speak of marriage again for the rest of the evening . . . or the rest of the trip for that matter.

The evening passed under the cold and distant lights of memory, ticked away minute by minute. At the same time, another hour had unknowingly rescinded on Xuan's life clock. It now rested at ten.

Cabin Rental in Yosemite
Dawn on October 20, 2019

Thick mud was cascading down the mountain. The vehicle was almost full. I couldn't move, couldn't get my leg free . . . couldn't stop any of it.

I was hauled out of my dream like a thrashing fish out of water as their gill arches collapsed—suffocating, sucking for air as my lungs filled. As I woke to the sound of roaring thunder, it took a while for my mind to surface and my eyes to focus.

The first thing I heard over the storm was the rhythmic sound of breathing that was not my own, and a voice trying to break through my terror.

"Take a deep breath, Cassie. You're okay. You're safe."

I obeyed.

"Again."

I did so. This time his face came into view. My chest expanded as I reached for his hand, needing to touch something.

"Breathe. You're here, you're with me. Safe. I promise I won't ever let you go. Or let anything happen to you."

I turned toward the cabin window and saw the rain coming down in torrents. The wind had picked up, howling like the dead. Groggy, I lay with a pang of fear in my chest as the thunder boomed across the stormy valley. I had awoken to the patter of rain, thanks to my PTSD. Rushing water always made me remember Colombia and the mudslide.

I closed my eyes, fighting nausea. Xuan rubbed my back until the feeling subsided as I sprawled over the edge of the bed. My mind took a while to try to forget. When I was finally able to move, I twisted back over and faced him. The sight of that face reminded me. *I made it out. We survived. This isn't just a dream. This is real. I'm here because Xuan rescued me.* I repeated these statements over and over.

The cabin was warm, the woodburning fire mere embers. Xuan wrapped his arm around my bare chest, a precise reminder of our declarations of passion and how, exactly, we'd spent the late hours of the night and a few hours around dawn. We hadn't made love since that night on the beach—he'd been either too tired or too sick. But this time he had energy, and being with him was better than I'd remembered. I focused on that, not wanting to think about the storm or my nightmare . . . only him.

I thought back to the last few weeks of our adventures. Xuan had been feeling good the last few months. We'd survived skydiving and kayaked Emerald Bay in South Lake Tahoe. We'd even taken Mei wine tasting in Sonoma County and ridden in a hot air balloon in Napa, luckily right before fires hit the region. Xuan had continued his treatment at the hospital and had been mostly bedridden at home when we weren't out exploring. I worried about him pushing himself so hard, but Xuan insisted. He kept saying that you only have one life to live. His bucket list was like a holistic remedy.

"We can go back to sleep if you want," he said softly. I felt his smile in my ear.

Sleeping would be futile. I was afraid the sound of the rain might drag me back into that hell where I'd been trapped. No, there was no point in trying to sleep. I wanted something to distract me, take my mind off the rain. The storm outside seemed endless—the wind howling, and then howling and howling.

Xuan gently ran his fingers across my skin, like a musician, in way of invitation. In answer, I flung my arms around his neck, my hands plunging into his disheveled hair. I was surprised he hadn't lost his hair with the pills, but the doctor said not everyone did.

I had different ideas of how to spend the remainder of the morning. Xuan kissed me. My tongue met his, hungry and searching as I let out a sigh. My hands slowly slid from his hair, down his chest, downward.

Xuan gave me exactly what I wanted, gave himself what he wanted, over and over and over, as if this might last forever.

Part Four: Entwined

CHAPTER TWENTY-SIX: ALL HALLOWS' EVE

Seabright, Santa Cruz, California
October 31, 2019

It was seven o'clock in the evening, on All Hallows' Eve, and the little monsters and ghouls were out to play. They must have been desperate for sweets, since they were outside despite the smoldering fires that raged across the state.

I sat at the window and waved as I watched a few small chaperoned groups walk up and down our block. The night was dark save for the faint glow of grinning jack-o-lanterns, which illuminated the pathway between candy-giving houses. Even the usual soft halo glow of midnight blue from highway lighting was stifled by the smoke. I generally loved passing out goodies and seeing kids in their costumes, but this year I decided to set out two large bowls of candy, to try and prevent the smoke smell from entering Xuan's house.

After a while, I headed upstairs to start changing into my evening ensemble. We'd planned to leave his house around nine o'clock for Sky's annual costume party. I wasn't in the get-together mood, but Sky was expecting Xuan and me to be there. This was tradition. Xuan and I fought about attending. The effects of the fires all along California forced Xuan into a mandatory house detention, except for his trips to the Mary & Richard Solari Cancer Center. Earlier in the day, Mei had taken Xuan for more testing. Xuan's primary doctor strongly recommended he rest and not leave the house unless it was essential, not until the air quality improved from the fires. His mom had even purchased air purifiers to put around the house, but they didn't help much.

As a result of the fires, we'd stayed indoors. We binge-watched the Asian dramas: *Descendants of the Sun, Heirs, Accidentally in*

Love, and *Love 020*. We also read, carved pumpkins, baked caramel apples, and played Pai Gow—Chinese dominoes—to pass the time. But Xuan was growing restless with each day that passed, which was understandable. The daily AQI color had remained very unhealthy to hazardous since we'd returned from Yellowstone.

Mei and I both tried to persuade Xuan to skip that night's party. But he seemed absolutely determined to go, despite the fact some smoke still lingered in the air. It was as though he'd convinced himself that he had more energy than he actually did and he would be fine for a few hours if he stayed inside Sky's house.

I could tell he was beyond exhausted and not feeling well, and the fires were making the situation much worse. Going outside wreaked havoc on his lungs, hence our argument. The immediate effects were coughing and a sore throat. Mei and I were both worried going out would compromise his immune system. But he refused to stay home and miss the party. Or miss any more experiences for that matter, knowing he would only have a few Halloweens and Christmases remaining. Friends and parties were his mission . . . normality. He'd won the argument—we were going no matter what. I just worried he would run out of fuel.

"You make a sexy Little Red Riding Hood." Xuan appeared in his bathroom doorway. He wore a traditional ancient Chinese swordsman costume from the Han Dynasty. Inwardly I was already pining over how hot he looked. "Are you about ready?"

I still didn't think it was a good idea to go that night and I'd been cross with him all day because of it. But it was Xuan's choice. He had the right to choose how to spend his remaining time, and going tonight was important to him.

"Almost. I didn't get much sleep last night, so I'm trying to cover up the circles under my eyes."

"Did I keep you awake?"

"No. Your cat turned into a furry ninja, determined to claim my face as its ultimate resting spot," I said and then laughed. "I finally surrendered and let the lil' monster win. I guess I can add 'professional cat pillow' to my resume now."

"Sorry. He's done that since he was a kitten."

"No worries. He actually kept my neck warm," I reassured him. "I just need a few more minutes to finish my makeup, and then I'll be all set."

"You don't need it. You're just as beautiful without it."

"Liar." I almost laughed. "But thank you."

"Would I lie to you?" he asked sweetly.

Yes, all the time, if it's about your health and how you're feeling. I didn't vocalize what I was thinking.

Xuan placed his hand under my chin and gently forced me to look in the mirror. "You are more than pretty. You are beautiful," he whispered. "Now look at me."

I obeyed and saw the same thing in his shining, radiant eyes that I had seen a thousand times. *Love.* He leaned in and kissed me. My red lipstick stained his lips like paint.

Xuan continued to watch me in silence as I finished doing my makeup. Having him stand there was like a defibrillator that constantly jump-started my heart. When the time came, I just prayed I would be able to jump-start his.

"Xuan, do you mind not watching me? I can't concentrate with you staring."

He smiled. "Sure. After all, I would hate to be responsible for ruining your eyeliner."

From the mirror, I continued to watch him as I applied a dark and smoky eye shadow. He was as alluring as a sexy vampire. Finally, I finished. Truthfully, it was half-assed and I didn't do much with my hair, just gave it a slight curl at the end.

"Do you know what today is?" Xuan asked.

"Halloween?"

"Our anniversary."

"Our anniversary was a few weeks ago. Remember our trip to Yosemite?"

"Not the anniversary of the comet."

"What *other* anniversary do we have?" I asked. I made my way to the bed where Xuan was sitting.

"It's the anniversary of the first day I realized I was madly in love with you. That night, we went to your friend's Halloween party. I remember the black dress you wore. You had feathery black angel wings attached to your back and glitter all over your body like you were a fairy from *A Midsummer Night's Dream*."

"I dressed as a fallen angel that year."

"You were *my* angel. The most beautiful thing I'd ever seen."

"People don't have anniversaries for the day they fall in love."

"They should. I remember every day and every moment that was special with you. Love is fragile . . . a gift. And when you love someone, you should be the caretaker of their heart."

"Loving you has been the greatest gift I've ever been given. You know that, right?"

Xuan nodded and then pulled me close to him as if to reply. The feel of his lips on my neck was like an electric shock, making the little hairs stand.

"Stay still or I'll ruin your makeup," he whispered in my ear.

"I don't mind being fashionably late," I suggested.

"I wouldn't either, except I don't know if we would survive Sky's Titan-like wrath."

I sighed. "You're probably right."

"Don't worry. We'll still have plenty of time after the party."

Unwrapping his arms from my waist, I hurried to grab the picnic basket that acted as a prop for my costume that night and followed Xuan downstairs into the living room. He reached for my red cloak in the closet, then helped me to put it on over my costume—a white dress and red shoes to match, which looked as though they belonged to Dorothy from Oz. Maybe if I clicked my heels together three times we would magically be teleported back upstairs and into bed.

Glenwood Drive, Scotts Valley, California
October 31, 2019

In approximately fifteen minutes, it would be ten o'clock in the evening and we would be officially late for Sky's annual Halloween party at her house in Scotts Valley. We were driving 20 MPH below the speed limit on Highway 17 due to low visibility. The sky was the perfect hue of black and ash cloud gray, choking out the new-born starlight.

On the ride to Sky's, Xuan didn't say much. He looked pale, gutted. The air outside was thick from smoke coming from the different fires around the state. The smell of sulfur from still-burning fires lingered in the air, turning the sky cold and ash gray.

I watched raindrops hit the glass as we turned down Hawks Hill road, which was up Glenwood Drive.

"What did the doctors say this morning?" I'd asked him earlier, but he refused to tell me. Probably so I wouldn't insist we skip tonight's party. I knew he was scared to find out if the cancer was spreading. We had to wait for the results. It felt as though we were always waiting for something these days—waiting at the doctor's office, waiting for results, waiting for rain.

"Do you really want to know?"

"Of course." I felt as though I was inside the eye of the storm. The eye was calm. Too calm, I agonized. I tried to chill in preparation for the next unexpected challenge. *I hate surprises. I hate the waiting, the not knowing.*

"They aren't one hundred percent certain," he said.

"Maybe a crystal ball or psychic—"

Xuan interrupted. "But the pills may not be working as much as we hoped. It looks like I may need to do systemic chemo. The scans showed more cancer."

Damn it. I knew Xuan didn't want to do chemo. "I'm sorry. I know that wasn't the news you were hoping for." I was positively crestfallen, stunned even, as I looked over at him. Like looking at an hourglass with time running out. Four months had passed since Xuan had started the cancer warrior pill osimertinib. Treatment had been grueling, physically and emotionally. The little tablets took a toll, but they also gave Xuan energy, off and on, to travel, to live. Xuan's bucket list was not a placebo. It was a drug with a crash that would follow, just like what happens when you have too much sugar or caffeine. Each time we accomplished a wish, he came back with diminished strength, but he was living life. Like a drug, he was hooked on the rush. *Will he still have the same vigor on chemo?* A huge lump knotted in my throat.

He squeezed my hand. "Let's not think about that right now. Not tonight." His voice was hoarse. Whether from the smoke or the thought of doing chemo, I didn't know.

Xuan searched for parking and found a spot close to the front of the house.

"Wait." He gently took hold of my arm as I attempted to exit the car.

I turned to look at him and smiled. "You okay?"

"I got you something."

"Why?" I asked.

"What do you mean why? Because I love you. It's an anniversary present. It's not a yacht or trip around the world," he joked.

I didn't know what to say.

"Just open it."

I took the small box from him. Unwrapped, I saw a silver, oval-shaped locket. Opening the locket, I saw Xuan's picture inside. The inscription *Forever and Always* was engraved on the back of the necklace, with our names inside an infinity loop.

"It's lovely." I fumbled to take off my small cross necklace so I could replace it with his.

"Let me," he said.

"I can do it."

"I know you can do it, but that's not the point."

"You know I love you, right?" I asked.

"Of course I know," he answered softly.

"Good. Because I love you."

"You already said it." He beamed.

"Maybe I want to say it again. It's a free world. A girl can tell her fiancé she loves him as many times as she wants."

"I'll never grow tired of hearing it."

I checked the dashboard clock. "We're late."

He finished putting the necklace on me. "I don't mind waiting in the car a little longer. You can continue telling me how in love with me you are."

After a few extra stolen minutes, Xuan came around and opened my door for me. Hand in hand, we walked up the steps to the party, where music blared from inside the house. As if at a masquerade ball, Xuan would wear a mask, pretending he was feeling okay that night.

When we finally made it inside, the living room and hallways were packed with people in costumes dancing and holding drinks. Casual insinuation and introductions were forgotten as people shuffled between rooms. Jungle juice sat in a witch's cauldron with dry ice foaming out for a steamy effect. Amanda must've been controlling the music, because Shakira had just ended and then "Mi Gente" by J Balvin blasted from the speakers, a perfect reminder of our time together on our study abroad.

After we greeted our friends, Xuan took my hand. He smiled. "Care to dance?"

I suddenly wanted to dance with him very much. To be reminded of Colombia and how it felt to be held in his arms for the first time. We were standing at the edge of the crowded dance floor.

As he moved, I matched him step for step. I felt him caress me hard as I yielded to the light pressure that drew me close. We continued to dance in sweeping figures across the tight space. We had taken up Latin dancing classes as a hobby and had been going once a week, at least until the diagnosis. Several people at the party stopped to watch us.

One of my favorite songs, "Dulcito e Coco" by Vicente García, came on. Xuan gently folded me into his arms. This time the Dominican beat was slow, seductive, as Xuan spun me around in sync to the beat. I matched his steps, side by side, as Xuan continued to hold me lightly by the waist. Then he spun me again.

When the music stopped, Xuan released me from his embrace but still continued to hold my hand. Heated, we made our way toward the tables for a drink.

"Xuan, right?" A female in a yellow Cher costume, from *Clueless,* tapped his shoulder.

I remembered her mermaid-colored hairstyle, with vibrant colors like a peacock. She was the girl from the beach. This time, Raylan wasn't with her.

"Yeah." Xuan stuck out his hand. "Sorry, I don't think we've met."

"I'm Emma, Raylan's girlfriend. He told me you have cancer. I'm sorry. That must suck."

"Thanks, Emma."

"So, what are your odds?" Emma asked.

I felt like a cat ready to pounce. Questions like this were expected from loved ones. But when they came from a practical stranger, they were *not* okay. Xuan had been really open with our friends. The people we were closest to deserved to know what was going on. But that didn't mean he wanted to spend his night divulging sensitive information to random strangers. Being given the label of "girlfriend" did not give Emma a special place in our lives. I looked her up and down and was ready to say something sarcastic, but Xuan squeezed my hand as if he knew I was livid at the girl's insensitivity. He took the high road.

"Who knows? Maybe a couple of years if I'm lucky."

"My friend's dad had your type of cancer. He died a few years ago."

Xuan offered his condolences. My metaphorical cat claws were drawn. This was not an appropriate party conversation or topic. Even cancer patients get "cancered" out.

"My aunt had ovarian cancer," offered Emma. "I tell everyone to try juicing and doing yoga. I really ramped up her vitamin K. She's cancer-free now because of the lifestyle changes. You should try that."

My cat-woman personality was coming out, walking a fence, and I wasn't quite sure which side I was going to land on.

"Maybe," Xuan said politely.

Xuan was such a better person for taking the time to talk to Emma—always patient, dignified, and kind. But he looked as though he couldn't take any more "advice."

"Holy Saints, that's enough, Gemma," I snapped, purposefully saying her name wrong for effect. "I don't know if you're just acting like Cher Horowitz or if you *are* that naïve, but we're at a party, and my fiancé didn't come here to talk about his diagnosis. Cancer is complicated. And foisting vitamins and supplements and unsolicited advice onto people undergoing treatment isn't really respectful. So spare us your remedies and please go dance, drink, or drop dead for all I care."

"I'm so sorry. I wasn't thinking." She seemed genuinely apologetic.

"No worries," Xuan said. "You're not the first."

And she wouldn't be the last. A lot of people had offered him tips, as if he should forget what his doctor said in order to try X, Y, or Z. It seemed like everybody thought they knew better than the professionals who'd actually studied medicine, and patients' blood work, and thousands of dollars' worth of scans and pathology reports, because someone knew someone who was magically cured by a more natural, holistic approach and had gone into remission because of it.

Just then Sky walked into the living room. She became an easy excuse to get away from Ms. Insensitive.

"Oh, look," I said. "There's Sky. Sorry, Gemma. We need to go say hi to the host. Thanks for your little cancer warrior tips."

Sky was wearing a very real looking *Juno* costume from the 2007 movie. Sky's short hair was pulled back into a ponytail, like the character from the movie. "I like your outfit, Sky." I noticed that Sky's waistline had changed. She almost looked like she had a small baby bump forming.

"Thanks, you look all right yourself," said Sky.

"Sky, are you pregnant?" I asked quietly.

"Nick and I've been seeing each other for a while and now we're pregnant. He's dressed as Bleeker somewhere around here, but he might've already changed into his police uniform for his work shift."

I leaned in and kissed Sky on the cheek. "Congrats! I had no idea."

"Thanks. We just barely found out, and you've been super busy with your own stuff. We didn't want to bother you guys."

I felt guilty. I'd been so occupied with Xuan that I hadn't made time for my friends.

"How far along are you?" Xuan asked.

"Four months. And my bladder control's already ruined! My hormones are doing the crazy dance. You guys should wait to have kids. Being pregnant ruins your body and your sanity," Sky teased.

The comment was made before Sky realized what she'd said. *Pregnant.* The word and image shifted through my mind. I'd never really thought much about the possibility.

"Oh, Cassie, I'm so sorry. I didn't mean to say that!" Sky apologized.

"It's okay, really. I'm just happy for you." Honestly, I was still too young. I did want them, *someday.* I just thought that would happen later, once Xuan and I had finished our Ph.D. programs, settled into established careers, and saved a little money. But that would never happen now, and I was envious. Sky and Nick got to have a family and we would not . . . not ever.

I'd taken birth control because the doctors had recommended we not try to make a baby during the treatment. Xuan wouldn't want to have a child before he was married. And with such a limited amount of time in this world, having children was not in the cards. This realization made me sadder than I expected. *Since when have I started thinking about babies and being a mother?* The answer was staring me in the face. Since the possibility had been taken away from us.

"Where's Nick?" Xuan asked. "I need to go congratulate the father-to-be."

"Halloween is a busy time for DUIs, so he has to work tonight. But I don't think he's left yet. You can probably still catch him."

Xuan kissed Sky on the cheek and then went to find him.

"Where's Roxy?"

"In the kitchen. She's helping me out with the food. She and her girlfriend had a big fight this morning so she's cooking her feelings away."

"I thought she was still with Keith?" She'd been off and on in relationships for a while, but she'd seemed happy with him.

"They've been over for a while. She started seeing a girl named Amren from her yoga class."

"Oh." Roxy was dating someone new and Sky was pregnant—proof that I'd been a terrible friend to both of them over the past few months. "That's good. I always thought Keith was kind of a tool."

"Yeah. I didn't like him very much either. But Amren's great. I told Roxy to invite her to our annual Christmas party."

Roxy was bi, and in my opinion she was—and still is—a total badass. Of all my childhood friends, this girl's my bestie. Even when we were young, I knew deep down that Roxy was going to conquer the world. Her brilliance, coupled with her unwavering commitment to feminism and human rights, made her truly exceptional. And she cared, *really* cared, about animals and the pressing issues in our world. She wasn't just one of these people that wore shirts and posted awareness videos online. She dedicated her weekends to protests and taking action. And I loved that she was hooking up with Amren, or whoever this girl was, if she made Roxy happy. I loved her. I loved all of her. Hopefully Amren would see how awesome Roxy was and make her feel special.

"Can I help you guys?" I offered.

Sky took my hand. "Of course. I'm glad you're here, Cassie. I wasn't sure if you'd come, what with the fires."

If it had been my choice, we wouldn't have. "Xuan insisted. It's tradition, after all."

I followed Sky past the fog machine and strobe light as we squeezed through the thirty-odd people crammed in the living room, now decorated as a woodsy haunted house, to get to the kitchen.

"Cassie. When did you get here?" Roxy was dressed as a Greek goddess.

"A few minutes ago. How are you?"

Roxy was violently chopping fresh basil. "The little pregnant girl's been working me like a slave for the last few hours. I just barely finished the guacamoldy eyeballs and oreo graveyard cake."

"What are you making now?" I asked.

"I'm making the sauce for a lasagna."

Sky reached for a chocolate-dipped raspberry-coconut macaroon, unfazed by the comment.

Roxy held up her knife. "You better get out of here, pregnant girl, before you eat all of my hours of hard work."

I tried to laugh, but it was forced.

"What's wrong?" Roxy asked. "Are you okay?"

"Fine," I lied. But my voice was so full of disdain that Roxy could read me like a book. "I just had a little run-in with Emma." Pushing my anger off on Emma was easier than to chit-chat about the reality of cancer life. "So what can I do to help?"

"Help? What? You should go enjoy yourself. Be with Xuan."

"I want some time alone with my best friend, and Xuan can use some time with the guys. I think he wants to forget for a night and believe that it's all going to be okay."

"That's understandable," said Roxy. "Is he feeling any better?"

"Depends on the day," I said. "But these fires are definitely not helping."

The sound of footsteps came toward the kitchen. "Cassie?" Xuan seemed taken off guard. "There you are. I was looking for you."

"Well you found me," I said. "You okay?"

"Yeah, of course, *bǎobèi*." Xuan turned to my friend. "Hey Roxy."

"Hey," Roxy answered back without taking her eyes off the lasagna.

"Do you need help?" Xuan asked.

"Can you find Amanda and tell her I need help keeping Sky away from the kitchen?"

Xuan bowed his head slightly toward Roxy and said, "Sure. No problem," and then looked at me. "Raylan's here. You should come say hello while I go look for Amanda."

"I'm talking to Roxy," I told him dismissively. "You can tell him I said hello and Happy Halloween."

"Okay. Enjoy girl time. I'll see you in a while." He walked out without another word.

"What's up with you guys?" Roxy asked, still being overly attentive with the lasagna, never looking me in the eyes. "Don't you find it odd how close Xuan and Raylan are?"

"Yeah, I do. But Raylan's been supportive. He's been a great friend to Xuan, so I can't be upset that he's sort of in our lives now."

Roxy sighed heavily, sadly. "I still think Raylan is in love with you."

"That's not funny."

"I'm not smiling."

"Why do you think that?" I knew Raylan still had unresolved feelings—he'd told me as much when he admitted he'd come back to Santa Cruz for *me*. What I didn't realize was he hadn't let those feelings go once he befriended Xuan. And that they were now obvious to the people around us. *Does Xuan see what Roxy has seen? Does Emma? Maybe he's still interested because I'm like forbidden fruit. People always want what they can't have.*

"I see the way he watches you. He can be with Emma or one of his many *girlfriends* but the moment you walk in the room he lights up—like there's no one in the room but you."

"We're so opposite that we argue about everything, all the time. He likes to yell at me."

"Cassie, I have a really good sense about these things, and I'm telling you, my Cupid senses are tingling."

"And what are these magical superpowers telling you?"

"That the boy never stopped loving you."

"I don't know, maybe. But it doesn't matter now. It took me leaving and going to an entirely different continent for me to stop thinking about him. That's when I found Xuan. He helped mend the broken pieces of my heart, and that's when I finally got over Raylan. I was able to open myself to the idea of being in another relationship after my near-death experience in Colombia. Raylan made his choice a long time ago and life took us in separate ways. I haven't thought about Raylan a day since then." *Right. It wasn't meant to be. We gave it a go, and it didn't go anywhere. Life goes on.*

"I know the past story. I'm just not certain of the future."

I looked Roxy straight in the eyes, surprised by her audacity. "Holy Saints, Roxy, I'm with Xuan. I am in *love* with him. And nothing I ever felt for Raylan compares to how I feel for him." Most of my friends didn't believe in destiny. Nothing supernatural, nothing sent from above . . . no magic, no fate, just life, circumstances, and probability. But there were many signs from the universe pointing to Xuan. I never thought my love story would begin as a blockbuster, but everything that happened seemed like a big neon celestial sign that we were meant to be together. My friends would never understand, not really. If I hadn't met Xuan, I would likely feel the same as them.

"Yeah, but he won't be here forever, Cassie. Then what? You can't go through this life alone."

In related news, I was about to murder my best friend. "Actually, I can. A lot of people choose to be alone, and I have no intention of ever being with anyone else, Roxy. Xuan is my one and only. There will never be another person for me in this life, and I expected you of all people to understand."

"Xuan wouldn't want that."

I felt shocked at the words coming out of my best friend's mouth. My subconscious was screaming. They all knew the truth, that Xuan would die, but it was still hard to hear. And it was especially hard to hear that my best friend was talking about me hooking up with some other guy while Xuan was still alive. It was just cold and wrong.

"Excuse me," I said. "I need some air." I imagined incinerating her with my eyes as I waved goodbye.

Without waiting for Roxy to reply, I hurried to find Xuan. Music drowned out the chatter and laughter in the living room. Two girls from campus were dressed as gypsies and danced almost hypnotically to the music. They glided with triumph through the sea of faces, demanding attention everywhere they went.

I heard several whispers talking about Xuan's cancer—his fate. It was hard not to scream at all of them, to remain silent and zen-like. Someone had even said to him, "Best of luck on your journey!" The comment had been tossed at him like bon voyage confetti. He was dying of cancer, not going on a Caribbean cruise. I held my tongue for Sky, because this party was important to her, and for Xuan. I pretended to be sweetly and blissfully oblivious to all the comments because recreating a scene from Stephen King's *Carrie* would be the last thing Xuan would ever want. When it came to clueless cancer comments, Xuan and I had heard many, all tumbling out of the mouths of colleagues, friends, other patients, strangers, and even loved ones, like Montezuma's verbal revenge. Some were universally annoying, others more individually perturbing.

Spotting Xuan, I made my way toward him. He was holding a red Solo cup in his hand. We both knew of the potential downside of his pills and alcohol mixed. Side effects? Oh yeah. But that was his choice.

Luckily, Xuan didn't seem to notice the whispers about his cancer and death. Or he was just better at pretending than I was.

"Xuan, I need to get some air. I'm going to step outside for a minute."

"Want me to go with you, *bǎobèi*?"

"No, the air outside's dangerous. You should stay inside." Xuan's smile was gone and his heavenly face morphed to serious. My comment had hurt him. I could see the pain in his eyes, but he didn't say anything. *Dammit.* "I'm sorry. I just want a few minutes alone, if that's okay?"

"Of course, Cassie. Take all the time you need."

Chapter Twenty-Seven: A Storm of Emotions

Seabright, Santa Cruz, California
October 31, 2019

Intense rain beat down like tiny drums across my body. I knew I was being silly to be standing in the middle of the storm, breathing in hazardous air, but I simply did not care. I had to escape the crowd for a few minutes, even if that meant my hair, makeup, and dress would be ruined. Inside the house, I felt as though I was having an anxiety attack and I could barely breathe. All I could think about was Sky's comment about having a baby. And then Roxy's comment about Raylan and how Xuan wasn't going to be around forever. That mixed with the possibility of chemo and everyone's comments and I reached some mythical inner limit. I had no control over the situation, over any of this. Everything felt out of balance.

Saints, I'd make any bargain, I'd sell my soul to the dark spirits on this damned All Hallows' Eve, if they would spare Xuan. I was beyond angry—babies and dating Raylan. I wanted to scream. Something about the storm felt nice, almost familiar.

"What the hell are you doing? Are you crazy?"

I knew the voice even before I looked at him. Slowly I turned to face Raylan.

"Well?" he asked. He was wearing the same tight all-black shirt he normally wore, refusing to dress up for the occasion. Though on that night, he could pass for one of the T-Birds from *Grease*.

I said nothing. He was the last person I wanted to see right now, especially after Roxy's observation.

"Has the storm made you mute?" he asked.

"Go away, Raylan."

"Well at least you can speak," he said mockingly. His voice was thick with an emotion I couldn't quite register.

"Please go away. I just want to be alone for a minute," I begged.

"I can't leave you. You've been out here for almost twenty minutes. Xuan was going to come and look for you but I didn't want him to get sick in the rain and this air. I told him I'd find you."

"Great, you found me. Now you can go."

Raylan grabbed my arm. I tried to free myself but he wouldn't release me. "Cassie, stop acting like a child." Raylan dragged me underneath a large willow tree which helped shield us from some of the rain. My wet blonde hair was now brownish, plastered to the side of my costume. I grabbed the tips and twirled a strand of soaked hair around my index finger.

"What's going on, Cassie? You can talk to me."

"*Nothing*!" I said emphatically. "Absolutely *nothing*. I just wanted to be alone and get away for a minute."

Raylan stood there, not buying what I was selling. "Explain. Why are you out *here* in the rain?"

"I can't. It's too difficult."

"I have an IQ higher than a vegetable, Cassie. Try me."

"Bad idea."

"Why? Because we dated? Cassie, I know how you're feeling. I've seen the face of death and I know what it does to people. I'm the only one at this party who truly knows what it's like to have the Grim Reaper constantly looking over your shoulder."

"Why do you want me to talk to you?"

"Let's just consider this a step toward the newly reformed friendship."

"I take it back then. I don't want to be friends."

Raylan smiled. "Try me, just this once. If you don't like talking to me, I'll never ask you to do it again after tonight. Just be honest about how you feel."

I looked into the bluish-green eyes of Raylan and sighed. A small part of me wanted to be able to confide in someone. Xuan trusted Raylan, and I'd decided to give him a chance at being friends.

"I just couldn't breathe in there. I feel like a heavy weight's been gathering inside me. And then tonight Roxy and Sky said things that made me think about the future, like having kids and moving on. I tried to let it go, but then I watched as people I've known for years pointed and talked about Xuan, like he was a walking corpse. The pain I've gone through these past few months is nothing compared to the pain he'll feel if he realizes his own friends are treating him like the plague."

"So? Couldn't you just stand under the doggone porch? Did you have to come out into the middle of the storm?" he demanded.

"I wasn't thinking. I didn't want Xuan to see me upset. He's been through enough. That's why I needed some air. And when I saw the storm, I realized I wanted to be in it, because that's how I feel on the inside . . . like a storm is raging."

"So you came out here and made Xuan worry about you? You've got to be stronger, Cassie. I can already see that you're breaking. But what you're facing now is nothing compared to what's coming. Watching the person you love die is going to be the hardest thing you ever have to do."

"Don't you think I know that already, Corporal?" I yelled.

"You don't know, not yet. Xuan's still alive, Cassie. He hasn't died. You haven't lost anything *yet*. But you will."

I began to cry and dropped to my knees in the mud. My white dress was instantly ruined.

"You can't act like this," said Raylan. He reached down with his two freakishly long arms and picked me up, effortlessly lifting me off the ground like a rag doll.

"I just . . . I can't. I don't know how to do this, Raylan."

"What?"

"Any of it."

"Cassie, you need to understand that he only agreed to undergo treatment because of you. He made this choice solely for you, and no one else. Despite being aware of the limited time he has left and the financial burden the treatment will impose on his family, he chose to stay by your side."

I knew, had known the moment he'd agree to undergo the treatment. I hated myself for being the cause of his pain.

He continued to push. "Xuan is doing the cancer therapy stuff even though he didn't want to. He loves you *that* much. And because you asked him to do this, he is. And one day, because of love, you will stand by Xuan until the end and you'll have to watch him die. And because he loved you, you will eventually have to let him go, because that's what he would want."

"I know."

"Honestly, I don't think you do understand. Not yet."

"He's getting worse, Raylan. He's been doing the pill for a few months and he's already going downhill. The doctor told him he may need to do chemo. But I don't know if he will. He may choose not to. I'm scared."

"He'll do the chemo. At least for a while."

The conviction in his voice surprised me. "Has he said something to you about it?" *I wonder, is this a side effect of losing the one you love? Is Raylan the messenger, a middleman now?*

"He hasn't said anything about stopping. But think about it. If you have a few years or less left to live, are you going to want to spend that time at hospitals, being poked with needles?" asked Raylan. "Not me, not a chance."

"No. You're right."

"Xuan's done really well so far. But this is only the beginning if he has to go through chemo. He's been brave, but he's also put up a false bravado around everyone, including you. How long do you think that's going to last if his disease is progressing?"

I'd already considered that and it scared me. I knew that day might eventually come and I wasn't sure what Xuan would decide when it did.

"The people inside that house, and the people you call your friends, don't understand. They can't. They'll never know how tough it is—to be the one who has to watch someone die. To live day after day, not knowing what tomorrow will bring. But I know what you're feeling and going through, and you're not just brave or special. You're extraordinary. You'll get through this, Cassie."

I pulled my hair back, trying to keep the soaked strands from blowing in my face, "I need a few minutes alone and then I'll come inside. If anyone asks, just tell them I lost a piece of jewelry getting out of the car and I came to look for it."

"Sure."

"And Raylan . . . thanks."

Inhale. Exhale. Be brave, bold, fearless. I took a few more deep breaths and then gathered myself and went to my car and opened the door as if to grab something in case someone was watching. I shut the door to the vehicle and then walked back toward the party. The rain had undoubtedly drenched my costume. I could have passed as a drowned rat, but I didn't care anymore. When Sky, Amanda, and a few others asked me why I went outside, I lied about dropping the anniversary necklace Xuan had given me. That was better than people thinking I'd been crying.

Seabright, Santa Cruz, California
November 1, 2019

Xuan and I were quiet on the drive home. The musky fragrance of his cologne mingled with a slight aroma of tobacco from the celebratory Cubans the guys had lit up in the greenhouse before Nick had headed off to work.

Once back at Xuan and Mei's house, we both peeled off our wet clothes and changed into dry robes. I brewed tea using the leaves and strainer in the kitchen. I tried to remember the exact steps of the art of Chinese tea, but I was too tired and stressed out to remember everything. *Perfection is overrated.* So I let it be tea time with a few flaws, brewed by a coffee enthusiast.

"Let's watch a movie tonight, *bǎobèi,*" said Xuan.

I turned around and he was standing in the kitchen entryway with his robe open. His milky-white good looks, as well as his naturally toned body, left me wanting to wrap myself around him.

"A movie? It's almost three."

"Yes, a movie. I want to lie here on the couch with you and do something normal for a while."

"What did you have in mind?"

"How about we watch a Chinese film? My eyes are kind of blurry tonight, so I thought it would be easier to just listen to Mandarin."

Slightly depressed, I wondered how many more movies Xuan and I would get to see before he was gone. "Of course," I said.

Xuan popped in a Chinese film his mom had bought a few years ago and I turned off the lights and grabbed a blanket from the cupboard. Xuan put the English subtitles on for me. A delicate, warm arm looped around my waist as the movie began. I leaned my head against his shoulder as we slumped down on the couch.

The movie we watched was called *The Left Ear,* and it was a Chinese story about a seventeen-year-old girl named Li Er. I remembered closing my eyes and drifting in and out of sleep to the sound of Mandarin in the background. Sometime after Li's friend died in the movie, Xuan and I both fell asleep, intertwined like two felines.

We stayed on the couch for the rest of the night. I wondered if the movie we didn't get to finish had a happy or sad ending.

As we slept, the old clock chimed on the hour. Somewhere in my head, I could hear nine echoing chimes as if in warning. Xuan's eternal clock was inching its way down to the next hour of nine. How quickly would the bell toll if he refused to do chemo?

The next morning, the entire block woke up to hate-filled messages and pumpkin guts all across their yards and cars. The Blink cameras showed three hooded figures riding their bicycles up and down the street at 4 AM., smashing pumpkins. The messages were white separatist in nature and targeted different various ethnic backgrounds—Blacks, Asians, and Mexicans. A few were anti-Semitic. A letter was taped to Xuan's front door.

"I don't get it," Xuan said. "Who would do something like this?"

Haters like Brett, obviously.

I shook my head, realizing that I no longer had a choice. Despite Xuan's usual composure and unwavering nature, I knew that the conversation I now needed to have with him about the hate mail we'd been receiving for the past few months would deeply affect him. But there was no avoiding it any longer. I needed to show Xuan the letters I had saved. It was time to tell him the truth.

"Xuan, there's something I need to show you."

Chapter Twenty-Eight: Hymn of Two Souls

West Cliff Drive, Santa Cruz, California
November 28, 2019

Thanksgiving Day. I sat lazily on the porch of my house with a blanket, a hot cup of cocoa, and a book. Leaves were quickly changing into yellows, reds, and oranges and falling to the ground in crispy, crinkly piles. Despite the holiday, I was alone. This year my mother had accepted an invitation to a friend's home and had flown to San Diego, since my father was still deployed overseas. Stella had okayed that with me before accepting the invite. At the time, I'd assumed I'd be spending the holiday with Xuan.

I didn't know that Xuan would decide to go camping with the guys. Despite the family holiday, Raylan and Beom had swayed Xuan into some much-needed guy time and left for Sequoia National Park to hike and camp. Raylan didn't want to be anywhere near his blood relatives on any holiday, really, and Beom's family was in South Korea.

I used the time to catch up on all the coursework I'd been assigned just before the holiday break and then rewarded myself by staying in my pajamas and slippers the entire day, unmotivated to get up from the rocking chair on the front porch. I'd only left the house that morning to buy a pumpkin spice latte.

A minute went by, then another, followed by an hour, and then an entire afternoon. When the brightness of the November sun began to fade, I put my book down and stretched before retiring into the warm kitchen to microwave the plate Stella had made for me before going out of town. I had accepted that Thanksgiving, the biggest food-centric holiday of the year, would be rather boring this year, and I fully intended to focus on eating my feelings away regarding 2019 with extra helpings of my mom's renowned twice-baked potatoes and whipped-cream-towered pie.

I could hardly feel syrupy sweet gratitude and joy by myself, but I still planned to serve up a portion of thanks despite not having a traditional Thanksgiving this year. I had a lot to feel thankful for, despite Xuan's diagnosis. The fact that he was still here, and alive, was reason alone to feel thanks. So I ate, and filled up on sweets, before blowing out a pumpkin-scented candle and heading upstairs. Sprawled out across my mattress, I talked and gave thanks to God before falling into a non-turkey-induced sleep.

Note to self: Practice sweet gratitude eight days a week and then some.

A knock resonated from the door. "Hey, beautiful, Happy Thanksgiving."

I opened a single sleepy eye, and poof, just like magic, Prince Charming was standing in my room. "Am I still dreaming?"

Humor danced in his eyes as I looked at the clock, which read 5:00 PM. Still Thursday night and still Thanksgiving. I wasn't expecting Xuan to stop by that night, or even be back in town from camping for a few more days, and the sight of him unnerved me as he wore a black suit and was clean shaven. *They must have finished early. Or maybe it was too cold for Xuan to camp.*

"What's wrong? Are you okay?" I asked.

"Does something have to be wrong in order for me to want to see you?"

"You're back early and you don't even smell like campfire," I said accusingly, still not sure what to make of his suit. "And you look like you're headed to prom."

"We did get back early, so I went home first to shower and get ready before coming to see you. I figured you'd prefer me showering and putting on cologne instead of taking you out while I still smelled like a black bear's armpit."

"Ready for what? Where are we going?"

Concentration settled over his face. "Can I come sit with you?"

"Of course." I tried to hide my hair with a pillow but he moved it away. "Xuan, I'm a mess. I haven't even showered."

Xuan put his hand on my shoulder. "I don't care how you look. I came here to see you. All of you."

"I'm happy you're here—home. Did you have a good trip?"

He hugged me. "It was one for the books."

I turned to face him and in response he leaned down to kiss me. My mind went blank for a split second—complete, utter space-like void and all I could think about was Xuan and how much I had missed him. After he pulled away, I touched my lips, and felt his lingering warmth.

"You taste like pumpkin," he observed.

"It's probably the piece of pie I had."

"Just a single slice?"

He knows me too well. "Fine, it was more like half of the pie dish and a can of whipped cream." In actuality, I never specified how big the piece was in my original statement, so it was still technically just one *extra-large* piece.

"That's my girl."

"So how are you feeling?" I asked.

He smiled. "Selfish." Xuan took my hand. "Will you come with me, *qīn'ài de*?"

"Where do you want to go?"

"That's a surprise." He handed me a large box. "Just get showered and dressed. Then come take a drive with me. I'll be downstairs waiting. Take your time." He stood and then looked back toward me.

I was still blushing as he left the room. I could hear Xuan's footsteps headed down the stairs as I opened the box to find a dress. I held it up—it was a long A-line V-neck with a dramatic cutout back. The color was a deep burgundy, and it had with a sweetheart lace. The dress was beautiful. I held the satin garment in my hands, unable to imagine where he could possibly be taking me in this. But then again, we'd dressed up ridiculously fancy for our date on the Wharf. Maybe he was taking me to another restaurant for dinner.

After quickly showering, I started to curl my hair. Satisfied, I sprayed the heck out of my hair and put on lipstick and gloss. The final touch was a dark, smoky eye shadow. As I walked down the stairs, Xuan met me at the base of the stairwell, holding out a beautifully coordinated pashmina to wrap around my shoulders and then took my hand in his.

"Are you going to tell me what we're doing?"

"Nope, still a surprise. But first I have to stop at my place. I forgot something."

Seabright, Santa Cruz, California
November 28, 2019

Halfway to Xuan's house, he pulled the vehicle over. We sat facing the ocean. The luminous milky moon was full, reflected in the waves over the darkening evening sky. Taking my hand in his, he leaned over and kissed me. "Cassie, do you remember the first time I kissed you?"

"Of course. I'll never forget." I paused. "Xuan, why are we taking a trip down memory lane?"

"I don't know. I've been thinking a lot lately about how we met and how our paths crossed. I guess in the end you start thinking about the beginning."

I squeezed his hand.

"Cassie, if you'd known back then that this is where our paths would lead us . . . that I would get sick . . . would you have still chosen to be with me?"

Did he seriously not know the answer? How much I loved him? "Xuan, I do choose this path, every night, in my dreams. I cannot imagine my life any differently. When I dream, it's always of you."

Xuan smiled and nodded. He didn't say anything else, as if my answer had been enough. He put his foot on the pedal and shifted into reverse. We passed the empty glow of blinking neon lights from homes and businesses in the city. After driving a while, we pulled into Xuan's driveway. The house was dark on the inside. There was no sign of Mei's car.

Xuan got out of the vehicle and then hurried to open my door. Taking his hand, I slid out of the car. Then Xuan moved to stand behind me and placed his hands over my eyes.

"I thought you had to grab something?"

"Just trust me," he whispered.

In my mind, I heard the distant echo of a memory—him asking me to trust him and take his hand during the mudslide. As always, I placed my trust in him and he led the way, occasionally telling me which foot to use and when to turn. Xuan's hands never left my eyes and yet I heard the rusty gate open to the backyard.

"I'm going to take one hand off but you have to promise not to peek. Deal?"

"Deal." I kept my eyes shut tight, even though I felt like a child on Christmas Eve, wanting to look.

Beside me, I could feel Xuan shift. It felt like he was fumbling with something, maybe his cell phone. A few seconds later, the song "Iris" began to play, by the Vitamin String Quartet. The song began to fill the air from the outdoor speakers.

"Ready?" he asked.

I nodded, unsure of what exactly I was supposed to be ready for, or what this was all about.

Then, softly, he removed his remaining hand. And as I opened my eyes, hundreds of glowing string lights captured my attention. Dangling lights stretched across the yard against a backdrop of deep-blue sky, freckled with luminous stars. Sunflowers hung from the trees in the backyard. Several tables were set up with maroon tablecloths and rustic brown table liners, like the European colors that would've been at our fantasy wedding.

"What is all this?"

On cue, several familiar faces of friends and family came out from hiding in the dark home. "Surprise!" they yelled as they came out cheerfully from the French doors. Someone turned the light on inside of the house.

I turned to Xuan. I felt stunned as I speculated there were about forty people who had joined us. Aunts and uncles, cousins, and my grandparents—all were there to surprise me.

The sliding door to the back of the house opened again. This time Mei and my mother came out. Both women were dressed in fancy attire. That and the table decor made me think of a wedding. But Xuan was so adamant about not getting married because of his cancer. *Could it be?*

He looked down at me and I could see the faint glow of the heavenly orbs in his eyes. And in them I saw the past, present, and future were all the same thing—all intertwined by a long thread.

"Cassie, if I had one wish left to be granted, it would be to dance with you under the stars and to call you mine."

"I *am* yours."

"And I'm yours, in this life and the next. My life will never be complete without you beside me to share it. I know we'll never get the chance to grow old together, but if you agree to it, then I want to be selfish with you. Tonight I want to write our own happy ending, even if that version is short. I don't think I can bear another day of my life to go by that does not have you in it as mine completely."

"What are you saying, Xuan?"

Xuan got down on one knee—a second time—in front of everyone. "Marry me tonight, Cassandra Temperance Steel. Marry me, here and now, in front of all our family and friends. I don't want to part from this world without you being called my wife."

When I looked into his eyes, I could see a reflection of the two of us and the life I'd hoped we would share together. This was exactly what I'd prayed for with every fiber of my soul. All I wanted was him, every day, for as long as God allowed. "Yes, I'll marry you," I whispered.

He lifted me off the ground and spun me in a complete circle.

"But how are we going to get married? We need a marriage license from the State of California."

"I picked up the application and filled it out today, but we'll both have to go to the County Clerk's office tomorrow and show proof of identification. After the ceremony, we'll get it signed. Once it's turned in, we'll receive a marriage certificate."

"Sounds like you have it all planned."

"I do. But there's one thing we need to talk about before we get swept away."

"Okay."

"I know you and I talked about last names a while ago, and we were planning to do a combination of both our last names, but I think given our circumstance and time frame, you should keep your name as Steel. Remember, it's not very common in China for husbands and wives to change their last name. My parents didn't. I just think it will create more of a hassle for you in the long run, when I—I . . ..am gone."

"Oh." I didn't want to talk about his death right now. Not on my wedding night. "Are you sure? I was really looking forward to taking your name or doing a hyphenated version."

He smiled and kissed my cheek. "I'm sure. But we can talk about it again later tonight and make the decision together before we go to the clerk's office tomorrow."

"Okay," I said, a little disappointed. We had talked about me keeping my last name before, but we had settled on Zhang-Steel. Traditionally, unlike in anglophone Western countries, a married woman kept her name unchanged, without adopting her husband's surname. In China, there was no legal procedure to follow in order to change a name. Given the fact that Xuan was willing to budge on the wedding, I was okay with keeping my last name. It didn't really matter what I was called—all I cared about was being married to him.

"Who will officiate?" I asked.

Xuan turned me toward the direction of the house and the large weeping willow tree. Under that tree stood a tall figure, bathed in the warm-white light of hanging globes. Command Sergeant Major Steel was standing in his U.S. Army Dress Blues under the willow tree.

"Dad?" The sight of my father shocked me. I felt taken aback, dumbfounded. I was momentarily paralyzed with happiness, and any lingering anger I had towards him vanished instantly.

Xuan let go of my hand, and I ran over and jumped into my father's strong arms.

"I love you, baby girl," my father whispered, his voice filled with affection and warmth. His presence felt sturdy, more resilient than the last time we had been together. Strands of straw-white hair intermingled with his light-brown locks, a visual reminder of the passing years.

"I can't believe you're here." Tears welled up in my eyes as I held onto him tightly, cherishing this precious reunion. "I've missed you, Dad. How long are you home?"

"Two weeks," he replied, a hint of melancholy in his voice. "I have to fly back on the tenth of December."

As a pause lingered in the air, he spoke again, his tone tender and sincere, reflecting the weight of his remorse. "I love you more than anything, Cassie." My father's voice held a tender tone, brimming with warmth and sincerity. He stood before me, his remorse evident in his eyes. I just wanted to be here tonight to apologize and express how deeply sorry I am for my actions. Sending Raylan here was a mistake, and I acknowledge that now. You were right about everything, and I never want to lose you as my daughter. I'm asking for a ceasefire. Can you find it in your heart to forgive me?"

His words melted away any lingering bitterness I held in my heart. After a brief moment of silence I said, "There's nothing to forgive."

With those heartfelt words, a profound transformation washed over my father. Like a gentle breeze sweeping away the weight of past conflicts, his stern expression melted away, replaced by a radiant smile that illuminated his face. In that moment, the weight of years seemed to lift, and a subtle transformation took hold. The creases that had etched themselves upon his forehead appeared less pronounced, and a newfound lightness seemed to grace his features.

Overwhelmed by emotions, I whispered, "I love you, Dad."

As his embrace tightened, he whispered, "I love you too." He continued, "Xuan contacted me and told me about his plans. He asked if I could arrange leave to attend the wedding tonight and he also asked if I would be interested in officiating the ceremony. I actually got ordained online a few weeks ago. It's amazing how easily you can do things online these days, isn't it?"

He was there to officiate our wedding. *Am I dreaming?*

Xuan walked over to my father. Command Sergeant Major Steel took Xuan's hand in his, looked into his face, and apologized. "She's my only little girl, and I've struggled with the idea of ever letting her go from the day she was born. It's hard for me to think that anyone in the world could ever deserve her but I'm glad she found you. I've never said this, but thank you for saving my daughter. For taking such good care of her while I've been away. I will be proud to call you my son. You have my complete blessing."

It wasn't quite a Grammy Awards apology, but it was the first time in my life that I'd ever heard my father apologize for anything. My father stood there in his formal military uniform and unconditionally accepted Xuan, also a first. He was sorry for his behavior motivated by his idea of the right man for me. Maybe he finally understood.

"It's been an honor, Mr. Steel."

I embraced my mom, who had lied about San Diego, before folding myself into Xuan's arms once more. I quietly whispered, "How's all this possible?"

"With a little help from our family and friends."

"Did you even go camping?" I turned to Xuan.

"We did for a night. That was my bachelor party of sorts."

"I'll take rugged adventure over hired stripper any day. Though I'm surprised the guys didn't have a wilder evening planned."

"Oh they had plenty of interesting ideas. They were sorely disappointed when I rejected them all."

The night was wonderful for an outdoor wedding. Xuan swept me from one gathered group to the next. A woman bathed in gold came out and took a seat at a piano keyboard. Behind her a second woman, dressed in similar fashion, came to sit nearby with her violin. The pianist's fingers began to dance across the keyboard, giving it a voice. Her hands were a work of art, speaking a language that predated words. Sweet strains of classical music and classic rock favorites played by the duo drifted through the small crowd.

Xuan led me to a long table. "This moment is important in Chinese tradition. It will mean a lot to my mom. Do you remember what I taught you about the *jing cha,* the Chinese tea ceremony at a wedding?"

"It's been a while, but I remember."

Xuan called over my parents and Mei. The Chinese tea ceremony was intimate and only for close family.

The Chinese tea ceremony was an important traditional time when the bride and groom expressed their respect, gratitude, and appreciation for their parents' love, support, and effort in raising them.

A dark red tea set with a double happiness symbol was already placed on the table for the tea ceremony—my official welcome into the Zhang family. Mei placed a laptop on the table so Ji-Hoon could be a part of the ceremony.

Xuan attempted to clarify the procedure to my spectator relatives. "We utilize black tea that is sweetened with dried longans, lotus seeds, and red dates." He flashed a grin in my direction before facing my parents, straightening his posture. "This ritual signifies the coming together of our two families. It would be an honor for my mother and me to share this with you."

My father nodded thoughtfully at the offer.

I handed the teacups to Mei and my mom and dad then poured the tea. Tradition required the groom's family to be served first. "Please drink tea," I said as I bowed my head slightly and filled the cups.

Ji-Hoon was seen on the computer screen, sipping from a teacup he had brewed.

Mei's face lit up with delight, her eyes brimming with happiness. "I am happy to be drinking my daughter-in-law's tea," she exclaimed. With a graceful motion, she took one last sip from her cup.

As our tea ceremony neared its end, Mei gracefully reached into her pocket, retrieving an ornate red envelope adorned with intricate gold lettering. With a warm smile, she extended the small packet to both Xuan and me, bestowing upon us her blessings for a life filled with good fortune. This was called *hong bao.* This simple act held a profound meaning, reflecting Mei's acceptance and support for our marriage.

Xuan and I decided to postpone opening the envelope until a later time. When we finally did open it, we were completely taken aback by what we found inside. To our astonishment, the envelope contained not only a generous sum of money but also the deed to the fully paid-off house in Santa Cruz. We would spend the next few weeks dealing with the paperwork to get the house transferred over into both our names. I didn't know what to say. It was an unbelievable gift.

Following the tea ceremony, Xuan and I made our rounds, shaking hands and embracing all of our guests. When I reached Raylan, I felt a sense of gratitude wash over me. I knew Raylan was partly the reason this evening was happening. Xuan had told me about the tireless work that he'd put in over the past week to prepare the yard for tonight's celebration. "Raylan, I want to thank you for everything. From the yard preparations to your unwavering support, we couldn't have done this without you. We are both so grateful to have you in our lives, and your presence here tonight means everything to us."

He nodded. His hair was getting longer and now swept forward over his eyes. "Are you happy?"

I whispered my affirmation, "Yes, there are no words." Raylan placed his hand on my shoulder, but then hesitated and withdrew it. I saw his reluctance and stepped toward him, giving him a huge hug. "Thank you so much. I know you helped Xuan arrange this."

When I looked into his face and eyes, I could see the genuine meaning of this gift. It was his way of letting me go, because he wanted me to be happy.

My father looked at Xuan. "Should we start getting everyone in place?"

Xuan looked at me. "Are you ready?"

"I couldn't be more ready."

There was a lot of commotion as my father began giving everyone directions. Xuan began to explain to my father that I wouldn't be taking his last name during the ceremony. My father was very traditional, but he seemed to understand and assured Xuan he would explain to our relatives why I would be announced as Mrs. Steel so they'd understand the Eastern wedding tradition of name taking. While Xuan did that, Stella whisked me inside the sliding doors of the Zhang house, and into the living room where Roxy, Amanda, and Sky were waiting in long burgundy bridesmaid dresses.

Hanging from the door of a corner bedroom was a breathtaking wedding gown made of full tulle and delicate lace. As I approached the dress, I gasped at its beauty. The material was so soft, with textured lace and layers that seemed to flutter like petals around the deep sweetheart bodice. I remembered seeing the long ivory, strapless dress at Bridal Rogue Gallery, which was available at a boutique in either London or York. This was one of the dresses that I had printed out and circled in a bridal organizer where I kept cut-outs and ideas.

Stella smiled. "Your dress is *something new.*"

"How's this even possible?"

"We had it shipped from the UK. You and Roxy have been the same size for years so we were able to have her stand in for the fitting. Your Aunt Iris came from Sacramento to help with the alterations."

I slipped out of the dress Xuan had given me to wear at my parent's house and into a petticoat before my mom and friends helped me with the wedding gown. Roxy was there to balance me and button the back of the dress. After I dressed, Amanda handed me a blue leg garter, the *something blue.*

Sky handed me a jewelry box with a matching marquise-cut diamond earring and necklace set. "Your *something borrowed.*"

Amanda ushered me towards a chair to sit. My nerves jangled with anticipation, as she stood behind me, makeup brushes at the ready. With gentle, practiced hands, Amanda began to work her magic. She started by carefully applying a sheer layer of foundation, smoothing out any imperfections. Next came the delicate task of shading and highlighting. Amanda worked with deft precision, carefully applying each stroke of color, enhancing my eyes and other features.

As Amanda worked, Sky and Roxy pulled up a chair next to me. We all chatted softly, and they attempted to sooth my anxieties and share in my excitement. We laughed and reminisced about old times, and they all promised to take me to Las Vegas for a delayed bachelorette party after the holidays.

As the transformation took place, I began to relax, my tension melting away under the gentle ministrations of my three best friends. And when the final touches were complete, and I was finally allowed to look into the mirror, I gasped in amazement at the stunning reflection looking back at me.

"You make a gorgeous bride, Cassandra," Stella said as Amanda finished working her magic. "Here, this is for you." She handed me a waltz-length lace mantilla bridal veil. The lace was one tier along the edge. "This was mine from when I married your father. This counts as *something old.*"

Mei came in to check on us and Stella went to check on the outside preparations. Mei took my hand and I sat beside her. A second box sat on the coffee table. Inside was a red & gold Chinese dress. "I also wanted to give you something before the wedding. It's a typical Chinese wedding dress. Wearing a red wedding dress has been a Chinese wedding tradition since the Ming Dynasty. In Chinese culture, the bride wears a red wedding dress to celebrate the joy and happiness of the marriage."

I held the romantic dreamy A-line dress made with soft, breathable lace and tulle fabric adorned with elegant gold floral embroidery and finished with a dramatic cathedral length train. "It's beautiful, Mei."

"I know you already have your ceremonial wedding dress, but I was hoping you might consider wearing this when you leave here tonight. Xuan doesn't know I bought this. It's supposed to bring luck and happiness. I thought it would be a good surprise if you changed into this before the limo comes to pick you both up at the end of the reception."

I hugged her. "Of course I'll wear it. Thank you for allowing me to be part of your family."

"I cannot express my gratitude enough for the adoration and devotion you have shown towards my son. Your unwavering commitment to him, especially in light of his cancer diagnosis, is a testament to your remarkable character, Cassie. Your willingness to stand by him through the trials and tribulations of this disease is both admirable and inspiring. It's not often that we find someone who's willing to love so deeply and unconditionally, and I'm grateful that my son has found that in you. I couldn't ask for a better daughter-in-law. Thank you for loving my son."

My heart was overflowing with gratitude. I knew that without Mei, I wouldn't be standing here, marrying the love of my life. "Thank you for accepting me into your family."

Tears glistened in her eyes as she smiled at me, her love for her one and only son radiated from her. "You don't need to thank me," she said. "I'm just happy to see my son so happy."

I felt a lump forming in my throat as I spoke again, my voice barely above a whisper. "I feel so thankful and blessed to have him in my life," I said. "He's everything to me."

She nodded and then let Amanda come to the rescue with a few touch up duties around my eyes.

"They're almost ready outside," said Roxy. I stood up from the couch as she handed me a large, cascading floral bouquet overflowing with stunning blush-pink, champagne, and burgundy flowers. Peonies, ranunculus, burgundy orchids, safari sunset, and roses. The profuse greenery was seeded eucalyptus, agonis, silver dollar eucalyptus in gray-green tones, and eucalyptus berries. My best friends grabbed smaller pieces that were the perfect moody palette of deep burgundy and natural blush-pink and champagne tones.

"Before we start, I just want to say thank you. To all of you. I'm still so stunned that I just don't have the words to tell you how much I love each one of you. I know I haven't been a great friend lately, so thank you for being here and for making this night perfect. You've made my dream wedding come to life, and I will never forget what you all have done for me and Xuan."

My friends gently embraced me. It was a moment of pure magic, shared between me three dearest friends. And as we hugged each other tightly, tears of joy streaming down our faces.

"Okay, let's all let go of the bride before I have to redo her makeup for a third time," teased Amanda.

Stella dabbed her eyes with a handkerchief and I kissed her wet cheek.

Sweet notes of piano filled the room as my mother looked at me. "It's time, sweetheart."

After that everything quickly fell into place.

Chapter Twenty-Nine: The Vow

Seabright, Santa Cruz, California
November 28, 2019

The pianist began playing Pachelbel's "Canon in D major."

"That's my cue," Stella said as she wiped away one final tear. My bridesmaids met the groomsmen—Beom, Nick, and Raylan—and walked down the aisle together.

As I stood just inside the house door, at the threshold of the aisle, my heart raced with anticipation. I felt a rush of emotions swirling inside me.

Waiting for my cue, I stood alone inside the house, my hands trembling. My dress around before me, a vision of lace and tulle and silk. My hair was perfectly coiffed, and my makeup expertly applied. But in that moment, I was filled with an overwhelming sense of anticipation and wedding jitters from the surprise of it all. I knew that my life was about to change forever. I was about to become someone's wife. The thought was both thrilling and terrifying. *What if I couldn't live up to the expectations?*

I took a deep breath, trying to calm the fluttering of my heart. Closing my eyes, I tried to picture the groom, waiting for me at the end of the aisle. I could almost feel his love radiating towards me, and in that moment, I knew that everything would be okay.

I took another deep steadying breath, and when I opened my eyes again, a sense of tranquility settled over me. I was ready for this. I was ready to take this step, to start this new chapter in my life. I knew that there would be challenges ahead, but I was determined to face them head-on, with my soulmate by my side.

Then my father asked everyone to rise. Now it was my turn. And with that, I stepped forward, ready to begin my journey into forever as the soft strains of "A Postcard to Henry Purcell" by

Jean-Yves Thibaudet began to fill the air. I felt my heart swell with emotion as it beat as fast as a hummingbird's wings. Taking a deep breath, I came out of the house. I felt as though I was stepping into Shakespeare's *A Midsummer's Night Dream*. My gaze darted around the garden, taking in the beauty of the venue, the smiling faces of my friends and family, and the delicate flowers that adorned the yard on small Roman style pillars. An ivory runner had been placed down the center of the yard, sprinkled with cream colored rose petals. The yard was lit by hundreds of candles and lanterns. Everything was perfect. The colors, the atmosphere, and my family and friends there as witnesses. But my attention was quickly drawn to the end of the aisle, where my future awaited me.

Xuan stood under a large archway with dangling vines and twinkle lights. His adoring eyes watched my every move and my heart swelled with pride and devotion in response. The friends who had stood beside him, despite his cancer, now stood beside him as groomsmen.

Everyone stood silently in respect as I made my way down the aisle. I took a deep breath, feeling a sense of calm wash over me. I thought of the journey that had led me to this moment—the moments of joy and the moments of sorrow, and the love that had sustained me through it all. I knew that in just a few short steps, I would be joined with the one I loved, and that our lives would be forever intertwined.

I felt the soft fabric of my wedding dress brush against my legs, and the gentle pressure of my cream rhinestone sandals against the ground. I walked forward, my eyes locked on my future, feeling a sense of wonder and joy fill my heart at the enraptured look on Xuan's beautiful face. And as I reached the end of the aisle, and took my groom's hand in mine, I knew that this was the moment I'd been waiting for. This was the moment that would change everything.

My father began the ceremony in the traditional way. "Welcome, family, friends, and loved ones. We are gathered here today, surrounded by the beauty of creation and nurtured by the sights and sounds of nature, to celebrate the wedding of Zhang Xuan and Cassandra Temperance Steel.

"Xuan and Cassie, please join hands, look at one another now, and remember this moment in time."

With that, he led us through our vows.

Command Sergeant Major Steel asked, "Do you have rings to exchange?"

Beom moved forward to hand Xuan the rings his mother and mother-in-law had helped pick out.

My father thanked Beom. He continued. "Your wedding rings are a symbol of your promise to one another. The ring, an unbroken, never-ending circle, is a symbol of committed, unending love."

We slipped the rings onto each other's fingers.

"You may now share your first kiss as husband and wife."

I threw my arms around my husband. His eyes, the smell of his cologne, the feel of his soft lips pressing against mine—everything about him invaded all my senses as he went for an unexpected dip. He pulled me back up, claiming my mouth with such intensity that it nearly felt as though I was taking a bite of forbidden fruit.

"Congratulations. Friends and family, I now present to you the newly married couple, Mr. Zhang Xuan and Mrs. Cassandra Temperance Steel. Let's hear it for 'em!"

A wave of warmth spread across my skin. Xuan never let go as he continued to hold my hand in his. In front of everyone, we'd promised each other love and devotion, in sickness and in health. There were worse things than death, like not ever experiencing love such as we shared. Marrying Xuan was one of those life-changing moments, something so hugely consequential that it was written in the stars. That night, right then, was the most wonderful moment of my life. This would be the beginning of a new life that we would face together, in all our human frailty and flaws. My soul was now tethered to Xuan's like a never-ending kite string.

Mei had set up her laptop on a chair so her husband and other family members in China and Korea could log on to see the entire service and be a part of the festivities. Even though he was far away, it was important for my new father-in-law to be able to watch the ceremony and see his only son get married. At the back of the yard, my uncle had been videotaping the entire ceremony, and my aunt, who was studying photography at the Academy of Art University in San Francisco, had taken pictures of the entire wedding. I would never know how much planning had gone into this night, and how many people had come together to make it happen, but the thought filled my heart.

From the corner of the garden, the pianist stood and faced the crowd. "Now it's time for Mr. Zhang and Mrs. Steel to share the traditional first dance as a married couple. If everyone would please clear the dance floor."

Xuan held out his hand, palm upward. "Come dance with me, my beautiful wife," he said, then waited for me to take his hand.

He led me to the temporary wooden dance floor in the backyard, under a flower-adorned marquee framed with hanging petals. Everyone else proceeded toward the center stage of the garden, watching us. The violinist and pianist began to play a duet to the cover of Ed Sheeran's song "Photograph." If I could, I would dance with him all night and play a song that would never, ever end.

Xuan grinned. "In case you're wondering about what happens after, we have a limo that will take us to the Chaminade Resort in three hours. My mother booked us a suite for our honeymoon night. But I think I should warn you that, when we arrive, it's likely the bed will be dressed in red-colored bedding with pillows to match and a mix of dried fruits and nuts somewhere nearby."

"Really?"

"Yeah. It's an old tradition. The combination is supposed to symbolize a blessed and sweet and long-lasting marriage. I'm sorry. She got hold of the room keys. You know my mom. There's no stopping her when her mind is set on something."

"Why are you apologizing? I love it, Xuan. Everything. I love your family and all your traditions."

"I'm just sorry I can't take you on a real honeymoon."

"Xuan, you always have a way of making everything beautiful. Everyday I'm with you feels like a honeymoon. Being with you isn't about going on some fancy trip. It's about you and me and being together every day. I want my day to begin and end with you. To share in the little moments."

Next my father cut in. "May I have this dance, Mrs. Steel?" "I Don't Want to Miss a Thing" by Aerosmith came on through the speakers. I took his hand and remembered a time when I was younger and had to step on his shoes. That night we glided across the dance floor. And I knew that, despite our fight, I was loved and adored by my father. Even though he'd been gone much of my life, people were able to sleep peacefully at night because of men like him—I was proud of him. The years spent apart, and the sacrifices my parents had made, were hard, but loving Command Sergeant Major Steel again was easy.

Xuan took his mother onto the dance floor after our song ended. A Chinese singer and songwriter came on as they danced. The name in English was hard to pronounce—"Guo Junchen"—and it translated similarly to "Tell Me the Future," though that was not the exact title. Xuan and Mei had a special bond, and there was no better way to embrace and honor her than with a heartfelt mother-son dance.

As my husband twirled around the dance floor with his mom, Stella came over to join me. She reached out her tiny arm, wrapping it around me tightly. "You look absolutely stunning tonight, my darling daughter." She paused, wiping away a tear, and then continued, "I want you to know how incredibly proud I am of the woman you've become, Cassandra. One thing I've always admired about you is that you've never been afraid to follow your heart. I'm sorry if I haven't always listened to you. But no matter what, remember that I'm your mom and I'll always be here for you, now and in the future. And as for your groom," she said, a gentle smile playing on her lips. "I know that he's facing a difficult battle, but I also know that he's a fighter, and that he loves you with all his heart." With a final squeeze of my shoulder, my mother took a deep breath. "No matter what the future holds, I know you and Xuan will face it together, with love and strength."

"I love you, Mom. Thank you for this beautiful life."

As the night continued, everyone ate and drank. The wedding cake was a simple, rustic design similar to something I'd cut out of a magazine months ago.

"Together," Xuan said as he placed his hand on mine and together we sliced through the first piece of tiered semi-naked cake with a layer of frosting.

After the cutting of the cake, everyone took to the dance floor to end the night. Once again, I found myself in Xuan's arms as we slow-danced, gradually swaying back and forth to the music. For me, time was stretching like the universe.

"You're mine now," Xuan whispered in my ear. "And I have no intention of letting you go or sharing for the rest of my life, *qī zi*."

"*Qī zi*? I haven't heard that word before. What does it mean?"

He smiled and then explained. "In Chinese, *qī zi* is generally considered to be a formal word for wife, reserved for times like today. After today, *lǎo pó* will be more common. It's less formal, and similar to wifey."

He was calling me his wife, and I absolutely adored it. I asked him to teach me the Mandarin word for husband, and I eagerly practiced its pronunciation in a sentence.

"Now you're mine, *zhàng fū*. And no matter what lies ahead, through thick and thin, in sickness and in health, my love for you will never waver. I wouldn't trade a single moment of our time together."

"Wǒ *zhǐ shǔ yú nǐ*." I had heard him say this before and knew it meant "I only belong to you."

"Thank you for tonight—this has all been like a dream."

We continued to dance to a mix of English and Chinese songs, this time to another song from one of my favorite Chinese dramas, "Accidentally in Love." The song was sung by Guo Junchen, and the song title was translated as "Star" in English. This was followed by the song "Yang Yang—Just One Smile Is Very Alluring" by Liuzki.

When I threw my bouquet, Sky collided with Amanda and the flower girl in front of her as she tried to catch it. Xuan took the blue garter off with nothing but his teeth to Michael Bublé's song "Feeling Good." Beom stood at the back of the yard and blushed an embarrassing shade of red as it fell into his hands.

Nick and Sky came up, hand in hand. They looked happy. "Sky's feet hurt and she's getting tired, and I've gotta work tonight, so we're going to head out."

"Thank you so much for everything." I hugged my friends.

Sky leaned in. "Make sure you open the gift from me tonight. It's the small, sparkly pink bag, *specifically* for your honeymoon." Sky turned to Xuan. "I didn't get anything for you, but I think it's more a gift for you than it is for her." She winked.

"Don't worry," Nick said. "I got a matching one for you too, bro. I thought you'd like to model it for your wife later."

A surprised laugh came from my throat, one which was echoed by Xuan. "Please tell me you're joking."

"I guess you'll find out."

I felt my skin pulse at the thought of what could be inside that little pink present.

Xuan folded me back into him like the darkness of night, only stopping to talk to family members who continued to call Mei on WeChat to offer us their congratulations and blessings, and to dance with my father, or with someone asking to cut in.

I felt like I was watching myself in a dream, except this was not a dream. This was real. I had everything I'd wanted—and yet none of it was the way I'd imagined it would be. While many constellations had wheeled past the dance floor, the Northern star remained, slightly dimmed by Jupiter and Venus, the two brightest planets in the sky. The spectacularly bright Venus, once known in ancient Rome as the Goddess of Love, was positioned above Jupiter, allowing it to reign over the night sky.

Amidst the joyful chaos of the wedding reception, Xuan and I were able to step away from the throngs of people and found a secluded spot on the dance floor. The music was still playing, but we moved together in a peaceful quiet. As we danced, I felt a sense of calm wash over me. Xuan's movements were fluid and effortless, and I followed his lead with ease. The world around us faded away, and for a few precious moments, it was just the two of us, lost in the music in a peaceful quiet. I prayed that God would look down on us and see the beauty of our existence, and the trueness of our love. I prayed that He would decide to spare Xuan and leave us alone for many years. I prayed for a miracle. I knew I was being greedy as I'd already been blessed with so many. But this was my wedding night. I was allowed to be a little selfish.

We continued dancing as a swift gale wheeled through the hills of Santa Cruz. Xuan leaned down to whisper into my ear, his lips lightly brushing the helix. "Once upon a time there was a boy, and he loved a girl very much. He was sad because he didn't think the girl noticed him. Until one day the universe intervened and a beautiful comet brought them together after a tragic accident occurred that day. The boy and the girl found comfort and friendship in each other that night. And something new and extraordinary began to blossom under the heavens, something that would burn with such brightness that all the stars would be in awe. And the boy fell madly in love with the girl and promised to always find her, in this life and the next."

"That's my favorite story."

Xuan smiled. "It's the best one I've ever told, Mrs. Steel."

CHAPTER THIRTY: THE SACRIFICE

The Mary & Richard Solari Cancer Center
December 5, 2019

Reluctantly, Xuan had agreed to start systemic chemo. He met with his cancer doctor and surrendered. He loathed the idea, infusing poison into his body, but he did it for me—his wife.

He sat in comfortable, loose clothes on a chair upholstered in dark-blue vinyl in the chemo room, his arm resting on an armrest as we watched the new Spider-Man movie. An IV tube was snaking its way into his vein. Next to him was the stand for the infusion, dripping poison into his body.

Several people sat in the rows of chairs, as if they were sitting at a movie theater. A few people had pulled a curtain for privacy but most sat in full view, bored with tablets, smartphones, or magazines to help pass the time.

Xuan's eyes were closed for a few minutes, his face peaceful, but I could see the strain in the way his hands gripped the armrests.

I wanted to say something, to offer some kind of comfort, but the words caught in my throat. So I simply took his hand in mine, squeezing it gently. Xuan opened his eyes and looked at me, a small smile tugging at the corners of his pale lips. It was a smile that didn't quite reach his eyes, but I knew that was all he had to offer right now.

The chemo drugs continued to trickle into Xuan's veins, the transparent fluid vanishing into his body like a venomous serpent. I watched as his complexion grew faint and ashen, the color draining from his face. His breathing became shallow, and I could see the effort it took for him to keep his eyes open.

Time seemed to stand still as we sat there, watching the IV

drip. I felt a lump forming in my throat, and I swallowed hard, trying to push it down. I didn't want to add to the burden he was already carrying. But he turned to me, his eyes shining with tears. "Thank you," he whispered, his voice barely above a whisper. "Thank you for being here."

I squeezed his hand again, feeling the warmth of his skin against mine. "I'll always be here," I said, my voice cracking. "No matter what."

And in that moment, as the drugs pumped through my husband's body, I knew that we were in this together. That no matter what the future held, we would face it side by side, holding each other's hands, and never letting go.

Dominican Hospital, California
December 9, 2019

I woke up to the soft, subtle sounds of a nurse's presence, her footsteps resonating in the hospital room. As sunlight streamed in through the hospital window, I saw her carefully removing something from Xuan's arm. He had already undergone his first round of chemotherapy, but unfortunately, he had a severe reaction to the treatment. He started throwing up blood, causing great concern. Due to his condition, the doctors decided to keep him in the hospital for observation for a few days.

Blinking my eyes open, I was surprised to find Mei sitting attentively by her son's bedside. It appeared she had just arrived, likely after completing her work shift. As I sat up, stretching my tired limbs, I greeted her with a warm smile.

"Mornin', Mei," I said, my voice still laced with sleep. "I'm going to grab something from the cafeteria. Do you need anything?"

Mei looked up, her fatigued eyes meeting mine, tinged with subtle red lines tracing the blood vessels—a telltale sign of the sleepless nights and the countless tears she had shed in solitude. She shook her head slightly. "I'm okay, sweetie. Thanks for asking."

"Alright, I'll be back soon. Call me on my cell if you change your mind."

I glanced down at Xuan, his body curled into a protective ball under the hospital sheets, then quietly left the room. The sight of him like that tugged at my heart, but I knew he needed rest, and I needed to take a break as well. With a heavy sigh, I made my way out of the hospital room, the sterile scent of disinfectant filling my nostrils.

Reaching the elevator, I pressed the arrow button and waited for the doors to open. The elevator arrived with a quiet chime, its doors sliding open. Stepping inside, I pressed the button for the hospital cafeteria, eager to escape the somber atmosphere of the hospital room and find solace in a moment of respite.

After half an hour, I returned to Xuan's hospital room, carefully balancing two steaming cups of coffee in my hands. I wanted to do something for Mei, my new mother-in-law, even if it was just a simple gesture to show her that I cared.

"Hey, Mei," I said softly. "I brought you a cup of coffee. I thought you might like it."

Mei's eyes were wet and she held a crumpled-up tissue in her hand. She looked lost, confused, scared.

Setting down one of the cups of coffee on the bedside table, I gently placed my hand on Mei's shoulder. "Mei, are you okay?"

Her voice trembled as she tried to find the right words. "I . . . I don't know, Cassie. Everything feels so overwhelming right now. Seeing Xuan like this, it's . . .it's breaking my heart."

I squeezed her shoulder reassuringly. "I understand, Mei. It's a difficult situation for all of us. But we'll get through this together."

Mei nodded, her tears still flowing. "Thank you, Cassie. I can't imagine what I would do without your support. I'm incredibly grateful that my son has you in his life."

She picked up the cup and took a few slow sips, allowing the warmth and aroma to comfort her as she sought to regain her composure. We sat together in silence for a while, the only sounds in the room being the gentle beeping of the monitors and the occasional rustle of tissues.

"Any change while I was gone?" I inquired, breaking the stillness that enveloped the room.

"He opened his eyes for just a few minutes and then threw up."

"Did he ask for me?"

"The first thing he said was your name, but then he fell back asleep. Go home and shower. Get some sleep, xífù." She was calling me her daughter-in-law.

"Oh, but I should be here when he wakes up if he was asking for me. I'll go home in a while. Let me stay with him for right now just in case he wakes up again."

"Sweetie, it's okay to leave him for a few hours. I'll call if there's any change. Take a drive and get out in the California sunshine. Come back around lunchtime and then we can trade off."

Just then a team of doctors swept into the room. "Good morning! How are we doing today?"

"Xuan woke up a few minutes ago. Other than that, he's been out of it," Mei said.

"When he wakes up again, let us know. We have to take him downstairs for testing."

"More tests? How long will these tests take?" Mei asked.

"A couple of hours."

With that, Mei's fragile composure gave way. Her answering expression was like a crumpled piece of scratch paper thrown into the trash. Tears fell from her cheeks and chin onto her shirt and pants. I hesitated at the door, torn between my instinct to stay by Mei's side, and the understanding that she needed space to process her emotions. Sensing her desire for solitude, I reluctantly decided to respect her wishes.

This must be how the Titan Atlas felt bearing the weight of the celestial sphere on his head and hands, a burden given to him as punishment by Zeus. Love sometimes can feel like the weight of the world has been placed on your shoulders, and you can do nothing but carry it because you love.

Dazed and fatigued, I wandered through the bustling corridors leading back to Xuan's unit, the weight of exhaustion tugging at my every step. The hospital seemed even busier than before, filled with the constant movement of healthcare professionals, patients, and their loved ones. As I passed by open doors, glimpses into other rooms revealed scenes of solitude and anxiety—elderly patients by themselves, children anxiously waiting by their parents' beds. The nurses, always in a hurry, formed the heartbeat of the healthcare system. Their kind demeanor was evident as they tirelessly hustled around the main station, reaching for charts, visiting patients, and responding to emergencies.

As I entered Xuan's room, I skillfully held two cups of steaming black tea and a white sack of food, careful not to spill anything. With a gentle smile, I announced, "I'm back, and I brought lunch."

Mei, her emotions still evident on her face, gratefully accepted the cup and the small bag. Leaning over, I kissed Xuan, who was still asleep like a prince.

Turning to Mei, I asked, "How are you holding up?"

"Barely keeping it together," Mei said, her eyes bloodshot, swollen. I reached for her hand and squeezed it and then took a seat in the chair next to her.

"Xuan's a warrior. He'll make it through this."

"I know. He's always had such an inner strength. Truthfully, I don't know where he gets it from."

"From you and Ji-Hoon."

She adjusted her hand on mine. "Xífù, you look tired. Did you not take a nap at home?"

"I slept for an hour. I'll be fine."

"You need to take care of yourself, for my son."

"How is he?"

"No change. He's been in and out of consciousness. He doesn't make much sense when he's awake. I feel so helpless. It's hard for a parent to watch their child go through something like this."

"I can't even begin to imagine how you feel."

She gave me a sad smile and then handed me a letter addressed to Xuan which had arrived from Ji-Hoon in China. "Give this to him when he wakes. I need to call my husband and family and then head into the office. I probably won't be back for a few hours."

"I'll be here."

I waited until Mei was gone before I lowered my head onto my husband's chest. An IV needle was sticking in the crook of his elbow. Every time a nurse came in to poke Xuan with more needles, like he was a pincushion, I felt empty, guilty. I became suddenly, keenly aware of how small I was. There was nothing I could do but sit by Xuan's bed and hold his hand. Life is fragile.

"Sorry, Mrs. Zhang, but I need to wake your husband." The nurse had brought Xuan some of his scheduled meds. It was actually Mrs. Steel, but I didn't have the energy to correct her. Xuan and I *did* talk about me changing my last name after our honeymoon night. No matter what I said, he strongly felt it was best for me to keep my name the same, so I didn't argue with him. It was a moot point. I had gotten what I wanted—him. That's all that mattered.

Xuan sat up groggily and took the cup of pills. I almost wanted to yell at the nurse for waking him, but I knew she was just doing her job.

Every morning Xuan took more medicine, followed by a tray of hospital food he could barely stomach. Xuan had experienced short periods of being awake and alert. During those times when he did feel good, he liked to get up and move around, so we'd walk the different floors of the hospital together. He loved going to the maternity ward and visiting the babies who wriggled around behind the glass.

All the nurses on this floor knew Xuan by name, and he liked joking with them during their shifts. His jokes were like his armor. I knew he needed his wit now more than ever. Xuan was growing restless with each passing day. He wanted to be home.

"How are you feeling, *lǎo gōng*?" This also meant husband or hubby, but was less formal than *zhàng fū*.

"How do you think I feel?"

"I bet not very well. Especially now. After the tests, I mean."

"I feel like a lab rat. Everything they do hurts and gives me such a huge headache."

"I'm sorry. I'm here if you need anything."

Xuan's eyes bore into mine, his gaze filled with a mixture of anguish and accusation. "Is *sorry* all that you can say?" he challenged, his tone cutting through the air like a sharp blade.

I struggled to find the right words, grappling with the weight of guilt and the ache in my heart. "I don't know what the right thing is to say," I admitted, my voice tinged with vulnerability.

"Being sorry won't change any of this. You should have let me die my way, in peace. That's what I wanted."

Xuan's words cut through me like a hot branding iron. This was the comment I had been dreading, and it seared into my heart.

Guilt gnawed at my insides as I acknowledged the truth of his words. Back in May, at the end of that fateful month, I'd thought only of myself, pushing him towards treatment without fully considering the toll it would take on him. "I know," I replied, my voice hollow and frigid, mirroring the coldness I felt within. It was a painful admission of my role in his suffering.

I reached out, gently grasping his hand, acutely aware of the pain he endured, a suffering borne out of his love for me. I would never forget the look in his eyes, never stop beating myself up for asking this of him.

A part of me wanted to tell him it was okay to stop the treatment, to spare him from more pain. But another part of me, scared and unsure, couldn't bring myself to say it out loud. I couldn't bear the thought of losing him, not yet. It was selfish, I know, but I wanted him to hold on and keep fighting for as long as he could.

"Why me?" whispered Xuan.

"I don't know," I replied honestly, the uncertainty echoing in my voice. It was the only response I could give, because I didn't know the answer. Nobody did. *I could've died in the mudslide. Why not me? I couldn't answer that. Not then. Not now. Why do only the good die young, as the lyrics to that song go?*

Coldness crept up my spine. I couldn't form the words necessary to explain this. I reached for his hand. I knew he was in pain. He was suffering because he loved me. I would never forget the look in his eyes, never stop beating myself up for asking this of him. Part of me wanted to give him permission to stop treatment, but I was also too afraid of what would happen if I voiced how I felt. I just couldn't lose him. Not yet.

A sad frown twisted in the corner of his mouth. "Cassie, I think I want to be alone right now." He curled in a ball on the bed, withdrawing from me and the world.

Silently, I pleaded and begged. *Please don't push me away. Don't send me away from your side.*

"Okay." My jaw began to quiver. "If that's what you want." I felt hurt, like I was trapped in some nightmare and I was the bad guy. I was the villain, not the hero, in my own real-life comic book. But as I stood up and turned and walked toward the door to leave, I felt his eyes on me.

"Wait!" he yelled, panicked. "Please don't go, *lǎo pó*. I don't want to be alone. I should never have said that. I didn't mean it! Stay."

I turned back around and walked to the hospital bed where Xuan was lying. I took his hand in mine, feeling relieved that he wanted me to stay with him.

"I'm scared, Cassie. It hasn't been that long. I already feel so sick and tired, like a grumpy old—"

"Cat?" I smiled. "Don't worry about me. You've always been my rock. Now let me be yours, *lǎo gōng*." This was the informal term for husband or hubby in Mandarin.

Xuan's eyes held mine without pity. "I can do this."

Is he trying to convince me or himself? "I know you can."

Xuan said the food was miserable, but I took a taste and didn't think it was that bad. The doctors had warned Xuan that his meds could alter his tastes. Sometimes for a year, maybe longer. We had met a few patients who still had no sense of taste after several years. Many of them had told Xuan that even the texture of some foods in the mouth felt gross.

Suddenly, it hit me—I'd completely forgotten about the sealed envelope Mei handed me before she left. I rummaged through my bag, found it, and made my way over to Xuan. "Hey, check this out. I've got something for you."

"What is it?"

"It's a letter. From your father."

I didn't fail to note the light that gleamed in my lover's eyes as he read the Chinese script. Xuan scanned the words to the letter over and over. He still looked tired, but his cheeks had a bit more color, and he was moving with greater ease.

"Well, what did your father say?"

Xuan touched the edge of his mattress and beckoned me to sit beside him, a feat made awkward with the IV and medical tubes. "He's trying to arrange to come to America, but he has to go through red tape because of the issues with his visa. He's hired a lawyer."

The letter from Ji-Hoon was a blessing, and it gave him a newfound reason to keep fighting. More than anything, he wanted to see his father in person. I settled for a deep but brief kiss as he began to close his eyes, the letter still held tightly in his hand. It was as if the letter had infused him with revived hope, like the striking of a resounding bell, as his internal clock hour counted down and struck eight.

Chapter Thirty-One: The Tree Farm

Seabright, Santa Cruz, California
December 18, 2019

I loved Christmastime with Xuan—the smell of evergreen trees, the familiar colored-glass ornaments, my mother's homemade sugar cookies we would frost together, and the wood logs that were hauled from outside to replenish the fire in the living room grate.

I kept myself busy with holiday baking as I waited for Xuan to wake up. The aggressive chemo treatment was a necessary weapon in his battle against the monsters within. The initial cycle had taken a toll on him, leaving him fatigued, nauseous, and in pain, plagued by cramps, chills, and night sweats. However, since his release from the hospital, he had been progressing well, and his spirits had lifted.

Happy to have him home, I lit one of our favorite cinnamon and spice scented candles. I danced around the kitchen—now *our* kitchen—as I kneaded dough for baking. *It still feels strange to say* our *when referring to the house, cars, bills, and even our fluffy butterball cat.* And then of course, there were the words, *his wife – lǎo pó,* which seemed to cast a magical spell over me every time he said them. Completely and irrevocably in love, I was determined to make this holiday season special for Xuan. But it was also special for me, as it marked the first Christmas I would spend with my husband, happily married.

The weekend after we got married, Xuan helped me pack and move into our little yellow house. The transition from dating to marriage had felt sudden, but it had been amazing. At times, it still felt surreal to me. I only had a suitcase of clothes and a box of personal items to move from my parents' house. Despite Xuan and Mei's encouragement to feel at home, I didn't want to intrude.

Xuan had captured my heart with a powerful enchantment, and I felt truly blessed to share this life with him. As I placed the dough in the oven, I knew that our love would rise and expand, just like this first batch of Christmas cookies.

With Led Zeppelin's Immigrant Song playing in my EarPods, I continued to dance around the kitchen, the clatter of bowls and utensils blending with the rhythm. Lost in the music, I was oblivious to Xuan sneaking in like a mouse searching for crumbs. Suddenly, he appeared behind me, his arms enveloping my waist. Startled, I dropped an egg, its delicate contents splattering on the floor.

"Ho, ho, ho . . . it's beginning to smell a lot like Christmas."

"Is it too much? I can blow out the candle if you don't like it," I offered. After Xuan began chemotherapy, certain smells, particularly those associated with food, triggered and worsened some of his symptoms. Last night, the smell of cooking meat made him feel nauseous.

"I like the smell, *lǎo pó*. I just wish actual cookies were involved."

"It's nine o'clock in the morning. I'm just getting started on the snickerdoodle recipe." I turned around in his arms to look at him. Xuan was wearing a knee-length woolen winter coat and a pair of men's skinny jeans. I noticed he'd set an axe on the counter.

"Going somewhere, Mountain Man?"

"Let's go to a tree farm. And when we get back, you can bake me your special snickerdoodle recipe," he suggested.

"A tree farm?"

"We need a Christmas tree," he declared. "A real one." The previous year, we'd put up a three-foot plastic tree. "This is our first one as a married couple. Would the missus be opposed to that?"

"Not at all."

"I found a place near here called Patchen Old Town Christmas

Trees."

"Great idea."

Xuan held up his axe. "Let's go hunt a tree!" He sounded excited as he dipped his hand in flour and dotted my nose before leaving with his axe.

I cleaned up the messy egg spill on the floor, placed the dough in the fridge, and hurried to get dressed while the first batch of cookies was baking in the oven. Cutting down our own tree was as Christmassy as cookies and gift wrap.

Xuan and I were dressed and ready to go, after the oven timer went off. Mei took a moment to look me over. "You should dress warmer, xífù. You're not wearing a jacket, boots, or gloves. I don't want you to catch a cold."

"My jacket's in the car. I'll be fine," I replied confidently.

She shrugged and kissed us both on the cheek, promising to be home early enough from work to help decorate the tree.

Patchen Old Town Christmas Trees
December 18, 2019

After a seventy-minute ride, we finally arrived at Patchens' Christmas tree farm. As soon as I stepped out of the vehicle, the cold air hit me, and I began to feel it seeping into my bones. I should have listened to Mei's warning to dress warmly, but it was too late now. Xuan and I started our search for the perfect tree, but my discomfort was growing with every passing minute.

"You're shaking like a leaf," Xuan observed, as he leaned in and blew warm air onto my hands. "Here, take this." He reached into his pocket and retrieved the white O'Neill beanie that Mei had insisted he pack, just in case.

The crisp air carried the sweet scent of pine needles, blending with the delicious aroma of roasting cinnamon chestnuts wafting from the entrance shop. The affable owner of the farm offered visitors a tractor ride out to the tree fields—organized by type, including Douglas and Fraser firs—and saws to cut down your choice if you didn't bring your own, a ride back, a needle shake and netting, and free hot chocolate. It was a good deal.

This was a first-time experience for both of us to chop down our own Christmas tree, and it felt almost Ralph Waldo Emerson-esque. It also gave us the opportunity to escape the traffic and chaos that had engulfed the city during the bustling holiday season.

Xuan was clearly enjoying the outdoors and fresh air, so we opted to skip the tractor ride. With two weeks left before Christmas, many of the trees had been purchased. A date earlier in December would've been better in order to beat the choppies and come-latelies and get prime selection.

Xuan and I meandered through the lanes of trees, admiring their various shapes and sizes. Some were tall and slender, while others were short and plump. Each tree seemed to have its unique personality and character. We continued to wander through each row, perusing and evaluating our options, taking into account fullness and branch-and-needle coverage, and making scientific-ish comments about whether or not it really *looked* like a Christmas tree, which probably had Emerson rolling in his grave.

There were plenty of trees that looked nice but weren't the perfect fit. So we kept searching, taking an analytical approach to choosing just the right tree. Hand in hand, we wound our way through the crooked paths of the farm, assessing each tree we came to. We stopped in front of a Douglas fir. Its fullness made it prime for decorations and other ornaments, but the top of the tree looked slightly crooked, so we passed on it.

As we continued to stroll up and down aisles, we watched children riding piggyback or running around the farm, their excitement palpable.

On the second-to-last row we spotted a beautiful spruce tree with a perfect cone shape. Xuan and I both stopped. The six-foot-tall spruce stood before us, the branches chaotic yet orderly, reaching for sunlight. The color was healthy. The tree was thick, but there was room for ornaments. The soft morning dew rested on the pine as light reflected, looking like crystals.

"This is it," I exclaimed. "This is the one."

"I was thinking the same thing, *qīn'ài de.*"

Once we settled on our tree, we needed to do a needle test. Xuan grabbed six inches from the outer end of the branch and pulled on it lightly. The needles didn't slide off in our hands, which was a good sign.

We took pictures of our chosen tree and asked a passerby to snap some of us in front of the spruce. After we got a few nice smiling pictures as a couple, we made goofy faces for more candid photos as we chopped away for nostalgia. I laughed at my failed Paul Bunyan-style attempts before Xuan took the ax from me.

"May the Forest be with you," I joked, adding a playful twist to a popular phrase, as he began chopping away at it. I took on the role of an overly enthusiastic supervisor, complete with comically serious facial expressions.

This memory was one of those defining moments for us as a married-couple, marking a milestone in our first holiday season together as husband and wife. It served as a rite of passage, a significant event in our first year of marriage.

I had never personally cut down my own Christmas tree before, but from that very moment, I made a heartfelt promise to myself. Every year thereafter, I would come back to this place to select my tree, turning it into a cherished tradition. It would serve as a tangible reminder of our first Christmas together as a married couple, a memory that would forever hold a special place in my heart, even if Xuan was no longer with me.

Finally the tree came down. Using our own sap-covered hands, we hoisted it back to the register in triumph and waited in line to pay, as Crosby chimed in over the speaker with his baritone rendition of "The Little Drummer Boy," setting the mood. His voice was like a familiar calling that Christmas was near.

After the tree was wrapped, the workers threw it on top of my jeep and tied it down before we drove away with the Trans-

Siberian Orchestra's "Christmas Eve/Sarajevo 12/24" blasting from the radio. I was unprepared for how happiness would impact the passing of time—it rushed by, slipping through my fingers and crystallizing into unforgettable memories.

Despite the two massive C's hanging over us—cancer and chemo—Xuan seemed perfectly happy to be there, with the world at our feet.

Seabright, Santa Cruz, California
December 18, 2019

Once we arrived back at our house, we snuggled up in the living room and basked in the cozy glow of a newly lit fire. It had been a wonderful day.

As we waited for Mei to join us so we could decorate, Xuan retrieved a book of poetry that we'd been reading together every night before bed. I sat in his arms and nestled into his gentle embrace as he recited a passage from The *Coming of the Ship* by Kahlil Gibran. *"Yet I cannot tarry longer. The sea that calls all things unto her calls me, and I must embark."*

Inside the living room, the fire continued to fizzle and crack as it spit out delicious warmth. The boy I loved sat beside me on the couch, his head resting against my shoulder as the coziness of the space enveloped us both.

Eyes fluttering open and then closed, Xuan put the book down and rested beside me as we wedged ourselves into the tight space of the couch. The heat of his body pressed against mine and his presence was a comforting warmth in itself. Soon, he drifted off into a peaceful slumber. The soft glow of the firelight illuminated his serene and beautiful face. This room, our safe haven, felt like home, and I knew that I was exactly where I was meant to be, with the person I loved most in the world.

I stayed awake a while, taking in the piney smell wafting through the room. The bare tree stood near the window, an anchor to the present, like a bookmark or stamp that helped me mark this page of time. Everything was happening too fast, like an amusement-park ride. I wanted everything to slow down, not speed up.

The passing of the season had happened too quickly. Without much effort, the crackling, dying leaves had fallen in the front yard and now laid underneath a blanket of frost that covered everything with its shine and gloss. The chilling shadow of the season had crept up on us, stealing all signs of life from the summer land. I just hoped Xuan would still be there in our yellow house to see spring and the birth and regrowth of life. I wanted more of this, of him and experiences like today. I wanted to make my husband happy, as he had made me.

Be here now. Be here in the present

As the minutes ticked by, I felt my eyelids growing heavier. The rhythm of light afternoon raindrops mixed with the sound of Christmas carols was hypnotic, and my mind drifted off into a dreamlike state.

"Wake up, sleepies, the pizzas are ready!"

Mei had returned to find us on the couch. She'd already cooked three medium pizzas—Hawaiian, margherita, and Canadian bacon with olives—before deciding to wake us.

I opened my eyes to Chairman Meow sprawled out on the floor, on his back. The parody song "Catnuts Roasting on an Open Fire" came to mind as his fat bottom faced the direction of the living room fire. A connoisseur of comfort and luxury, the Persian was certainly the king of the house, an example of sovereignty and sophistication, minus the civilization. I'd even found Mei a coffee cup for Christmas that said *Dogs have owners. Cats have staff.* The quote was a precise personification of Chairman Meow, who was a perfect ball of long, thick fur like an oversized cotton ball.

Mei had put a stack of mail on the coffee table. "Anything from the Hater Grinch?" I asked.

"Nothing. Maybe he grew a small heart?" Mei suggested.

"Wishful thinking, but highly doubtful."

"So why nothing?" she asked.

"I think they're waiting for everyone to forget, to cool off."

Still, it had been eerily quiet since Halloween. Maybe that really was the last of it, since the act had crossed into vandalism.

"Let's not ruin our Christmas thinking about them," she suggested, trying to lift our spirits. "Maybe Santa will bring that person a new soul—one filled with kindness and compassion."

"You're too nice, Mei," I said shaking my head. "Personally, I hope the person gets a visit from Krampus this year instead of Santa. He knows how to deal with the wicked." I shuddered at the thought of Krampus's twisted horns and long, pointed tongue. He was a fearsome creature, but I couldn't think of anyone more deserving of his wrath than the person who had caused so much pain.

Mei frowned. "Let's just hope that person has a change of mind this Christmas, and their heart grows three sizes like the Grinch's did."

Beside me, Xuan felt warm, flushed with a slight fever . . . or maybe he was just hot from the fire. "Are you all right?"

"Of course, *lǎo pó*." He waved me off and began to stretch from our catlike nap.

We brought boxes of decorations and ornaments inside and then hurried upstairs to change our clothes. Xuan was wearing a black-and-red plaid shirt and I dressed to match him.

"Xuan, help me drag the box of decorations inside," requested Mei.

"Let's start with the lights," I suggested as I took a bite of the Canadian bacon with olive pizza.

Xuan plugged in the stand, and Mei began to hand the lights to him as he wrapped them around the tree.

The ornaments Stella had given us were all coastal themed. Stella had promised to save the sea ornaments for my first year living on my own and stored the box in the shed. We decorated our tree using the nautical blue-and-white palette and sea-themed ornaments, in turquoise, blues, and off-whites, and blue spheres with rope, mermaid-blue string beads, and naturally bleached starfish, all reminders of the first time Xuan and I made love on the beach.

As we hung the ornaments and strung the lights, I thought about how the old traditions would blend with the new ones that my husband and mother-in-law and I would create together. Mei had always planned to return to China after our wedding. But when Xuan was diagnosed with an illness, everything changed. We were all adjusting to a new reality, one that required us to come together and find new ways to celebrate and cherish the time we had with each other.

Like Xuan, Mei was a Sinatra fan. "Have Yourself a Merry Little Christmas" was followed by several a cappella versions of Christmas favorites by Pentatonix as the music continued to quietly play in the background. Seashell angels adorned the decorated tree like beacons of hope, sending the message that we were not alone. An elegantly glittered six-point star sat on top, made from a metal frame and accented with a large oval-shaped acrylic diamond. The tree topper was an intricately unique design, an impeccable finish to our tree.

A tall, perfectly formed and decorated tree stood before the window. Chairman Meow eyed the dangling balls with immediate interest, as if they'd been put up just for him. I just hoped the tree would survive the battle with the cat and that he wouldn't decide to use it as a fresh scratching post.

Mei held up her glass of mango margarita. "To family—old and new."

The amusement and happiness in Xuan's eyes sharpened to complete joy. I tried to cling to every moment of here and now.

We all drank to that.

The house was decorated colorfully, but tastefully. I looked forward to *The Nutcracker,* in just two more days. We planned to attend the candlelight church service at Twin Lakes on Christmas Eve, where Xuan and Mei had agreed to join me and my mom. I felt the longing for Candlelight Christmas Eve, when we would celebrate the light that came to the world in Jesus, the light that shined in the darkness, a darkness that could never overcome it.

Despite all the happiness and joy of the season, Xuan's internal clock had continued to count down. The hour hand now rested at seven.

CHAPTER THIRTY-TWO: OPERA HOUSE

Seabright, Santa Cruz, California
December 20, 2019

Like many families touched by cancer, I had come to understand the value of focusing on the present. Planning for the here and now had become a form of therapeutic medicine. As a surprise, I had procured two tickets for the enchanting holiday performance of *The Nutcracker* at the San Francisco War Memorial Opera House. It was another item that Xuan could check off his bucket list.

Although I had offered to buy tickets for Mei and my mom to join us, my mom already had prior commitments, and Mei had a tight schedule. Within half an hour, she needed to rush to the airport for a morning meeting in Oregon. However, she remained optimistic about returning on Monday, provided everything went smoothly.

Earlier today, Mei asked Xuan to jot down his top three choices for a mini-vacation. With Xuan out of the hospital and making progress in his treatment, she wanted to celebrate the New Year in style and divert his attention from the chemotherapy. Mei was typically meticulous and preferred booking in advance, but Xuan's ever-changing schedule had made it tricky to plan ahead. Nevertheless, Mei was determined to organize a trip for all of us, and she even extended an invitation to my mom.

Xuan's New Year's Eve preferences included New York City, New Orleans, or Los Angeles. However, given his desire to go skiing, Mei also considered renting a cozy cabin in Park City, Utah, or Lake Tahoe as viable alternatives.

In a sense, we all saw the New Year as a chance to bring closure to the experiences of the past year and embrace both the possibilities and challenges that lay ahead. The idea of traveling during the holiday season filled me with excitement and a sense of anticipation.

Before Mei left for the airport, she wholeheartedly devoted herself to exploring the trip options that Xuan had written down. With only eleven days remaining until the New Year countdown, securing reservations and flights would be challenging, considering the time of year.

As Mei busily searched for suitable hotels and plane tickets, Xuan and I were busy getting ready to leave for the evening ballet.

It was nearly time to go. My phone rang as I put the finishing touches around my eyes. I had taken my time to get ready for the ballet, wanting to look oh-so-perfect for my husband. It was Roxy. I answered and put the call on speakerphone. "What's up?"

"Cassie, I was worried you wouldn't answer!"

"Xuan and I leave in about thirty minutes. We have the ballet tonight at seven."

"Help? I've been Christmas shopping four times this week. I keep seeing all these wonderful presents and I just keep thinking of how good they would look on me, and then I buy them. Sky came with me yesterday, but she kept dragging me to the baby aisle. And then she said her feet were swollen like sausages and bailed. I still have a ton to buy for people and I can't decide what to get. Will you go with me? I'm completely hopeless."

I did have some last-minute shopping I needed to get done, even though I dreaded the idea of going to the mall on the weekend. "Sure. Tomorrow at noon?"

"You're the best! Send me pictures of you and Xuan at the ballet tonight!"

Gliding to the mirror, I observed the ethereal silhouette of the hand-embroidered dress. The dress was long and the body was as black as night. Spaghetti straps and a fitted corset-styled bodice with a V-neckline showcased a boning structure, which set a romantic tone. My hair was unbound and swept forward over the bustline of the dress. Last but not least, falling from the waist, just over the black fabric, was an elegant lace that was a light turquoise, the color of the comet's tail we had seen in Colombia, our unforgettable connection to the cosmos.

I grabbed my black purse and gave Chairman Meow chin rubs as he lay curled up on the toasty bed, before descending the stairs. Mei's cat often reminded me of a funny meme—*In ancient times, cats were worshiped as gods, a fact they have not forgotten.*

Xuan waited at the bottom of the staircase, wearing a classically tailored black-and-white suit and holding a wrist corsage in his hand. Saints, he was gorgeous.

He reached for me, I looped my arm around his, and it took all of my self-control to not stay home and take him back upstairs, despite the fact I was excited to see the hundred-year-old Russian ballet.

Xuan let out a breath. "I think the words *incredible* and *radiant* don't even begin to describe how you look tonight."

"You're quite the stunner yourself, *lǎo gōng*."

Mei took pictures of us in front of the crackling fireplace and the beautifully decorated Christmas tree, its branches shimmering with twinkling lights and delicate ornaments.

"You two have fun tonight. Take a few pictures for me," Mei said.

"We will," Xuan replied.

"I'll have everything sorted out for our New Year's trip before I return. I think I can make New York happen. But if that doesn't work, I found a cabin up in Deer Valley, near several different Utah ski resorts," Mei explained.

"Both sound perfect," I reassured her. "Have a safe flight."

"Love you, Mom. Call me when you land."

We said our goodbyes and then headed out to the car, ready to embark on our adventure in San Francisco.

"Here, let me get that for you." Xuan opened my car door and held out his hand to help me inside, a man who still showed his moral character well after the honeymoon stage. I admired him all the more for it.

As if he knew exactly what I was thinking, as he got into the car he whispered in my ear, "I can't wait to get you back home to *our* house, Mrs. Steel." An invitation for later.

The sound of his voice was enough to make my skin heat. Oh, I completely agreed. My one-month honeymoon hormones were doing a happy dance. This was going to be a long hour-plus drive tonight.

As we drove to San Francisco, the curve of his divine mouth stayed curled in a seductive smile, as if he knew precisely what I was thinking. "My mom is going to be gone for the entire weekend to Portland," he said, his voice dripping with playful anticipation. "That means we have the house to ourselves for the next three days."

I couldn't help but play along, "How will we ever fill the time?"

"Oh, I can think of a couple of ways."

His words lingered in the air, igniting a rush of excitement within me. The possibilities were endless, and my imagination began to run wild.

As we parked in the parking garage, he brushed his fingers against my skin purposefully as he grabbed his wallet from the center console to pay for parking. He was playing with me, and I couldn't be more delighted.

The War Memorial Opera House, San Francisco, California
December 20, 2019

As we approached the War Memorial Opera House, I was struck by the grandeur of the building. The entrance was adorned with ornate carvings and intricate detailing, showcasing the artistic beauty that lay inside.

"This place is a gem," I said. I had never been there. I loved the art and culture atmosphere in San Francisco.

"We should definitely come more often."

The doors were tall and imposing, made of rich, dark wood that gleamed in the sunlight. Above them, a sign proudly displayed the name of the theater in bold letters, beckoning patrons inside.

As I pushed open the doors, I was enveloped in a sense of elegance and sophistication. The foyer was spacious and airy, with high ceilings and marble floors that gleamed underfoot. Crystal chandeliers hung overhead, casting a warm glow throughout the room. To my left, a grand staircase led up to the balcony level, its polished handrails and plush red carpeting a testament to the theater's commitment to luxury.

To my right, a row of gleaming glass display cases showcased memorabilia from past productions, adding to the sense of history and reverence that permeated the space. In the center of the room, a grand piano sat, its polished wood gleaming in the light. A pianist played the tune Trepak, from the second act of Tchaikovsky's ballet, adding to the ambiance and setting the tone for the performance to come.

"It's almost time, lǎo pó. We should probably go find our seats."

"Okay, but first I want to get my mom and Stella something."

Xuan and I walked down the festive halls of the theater. Large Christmas trees and statues of nutcrackers lined the hallways. I passed a table of trinkets and could not resist buying a small nutcracker for each of our moms before we made our way toward our seats on the other side of the theater.

The theater was packed and shortly after we were seated, the curtains opened.

Xuan grinned, his eyes gleaming with anticipation. "I've heard so much about this ballet. I've always wanted to see it performed."

The San Francisco Ballet Orchestra began playing Tchaikovsky's mesmerizing score, filling the theater with its melodic beauty.

I found myself captivated by the exquisite faces, the stunning costumes, and the elaborate sets. The story opened on a cold winter night at a Christmas party. The stage was full of the youngest dancers—little soldiers and mice.

The music continued to carry us away, whisking us through different realms, as the enchanting story unfolded right before our eyes.

I couldn't help but wonder *is it all a dream?*

I craned my neck to see as children sat on the edges of their seats. Little girls in sparkly dresses watched the ballet dancers, surely dreaming of becoming just like them. The dancers were graceful, as if their bodies and art had been made to speak, as if communicating with the soul of the audience. There was only enough of a pause for applause between scenes before the music began to hypnotize us all again.

Xuan and I exchanged delighted glances, occasionally sharing whispers about our favorite scenes and characters.

The Sugar Plum Fairy was the queen of the Land of Sweets. She had gathered all of the different treats to dance for their honored guests. Everyone in the hall was quiet and still as the melody floated through their dreams.

For a moment, I thought it would be lovely to dance ballet under the stars and city lights. I could not imagine the pain and blood beneath those silk dancing slippers as they wove together in patterns, blending, lifting, bending. I reached out my hand and leaned against my husband as we waited for the Sugar Plum Fairy to grace the stage.

Xuan's body was like a smoldering fire as I touched him. *He shouldn't be this warm.* Turning my eyes, I caught him struggling to breathe. Something *was* wrong. "*Lǎo gōng,* are you okay? You're burning up."

"I'm sorry, I need some air." Xuan abruptly stood, to the shock of several guests behind our seats.

I quickly grabbed my bag and followed him. I didn't speak or ask questions until we were outside the doors. When we exited the theater into the lobby, two ushers in red vests eyed us. "You won't be able to get back inside, until—"

The man didn't finish his sentence. Xuan gritted his teeth as he took a few more steps forward, pain seeming to lash down his body.

I reached for him. "Saints Xuan, what's wrong?"

He leaned heavily on the railing of the hall, letting his balance readjust while he gasped in air. His hands shook as he held himself upright. Emotion rippled over his pale, sweat-beaded face as he sucked in air and raised his eyes. He winced as he met my stare and I heard his sudden ragged intake of breath and a single word, "Cass," before he grasped for his throat.

Panic. Panic indeed flared in my eyes as I watched his lips pronounce my name.

"Xuan, talk to me. What's going on?"

He then took a step toward the exit doors and stumbled.

"If you're sick, let me help you sit down."

He looked back at me, toward the sounds of my voice, and squinted his eyes. I reached out my arm to try to grab him—too late. A gasp tore from his lips, as if in pain. Then he collapsed. I lunged forward as soon as I realized he was falling, but I didn't make it in time. He hit his head hard on the metal railing as he fell.

"What's wrong with him?" a woman asked.

I turned to the short, senior woman who'd given us the eye for exiting during the ballet. I wanted to lash out an expletive or two, but I didn't. She was just an innocent bystander who had her hands free to call for help ASAP. "Call 911!" I begged.

"Xuan!" I yelled. But he was unresponsive. I saw blood from where he'd hit his head. "Hold on. Help is coming."

Not seeing him take a breath, I began mouth-to-mouth as I waited for the paramedics to arrive. Every second, one by one, passed by with horrific clarity. *Don't leave me now. I'm not ready to lose you.* As I breathed into his mouth, his motionless lips did not meet mine.

San Francisco Hospital, California
December 20, 2019

I rode in the ambulance and watched in fear as each agonizing second passed on our way to the hospital in San Francisco. The ambulance zigzagged, rushed through traffic lights and past pulled-over cars en route to the hospital. The drive to the medical center seemed endless.

The paramedics were able to resuscitate Xuan. He'd briefly regained consciousness in the ambulance, but he didn't respond to any questions. He didn't seem to understand what anyone was asking him. And when he gazed at me, I saw an unfamiliar look in his eyes. Once we reached the emergency entrance, he was taken away and I was left in the waiting room.

I called Mei and Stella and, through tears, explained what had happened. My mother assured me she would be on her way as soon as possible. Mei had just landed in Portland and would catch the next return flight home. I promised to keep them updated, but there was still no news to tell them.

"Mrs. Zhang,"

"Yes," I quickly stood.

"Doctor, how is he?"

"Your husband suffered a traumatic head injury that requires emergency surgery. When he fell and hit his head, it led to a bleed needing decompression. His body is fighting a fever of 103 degrees, and his oxygen levels and blood pressure are still critically low. We're doing all that we can. Once we've treated his head injury, we'll need to do a procedure called a pleurodesis and remove the buildup in Xuan's lung."

"Um, what's a pleurodesis?"

"Xuan has excessive fluid in the pleural space, decreasing his respiratory status and increasing his oxygen needs. The excess fluid in the pleural space is called pleural effusion." The doctor pointed to a chart of the human body. "See right here? The pleural space is this thin gap between the pleura of the lung and the inner chest wall. The pleura is a double layer of membranes that surrounds the lungs and inside that space is a small amount of fluid. The fluid prevents the pleura from rubbing together when he breathes. Simply put, when this happens, it's harder to breathe because the lungs can't inflate fully. The excess fluid is creating an inflammatory response."

I'd heard the doctor's words but really only comprehended head injury, to low oxygen and harder to breathe, as I was on the verge of a panic attack. "How long will he have to be in the hospital?"

"That will depend on his head injury and oxygen levels. Patients generally discharge in two to three days after a pleurodesis, depending on pain control and complications, but he'll likely need to stay for a few extra days so we can monitor him. We'll try our best to have him home before Christmas."

"I understand."

"I've reached out to his doctor and an oncologist at Dominican for his records and to discuss the medications your husband is currently on and his condition. First we need to deal with the bleed. I'll have the nurse bring you the consent forms for treatment."

"Do what you need to, doctor."

Stella arrived, with Raylan, almost two hours after my phone call. She couldn't drive at night with her vision, so she'd asked Raylan to bring her. She'd thoughtfully grabbed a change of clothes for me, knowing I'd dressed up for the ballet this evening and might be at the hospital for a while.

Sometime around 11 AM Xuan was stabilized but had been placed in an ICU room. He was currently unconscious. A face mask was giving him oxygen. He was propped up in a near-sitting position on the hospital bed. The sound of *M*A*S*H* played in the background on the TV screen—one of my all-time favorites. The nurse continued to come in and monitor his heart rate, oxygen levels, and blood pressure. She was cheerful and chatted with me every time she entered, trying to make me feel at ease. Her report that lab technicians would come to draw more blood and do simple routine procedures made me envision more vampires.

Mei arrived later that morning on the first flight back she could get. We took turns visiting the hospital ICU room due to the hospital's visitation rules. When we weren't with Xuan, we waited together in the chapel. Stella had been by my side all night, and Raylan had also chosen to stay. Beom had picked up Amanda and Roxy, and together they drove up from Santa Cruz.

When it was my turn to visit my husband again, I stood and paced the room to stretch my stiff back and legs. I moved quietly through the room filled with pulsing and beeping monitors. As Xuan slept soundly, I bent my head in silent prayer. Please . . . . save him. If you let him live, I'll happily give up the rest of the time I have left alive. Take *me* and let him live. That was almost an exact replica of the prayer Xuan had repeated to me during our dinner at *Riva Fish House*. He had asked God to spare me in Colombia, and to take him in my stead. Now I'd ask for the same thing.

The days leading up to *The Nutcracker* had been close to perfect—picking out a tree, decorating the house and tree, and then going to the ballet the night before. When I was with Xuan, I felt as though the entire world faded away. *Maybe I caused this by pushing him too hard during the past months. Maybe he fell because he was dizzy and tired because of me. Maybe this is our penance to pay. Maybe . . . .*

I held his hand and whispered, "Please wake up, *lǎo gōng*." I couldn't bear to see him like this.

Perhaps I'd believed in the unstoppable magic of love too much, just like in classic romantic stories I'd read growing up. A small, childish part of me actually believed that the end would somehow not come, ever. That our love would wrap us in a magical spell that would keep us together—in our own version of happily ever after. I'd settle for happily as Xuan's inner clock continued to count down to six.

Chapter Thirty-Three: Pediatric Ward

San Francisco Hospital, California
December 22, 2019

I often wandered through the hospital corridors in limbo. I liked to see the newborns or visit the sick kids. It was hard not to feel restless—*stuck,* like my feet were dragging through mud pits or quicksand, maybe even a little trapped inside. Needing to get away from the room but unable to go too far in case something changed with Xuan, who had still not awakened, I headed to the pediatric ward where the kids were all anticipating the arrival of Santa Claus.

Several of our friends had stopped by again, as well as some of Xuan's foreign-exchange friends. Most of them only stayed long enough to drop off flowers and magazines, but it was the thought that counted. The holidays were typically a busy time for everyone.

Raylan had also come to visit, his beach-style hair messy, probably from catching a few waves at Steamer Lane. The swell was up, creating the greatest year-round surfing experience, despite the cold.

After spending hours surrounded by beeping monitors that showed no signs of change, we both longed for a break to stretch our legs. I suggested heading to the children's area, which had become my go-to spot when I needed a change of scenery and some physical activity.

"You want me to come with you?" he asked.

"Sure. A twofer."

"Okay, let's go."

We walked together as I explained the process required to see the kids. "We need to fill out the paperwork for you at the desk. Then they'll ask us to wash our hands and sanitize. They should all be in the rec room now."

"You've done this before, haven't you? You seem to know the drill."

"I volunteer with the kids at Dominican, but I've been spending a lot of time here the last few days since Xuan was admitted. I've gotten to know most of the kids here already."

"What are they sick with?" Raylan asked.

"Different stuff. A few of them have cancer."

We walked down the corridors to the end of the hall, where two doors opened into a good-sized room. The kids, in their patient gowns, were crowded around a flatscreen TV watching *The Grinch.*

When we entered the room, one of the kids turned around and peered at us, as though we were from another world. One boy, about nine, with red curly hair and freckles, caught my eye. He reminded me of a first-year Ron Weasley. Next to him sat a girl, about the age of six, who had no hair—bald, beautiful, and bold. She was fighting the monsters, like Xuan.

"Cassie!" they shouted happily when they saw me.

Several other kids turned their heads.

"Hey, Aiden, Kieran, Sarai, Elizabeth," I said in response to the first four kids who ran to me. "How are you all?"

I introduced Raylan to the kids one by one, by name. He stood in his typical black shirt, looking uncomfortable.

One of the younger boys sat staring at Raylan's tattoos. "Cool! I want one of those when I grow up."

"Maybe you will someday," Raylan said.

"How's your husband?" another one of the kids asked. "Is he all better now?"

"Sleeping like a prince," I said.

"I hate having cancer," one of the girls said. Another one of the kids nodded in agreement. "You feel so sick. You can't stand up.

Your hair falls out. You get sores all over. And you look really gross, and scary. I wish to become like Bella, but instead, I feel like a beast."

"I didn't know chemo affected you that way, but I think you're beautiful," Raylan admitted. "You look like a princess to me."

"Well, it does. There are lots of side effects. But that's the way it has to be because without it, you'd be with the angels."

They asked Raylan a lot of questions as we sat and played board games.

When it was time to go, so the kids could start winding down for sleep, we both left with the promise we would return soon. I wanted to do something unforgettable for them, something the kids would remember forever.

"I'm glad you came with me." I turned to Raylan and smiled. "They're good kids. So sweet and innocent. They almost had me in tears a couple of times."

"Me too. Thanks for allowing me to tag along."

"Raylan, what are you doing for Christmas Eve this year?"

"Nothing. I used to go to Mass, but I haven't been since I returned from the military. My mom's gone, I haven't heard from Jace in years, and my father was caught selling, so he's in prison. Again. The only family I really have left is Nick, so I'll probably go to his and Sky's house for dinner on Christmas."

"That's nice he doesn't have to work Christmas. I'm sure Sky's happy to have him home."

"I think he does have to work the graveyard shift, but it's not until after dinner."

"Do you at least talk to Jace on the phone during the holidays?"

"He sent us a Christmas card several years ago. That was the last time I heard from him."

I decided to tell him about my sudden, not yet well-thought-out, Christmas Eve surprise just in case he wanted to help. "Raylan, how would you feel about spending time with the sick kids at the hospital after you go to dinner at your brother's place?"

"You mean come here? And spend time with the kids I just

met?"

"Yeah. It's the holidays. Sometimes small acts of kindness, can make a big difference in brightening their day and letting them know that they're not alone."

Raylan looked at me and his eyes opened wide as if he was up for anything out of the ordinary. "Sounds like a great Christmas."

"Good. Because I have an idea and I'd really love your help." And at that moment, I knew I had made the right move by allowing Raylan back into my life. It was time to fully accept him and trust him. I had been apprehensive when he initially returned, after I found out about my father's former intentions to break up Xuan and me. Despite all that had happened, Raylan had turned out to be a good guy. I'd misjudged him.

Hello, forgiveness.

Part Five: The Invisible Thread

Chapter Thirty-Four: The Light of the World

Twin Lakes Baptist Church, Aptos, California
December 24, 2019

Christmas inspired faith—in God and in His goodness, truth, and beauty, which was genuine and real but not always apparent or visible. Stella practically dragged me to the intimate, brief 5:30 PM Christmas Eve service at Twin Lakes Baptist Church, where we lit a candle for Xuan. The traditional candlelight service was slated to commence half an hour later, but the church had offered this pre-service for as long as I could remember. However, its roots could be traced back to Europe in the 1600s. The act of lighting a candle for a loved one served as a reminder that I was not alone in my grief—not the first person to lament over a loved one, nor the last.

We walked toward the main entrance where the service was being held. The night before, winter had plunged its vampire-like teeth into what was left of nature's trembling, dying heart. There was no leaf rustle, no birdsong, no grass whisper. The frost seemed to extract its life force, leaving the clay soil cold and drained, just the way I felt. But still I was trying—for my mom and because it was our cherished Steel family tradition for years. Christmas wasn't just a season. It was a peaceful feeling that overcame us as we gathered to celebrate the one born King. But I didn't feel amity, not this year. Reluctant to leave Xuan's side, I felt like a loyal canine, anxious that something might happen while I was away. Despite the passing time, he remained unconscious. Following his surgery, he required multiple blood transfusions, as if he was at the mercy of vampires. I sensed Mei needed some alone time with her son as she called her husband and family on WeChat to give them updates. So I let my mom drag me to church.

The service was always beautiful and the church was decorated with such ambiance. This year was no different, but I'd been looking forward to attending because Xuan and Mei had agreed to come with us.

"I went to check on Chairman Meow. Your Christmas tree turned out lovely," offered Stella.

"Yeah, it's too bad Xuan won't be home to enjoy it."

"I remember when your outdoorsy father took me to the wintry woods to bring back our first Christmas tree together. That was the first and last time we were ever able to do that. He was deployed during our second year of marriage and then you were born. We opted for one of the fakes we could buy at a store and reuse every year. So, leave your tree up and celebrate when Xuan returns home. There's no rule to say Christmas has to be celebrated on the twenty-fifth. Celebrate even if it's next month when Xuan's released. And if the tree dies before then, borrow my fake one. Your father's set to come home in February. Who knows, maybe we can all celebrate Christmas together."

I looked at my mother's adoring eyes and knew she meant well. But my mother didn't understand. How could she? Sure, she was a military wife. But her husband was well . . . alive. Yeah, he'd been gone for so many major events that had left Stella longing. And I knew that she worried every time my dad left to go back overseas. There was always the threat of danger in the life of a soldier—but he wasn't currently dying. Pining and losing someone were not the same. After all this time, my mother still looked at my father like Xuan looked at me. I'd seen it at my wedding—the love in my mother's eyes and the anticipation that they would have years more together, especially now that my father was retiring. *Finally.*

We were handed a single candle before making our way up to the second-floor balcony, where we found seats. The candle was a meaningful way to symbolize the light of Christ coming into the darkness of the world—my world.

The room was full. Probably over a thousand had gathered in attendance.

A few members I had grown up with came over to talk to me and ask about Xuan, meaning my mother had been talking to her women's group about Xuan's cancer diagnosis. *Go away,* I pleaded silently.

I didn't particularly want to talk to anyone, so Stella did most of the talking for me.

Rose Davenport, an active woman in her nineties, came up and lowered herself carefully into the seat beside me. "You all right?" she asked.

"As well as to be expected." I forced a smile with a dash of honesty.

She placed her hand on my shoulder. I looked into her eyes, full of experience. She undoubtedly had been through life's ups and downs, hopefully more ups. "I know how you're hurting, girl. I've been down this road myself. I lost my sweetheart during the Battle of Okinawa in 1945. I've mourned his loss every day, over seventy years. We survive losses as humans. We have to do it because it's part of the circle of life. But that doesn't make it any easier."

She sounded as though there was something stuck in her throat, something hard and painful. The way she talked was as if Xuan was already gone. I wanted to say, "He's still alive," but I didn't. Rose's eyes were filled with understanding and wisdom. Rose had never remarried. She told me that she chose to stay single. Her husband was it for her, and his absence hadn't made her love him any less. *Not many people around me know how bad I hurt, but she does. Rose understands.*

"When God took my Edward, a part of me died. I wanted to crawl into that casket with him. I didn't ever think that I could make it without him. We'd known each other for most of our lives. We tied the knot shortly before he was deployed, you know.

Seems like a lifetime, but time always goes so quickly." Rose took out a pencil and paper from her notebook and began to write her phone number and name in perfect cursive. She placed the papers into my hand. "In case you ever want to talk."

I didn't say a word. I just grabbed Rose's hand and gently squeezed it.

The pastor came onstage, followed by a short greeting. Next the band came out and the music started. A male led the congregation in singing "O Come, All Ye Faithful" as a blue light descended onto the trees in the background and the stage. This was followed by "Gloria in Excelsis Deo," which was sung as a duet. The pastor began to speak. "Christmas is the perfect time to celebrate the love of God and family and to create memories that will last forever."

As I listened to the pastor read from Matthew and Luke, I felt comforted, despite being disconnected. Christmas was about believing in things that defied logic, such as the Son of God being born to a virgin in a stable filled with farm animals. The Son came to save us from our sins and rescue us from our transgressions, demonstrating his embodiment of love, generosity, and goodness through forgiveness. The religious significance of this service was the reminder of how simple the birth of Christ was. He was born in a small town in a tucked-away place, and candlelight in the modern day was just a reminder of something simple and meek and peaceful. That night's candlelight service served as a reminder of the true meaning of Christmas.

Ushers came up each aisle and helped light the candles at the end, which allowed each person in the row to pass their own flame to the next person. The light reflected in the faces of the people just as the light of Christ was supposed to be reflected in believers. The light of believers was magnified and the room held all the symbolism of the light when Christ was born. I looked down at my own candle, at the symbol of Christ's light and love for all.

After each candle was lit, the pastor and the members of the band and all the church members began to sing "Silent Night" together as one. We wrapped up the service singing under the calm and bright silent night. This was memorable, inspiring, and hope-filled.

As I sang the lyrics, I felt a small light fill the inside of me against the darkness of depression and weariness. Tradition said that the song "Silent Night" sounded through the trenches louder than the guns of war on Christmas Eve and Christmas Day of 1914, shortly after World War I began. And that night the song that fell from my lips was louder than the bullets of doubt and the trenches of fear. The light of faith was serenely beaming inside me, like a star that would never fall. My faith would get me through the nights and the tomorrows. My faith was more powerful than the war I'd felt inside myself, and God would be with me, beside me, until the end. I wanted to believe that.

I'd once again become childlike in my faith. To think with my heart rather than my brain. To embrace the tranquil stillness of a world beyond my own. So I sang, "Silent night, holy night. All is calm, all is bright."

Chapter Thirty-Five: Santa's Elves

San Francisco Hospital, California
December 24, 2019

Following the church service, Raylan and I returned to the hospital. We transformed into Santa's elves, then walked down the corridor towards the children's wing. As the families were set to arrive in the morning, we'd decided to carry out our plan on Christmas Eve. "Nice ears, Steel."

"Thanks." I would've preferred dressing like Arwen Undómiel or one of the other Rivendell elves from Lord of the Rings, but I said, "Not a bad look for you either, Corporal Thompson."

"I never realized it before, but you're kinda the perfect size for one of Santa's elves. If teaching doesn't work out, you could probably apply for a position in the North Pole."

"And you kinda look like Buddy from the movie Elf."

"I'll take that as a compliment. Will Ferrell has a direct line to my funny bone."

We'd secretly stashed bags of toys with the nurses and they'd had each one cleaned and approved the day before. We grabbed the bags of puzzles, coloring books, games, and new winter-themed Squishmallow stuffed animals for all the kids. My friends had helped take up a collection, a pay-it-forward event. A lot of gifts were cash and gift certificates. The response was overwhelming. Everyone wanted to be a part of a Christmas miracle for kids fighting cancer and other terrible monsters.

Raylan stood in the doorway for just a second, looking slightly overwhelmed. He was standing very still, his eyes half closed, his hands clenching and unclenching. One of the nurses saw us. "It's nice of you two to do this for them. Yesterday one of the eight-year-olds got very ill. Passed this morning. Many of the kids feel angry, or scared they may be next."

The room was quiet and dim. I thought about the children. I couldn't imagine being so young and practically living at the hospital with needles, monitors, tubes, and pills. I shuddered, thinking of the antiseptic rooms and white hallways, especially during the holidays and special moments that kids this age were supposed to enjoy. *Why does reality always have a way of rearing its ugly head?* They were all very ill. There was no forgetting, not even for Christmas. The hospital did an amazing job trying to bring in holiday cheer, but it wasn't the same as being home.

The kids seemed downcast as we entered the main hallway. Raylan and I stood there in our outfits as the kids came around the corner. Then the kids saw us standing there with bags full of fun toys, just for them. Before long they were jumping for joy and shouting with delight as they circled around us.

"Merry Christmas!" I called out.

"And happy Hanukkah," shouted Raylan.

We'd done our detective work with the hospital staff. Two of the kids were Jewish. And since Amanda had been raised Jewish, she was able to help toy hunt with the money and donations we'd received, buying Hanukkah presents for those two and dreidels for all the kids to play with. I wanted to make this night special for all the kids, for all faiths and non-faiths. The kids—of all ages and races—gathered around me in a circle. I read *Twas the Night Before Christmas* by Clement Moore, a classic and a childhood favorite I could almost recite by heart.

"This is the best Christmas ever," one of the little girls shouted.

Raylan's smile began slowly. Then it broke out across his face fully, lighting up his eyes as he helped hand out the toys. "And what would you like for Christmas?" Raylan asked Sarai and Elizabeth.

Sarai responded, "I just want to go home and be with my family for Christmas."

Sarai's words hit me like a ton of bricks, leaving me shattered and broken. Raylan's expression told me he felt the same. Aiden, Kieran, and Elizabeth all nodded in empathetic agreement. It was as if the kids were all hit by a wave of homesickness that only Sarai had the courage to verbalize.

"I hope you will soon," I said.

The simple joys felt by children, joys that adults often took for granted or overlooked, deeply affected both me and Raylan. They were all sick, but despite their illnesses, they were here in the present and savoring each moment.

We spent the evening playing with the kids and watching Christmas cartoons until the nurses announced that it was past bedtime. When it was time to say goodbye, neither of us were in a hurry to leave the joys we had just taken part in. Raylan stopped me before going into the changing room. He whispered, "Cassie, it's been a long time since I've felt like this. I needed that. Thank you."

I replied, "You're welcome."

He hugged me then, short and sweet. "Merry Christmas."

I reached into my purse and handed him a wrapped package that had arrived via Amazon. It wasn't much. I hadn't been able to shop for anyone this year. "Merry Christmas, Raylan. Thank you for helping me tonight."

I'd often visited the hospital chapel to pray, seeking strength, wisdom, hope, and even a miracle. Without thinking, I made my way there after saying goodbye to Raylan.

By the time I returned to my husband's room, it was nearly midnight. Xuan had been moved to a different floor, meaning the three of us could be in the room together during visitation. Mei was dozing in the chair and Stella was standing in the corner with a small tray of hot chocolate. Growing up, our quintessential holiday tradition on Christmas Eve was to go to candlelight service, then drive around and look at displays of lights in Scotts Valley and Santa Cruz. We'd then head home and video call my dad so he could watch us open a few gifts. Before my mom sent me to bed to wait for Santa's arrival, she would make us homemade hot cocoa with a large dollop of whipped cream and then we'd stay up and watch the Grinch or another holiday favorite. We always baked Santa sugar cookies and set out a tray of carrots for the reindeer. While Raylan and I were busy playing dress up, my mother, who was a creature of habit and a stickler for adhering to traditions, had stumbled upon a cafe called Dandelion Chocolate that was still open. She had made a trip to the cafe to buy three ample servings of hot chocolate, each topped with extra whipped cream.

Stella spoke in a hushed tone to avoid disturbing Mei as she said, "Honey, I'm going to go find us some extra blankets. There's a bit of a chill in the air."

"Need help?"

"Stay with your husband. I'll manage." Stella wasn't very good at just sitting, so she made it a habit to keep herself busy when she visited the hospital. She'd taken it upon herself to make the room look cheerful. Stella had even gotten permission from the nurse to bring in a small fake tree for Xuan's room, along with a string of lights. The yuletide touches made the room feel more homey. Like my mom, I loved Christmas. I hadn't expected our first Noel as man and wife would be spent in the hospital.

I gently leaned over the hospital bed, my heart heavy with emotion, and pressed my lips tenderly against Xuan's forehead. "Merry Christmas. I love you." My hand passed over my husband's cheek and then his chest to feel the heart beneath where a phantom thread lingered, endured, unbroken, uncut. I wanted to pull and tug on that phantom bond, to coax it like a cat playing with string. *Come back to me.*

His strong echoing heartbeat in his body was the only response.

I drew my chair closer to his bed, needing to maintain that physical contact with him. As the quietness enveloped us, I started sharing everything with him—my fondest memories of our time together, how I had fallen head over heels for him, and what our relationship meant to me. I also talked about the endless possibilities of the future that we still had before us, and all the things that I was looking forward to experiencing with him.

And in return, the constant beeping of the monitors changed—became atypical. I couldn't move, couldn't breathe, as I stared down at his body in silence.

Xuan's chest rose and fell, his features the same, but then his eyelids and eyelashes began to flutter. I heard my breath catch . . . was it possible? Was he waking up? Groggily, he came to enough consciousness to slowly open them, but it was a struggle.

When his eyes finally met mine, I inhaled, hard. *Exhale. Inhale. Repeat.* I could barely believe it, hadn't let myself believe it, until I looked into his face. Seeing his eyes fully open had nearly knocked me breathless. Lightheaded, I got up from my chair to sit on the bed next to him.

"Xuan—" For a moment, I forgot how to talk. There was a kernel of light shining beneath his open eyes—recognition between two souls. Any lingering fragment of my soul that hadn't already belonged to him surrendered entirely in that moment at the sight of him.

I couldn't stop trembling. My hands shook slightly from the overload of emotions. "Hey there, sleepy. You're finally awake," I whispered. My voice broke as I brushed his hair back. I took a minute to steady myself.

He seemed as though he had something to say, and with a slow, deliberate movement, he raised his left hand towards his face and gently removed the oxygen mask that had been covering his mouth.

"Wa-water," he finally rasped. His mouth had to be dry.

"Don't speak if it hurts, *lǎo gōng*." I held up a cup. He was too weak to take it from my hands.

"It-it's okay."

"How do you feel?" I gently guided the straw toward his cracked lips.

"Horrible," he admitted. "Everything's spinning."

"I'll call the nurse." I pushed the call button and then reached down to wake Mei. "He's waking up."

Mei let out a choked sound of relief and joy and quickly got to her feet. She hurried to Xuan so she could see him before the nurses came in. "Hi, baby. Welcome back."

"Hi, *mā mā*."

Mei and I stepped aside as the nurse entered the room to check Xuan's vitals. Shortly after, the doctor joined us, carrying Xuan's medical file, which was as thick as an old phone book. Most of Xuan's records were electronic, but on occasion, the doctor would bring in a large stack of paperwork. "How are you feeling, Xuan?"

"Dizzy. A little numb. My throat and chest hurt."

The good doctor, whom I'd nicknamed The Messenger in my mind, nodded. "It was touch-and-go for you." He began to explain the head injury that had caused bleeding and fluid buildup in his lungs. His oxygen levels had improved, but the doctor wanted to keep him overnight. He said Xuan could possibly go home as early as the next day.

Xuan nodded, his face etched with exhaustion. He reminded me of a resilient cat, defying the odds and bouncing back from near-death, as if embodying the age-old belief in a cat's proverbial nine lives.

After the doctor and nurse left, I reached out and gently took his hand in mine once more. "If you can, try to get some rest," I suggested softly.

"You'll be here when I wake up?"

"I'm not going anywhere *lǎo gōng*," I said. "Promise."

He loosened a long breath, his body seeming to settle, calm. He closed his eyes and fluttered in and out of consciousness for the remainder of the night.

I bent my head in prayer. I thanked God, truly believing that He'd heard my prayers. By now, tears of happiness had filled my eyes. The only thing I knew for sure—could count on—was that tomorrow a new and glorious morning would come, for this was a holy night. I silently repeated the words I had sung—*Silent night, holy night* – and my heart rejoiced in the stillness and beauty of those gentle words. In its own way, all was calm, all was bright.

Chapter Thirty-Six: First Noel

San Francisco Hospital, California
December 25, 2019

When I woke on the morning of the twenty-fifth, my hand was still holding on to Xuan's. He was awake. I'd been so scared I would wake to find this had all been a dream. The bleak feeling of despair that had unfurled in my stomach had vanished. And it was Christmas.

There were obvious signs of the holiday at the hospital. Music played up and down the halls. Doctors and nurses wore holiday-themed scrubs decorated with candy canes, reindeer, and tinsel-and-light-trimmed elf hats.

Stella and Mei had left sometime in the night and headed back to Santa Cruz to grab a few things and shower. They were due back any moment now. Despite the two-and-a-half-hour drive, Stella had made several trips back and forth between San Francisco and home, whereas Mei stayed at a hotel near the hospital. My mother never could sleep in hotels. She hated being away from home for too long. The mornings my mom did return to the hospital, she'd often come with a box of breakfast pastries she'd purchased from a local shop in the Bay area, Jane the Bakery. As for me, I never left Xuan's side.

"Merry Christmas, my beautiful wife." The hospital window allowed a streak of light in, making his eyes appear paler in the sunlight.

My heart tightened to the point of pain. "Merry Christmas, sweetheart." I smiled and kissed his temple.

His hand slid down my back and he pressed me toward him on the bed, returning the favor. My heartbeat picked up speed.

"Does it—do you hurt?" I remembered how much my body

ached from head to foot when I was in the Colombian hospital. He was the strong one. I was weaker then. But despite our polar differences, we both were survivors, time after time.

A smile spread across my husband's face. "Not much, *lǎo pó*." He pulled me gently toward him until I was sitting on the bed. The doctor had exchanged his oxygen mask for nasal prongs, making it easier for him to breathe and talk.

"Thank you for staying alive," I whispered.

His voice was soft, as if he were speaking inside a church. "Everything's fine now, *qīn'ài de*. I'm fine."

"Xuan," I whispered. "I thought I'd lost you."

His face was close to mine. I could feel his heart pounding in his chest. "What happened?" he finally asked.

So I told him.

"I don't remember any of it." He was instantly more alert as the fogginess around his memory lifted. He seemed to remember passing out at the ballet. "I'm sorry I ruined our chance to see *The Nutcracker, bǎobèi*," Xuan said.

"We still have plenty of time."

"Maybe."

"Everyone's worried about you. They all said to tell you hi and that they've been pulling for you. Several of them have all stopped by to see you while you were asleep—especially Raylan." I smiled.

Xuan glanced up at me. "He did?"

"Yeah. He's fond of us. He must have finally found his heart, like the Tin Man, after all these years. He's quite emotional when it comes to you."

Xuan smiled and then began to cough just as Mei and Stella appeared in the doorway, with an armful of gifts and a glass dish of cinnamon cake.

Mei received an incoming call, prompting her to quickly put everything down before answering it.

I glanced at the gifts cradled in my mom's arms. She had gone slightly overboard, but her heart was in the right place. She wanted nothing more than for the four of us to be together as a family—at home or in the hospital. I still planned to celebrate Christmas with Xuan once we got back home, like my mom suggested, but we also decided to make the most out of the situation. After all, it was Christmas.

"Thanks for coming, Mom," Xuan said to Stella. "I appreciate you being here."

"You're my son-in-law. There's nowhere else I'd rather be than here, with my children, on Christmas."

Mei was still on the phone with the family, telling them the good news. Xuan talked with his father at length through video chat. Xuan wanted to wait until he was home before opening *all* the presents. That would be more comfortable for all of us so we each opened only one.

Xuan held something out from under the covers and handed me a small square box.

"I asked my mom to grab this from the house."

When did he manage to ask her? It must have been sometime after one, when I finally fell asleep. That must be why Mei traveled back to Santa Cruz with my mom.

For a moment I just stared at it, wondering if any of this was real.

"Aren't you going to open it?" he asked.

Carefully undoing the packaging, I saw two small red bracelets inside black satin wrapping. Each bracelet had an adjustable string and a single Chinese charm dangling from the middle.

I reached for a bracelet but his long fingers beat me there.

"May I?" he asked.

"Of course." I handed him the box, and he gently took my left wrist in his hand, then slid the red bracelet into place.

"What does the charm mean?"

"Soul mates."

He continued to hold my wrist and examine it. I could hear some strong emotions burning under his casual tone of voice as he said, "In China there's a legend about an invisible thread that ties all those whose lives have been intertwined together. It is said that this thread is governed by the Chinese God of marriage, Yue Lao. This bracelet is common for lovers to wear in China and other cultures—it's a symbol for the eternity I've promised you. The red thread of Fate will bind us together so that we can find each other in the next life."

I stared up at the face of the man I was unconditionally and irrevocably in love with, his eyes so full of life and emotion that they seemed to smolder just under the surface. Taking out the second bracelet, I put it on him and adjusted the string.

"Xuan, it's beautiful. You're beautiful." I kissed him and his lips were gentle against mine. Exultant. When I pulled back, he was almost glowing—his angelic face brilliant with joy and adoration.

When you live in a sunny state, everyone wishes for a white Christmas—for a miracle. But I got mine, wrapped in a red bow and delivered by the powers that be. I heard the faint sound of nearby churches ringing their bells to welcome Christmas from somewhere down the street. The melody was a message of peace on earth and goodwill to men.

I kissed my prince's hand. Then he reciprocated.

Sometimes all you had to do was believe. And I did.

EPILOGUE: THE FATES OF OLD

Looking down at the red bracelet that now adorned my wrist, I couldn't help but think about the Red String of Fate and the invisible thread that now bound Zhang Xuan and me together for eternity. Xuan had always said we were fated to meet each other in this life. Before Colombia, I wasn't what you would call a firm believer in Fate. But the more I think about it, I realize fate is not a new concept. Many cultures around the world consider fate to be something supernatural, in the realm of the gods.

The very thought that an invisible, unexplainable guiding force can be at work in our lives has existed for thousands of years. In ancient Greece, Fate was portrayed by three women who oversaw your birth and death. They controlled your destiny, until the end, when the thread—your tether to this world—was cut. That was a silly idea, a myth created to explain the mundane world around them like the story of the abduction of Persephone by Hades, which was created to explain the seasons. But other civilizations were not so different in their beliefs. In Egyptian myth, Shai was the ambivalent deity who controlled your destiny. In Norse mythology the Norns were responsible for shaping the course of human destinies. The Norns were said to spin the threads of fate at the foot of Yggdrasil. In China, the myth of Yuè Lǎo, the old lunar matchmaker god, was meant to explain destined lovers, regardless of time, place, or circumstances. And then there was Siming, who was the Chinese deity who made adjustments to the human lifespan. What was interesting was that all of these civilizations and cultures had a similar concept—there are no coincidences in life. The Fates were very much alive.

I couldn't help but wonder if, somewhere out there, the fates of old were watching. Maybe they were up there laughing at us over a good glass of wine. Maybe they were sitting there stewing in jealousy over our ability to love so intensely as mortals. I could picture them in my head—their divine hands at the spindle, spinning thread, twisting the red fibers of our lives and death, as Xuan's internal clock was now inching its way forward to five, never back. But our story wasn't finished, not yet.

ACKNOWLEDGMENTS

First of all, I need to thank *you*, dear reader, for having the courage to pick up my book—so, thank you! I am forever grateful. I'm honored you've chosen to spend time with my words and I hope that something here resonates with you. Your kindness, generosity, and support mean the world to me. Thank you for taking these characters into your hearts, and for allowing me to do what I love. This book was extremely difficult to write for a variety of reasons, and I am honored to have you as my readers.

I've had the opportunity to work with five fantastic editors over the course of this novel. The constant support, hard work, and talent of the following five women made my dream of publishing come true:

To Brigit Vries at eXtasy—I am deeply grateful for your unwavering dedication and invaluable contributions in shaping this book and allowing me to make changes up until the last minute. Your meticulous attention to detail ensured that every word and sentence was finely crafted to create the best possible reading experience. I am grateful for your willingness to accommodate my requests for changes, even up until the last minute. Your flexibility and understanding allowed me to refine and polish the book until it reached its full potential. Your steadfast support and guidance have been instrumental in elevating the final version of the book before it went into publication. Thank you!

To Julie Hayes at eXtasy—Thank you for your insightful and genius editorial guidance. We haven't been working together that long, but it's been such a pleasure! Your feedback and insight elevated the story to the next level. *Fated to Love You* wouldn't be what it is without your feedback and wisdom.

To Cal Orey, M.A., Healing Powers series author. Cal Orey is a best-selling author, journalist, and gifted storyteller. I want to thank Cal, who supported me and the characters through this journey. I would not be here without her wisdom and advice. She helped build me up and break me down in every way I needed. Her immediate response was my first breath of relief. Someone liked this book. As a first-time author, it was challenging to know what to cut out of the story. It was her guidance that led me to create a second novel and break the original into a trilogy.

To Audra Gerber—You were my fairy godmother. Thank you for working so tirelessly to make so many of my dreams come true. Your editorial genius and deep understanding of the characters made the book into a much stronger version of itself.

To Cydnie Dial—Thank you for sticking with me, and for the years of emails, critiques, and Jedi wisdom. You were the first person to ever read *Chasing the Comet*. Your advice and feedback kept me going over the years. Thank you for being a brilliant, lovely human being. I felt truly lucky to have your guidance as you looked over my first and second drafts of *Fated to Love You*.

Fated to Love You was an ambitious project for me, and there were several people involved in making sure I finished this book. I want to say thank you to the individuals at eXtasy Books:

To Jay Austin at eXtasy—Working with you has been a true pleasure and a blessing. Your expertise and passion for the written word have shone through in every aspect of the publishing process. Your commitment to excellence and your commitment to helping authors like me bring their stories to life is truly commendable. I cannot thank you enough for your unwavering dedication, your meticulous work, and your unwavering support. This book would not be what it is today without you.

To Tina Haveman and the entire team at eXtasy—Thank you for your wisdom, hard work, and generosity. You helped me turn this manuscript into something humble and beautiful. Thank you for taking a chance on me as a first-time novelist and the Chasing the Comet series. And to Martine Jardin at eXtasy—Thank you for the cover. I'm sorry I was such a demanding client.

This book, in this form, would not exist if I hadn't had the opportunity to ask complicated questions about my main character's cancer diagnosis and treatment options. I am indebted to the following medical staff members for their help and support:

To Kevin Kimbrough, Dignity Health External Communications Manager—thank you for taking the time to set up a meeting so I could ask questions about my fictional character's cancer diagnosis and treatment. There are simply no words in the English language to express the gratitude I feel, and there will never be a way I can repay you for your time.

To Dr. Michael Alexander, Dominican Hospital Oncology Medical Director—Thank you for taking my phone call and walking me through medical terms related to the story. Your help changed my life and made the Chasing the Comet series more realistic. I hate to admit that when I came to you for advice and feedback on the progression of my character's diagnosis, I thought I had a good handle on the medical timeline of symptoms and treatments, based on internet research, and I couldn't have been more wrong! Thank you for sorting me out.

To Dr. Gary Shwartz, Thoracic Surgeon and ECMO Director—thank you doesn't seem adequate for all you've done for me, and how much I appreciate your help in understanding Stage III and IV Lung Cancer. You arrived at the precise moment in my life when I needed you and your expertise the most, and I thank the universe every single day that I was able to connect with you. You helped make the story realistic with the diagnosis, treatment options, and timeline.

To the administration, doctors, and staff at Dominican Hospital and the Mary & Richard Solari Cancer Center in Santa Cruz—this novel simply wouldn't be the same without all of the dedicated staff. Thank you for your hard work and commitment to the community. Your continuing bravery and compassion do not go unnoticed.

To the hospital staff members in the San Francisco Bay area—Thank you for responding to the city's health crises and working to improve the health and well-being of all.

Next, I want to offer an enormous thanks to the following

people, without whom this book would not have been possible:

To my parents and husband—Thanks for putting up with me as I wrote this book, especially through dinners, dishes, movie nights, and weekends. I love you all.

To my brothers, Zhang Xuan—Jimmy, Beomgyo In, Zhou Zijie—Joe, Scott Wang, and Beckham Wang, I know we're worlds apart now, but you are in my heart and memory. And to my closest friends: Gelsey and Brandon Ermini, Amanda and Eric Smith, Zach Horton, Wu Can, Kat Zimmerman, Jakie Deily, Nate Martin, Daniel Nieto, Jonathan Sanchez, Mitchell Harrison, Sean Kienke, Justin Larsen, and the Bodell family—I wouldn't be the person I am today without each one of you. Thank you for the years of love and support, and for sticking by me through it all—the darkness and the light.

To Debbie Cotton—years ago, you believed in this story before anyone else. Thank you.

To my childhood friend and elementary school desk mate, Elliott Bliss—Your art is such an inspiration to me on so many levels. It always reminds me of home.

Next, I wanted to say thank you to the following native Spanish and Mandarin Chinese speakers. These four individuals helped me with language barriers and were irreplaceable. I included foreign language in conversations throughout my novel because it was important to me to stay true to the characters and their culture. The problem is, sometimes language can be difficult . . . especially when we don't understand it, and other times we want to swoon over sweet nothings whispered in French, Italian, or Spanish, which is just one of the many ways my husband won my heart. So thank you to the following four individuals who answered questions about culture, language, and the expressions of endearment and phrases in Spanish and Mandarin Chinese:

To my lovely sister-in-law Gabriela Suarez Cepeda—You are a brilliant ray of sunshine. Thank you for looking over my Spanish and for reading the chapters related to Colombia.

To my husband, Brayan—You gave me the courage to

continue writing and always answered my questions related to Colombia, even when it was late at night or you were busy. Thank you for looking over my Spanish a second and third time. I couldn't ask for a better partner.

To Zhou Zijie and Wu Can—Thank you for looking over my Chinese translations. I'm so proud of both of you and everything you've accomplished. You've been such a big part of my life.

Lastly, I want to express my gratitude to the sensitivity readers who provided me with alternate perspectives on the diverse characters portrayed in the novel and the groups they represented. Writing about culture is a complex and constantly evolving experience, and it can be challenging to do justice to a culture that is not your own. Cultural sensitivity and awareness are hot topics in the present time, and it was crucial for me to demonstrate cultural competency while writing about Chinese, Colombian, and Italian cultures throughout this series, including different languages. Your valuable input helped me achieve this goal, and I'm grateful for your valuable input.

Author's Note

As a dedicated world voyager, history teacher, and first-time author, I hold a deep respect for diverse cultures and strive to avoid cultural appropriation. Growing up, my remarkable parents imbued in me a deep curiosity about the world, which led to my spending over half my life steeped in various cultures. Through my travels, I have gained a profound appreciation for the diverse and fascinating ways in which people live, think, and create. My parents instilled in me an early love for maps, meeting new people, and exploring foreign lands, which has shaped the way I see the world and has greatly influenced my writing.

My novel is a tapestry of cultures, and the threads of Chinese culture and Colombian setting are carefully woven into the fabric. The Chinese culture has always fascinated me, and I've been fortunate enough to travel there several times. During my travels, I was captivated by the bustling cities and the breathtaking natural landscapes. I was enchanted by the ornate architecture, the intricacy of the language, and the warmth and hospitality of the people. In addition to my travels, I've also had the pleasure of hosting several high school boys from China, Taiwan, and Korea, who have become a huge part of my family. They've shared their stories, customs, and traditions with me, providing me with a deeper understanding of the culture. This experience has allowed me to portray the Chinese culture with authenticity and accuracy in my novel.

The setting of Colombia is equally important in my novel. My husband is from Colombia, and I was recently able to visit the area. The vibrant colors, the rhythmic beats of the music, and the delicious aromas of the food filled me with a sense of wonder and awe. The richness of the Latin culture was all around me, suffusing every moment with a special sort of magic that left an indelible mark on my soul. It was a transformative experience that I knew I had to incorporate into my writing, so that others could share in the same sense of discovery and delight that I had found.

The date December 2019 changed everything. Following the New Year, the pandemic swept the world and schools closed their doors. Not having to work three jobs, I found myself in a unique position to explore my passion for writing. I dug up an old journal from my high school creative writing class, where I stumbled upon a twenty-page story I had written as a junior, titled *Broken Dreams.* I breathed new life into the story, shaping the characters and plot into what would become my first publication.

The *Chasing the Comet* series not only delves into the intricacies of contemporary romance, but it also explores deeper themes such as cultural identity, family dynamics, and overcoming adversity. The series takes readers on a journey through different countries and cultures, providing a window into the diversity of the world. With its diverse cast of characters and complex storylines, the series offers a nuanced and multifaceted portrayal of the human experience, while also exploring issues of racism.

I knew that in writing this novel, I had to stay true to the cultures and experiences that had shaped me. I was determined to weave these cultural elements into my writing, and in doing so, pay homage to the beauty and diversity of our world. This novel became my voice, my form of action, and my contribution to the pandemic years. My ultimate goal in writing this novel is to honor and celebrate these diverse cultures, and to share their beauty with the world. I hope my dedication to authenticity and accuracy shines through in every page, and I hope that readers will be transported to these wondrous places and cultures through my words.

Crafting a story around Cassandra Steel and Zhang Xuan presented a unique set of challenges. I was struck by the scarcity of representations of Asian-American biracial couples in literature and media, highlighting the systemic exclusion of Asian voices from American culture. It became evident that Asians had been underrepresented for decades, and they are not the only marginalized group. This realization motivated me to create characters that readers could genuinely connect with, despite the complexities of writing about cultures that are not my own.

Despite the challenges, I was determined not to alter or westernize my story. Even when other publishers rejected my manuscript, citing taboo topics such as mentioning the pandemic and featuring a Chinese male as the love interest, I remained steadfast in my conviction. I refused to change Zhang Xuan's race and ethnicity, even when offered a contract with a large publisher on the condition that I make him a Caucasian American. The publishers believed that this change would make my book more marketable, given the current tensions between China and the USA.

Admittedly, it would have been easier to give in to their demands and alter the race and ethnicity of my characters to fit the expected mold. However, easier does not always mean better. I felt a sense of obligation to the characters in my head and to my readers to create a novel that was authentic and true to the vision I had in mind. Changing Zhang Xuan's identity to that of a white male was not an option for me; it only fueled my determination to see Cassie and Xuan's story published.

As I wrote, I wanted to give Xuan and Cassie a depth that readers could relate to and fall in love with. Writing about a culture that is not your own is a significant responsibility, but it is also an opportunity to learn and grow.

To bring authenticity to the heartfelt love story of Xuan and Cassie in my novel, I knew I had to go beyond the surface-level research available on Google and Wikipedia. Culture, language, and religion are integral parts of our lives in this increasingly interconnected world, and I wanted to ensure that my portrayal of them was both beautiful and honest.

To bring these cultures to life in my novel, I spent countless hours researching and delving into the Mandarin Chinese and Latin cultures. I wanted to ensure that every detail was accurate and authentic, and so I spent two years traveling to the locations mentioned in the novel, immersing myself in foreign television, reading folklore, listening to music and comedy shows featuring artists from the region. Through my travels, I have tried the local foods and savored the sights, sounds, and flavors of different regions, which I have seamlessly integrated into the novel's setting. The lush landscapes, bustling streets, and vibrant cultures are all captured in vivid detail, creating a rich and immersive experience for the reader. Honestly, it's been quite fun to explore neighborhoods and try locally inspired recipes where my characters exist in the setting of this novel. I hope my experiences and love for people and culture are reflected in the pages of my novel.

As I close this chapter of my journey as a first-time novelist, I want to remind everyone to strive to be kind and to love one another. We are all human beings, and it is through stories like Xuan and Cassie's that we can come together and appreciate the unique experiences and perspectives that each culture brings to our world.

Thank you for taking a chance on me as a first-time novelist, and my characters. I hope that they have found a way into your hearts and that you fell in love with the story of Cassie and Xuan, as much as I did.

About the Author

Kayla Cunningham holds two education degrees, and she teaches history at the high school level and adult ESL, while also volunteering as a Hostage Crisis Negotiator. She is currently working on her Ph.D. in Teaching English as a Second Language and enjoys taking flying lessons with her husband. Kayla has a passion for traveling and meeting people from different cultures around the world. She hosted six boys from China and has traveled to Asia many times. She was born in San Luis Obispo and raised outside the city of Santa Cruz, California. She is an advocate of exploring issues of racism and current events, including the rise in Asian hate crimes caused by the pandemic. *Fated to Love You* is Cunningham's first contemporary romance novel. She just completed the second installment of the Chasing the Comet series and is currently working on a YA fantasy trilogy called *Storm Breaker.*

Website: https://kaylacunninghamauthor.com/

Made in the USA
Coppell, TX
09 July 2023